PLANESHIFTERS

CRITICAL MASS: BOOK II

GUNNAR C GARISSON

SHAPESHIFTER BOOKS, SEATTLE

Published by
SHAPESHIFTER BOOKS
Seattle, WA 98106

FIRST EDITION
April, 2013

FIRST EBOOK EDITION
February, 2012
ISBN 978-1-4524-4047-7

ISBN 978-0615806396

Cover art by Remy Francis,
www.rembrandz.com

Manufactured in The United States of America

This book is dedicated to the men and women of our armed forces, and to my father, Gary, whose selfless sacrifices and diligence have taught me what it is to serve your family as well as your country, and helped shape me into the man that I am today.

———————

"Nearly all men can handle adversity. If you want a true test of a man's character, give him power."

-*Abraham Lincoln*

PLANESHIFTERS

TABLE OF CONTENTS:

PROLOGUE: THORSSON KREY AND THE LEGACY OF THE NORTH CLAN

During the middle of the 21st century, even after a 25 year long war in the Middle East, mankind reached a pinnacle of growth and technological success, and ironically became the harbinger of his own destruction. With a global population of just over 11.5 billion, the sociological condition on Earth had reached a point of critical mass, and the growth actually flat-lined; the mortality rate finally equaling the birth rate due to disease, violence, starvation, and every other form of untimely death imaginable.

With the middle class all but extinct, the rich became richer; living, as always, in a world of excess. When the cities expanded outward as far as they could go, they started building upward, in higher and higher city levels, casting the poor to the underground to fend for themselves in virtual anarchy; reduced to a state of clan living similar to the dark ages, but fueled by the technology of the times, as they survived on the refuse of the upper crust in a constant struggle for the things the rest of the world takes for granted.

Brandishing his own form of strength and justice in an effort to live, rather than just survive, while holding tightly to a family borne sense of honor and dignity, Thorsson Krey and his North Clan thrived in the underground of a vast metropolis that used to be Seattle, Tacoma and Portland. The orphans of a larger group of free-thinking radicals, branded "Environmental Terrorists" and known by the government as the AFG, or Alliance For Gaia; the North Clan was, unbeknownst to Krey, being hunted and set up for extermination. As fate would have it, though, not all fires are so easily extinguished.

Fleeing into obscurity to fight another day, Krey manages to slip into a cryostasis program designed exclusively for the very rich to escape this decaying world in favor of a chance at a better life. Thinking he will awaken after 100 years to a new chance at a life worth living, he is instead thrust right past a chain of events that led to the very exodus of the last of mankind from their dying planet, and arises to find that he is not only no longer on Earth, but is now a slave to a new controlling hierarchy: a Fleet of survivors made up of the descendants of the AFG, combined with the elite of Earth who made it off world and now scavenge planet to planet in a desperate search for some kind of future for mankind.

Proving his worth to the Fleet, he is freed to assist them in their struggle with an indigenous race of telepathic "dragon" creatures who threaten to stop them from attaining the mineral they desperately need in order to press on to their next destination before the unstable system surrounding them self-destructs. A severe conflict of interest arises as he realizes they are causing this instability themselves, and Thor is faced with making the difficult decision to follow his own destiny and uphold his honor and integrity, or blindly follow orders and help to annihilate an ancient alien race that he discovers are far beyond the limited capability of which they are being painted as possessing.

Rediscovering a lost relationship across the vast boundaries of time and space, Thor meets Sky, who he finds to be much more than she seems as connections to his past emerge through her and throw his whole new life into a tailspin. Sympathetic to the plight of these creatures as well, she struggles with the leaders of her kind to help them find their last remaining traces of humanity as loyalties are tested and duty collides with honor, ultimately finding Thor abandoning all hope for his own kind, and coming to the aid of those who he was told were his enemy. They find, along with the few who remain dissident at their side, that you cannot stop the tides of fate, and are themselves now separated from the rest of humanity as they flee to protect Ar'Jvikkah, the offspring of the alien Queen and all that is left of a collective history passed down by this dignified elder race of travelers, who Thor discovers are connected in a very deep and historic way to the human race, on their own exodus... full circle, back toward what they believe will be a *healed* planet Earth.

<u>CHAPTER 1: PREMONITION</u>

It was now fully dark outside and the weather was getting progressively worse as she left the bar on foot and started heading back the way she came. She came around the corner by the overpass and paused in front of the side alley at the base of the ramp, digging in her cargo pocket for a hair tie to get her long, blonde hair out of her eyes as the wind picked up in random attacks, sometimes even blowing straight up. She suddenly had the overwhelming feeling that someone was right behind her. Before she could turn around, a gust of wind blew the leather fedora right past her leg where it spun around on its edge, then came to a stop and rested a few feet out in front of her.

She smiled, finally able to breathe again, and continued tying her hair back. "So, where have you been hiding out?" she called out loud, speaking well over the volume of the wind, but still not turning to look at him. No answer. She was overcome with a sudden bad feeling, and started to spin around to see what was wrong with him, when, YANK! Her head was jerked straight back by her pony tail, pulling her momentarily off balance. *Why would he do this?*

"Hey!" She dug her heel, regaining some posture, then reached back, grabbing the hand he was holding onto her with and pinning it to her head. She breathed in and squatted low, twisting her frame and pivoting on the balls of her feet with his hand trapped. His arm was twisted all the way under, 180 degrees, when she could finally see his face. She gasped when she realized this was not Dagaz!

She stood all the way up, nearly breaking his trapped arm, then took one step back. As his weight bore down on his lead foot, she suddenly released his hand and thrust a powerful kick right into his kneecap, breaking the joint straight back instantaneously. His scream echoed off the surrounding buildings, but no one was around to hear it. He mumbled something unintelligible, then passed out from the pain, quaking on the ground in his long trench coat. She stood above him, wide eyed, catching her breath and looking all around in a fighting stance until she was sure the threat was contained.

She knelt down over him and started going through his pockets. He was apparently some sort of wealthy topsider. Jackass probably came down here a lot, looking for prostitutes and was going to try to rape her, she figured. She resisted the urge to pummel him further in his sleep, and twisted around to see where that hat of his went; one hand still on his chest.

The sound was unclear, kind of like a hum from deep down inside her head. Everything shook sideways and there was a strange smell. She couldn't control her mouth and briefly had the sensation of biting her tongue. A strange echo rambled on in her head, like several different voices all trying to say the same word, but from different starting points, then everything started to fade into darkness.

He lay awkwardly strewn on his back gasping for air, the pain in his leg nearly unbearable. The spring loaded cuff-stunner he grabbed her wrist with was designed to shock the victim until turned off by the remote side, which still remained tightly enclosed in his hand. He broke concentration while struggling hard to get to his feet and fumbled the transmitter grip, sending it bouncing to the ground next to her rapidly convulsing body. He had no intention of turning it off anytime soon, and he smiled smugly through the pain at the way he stole victory from the jaws of certain defeat, but in the blink of an eye, the verdict was changed yet again.

"James Stanton!" the voice boomed from right above them. He clambered about in a panicked frenzy, and jerked with his whole body so hard that he literally crumbled back to the ground, scrambling to roll onto his back so that he could get a look at who was behind him as he grasped at his mangled knee. The man was wearing black business attire from head to toe, his arm outstretched toward him holding a TC Contender single shot competition pistol with night sights and a silencer leveled motionless right between his eyes. Stanton's mouth popped open, but he was unable to make a sound. Shocked into motion by the loud report, a pair of crows who were fighting over a nearby sandwich bag took flight over the top of the onramp and disappeared quickly toward the freeway above before the blast even finished echoing in the deserted junction.

Kait laid in fetal position on the ground, practically underneath the twitching corpse of James Stanton, with strong gusts of wind whipping her hair into her eyes, along with dust and debris from the roadside. She focused her entire will on maintaining consciousness and relaxing her convulsing body by tuning into the pitch of the obnoxious device's debilitating energy the way Thor had taught her. The lone gunman bent down next to them and dug a set of keys out of Stanton's pocket, then walked over to get his car that was left parked just on the other side of the deserted road and pulled up close to them, popping the trunk.

He scooped up a small laptop computer from inside the car and shut it in a briefcase along with some paperwork and folders, snatched Stanton's fedora off of the ground beside them, then carelessly tossed it all in the trunk, followed by Stanton, himself. She desperately struggled to do something, realizing the device had paralyzed her completely, except for the violent shaking. The man turned his attention back toward her and drew the long, single shot pistol from his shoulder holster and leveled it directly at her head. His dark eyes were cold as ice as he made momentary eye contact with her, and it was then that she realized this man was a solid professional, that she probably got caught in the middle of something that didn't even concern her, and that he was definitely going to kill her, nonetheless.

Just then, gunfire erupted from off in the direction opposite the bar… from somewhere in the alley. The man in black doubled over and was sent straight backward, losing his gun instantly as huge wounds opened up in several places on his chest, abdomen and neck. She completely lost her focus on the device and was taken over violently by the stunner's charge again. She faded out of consciousness and slipped immediately into a dream she had experienced numerous times throughout her young life….

She is flying over an area of untouched wilderness, somewhere in the mountains of the Pacific Northwest… feeling free, but on her way to do something, or meet with someone. The feeling becomes more urgent and much more vivid, and finally she is able to see her destination: a small cabin on a tundra covered hillside. Focusing in from high above, she can see Thor walking up the hill toward the house and she swoops down to greet him. Just as she reaches him, instead of continuing toward the cabin like he usually does, he turns around to face her.

Large wings sprout outward from behind him and he rises slightly upward off the ground, eyes glowing and arms out to the sides with his palms up. "Thor?" she asked, shakily, as the sky started to darken and the wind kicked up to an intensely strong howl. To her terror, she could suddenly tell by his energy and the way he was smiling that this wasn't really Thor. She lunged straight up, trying to break away using her own wings, but was quickly stopped by a blast of malignant energy from the palms of this doppelganger that sent her reeling over backwards with a sensation that could only be described as concentrated despair. She gasped and wept at the same time as the darkness surrounded her from within in a matter of seconds.

She was jarred awake to the sensation of falling hard onto the ground, then suddenly realized she was being carried, fireman style, over the shoulder of a huge man as he effortlessly ascended several flights of stairs. Upon reaching the top level, the man, dressed in some sort of official looking uniform, reached out and put his hand on a sensor pad next to a solid steel sliding door. It beeped, then whisked open, revealing a room with about 50 people in it, all of which she instantly realized she knew... *All of which were deceased!*

She suddenly became very frightened as she gazed into the eyes of one, in particular... her little sister. The five year old girl standing before her had died in her arms when she was a child herself, from complications with a severe flu attack, and now, as she lived and breathed, here she stood before her! As good as it was to see her here, in the flesh; Kait could immediately tell something was amiss. It *was* her, down to the very last detail, but her energy was somehow different... simply put, she was a cheap copy, at the very best. She was, quite simply, someone else. The gnawing feeling in her abdomen intensified as she turned to her benefactor, the man who had turned off the stunner and carried her here, only to realize that he was no longer in the room.

She tried to speak, but instead of words, she scarcely managed to utter something more akin to a grunt or groan. She was now becoming truly terrified, and she instinctively spun back around to her sister. She glanced downward and realized she was involuntarily hovering a few feet from the ground; the sensation of energy permeating the air around her. The hair stood on the back of her neck, and her arms slowly rose out to the sides, palms up, as her giant wings flapped gently out to the sides to stabilize her.

Looking at each and every terrified face before her, she realized something ominous was happening as she mentally recorded the looks of awe and terror from everyone in the room. She was becoming more and more detached from them. Within a few seconds, she didn't even recognize her own sister, and she had elevated her pitch to a point well beyond that of anything she had ever experienced or even imagined before. It came as natural to her as drawing breath... almost as if she had been doing this her whole life.

Turning her palms out to the sides, then over toward them, she unloaded. Screams of terror and the crashing sound of lightning and destruction filled the air as she tore the entire room and everyone in it asunder, leaving not so much as a remnant bone to tell their tale. In the metal sheathing of the opposite wall, she could hazily make out the reflection through the smoke and debris of someone she no longer recognized, hovering a few feet above the floor with glowing eyes and wings like a dragon flapping in the air out to her sides. Her hair had darkened and her whole body seemed to be engulfed in some sort of pure energy protective aura that fluctuated in hue as she breathed a sigh of momentary relief that this was over.

Gasping for air with her heart racing, she sat straight up in her new bed in the Captain's berth onboard the Phoenix and quickly looked around. She forced her eyes to focus as fast as she could; needing to see what was truly real. Thor was still sleeping soundly by her side, and it appeared everything was just fine, but still she had a hard time shaking the intense and lingering feeling of guilt and shame for what had just transpired, dream or not. She had the first part of this dream many times before, but never the rest. She was unclear what to make of it, and wanted to talk to Thor about it before it faded into obscurity as her dreams often do. She started shaking him, gently but persistently. "Whu... hmmm," he stirred, opening his eyes just slightly, then rubbing one of them. "Are we there yet?"

"Not just yet," she smiled, her middle length dark brown hair tickling his neck as she kissed him gently. "Do you still need more sleep?"

"I've been sleeping for centuries... hell no! I'm good... I hate sleeping!" he yelled softly with a smile

"I might be starting to get that way myself," she led in, grabbing his interest as he propped himself up slightly on his side, paying closer attention. "I just had one hell of a dream! You know how when you dream you're someone else, you can't tell it isn't you... it *feels* like it's you?"

"Yeah, I think so... why? What happened?" Just then, the intercom chirped twice and the voice of Ensign Bjorn Eriksson, their navigator, helmsman, and trusted friend, resounded from the speaker.

"Captain, there's something you need to see... You both better get up here as soon as possible

"On our way!" Thor yelled back, already strapping on one of his combat boots.

———————

They arrived on the bridge to find Bjorn typing away on multiple screens, obviously more than a little disturbed by something he had discovered. "Captain…" he nodded, barely looking up from his work, "Commander…" he added, gesturing at Sky, who returned the nod, and then looked at Thor and smiled, shrugging.

"Well…?" Thor prodded.

"Okay, let me see if I can break this down in a manner that makes sense at all…" He scratched the top of his head and the back of his neck as he continued to stare at the screen, fishing for the right words.

"Just bloody spit it out, man!" Thor intervened, sarcastically snapping his fingers several times fast, right in the Ensign's face in an effort to break him out of his trance.

"Okay… we have a potential problem. As you know, we have all but escaped the shockwave *and* the threat of getting caught in the gravitational pull of the singularity, and are cruising at our top speed with the addition of solar sails at very near the speed of light, but almost exactly one hour ago I was studying the singularity, and --"

"Singularity?" Sky asked.

"The black hole. I was studying it closely, getting *all kinds* of new data! We've never before seen one from this distance, not to mention recording it's birth in the universe, first hand!" He started smiling, speaking quickly and as excited as a giddy child at the wonder he was beholding. "The data coming in was incredible! I mean, --"

"Bjorn!" Thor yelled, reining him in.

"Yeah, yeah, right. Sorry. Anyway, I was studying it closely, and about an hour ago, there was an explosion of some kind… a secondary explosion, if you will, deep within the black hole. It was a sizeable burst of energy, and it seemed, at first, to be unidentifiable in nature. I couldn't see a ripple of any kind, or any shockwave strong enough to escape the gravitational field, so I assumed it simply 'imploded,' the way planets and small stars do when they are consumed by a black hole of this magnitude... Then I saw this." He clicked a few buttons and pulled up a screen showing the blast radius of a halo-style shockwave of some kind, surrounding the black hole's center in an almost perfect sphere, but slightly elongated in the shape of an ellipse. Then he showed them another one, this time at least twice the size, strongly exaggerating the ellipse in both directions, as if those sides were accelerating. "This one was taken 20 minutes ago."

Thor looked at Sky, then back at Bjorn, with an increasingly concerned look on his face. "What does this mean," he asked, "and why didn't it show up on a regular scan?"

"What it means is that we are about to get hit from behind by a shockwave composed of concentrated tachyon radiation traveling faster than the speed of light," Bjorn explained. "The reason it didn't show up on any of the regular scans is that tachyon particles are subatomic... if it wasn't for the concentrated nature of this blast, and the fact that I was scanning the singularity when it happened, we would probably not have noticed it until we got blindsided by the shockwave without ever seeing it coming!"

"When *what* happened?" Thor asked, a little puzzled.

"The blast... It looked, at first, as if something huge was emerging from *inside* of the black hole! I know this sounds preposterous, but its actual mass, the measurable part, that is, nearly doubled in size immediately before the explosion, as if something absolutely massive was trying to emerge *from the other side*, and then, BAM! It erupted like another supernova! The difference, this time, was that due to the already extreme gravitational pull of the black hole, the entire explosion was suppressed within the event horizon... that is to say, it was drawn immediately back into the black hole just as soon as it started to explode outward. Sort of an instantaneous implosion, per se. That's when I noticed the distortion on our view of the surrounding stars, and augmented the scan to include subatomic particles," he added, gesturing at the monitor, still frozen on the last picture of the tachyon shockwave.

Thor slapped him on the shoulder, "Good work! Now what? What's going to happen to us?"

"There's no way to be sure... This sort of thing has never happened in recorded history."

"Best guess...?"

"I've been running some simulations on our solar sails, and it looks to me that the only way to keep from getting run over is to try to *catch the wave*. Follow me on this.... We already bend the shape of our shield ellipses into solar sails, outside of the heliopause, to combine interstellar winds with our relative speed and enhance our forward momentum, yes? Now picture altering the parameters a little more to shape them into giant spinnakers and drogue chutes, in reverse, to catch as much of the solar halo that is being pushed forward by the tachyon wave, directly from behind, causing us to accelerate drastically *just before* the main body of tachyon radiation hits us, since, unfortunately, our shields won't catch, stop, or even alter subatomic particles... This should, by all my calculations, give us a fighting chance of not being shredded on a subatomic level by the universe's worst sandstorm, straight from the mouth of Hell itself!"

"Just how fast are we talking about?" Sky probed with a terrified look quickly replacing her light demeanor.

"If we manage to hold together, we will have accelerated to 1.2 times the speed of light," Bjorn reported, matter-of-factly, a nerdish grin playing at the edges of his lips.

"And what about the ramifications of traveling faster than the speed of light, in the first place?" she posed, mainly just for consideration. "Isn't that impossible?"

"In the physical world, yes... yet it happens in nature every day in planes of existence that can't be measured or quantified. Thought, for example. Our thought energy travels nearly instantaneously, projecting outward, omni-directionally, just like the energy from subatomic radiation!"

"Projects...? Explain how you can prove that!" Sky argued.

"Telepathy." Bjorn stated proudly, glancing with a grin toward Thor, who had an obvious light turn on inside his head right at that moment. "It can't be measured, quantified or proven... yet we all know better. Well, we do now, anyway!"

"Okay... supposing it *is* possible... aren't we going to become an experiment in time/ space disruption? There's a good reason everyone can't exercise telepathy!"

"The lesser of two evils," Thor interjected, staring hard at the monitor, then at Bjorn, who half-smiled again and nodded in agreement. "How long until it hits?"

"Two hours," Bjorn said, clicking on the terminal and bringing up an current screen showing a noticeable change in the short time since they had been talking. Sky closed her eyes and just breathed, her mind racing through possible connections to the dream she had not an hour earlier.

"Everyone make all necessary preparations. Meet me back on the bridge in one hour." Thor walked purposefully toward the door, softly brushing his hand over Sky's on the way by. "I'll tell Erük, I've just got one stop to make first...."

"McGinn?" Sky guessed.

"McGinn."

"I'll get Dr. Astrydd and meet you in the brig... we need to get all nonessential personnel back in cryostasis immediately! Hell, prepping all the chambers will take close to an hour!"

"Do you think we should? Given the nature of the problem?" Thor asked, directing the question slightly more at

Bjorn. Sky widened her gaze, shrugged, and exhaled loudly, rolling her eyes in uncertainty, then turning to Bjorn as well.

He stared at Thor for a moment, then at Sky, took a deep breath in and then held it for a long time, tapping on the edge of the monitor as if he was deep in thought. He slowly blew out every last bit of air he had been holding, then cleared his throat to speak....

"Aw, shit, guys... I don't know! I'm just a fucking navigator... damn!" Thor and Sky both burst into a fit of nervous, pent-up laughter, then sprang into action, both heading for the same door.

"Take that as a yes?" Thor nudged Sky playfully. "I'll just meet you back here... I'm going to give McGinn the code to my old quarters, as long as he can handle all this!"

"I'll get Astrydd and take care of the others," she smiled.

CHAPTER 2: KIERAN MCGINN

Thor placed his hand palm down on the already reprogrammed door lock scanner to the brig, then took a cautious half-step back as the huge steel door slid sideways on its well-designed magnetic tracks to reveal a small room full of anxious looking cryo patients, some thoroughly adjusted to their new lifeline, some not so much. A couple of the older, slightly frailer people were still in their cells, even though the energy fields had been turned off by Sky long before their escape from the Algol system.

The rest were either pacing around the room in deep thought, or huddled in a ring around the glowing central column of the cell room as if it was a campfire for the small amount of heat it generated, this being one of the many chambers onboard that maintained an uncomfortable, yet energy efficient 58 degrees Fahrenheit during deep space runs. All the rest followed suit... all but one. Off to the right, sitting back against the partition wall between two cells was Kieran McGinn. The well-built, 40 year old Irish man appeared, for reasons Thor could definitely understand, to be keeping entirely to himself, and seemed mildly entertained by the nearly inexhaustible supply of cheap entertainment around him.

"Top of the morning' to ya!" Thor yelled. McGinn looked up from his daze and smiled.

"Captain Thorsson Krey, is it, now? Good to see you, to be sure… good to see you!"

"Let's take a walk…." Thor gestured toward the door, trying very hard not to get into a conversation with anyone else, though he could tell they all had numerous questions for him. He held off until just before he shut the door behind him and McGinn, then turned back around to them and spoke directly. "Commander Davies and Dr. Astrydd will be with you momentarily and will require your full cooperation to prepare for the next leg of our flight… please see to it that they get it!" He placed his palm back on the door and it slid quietly closed, locking automatically, as no code was entered. "Follow me."

"Welcome to the future, eh?" McGinn laughed out loud, mostly just breaking the tension as he struggled to catch up with Thor, who was leading him quickly down a series of tight corridors.

"How long have you been awake?" Thor asked him quickly.

"About a week... I think. Time seems to be standing still in here! I still don't have any Goddamn idea where we are or what we're doing… All I've been told is to shut up and shovel this "crystal" shite, and next thing I know, were in a state of total mutiny and I hear your voice over the loudspeaker sayin' you're the new Captain! Nice twist of fate, by the way, but why were we not free in the first place? And where the hell is CryoKinetics in all this? Is this their boat?"

Thor stopped and stared at him for an uncomfortably long time. He could see that Kieran was absolutely clueless about where, and more specifically, *when* he was, but there was something else. He couldn't put his finger on it, but he'd seen this look before... in the underground. This man was hiding something from him, he was sure of it. He had another agenda driving him and it seemed to have something directly to do with him. He decided to play along for the time being and see what transpired... guard up, of course.

He took Mr. McGinn into the computer room where he spent his first week learning how to manipulate the ship's shields with his mind and laid the entire scenario on him just as Captain Parnell had done for him. He told McGinn of the exodus that led mankind to live on space stations orbiting the Earth, and how a fleet of self-sustainable bio-ships left to search for another inhabitable planet, orbiting potential prospects long enough to gather resources and raw materials, then setting off again, on and on, until the present time.

None of the planets so far have fit all the required criteria for prolonged settlement or terraforming, with the possible exception of Cheops, a rogue moon in the Alcyone nebula, so no new roots had been planted. He explained a bit about their last mission, about their timetable and about their problem with the indigenous creatures penetrating their energy shield. He told McGinn how he was tricked into helping the fleet perpetrate a global genocide and how the whole event, including the destruction of their world and the formation of a massive black hole in its place could have been avoided. Mankind had become nothing more than interstellar planetary parasites. "In short, Mr. McGinn, you are not onboard a boat, you are on an interstellar spacecraft heading back in the direction of what hopefully will be a healed planet Earth."

"What happened to Earth... to The United States of America? Is there any world government left in place at all?" Kieran asked, fishing for something in particular.

Thor had researched most of what Captain Parnell had told him on this subject, and knew the basic facts to be true, so he broke it down for McGinn, carefully leaving out his family's involvement with the AFG. "There was a 25 year Arab war that started in the late 21st century, depleting most of the world's resources, especially in the smaller, more anarchic countries that had very little to begin with. In an effort to guard themselves from extinction, several countries brought the conflict to nuclear capacity, ironically feeling it was the only way for their particular race to survive, then justified it with religious zealotry.

"The Earth fell into a nuclear 'autumn' that lasted 3 long years, at the end of which, the world's population had dropped to less than 1/3 that which it was at the beginning of the century. Some died in the war, some died of radiation sickness and disease, and many to the increasingly severe weather patterns and natural disasters created by the environmental disruption, but all of this paled compared to the carnage that followed.

"The chaos and desperation quickly turned an already violent race of divided people into roving bands of nomadic pirates that swept from city to city and across the countryside, raping, killing, and taking whatever they could, leaving behind scattered patches of defenseless victims with scorched homes that were spared nothing but their very lives, and sometimes not even that. As food supplies became contaminated, the soil no longer supported crops, and livestock and migrating animals fell prey to disease, they turned to the only food source they had left... *other humans!*

"With most of the world's soldiers dead, and those that remained turned mercenary and charged with the guarding of the palaces of the wealthy corporation owners and politicians, there was little hope of stopping this onslaught of devastation. It seemed mankind's ingenuity, combined with an extreme lack of foresight, had finally and ironically brought about his final demise.

"It was then that The Alliance For Gaia, a radical group of environmental activists, branded "eco-terrorists" by the government, who went underground to escape prosecution, came down from the hills en masse upon every stronghold in the western hemisphere and took them by storm. Not only weren't there sufficient numbers left to defend against such a force, but their timely coup de grâce was delivered completely by surprise, as they were believed to be all but disbanded and extinct for nearly a decade. The status quo had long since written them off as any kind of a threat and had no idea the Alliance had been preparing for this exact scenario all along by experimenting with new weapon technologies and tactics. Not only hadn't they been snuffed out and exterminated by the corralling efforts of the government, but they were stronger than ever.

"They grew, not in numbered pockets that could be identified and stopped, or branded as a cult of extremists by the government, but rather, as an idea; a ghost in the machine, living among those who didn't care or were distracted by their own agenda, quietly waiting for the right time to strike. Their strength *was* their anonymity. They used every manner of underground communication to spread the ideals of their cause like a brushfire... music, art, television, the internet... planning only in vague hypotheticals, until at the right time, when it was the only remaining option, the Revolution gave birth to itself! Those who were tuned in to the cause knew exactly what to do.

"There is always opportunity in chaos, and this sudden global shift of power was no exception. With the downward spiral the environment was taking, a new plan took root. A new Alliance was formed with the superpower from the East to build and launch a fleet of self-sustaining eco-ships to facilitate the escape of civilized man from this dying planet. All remaining resources were exhausted to meet this goal, and miraculously, it was accomplished. The Great Exodus had begun.

"Much equipment was salvaged during the construction process. Since it would have been far too inefficient to launch a fleet of this magnitude from the Earth, it was built almost entirely in space, orbiting around the Earth, while salvage crews collected everything of any use. Communication satellites, spy satellites, missile defense satellites, weapons, fossil fuel, just about everything left on the planet or floating around in space was collected, dismantled, then put to some kind of use... This, of course, included all of us floating human ice cubes on the massive CryoKinetics satellite!

"CryoKinetics had long since financially deteriorated and had clientele from every corner of the world, so our lives became subject to International Salvaging Claim law. The AFG's first notion was to leave us there, or shoot us down. After some heated debate, they chose to put us all in a state of deep freeze, excluding only the parts of the brain and soft tissue that would be irrevocably damaged by freezing, while keeping those parts under strict temperature control. This would allow for indefinite cryostasis with very minimal energy expenditure. They could then bring us along, and thaw us out as needed for slave labor; after all, to most of the Alliance, we represented the upper crust of the "elite" whose relentless self-indulgence and self-serving legislature and lobbying helped bring the Earth to this state of malignant decay.

"Within one year of star mapping, and improvements to fleet for extended self-reliance, all signs of civilized life on Earth had disappeared, and the Fleet decided to move on.... To make the rest of the story really short, Mr. McGinn, that was around 700 years ago.... It's the year 2749, not 2157... and we were extremely fortunate to have been thawed out at all," Krey grinned as he punched in a couple commands on the holographic computer terminal next to them and brought up a 3D image of the black hole, complete with an updated rendering of the incoming shockwave, then turned the base around so it faced McGinn, who was still sitting with his jaw wide open and a blank stare, "and that's not even the *best* part!"

"I'm truly afraid to ask," McGinn said quietly.

CHAPTER 3: THE GREAT TRAVELLER

Holding the elegant case just behind the hilt of the sword handle, with the curve of the weapon bent downward at waist level in his left hand, Thor bowed at the waist, eyes up. He stepped forward with his right foot, turning his toes outward with the heel in at a 45 degree angle in a traditional Japanese hanmi stance and drew his katana from the sheath with his right hand, slicing all the way across at neck level from left to right in the same fluid motion that it was drawn with, then reversed the footwork while rolling the sword around with the right wrist, crossing back over to the left side and wiping the blood from the blade as it is lined back up with the sheath and gracefully slid back in, edge upward, gravity keeping the edge from rubbing along the inside of the sheath and dulling the sword. Heels together, eyes up, he bowed at the waist.

The lights were at their dimmest setting in the Biodome, simulating nightfall for the nearly 5 acre ecosystem of fruit bearing trees, plants, crops, small animals and fish that lived in its meandering streams and fields. Thor liked to come here when he needed to think and practice kata. It was the only place on board that really reminded him of Earth. The smells and sounds were off a little bit, but they were close. Trees were still trees, and the blend of aromas emanating from the vegetable fields was close to euphoric. Where he came from, most everything was either man made or polluted, so this place was paradise by anyone's standards.

Being the main source for all of the ship's oxygen, there was also a natural boost to be had while practicing here. Standing centered among a series of small pools and streams used for natural filtering, Thor quickly drew his sword again, this time, rolling a fan block around to his right side while rushing forward two steps, finally thrusting the tip forward with the sheath held downward in his left hand, guarding his head in an overhead block. He smiled, sensing he wasn't the only one in the room anymore.

"How is the little one?" he asked, turning his right leg sideways behind the left, rolling backwards in a defensive chugari, ending with the sword guarding the overhead position with its handle high, and the tip pointed down and to the right, sending his ghost attacker's overhead strike sliding off his right side toward the ground, along the full length of his blade. Pivoting 180 degrees to the left on his heels to end up in a left hanmi facing the opposite direction, he sliced almost straight down, but slightly to the left, at what would be an attacker's left shoulder and neckline, a killing blow, then fan blocked with a roll to the right again, and finished off the attacker behind him with a thrust to the rear on his right side.

"Excellent," Erük answered from the top of a very large apple tree, with a mouth full of apple mush. "He grows more every day." He dove down gracefully, gliding in a very low swoop along the top of the grass that Thor was standing knee deep in, ending directly in front of him with a very skillful back-flip, landing perfectly on his back legs alone. Thor smiled and nodded, placing his katana gracefully back in its sheath, and grabbed Erük's right arm, gripping his forearm tightly, then pulling him in for a brotherly hug. Thor was just about to ask where the little one was when he saw him over Erük's shoulder.

He was diving straight down toward the pools with a mouthful of soft, baseball sized red fruit, and Thor cringed, pushing to get around Erük, unsure if maybe he wasn't falling, rather than flying. Erük stopped him, *"No need to worry, my brother. Remember, he is the son of Ar'Yiisah, The Great Flyer... just watch,"* he said, telepathically. The young Sand Dragon, or M'ahk Tehríll, meaning "Wind Walkers" in their native language, was only a few days old, but to Thor's amazement, had already nearly tripled in size and coordination! He landed softly in a small pool of water with a splash, chewing happily on the red fruit mush with what had to be a huge smile on his face, shining through as his cheeks bulged outward like a hamster, teeming with half chewed fruit. Thor smiled back at him and winked, relieved.

They had been staying in the Biodome for comfort, as it bore the closest resemblance to the caves they lived in back on their planet. Kept at a constant 75 degrees Fahrenheit at all times, it was also the perfect atmosphere for raising one of their young efficiently. Sky even came up with a way to saturate a closed-loop stream system with crystal to simulate their subterranean water system without contaminating the rest of the ecosystem. Being their primary source of nutrition, this was all they needed to stay healthy for the meantime, at least until more permanent quarters could be provided, though they had taken a serious liking to some of Earth's fruits and vegetables in the process.

Erük could tell from the onset of the conversation that there was something major on Thor's mind, so without even asking permission, he leaned in close, grabbing him by the shoulders, and locked eyes with him, just as he did the day they met, instantly absorbing all of his thoughts on what was about to transpire. Erük looked worried. He let go slowly and took a disbalanced step backward, clumsily turning to gaze at the young one standing next to him now. His curious eyes looked up at the 7 foot tall elder, trying to pry what was wrong out of him, but Erük was blocking him somehow.

"What is it...? What will become of him?" Thor asked without speaking.

"He's only been alive for a few days... this phenomenon might kill him."

"How can you know this? This sort of travel has never been done! Not even by us!"

Erük paused for a long time, then turned back around, looking directly at Thor again. *"We were not indigenous to that planet at all, my brother.... We evolved. We were not-- we were not always as we are now."*

"Who were you... where did you come from?" Thor asked aloud, suddenly more than a little intrigued.

"No one remembers. It is forbidden to talk about. Only the Queen carries this knowledge."

"You are from her bloodline, Erük, don't you share that legacy?"

"Not in that way, some memories have to be transferred directly. When she's dying, the old Queen will pass this on to one of her choosing. If they are of her bloodline, they will evolve to replace her. If not, they will carry it until one emerges who will."

Thor suddenly looked surprised, leaning over to see the young M'ahk Tehríll a little closer. "Your name is Ar'Jvikkah?" He smiled, looking back at Erük, "Why didn't you tell me this earlier?"

"He didn't tell me until just a moment ago... when I was worried for him."

"Why, what does it mean?"

"Great Traveler... as close as I can translate it. There isn't a word in your tongue for *Jvikkah*, it is simply how we survive and adapt... some of us change color to fit our surroundings, some of us can teleport short distances in times of stress, some can even join with the ether, or enter each other's dreams... This is all considered *Jvikkah.*"

"Join with the ether... you mean plane-shift? He's a planeshifter?" Thor asked, more bewildered by the moment at the seemingly unending complexity of these wondrous and misunderstood creatures.

"A *Great* Planeshifter, as his name would imply."

"Imply...? How do you get your names? He can barely formulate telepathic thought... surely he didn't name himself!"

"We receive our names from the collective... intuitively, at a very young age. We are born tuned into it, so listening comes natural."

"Amazing! But I thought your *collective* died with the Queen... How is it that--"

"It *never* truly dies, so long as one of her bloodline remains. She passed herself on to Ar'Yiisah. And Ar'Yiisah on to--"

"Sky," Thor smiled, nodding as he remembered the long stare Sky and Ar'Yiisah shared just before her passing.

CHAPTER 4: RELATIVITY

The three of them made it to the bridge to find Sky, Astrydd, and their new friend, McGinn converged around a monitor, hanging on Bjorn's every word, as he walked them through what he believed would probably transpire in just under a half hour. McGinn slowly turned around, having a hard time prying his attention from the monitor, or the front viewers above the control panel of the massive starship, showing an ever expanding universe go whipping by, star after star, as if they were watching an early Earth sci-fi show on large screen.

"Jesus, Mary and Joseph!" he yelled, stumbling backward over Astrydd's leg and falling down flat on his back at the sight of Erük and Ar'Jvikkah entering the room with Thor, who was now dressed in full battle gear.

"Kieran! It's OK... these are my friends! This is Erük, and this little guy is Ar'Jvikkah... They are the ones I told you about... The Sand Dragons, remember?"

"F-f-f-ff-fucking dragons? Christ, I'm sorry, I musta missed that much! Well, never mind me, I'll just be over here changing me shorts..." He smiled nervously, slowly getting

28

back up to his feet without taking his eyes off either of them for more than a second.

Ar'Jvikkah bounded across the room, obviously very glad to see her, and jumped up into the air when he got close to them, landing right in Sky's open arms and nearly knocking her straight over backwards with his rapidly developing frame. She laughed and smiled, scruffling the top of his head like a playful child. She had become as much of a surrogate mother to him as she could possibly be, coming from an entirely different species, and the two were already practically inseparable. This may have started out from a sense of guilt and responsibility for accidentally killing his natural mother, Ar'Yiisah, during the struggle for control of the ship, but it evolved very quickly into an undeniably real bond between the two of them. Thor had only just begun to understand how deep this bond really went.

"Ar'Jvikkah, eh?" Sky exclaimed, smiling and holding him up high, looking directly into his enormous eyes. "Well, *I'm* going to call you Vik, for short," she smiled, glancing over at Thor, who was staring at her and smiling like a proud father.

"We have much to talk about," Thor said mysteriously, still smiling at her.

"Yes, we do..." She looked quickly in McGinn's direction with a serious look on her face, not wanting him to pick up on it. Thor looked a little puzzled, trying to gauge the seriousness of the issue, but not really having much luck reading her any further. He decided to dismiss it for the moment. "You look nice," she said with a smile, changing the subject by gesturing to the traditional Japanese katana on his left hip, shoved through the belt of his battle uniform.

"Yeah, well, it keeps me grounded..."

"We knew there was something special about you when we went through your personal effects storage on your cryo tube, and all you had with you was a couple pieces of paper and that sword," she laughed, "everyone else packed it full of every kind of picture, money, jewelry... damn near everything imaginable, but all you brought was a sword!"

"Yeah, well... some things never change," he said, glancing back at McGinn, who was staring at him strangely, but trying to muster up a bit of a smile. "What did you bring with you?" he yelled over to McGinn directly.

"Oh, this and that, nothing much, really," he evaded, glancing nervously at Sky for some reason.

"Didn't you guys know each other before going in?" she asked, rhetorically.

"No, no... w-we actually just met that day," he said quickly, "Hey, Bjorn, could you show me the current timeline for the event? Maybe just leave it up on screen so we can see where we stand?" he requested, quickly changing the subject.

"He's hiding something... all of his thought has been bent on you, Thor," Erük said telepathically, such that Sky could hear as well.

They all sat down in various seats surrounding the holographic monitor, pretending to be contemplating only what was being shown and discussed by Bjorn and Kieran. *"I've picked up on that as well. What do you think it's all about?"*

"I hadn't had the time to tell you, but we only found one thing in his personal locker as well," Sky interjected, now somehow able to hear Thor as well as Erük!

"And what was that?"

"A single picture..."

"Of what?"

"Of you!"

There was an awkward silence that even Thor had trouble not allowing to stand out. All he could picture was that horrific scene at the North Clan stronghold that cost him his entire family. There was no doubt that it was a professional hit, *but why? And by whom?* He made one strong and concerted effort to revert his attention to the business at hand. *But first, "How can you hear me, and I hear you...?"* he directed straight at Sky.

"I'm acting as a conduit for the two of you... eventually, you will both be able to do this on your own... you both possess the raw ability already," said Erük, who was hanging pretty close to McGinn now, possibly trying to read him a little deeper while keeping him distracted.

"Anyway, Thor, there is one more thing... " She put her head down in her hand as if she had a headache, or was deep in thought, and focused as hard as she could. Thor started to get a mental image of some kind of barcode. As it got clearer, he realized it was a tattoo of a barcode on the lower neckline of a man, laying on his stomach. It had a small series of numbers he had seen before... He looked over at McGinn, who was conveniently facing the right way, but his new uniform covered that part of his neckline completely.

"McGinn?" Thor asked.

"Yes. While we were reviving him we noticed that tattoo, and a lot of scars... more than you." Just then, he realized where he had seen these marks before... On the man he had beaten down right in front of Thomas in the underground! When the man sprawled out face down onto the pavement, he nearly lost his coat and shirt, and Thor had noticed this same sort of mark on him while he was laying in the street, unconscious. He had heard of these people before, in underground lore, and even then he realized this man wasn't one of Cane's regulars, but he didn't look into it too deep at the time. Perhaps he should have... He couldn't help but wonder if maybe his family would still be alive if he had!

These people were, in almost every sense of the word, ghosts. It was rumored they were an assassin's guild that worked for the highest bidder, and in most cases, that meant the government. Not the official government, mind you, but the one that didn't like to answer any questions when it needed something done. They did the work that was too dirty for the CIA, and too secretive for the NSA. The only thing Thor couldn't figure out was what this guy was waiting for.... Then it all started to make some degree of sense.

He had probably been sent after Thor, at first, to find out how much he knew about what Stanton had uncovered, and who else knew about it... and secondly, to recover the money. What they didn't expect was his move into CryoKinetics, as well as everything that transpired after the original 100 year trip went bad. He wasn't sure why this man had followed him into the future in the first place.... Maybe they were supposed to rescue him afterward, but he seemed to be having a severe moral dilemma now that things had transpired the way that they had. For what it was worth, Thor saw enough good in the guy that he resisted the urge to protect himself by putting him immediately back in cryostasis, and rather, decided to try to get inside the man's head instead. *"Keep an eye on this man at all times, you guys... I'm not sure what he's up to, but I think he was originally sent to assassinate me."*

"By who?" Sky asked.

"Some pretty bad-ass mother fuckers!" he said aloud with a devilish grin on his face, making Bjorn and Kieran both turn around and look at him quizzically. "There's no paddling back in from this one, ladies and gentlemen!" he added, staring intently at the 3D hologram showing the wave approaching closer and closer.

Sky sat with Ar'Jvikkah on her lap, gently stroking the back of his long neck with her fingertips, causing him to make a noise similar to a purring cat, then looked over at Erük, locking eyes with him for a moment.

"Don't worry, Sky, nothing will happen to him as long as I am in control."

"And I will protect this little one with my life... as if he was my own!" She offered in return.

"I know you will."

CHAPTER 5: TACHYON STORM

The lights on the entire ship had dimmed to a dark shade of amber and the proximity alert siren was going off in a steady, maddening cadence. After a very short debate, the crew had made the decision to harness themselves in to their seats to brace for impact. Erük was sitting calmly with a particularly large chunk of Crystal in his lap and talons, attempting to use it to augment his control over the properties of the shields to include resistance to the tachyon radiation as well as the interstellar wave it was pushing forward. The flashing lights made the whole situation even more surreal, and things seemed to progress at a slower and slower rate, until, just before impact, time seemed to stand utterly still.

There was no telling if it was the impact of the wave, or the fact that they had seamlessly, but quite suddenly, surpassed the speed of light itself, but all at once, things started to change. Time had frozen, but for the moment and its meaning, movement was still possible. Then, as if all the energy from the entire universe had hit them at once, a great shove from behind was felt by everyone, accompanied by a strange noise, knocking McGinn and Thor both, up and over their seats in what seemed like slow motion, revealing that neither of them had buckled their harness. They finally landed, both of them on their feet, as if during the flight over their chairs they had gracefully regained some amount of aerial control over their trajectories.

Thor felt a rush of energy, the likes of which he had never felt before, except in his dreams, and instinctively tried to tune into it by raising his pitch accordingly. He felt suddenly as if nothing unusual was taking place, in fact, his focus seemed to have sharpened dramatically, and he drew his katana defensively, as he noticed Kieran reaching for something behind his back. He assumed it must be a gun, though it seemed to be taking forever for him to draw it. Thor looked around quickly and noticed that no one else was moving any faster than McGinn.

Sky murmured something Thor could barely make out, "Thor, watch out... he's got a gun," but it sounded like it was coming through a pitch shifter in slow motion.

He turned back to McGinn, who had the pistol out and almost leveled at him, and spoke directly to him, staring him in the eyes, "You don't need to do this! Everything has changed! *WE* are in control of our fate... not anyone else! Don't make me do it!" As if he hadn't heard a thing Thor said, or he was speaking some foreign language, McGinn's eyes remained glazed with misunderstanding and the pistol went off twice, sending two bullets spiraling directly at him. They were moving very quickly, but in what was still slow motion to him, and he could actually track them through the air.

He quickly pivoted 45 degrees at the last possible second, then sliced straight down, cutting the first bullet directly in half, right out of midair as the second one flew past his ear, brushing through his hair before slamming into the back of his seat, sending some of its filling into the air in a slow motion shower of confetti. The noise from the gun's discharge came seconds later and was greatly distorted, almost as if it was shot underwater. He quickly looked around, amazed that he seemed to be the only one operating in "real time." No one else seemed to be sharing this effect, but as he looked around the room, what he started noticing was much more bizarre than that.

People were phasing in and out of sight, apparently on the threshold of some kind of gateway between planes of existence. The lines between past and present, dream and reality, the physical and the ethereal, and space-time itself were crumbling before his eyes. One moment, he saw Sky, sitting with Ar'Jvikkah strapped across his shoulder to her chest, looking slowly around the room, mouthing something unintelligible, then he blinked and it was Kait, sitting there smiling at him! Caught up in the insanity of all of this, he suddenly realized he had been ignoring Kieran…

He spun around and saw him lunging at Sky with his pistol drawn, and without so much as a second thought or hesitation, Thor rolled across the floor toward them in a right chugari, using the momentum of the roll to add considerable force to his strike, as he came up out of it directly beside McGinn with his sword coming down from above, and cut right through the softest part of the midsection, just below his rib cage, completely separating the man in two halves. Thor cringed as he realized the very loud ringing in his left ear had to be the result of the gun going off again, and shocked out of his cohesion with the energy flow, he was now moving in slow motion himself as he turned in horror to see what had happened.

He could hear Sky screaming, but could not see her, only the flashing of the lights and a surrealistic blend of faces, flesh and voices in the darkening room, some familiar to him… some not. Through the corner of his eye he could see a cup of water spilling across one of the consoles. The water was pouring out in slow motion across the countertop, then when it reached the edge, it dripped... *upward*. His head was spinning and he was having a hard time remaining conscious, though the sound in the room was deafening, and growing louder. It started as voices, then distorted into abstract noises, vehicle sounds, industrial mayhem, and even explosions. It very quickly escalated to the point of complete and utter malevolence, and Thor succumbed to it entirely, collapsing on the floor, still holding a death-grip on his katana.

———————

Kait hovered above the aftermath of the carnage that had just been unleashed through her; huge dragon-like wings flapping gracefully, instinctively timed, even as the transition progressed back to her conscious self.

She floated softly back down to the floor, quickly regaining her sense of self. She was utterly blown away by what she had just done to them, but they weren't real... *were they? She wasn't real. This was a dream. It had to be.*

"Does it?" the voice boomed in her head, strong, yet somehow gentle.

"Does it, what?" she asked back without speaking.

"Does it have to be a dream?"

"I was just taken over by someone who destroyed everyone I know who already died... I am not even me... I think that it does!"

"Then, so be it."

"Who are you?"

"A friend."

"Why would a friend put me through this?"

"You can only move forward with your back to the past... but it was not I who put you through this, "

"Am I dead?"

"No, but you have no further use for this plane..."

"Who are you?"
"A planeshifter... like you."
"Will I see him again?"
"You already have."

Slowly, as if afflicted with the most severe New Year's Day hangover they'd ever experienced, each of them started to wake up, some lying on the floor and some still strapped to their seats. The body of Kieran McGinn was laying on the floor in front of Sky's seat, cut very cleanly in two, but for as critical of an area as had been severed, they were astonished that there was absolutely no blood. Not a drop. Thor slowly pushed his torso over to reveal something even more bizarre.... His eyes were completely white. No color, no pupils... nothing. Just white.

Sky screamed, and at first, Thor didn't look, he just assumed it was because of McGinn, but then there was a second one... almost a cry of pain. He spun around to see her holding her abdomen with a look of shock on her face. It was then that he noticed something was dreadfully wrong! Looking frantically around the room, he noticed that someone was missing... Erük's howl confirmed it, Ar'Jvikkah was nowhere in sight! He rushed over to where the young dragon had been sitting, strapped to Sky, and nearly ran right into Erük, when they both felt it at the same time... *Sky was pregnant!*

Thor and Erük huddled around her as Dr. Astrydd ran through several different diagnostic scans. Though very small, the medical facility onboard the Phoenix was top notch. From the bed that Sky was laying in, they were able to perform any scan, test, or even surgery with all of the necessary tools and equipment within arm's reach of the Doctor at all times.

Thor was amazed at the clarity of the scanning devices, more than anything else. It was apparently no longer necessary to interpret cross sectional data from CT scans or magnetic imaging for soft tissue, let alone utilizing harmful radiation to take x-ray pictures of bone density differences. Medical science had advanced to the point of being able to scan full body telemetry in one shot, then break down the views needed accordingly, whether it be a 3D shot of the entire body of soft tissue missing the skeletal system, or the complete reverse, and everything in between. The image was on the screen at the punch of a few buttons, or floating holographically near the patient for touch-relative identification. It was absolutely astonishing, the level of efficiency that mankind was capable of when his survival depended on it.

Astrydd stripped away the internal organs shrouding the view on the hologram, leaving only the obvious for examination... She was carrying the young dragon-child inside her, and she was pretty far along! He looked different than he should have, given his appearance at birth. Erük noticed this first, and spoke out. "He has evolved in reverse."

"Wh- What do you mean?" Sky asked shakily through teary eyes.

"We were not always as we are now." He looked up at Thor with a nod, "We were once very much like you...."

"How much?" Thor asked.

"I do not know for sure... It was-"

"Forbidden. Yeah, I remember. How the hell could this have happened, Erük?" Thor asked impatiently, holding Sky's hand tightly and stroking her hair. Dr. Astrydd looked up from the control module of her scanner with a shocked look on her face after scanning not only Sky, but Erük as well.

Astrydd cleared her throat and firmly sat the device down on the edge of the examination table, then looked them all straight in the eyes. "Because they have the same basic DNA. Exactly the same!" she concluded to the surprise of everyone in the room.

"Who? Sky and Ar'Jvikkah?"

"No, no, no…. Us and *them*!" she clarified, gesturing at Erük. "According to this, we're the same species! And that's not all," she added, looking around the room at each one of them, her face flushed white as snow. "Everyone in this room has the organs, skin, and muscle tissue of a 20 year old!" She continued around the room with the hand scanner repeating the test for accuracy. "I can't explain it, but it appears that we all have undergone some sort of mass regeneration…"

"Well, I'll be a cocksucker's lunch." Thor said with a blank stare on his face.

CHAPTER 6: RELATIVITY REVISED

On the way back to the bridge Sky took an understandable detour, letting go of Thor's protective grip for the first time since they left the medical bay. There were very few places onboard that were good for just being alone and thinking, but the Biodome was definitely one of the best. She had been coming here to read, think, or just hang out for as long as she could remember, and was probably more familiar with all the plants and animals in the many Domes like this one than anyone else in the fleet, including the engineers who designed these things. For her, it was a touch of a life she never had. She grew up hearing stories about Earth, but never experienced so much as a planet with an atmosphere until just a few years ago.

The last stop on their exodus was the planet Cheops, named after the greatest of the Egyptian pyramids back on Earth, due to the presence of a pyramid shaped mountain on its face that was so large, it was actually visible with the naked eye from orbit. The outer layers were identified as thousands of years of sediment and deposits of every conceivable origin, and eventually were stripped away by the Fleet's archeologists to reveal an actual constructed pyramid of unknown origin beneath the surface, mirroring almost exactly, the style, material, and proportional dimensions of the great pyramids of Giza in ancient Egypt. The most astonishing revelation was that after some very in-depth investigation, it was discovered that even this layer was simply nothing more than a shell for an internal structure... a natural pyramid of solid rhodochrosite growing from a hard mineral deposit, similar to a gigantic geode, rooted deep within the planet's surface. This particular crystal was known to grow in this shape back on Earth, but it was absolutely unheard of at this size and purity, leaving the Fleet's best scientists utterly baffled.

She was fairly young when they first arrived, maybe only 15 or 16 years old as her memory served, but already in full and loyal service of the Fleet Command. The first time she shuttled down to the planet her entire life changed instantly. Though the planet was cold and stormy nearly all the time, basking only in the distant glow of the surrounding seven stars, too far away to generate any noticeable warmth, along with the refracting light that penetrated and lit up the frigid blue nebula that surrounded them, and the hazy shrouded daylight of the ominous blue giant, Alcyone, she couldn't get enough of the feeling of extreme openness and the expanse of the heavens. It affected her so strongly she took her adult name from it. She was so captivated by this place that she spent most of her time here in a romantic daze, caught in the wonder and amazement of this intoxicating and exotic world to such an extreme that she could barely focus on even the simplest of her assigned tasks. Here, it seemed to her, *anything* was possible! It wasn't until about a week into their mission that trouble started brewing.

There were a small group of explorers among them who didn't exactly see eye to eye with Command, and took a pretty strong stance against them with regard to the handling of the strip mining operations underway on the surface. Delving deep into the caverns of the mountains that surrounded the pyramid on all sides for a rare variation of iron pyrite, or fool's gold, as it was called back on Earth, that was needed at the time to trigger the magnetic reactors that powered their engines, the ground crews had come into contact with some sort of indigenous life form. The creatures were nearly humanoid in appearance, at least so the workers thought, so efforts were made to communicate with them. It seemed no one could ever get close enough to get a real look at them, and all of the Fleet's sophisticated scanners came up with nothing possessing enough mass to identify as life at all… yet there they were.

The decision was made to simply continue to "mine around them," but as the crew's efforts started to encroach more and more on their natural surroundings, they began to change shape. What had always been encountered as a humanoid shape, standing in the shadows of the rock, just out of sight, staring at them and then running away when pursued, began to evolve into a series of more and more malignant forms. They were seen in the form of rock formations coming to life right before their eyes, clouds or mist that suddenly took human shape and then charged at the workers, and even as other humans… the worst recorded case being a woman walking all the way back to her shuttle with two coworkers by her side before realizing at the last minute that this was not her friend, but a doppelganger that had taken his form, leaving him nowhere to be found! The frightened woman and her partner didn't find out until the being actually tried to board the ship, and she noticed its feet weren't touching the ground. It fled immediately, and when they returned to the mine with a security team, the creature was gone… as was their friend.

A large party of them hunted for the man into the night, and had another encounter deep inside one of the shored up tunnels they had dug themselves. They were all carrying torches and light-sticks because the magnetic properties of the highly ferrous mountain range restricted the use of any closed cell power source anywhere near the mines, and rendered their spotlights useless. After about an hour or so, when they were just about to give up on that particular mine shaft, all hell broke loose.

The walls seemed to "come alive" and turn into every type of winged creature and crazy apparition the men could imagine. In the confusion, one man attacked one of them with his torch, and that's when they had an epiphany. These "ghosts," as they were being called, were susceptible to fire! The thing screamed a ghastly pitch that brought the men to their knees, some of them holding their heads and falling to the ground sideways, dropping their torches in the mayhem, but it didn't matter... The fire spread like it was spawned from hell itself, and when the air cleared and the smoke dissipated to some degree of normalcy, not a creature was left.

Two of the men died in the medical bay in the days that followed and most of the others were treated for third degree burns to every inch of skin that was exposed during the short lived, but very intense fire that engulfed them all. It seemed the stories of what transpired differed slightly from person to person; every tale slightly skewed toward a different fury from deep within the mind of the observer... ranging from bats, to witches, to ghosts or dragons, and all manner of twisted spectre and evolved life form. The one common factor that they all commented on was the smell.... It was said the smell of ether was strong in the air from the moment it all started until well after the fires were gone. The man they were looking for, a well-liked Journeyman named Nicolas MacAave, was never found.

Fleet Command made the decision to evacuate the colony, regardless of the fact that they had already started advanced terraforming procedures to stabilize the air and weather patterns on Cheops, and fire bomb the surface of the planet to speed up mining for the remaining Fleet, who were already charting the next leg of the exodus for the twin planets in the Algol system, nearly 15 light years away. This did not set well with the colonists, or the small group of miners and scientists who had already begun a more advanced study of these unusual beings, who, in their expert opinions, were merely acting in self-defense and had shown numerous signs of intelligence.

The group maintained that although the presence of a massive, long term polar storm encroaching within days would undoubtedly make colonization difficult, that the risks were outweighed by the benefits of finally having a home base from which to operate as a race of people. Fleet Command had been operating under the flag of Martial Law ever since the Exodus began, so the decision was made for them all without a chance for any further debate, thereby side-stepping the eventual establishment of a colony based House of Representatives as outlined in their long term protocol for colonization. The separatists believed that there was major ulterior motive driving Admiral Reid's decision to commit genocide and abandon a potential sustainable ground colony, however hostile, but since they could offer no proof, Reid used fear of the aliens to gain favor and public support, and so they stood alone, once more.

The facts were a little fuzzy to her at this point, but she did have some memory of a revolt and some kind of banishment taking place. The Fleet proceeded with the firebombing, and rode out the remainder of their tour with little incident until the end of the planet's solar cycle, bringing on a season of hostile weather and what was predicted to be a

50 year long storm forming from the tight rings of the equator, and converging on the poles. Their base that was set up on the southern pole near the pyramid mountain was abandoned, as was the colony, and the Fleet-wide decision was made to move on and catch up to the scout ships and Fleet Flagship, who had already departed for the Algol system at the onset of the storm. The terraforming efforts that would have softened the blow from the weather were destroyed in the firebombing, so there was no longer any good reason for the settlers to remain.

It was speculated by the so called "extremists" that the whole thing was a conspiracy their Commanders carried out to keep the Fleet from dividing. Prior to the entire chain of events, the same group of separatists had proposed, and even drafted some preliminary legislation for the birth of an independent colony at Cheops. They proposed that it even be granted sovereignty, due to the extreme physical separation from the rest of humanity that would take place by the Fleet pressing on. Reid did not like this, and made no secret of his desire to squash the entire movement right from its conception. He was not about to give up any power or control over his beloved Fleet without a fight; but what, exactly, he might be capable of was still a great mystery. Many people in his closest circles witnessed him plotting and scheming to discredit the separatists and their families, according to him, for reasons of Fleet-wide security and loyalty, but in the end, there seemed to be limits as to what he was willing to do, or even mentally capable of cooking up on his own.

This dynamic period of unrest gave birth to a lot of gossip from every corner of the Fleet, ranging from the plausible to the utterly absurd. It was even suggested by some that the indigenous "ghosts" were nothing more than fear based hallucinations brought on through the drugging of the miners and the search party by the management, and that the "spirit fire" that burnt the rescue crew was just a gas explosion set up by them as well, but even as young as she was, she knew the workers' stories had to be true.

She saw the many faces returning from work in the mines, many of which were her friends, and she knew they had seen something that couldn't easily be explained away; but in the end, the result was the same. They raped the planet, they got what they came for, the storm came, and they were on their way. This was just the way of things as far back as she could remember. Since she was a child she only had this one truth to count on... things would always keep changing, their leaders would keep on lying about it, and there would always be a future to stay busy planning for.

As they left, she could remember the main body of the lightning storm coming from all around them, attracted to their tiny ship like a magnet. Bolts of lightning were illuminating sections of sky randomly as she stared in wonder and relative safety through the front viewing shield at the mountains in the distance, the swirling clouds of gasses dancing violently around them, and the huge water spouts from the tempestuous ocean below, rising up to meet the heavens in a vortex of natural energy unleashed before them by the very Gods of this hostile world themselves. Much too young to appreciate the danger they were all in, she absorbed the experience to her very core; living a lifetime in each breath and for the first time in her young life, truly living in the moment. This was how she felt when she was with Thor. He was her storm, and yet, he was her mountain.

She was once again capable of living in the moment, and for all the conflict and strangeness the last few weeks had brought into her life, she felt as if she was exactly where she was supposed to be, doing exactly what she was supposed to be doing. She smiled, suddenly seeing the humor in this train of thought as she rubbed her belly, ripe with an alien life with whom she had already become familiar and began to love. She wasn't sure why not, but she was absolutely unafraid.

Looking high up in the dome's trees, she strolled along the edge of a tiny meandering stream, daydreaming about what it must feel like to be able to fly. Her mind flashed back in fragments to the dream she had, and for a moment she could almost *feel* the set of wings behind her, lifting the rest of her petite frame off the ground entirely. She slowly closed her eyes, smiling at the vivid sensation of weightlessness she was able to feel by simply thinking about it. Upon opening them, she realized too late that she was about to step off of the small grass plateau she was standing on into a small, but deep, pool of water, and as she started to fall forward, off balance, her right foot searching fruitlessly for a place to step, she suddenly found herself floating gracefully across the three foot drop to the other side without losing an inch of altitude! She gasped out loud, laughing a little, then looked quickly around the chamber to see if anyone was watching.

It felt similar to the zero gravity work she had done in the past... outside the carrier, but minus the suit and extreme cold. Unsure what just transpired, she looked back at the pool. *There was no wake!* She hadn't even touched the water at all! Staring for a moment in disbelief, she started noticing things in the water she had never been able to see before.

There were the small transparent fish, about the size of guppies, that she had seen before, and actually helped stock into the system, but among them, unseen by her eyes before this, were even smaller creatures, similar to small sea horses. There were hundreds of them, and for some reason she was able to focus on the individuals without even bending down to get a close look. She looked around the dome, suddenly noticing all sorts of vivid detail she had previously taken for granted.

Looking back up into the trees she noticed some clusters of fruit dangling at the lower canopy level and was overcome with a sudden primal urge to eat them. As if she had done nothing more than blink, she suddenly found herself standing, not on the grassy patch in the field, but on top of the actual branch she was just staring at from below, holding onto the smaller branch with the cluster of fruit! She was shocked, and jumped a little bit out of her skin while looking down and reaching into the fruit cluster for something solid to grab hold of. Realizing a couple seconds into this flailing dance that she wasn't going to be able to recover her balance, she instinctively looked down for a water landing and shot outward with the last bit of control over the situation that she could muster, holding one arm protectively around her belly. In the same blink of an eye that put her on the branch, she was suddenly standing waist deep in water, with a huge splash shooting out 360 degrees out to the sides in a circular pattern, rather than up and out, as her initial trajectory should have produced.

She stood still in the water, unable to fully assess whether she had been injured or not for at least a good minute or so after the water stopped moving. There was no pain in her legs, there were no imprints in the mud under her feet, and there was never the sensation of falling, or even any time elapsed at all, though the branch had to be at least 40 feet up in the air and 20 feet out to the side! Looking down at her own hand, she saw the bright red fruit, dripping with water from the pool, and she laughed out loud, took a large bite out of it, then started to climb up out of the water, smiling ear to ear with one hand still on her belly.

———————

Sky arrived on the bridge to find Thor, Bjorn, and Erük huddled around a monitor staring quietly at the screen. Erük turned and watched her approach closely, still obviously amazed by what was transpiring within her, as well as her outward appearance.

"You hold within you the essence of our entire species, Sky, do you feel this?"

"Oh, I know, Erük, believe me! He's making his presence known, that's for sure," she said aloud, smiling and rubbing her belly softly.

"I'm not just talking about Ar'Jvikkah," Erük led. Thor looked up from his terminal and glanced at Erük, then at Sky, nodding seriously. She looked back at him, puzzled. He walked slowly over to Sky and wrapped his arms around her. She couldn't get over how much different he looked, even on the surface... It was as if they had lost 10 years' worth of aging in one day.

Bjorn, the youngest among them, looked up from the terminal and spoke out, his voice cracking a little as if he was going through puberty all over again, "We're quickly approaching the Alcyone system's outer planetary rings. I strongly suggest we cut our speed back to normal if we're going to use any resources from our older outpost...."

"Alcyone system?" Sky looked at him, astonished, "Older outpost...? Jesus, you don't mean--"

"Cheops!" Bjorn laughed, giddy as a child, "I can't believe it either! Isn't this amazing?"

"Amazing? We shouldn't be anywhere near Cheops for at least another 20 years of cryostasis! We haven't even been on course for 2 days!! Just how fast *are* we going?"

"Well, we're getting mixed readings from telemetry... none of the stars are where they're supposed to be...." He took a bite of some sort of composite fruit bar. "It's a bit hard to say." He mumbled through a mouthful of food.

"What the hell does that mean?" she asked plainly, as Bjorn continued to type madly on the terminal's keypad in front of him.

"Just a few more… cross reference points… and-" His mouth hung open as he stared blankly at the screen, not really wanting to tell them what he was seeing.

"What? Spit it out… and I don't mean your food!" she smiled, half yelling at him in a motherly voice. Bjorn took a moment to chew the last of his bite, then swallowed it and cleared his throat before proceeding, obviously buying himself a moment to digest what he was seeing, himself.

"According to all available star charts on this area, using our last recorded vector just before the tachyon wave hit us as a baseline… we are either transcending time-space through a quantum relationship with-"

"English… Please!"

He looked up at them with a shocked look on his face, his mouth still hanging open. "I think we've just went _backward_ in time… I think we're actually _in_ the past!" It suddenly got extremely quiet in the room, then it was Sky who slowly cleared her throat, grinning skeptically while shaking her head to one side only, in more of a twitch than any kind of actual fluid movement, and spoke.

"How far?"

"Probably only hours... I'll know more when we slow down… at this speed everything is coming in waves… as if we're phasing in and out of existence. I don't know how else to explain it."

"A wormhole?" she asked, starting to take him a little more seriously.

"I don't think so. It has something to do with breaching the speed of light… The light from the surrounding stars isn't where it would be if we were standing still. We are literally _outrunning time._"

"Explain," Thor demanded.

"OK, let me see… When you see the light from a distant star, you are actually _seeing the past_, due to the fact that it took (x) amount of time, usually many, many years, to become visible to your eyes from that distance, yes? Three things are moving... the star, the light from the star, and the vantage point... *us*. Well, in this case, the vantage point is moving faster than the beam of light, so there is a kind of temporal distortion taking place that cannot be quantified... at least not by me... at this time."

"Sorry I asked... I liked your first answer better!" Thor laughed, pulling his hand through his hair as he approached the front console and planted his fist down on it, breathing in deeply then exhaling, preparing for whatever came next. "Full stop. Let's see what kind of shite we've stepped in now..."

CHAPTER 7: CHEOPS

      Deciding not to give an overzealous assassin a proper funeral was a fairly easy decision, especially after he went after Sky, but somehow Thor felt a little less than civilized throwing his body out in the next waste purge. He talked it over with Erük and decided it would be appropriate to incinerate McGinn's remains in the medical waste incinerator, giving the man a "cremation at sea," so to speak. They both hoisted half of his severed body onto their shoulders and started down to the Medical Bay.

      "You know, Erük, I can't help but feel sorry for this asshole," Thor said, walking down the dimly lit corridor with the upper torso over his right shoulder, head to the rear. "He really was a pretty likable guy. I think he was just so utterly programmed in life that he couldn't let go of his charge, even after it was obvious that there was no need to carry out the hit... unless...." Thor started sliding through the whole scenario on some slippery slopes, doing little more than confusing himself.

"Unless what?" Erük boomed aloud, making Thor jump just a little since he was still not totally used to Erük's audible voice.

Thor pondered further before answering, still not completely sure of his train of thought. They rounded a corner and hit the button for the elevator. "Unless there's more to this than meets the eye.... Think about it, what was the logic behind him going into cryo to hunt me down in the future, unless the ones who hired him have a way of transcending time themselves? I know that sounds ridiculous, but why else would it matter? What would they have to gain from waiting to track me down? If they found me at CryoKinetics, why not kill me right there? It doesn't make much sense... If they just wanted the money back and me dead, why didn't he drop it after he realized what had happened to both of us? Why not let it go and get on with his life in the future? Anyone I could have told would be long dead anyway... It just doesn't seem like him! The guy seemed genuinely surprised when he learned what happened back on Earth, so why go after me now?"

"I don't know, my brother. Sometimes there is no *why*.... "

"Maybe he was just an idealist," Thor chuckled, "just couldn't live with the notion of leaving a job unfinished. It's not like he had a reputation to protect... there's not much demand for someone in his line of work anymore!" Thor started thinking quietly back to the conversations he and Kieran had prior to him turning rogue. His energy, his sense of humor, his background... Thor honestly believed that McGinn was "family" material, which in his experience did not grow on trees, and was something to be cultivated when found. He could count on one hand how many times in his life he met someone who he could really connect with, and this one tried to kill him. He wouldn't quickly forget him. It was as if he could feel his presence even now.

He put his hand on the pad for the medical bay door and nothing happened. He tried again... still nothing. He leaned forward to the small glass plane to breathe on it, hoping to wipe it clean if that was the problem, and gasped when he saw his reflection.... He dropped the corpse and spun around to Erük in shock, who was already sensing something was wrong. "Wha-" Erük dropped his half of the body and jumped back about five feet, slamming his back into the opposite side of the corridor in absolute surprise... Thor *was* McGinn! Down to the last detail, he had somehow taken the physical shape of Kieran McGinn to such a strong degree that the computer didn't even recognize his own biorhythmic signature or physical handprint, either of which would have opened the door!

He spun back around again to look at his reflection one more time, but by the time he adjusted his eyes to the small panel, he was himself again! He burst into a fit of animated but precarious laughter, turning back toward Erük while looking nervously around. "What the fuck was up with that? Did that really just happen?"

"It would appear you have natural adaptive abilities, Thor," Erük stated plainly as he leaned around Thor with one talon on his shoulder, inspecting him, front and back. Some of our kind develop this skill in various forms as a natural defense mechanism. It is called Jvikkah."

"What various forms?"

"Shape shifting, close range teleportation... even plane shifting," Erük stated.

"What exactly do you mean when you say, 'plane shifting,' are you referring to transcending planes of existence... *literally*?"

"Exactly. Plane shifting is when we change from one *form* to the next... not just physical appearance, but transcending planes of existence as well... for instance, entering the dream world while conscious, traveling the ethereal plane to communicate with the departed, and sometimes even transcending time itself. There are many planes of existence; some we know very well and have explored, and some we haven't. What you just did without even trying takes our species years of practice to master! We are all essentially born with the ability to blend in with our surroundings, in color and even texture, but to take on the form of another *entirely* takes much control over one's own vibration, and a very keen perception of the energy and vibration of others. I gather you've never done this before?"

"Never," Thor answered, looking down at the floor, but a million miles away. "Well... not exactly. Not to the eye. Only the manipulation of energies.... So why now?" he asked, somewhat sure he had an idea already, concerning the source. Thor reached back up and opened the door without incident, then hoisted the body back up to his shoulder and walked into the room.

"I'm not quite sure, but I'm sensing a change in us all," Erük said, picking up his half and entering the medical bay as well.

———————

Bjorn was typing madly on the keyboard in front of him, over and over, as if he was determined to produce his desired result by re-measuring the problem enough times. Sky sat nearby in one of the helmsman seats, half watching Bjorn, and half drifting off from complete lack of sleep. Her dreams of late had been so intense that she usually woke up feeling more exhausted than she was when she went to bed. They had all driven themselves nearly to the brink these last few days, partially due to the events at hand, but it was also customary to deprive oneself of sleep just prior to any expected cryo-sleep cycle to prevent the buildup and long term storage of adrenaline, the results of which can be extremely painful upon waking and add weeks to recovery time.

Sky yawned and looked over at Bjorn, smiling. "Have you made it say what you want yet?" she jabbed.

"What?" He looked confused. "Oh! Ha! ...That's funny. No, it's just-" He squinted further, then brought the view of the planet Cheops up on holographic. "Something's not right."

"What is it?" Sky asked, staring in wonder at the blast from her past now floating before her in the air of the cockpit. "Wow... I never thought I'd see that again!" The dark blue planet loomed before her, floating in the air holographically, but with enough resolution to give the appearance that you could reach out, grab it, and go for a three-pointer from right where you stood. Its frantic and seemingly random streams of wind and storm centers careened across the mountainous face of the planet and ripped through its valleys and ocean levels with the speed and intensity of Earth's most menacing hurricanes.

Near the southern pole, clearly visible even on the relatively small facsimile before them, was the great pyramid mountain: location of the pyrite mines and caves used by the early Fleet settlers for loading the refueling shuttles for the final exodus to Algol. She strained her eyes, but hard as she tried she couldn't make out any sign of the remnant settlements near the base of the mountain. Strange, she thought, even though almost all of the Fleet's larger structures had been scavenged and reconstructed as storage barges and skiffs for in flight transport of ore surplus and raw repair material, there should still be signs of the abandoned colony visible at this magnification. The extreme violence of the great storm that came in on their heels could have erased every trace of their existence, she figured. No sooner had she began to focus on that spot on the map, as Bjorn was turning it around again.

"Yeah, I know what you mean... Check this out, though." He turned the view about 90 degrees counter-clockwise, then pulled back, way back, to include the surrounding nine star cluster of the Alcyone system. The massive blue giant in the center was shrouded in its usual cloud of interstellar dust, reflecting its blue light in a fantastic show of cosmic beauty onto the surrounding planets and moons; some nearly engulfed by the center ring of gasses and particle matter spun into a giant disc around the brilliant orb, stretching forth from its equator by its tremendous centrifugal force.

Known as Alcyone, Eta Tauri, or "Atlas" to the ancient Greeks, this behemoth held sway over every celestial body in its grasp, including its diminutive binary counterpart, Pleione, Atlas's mortal wife, and her seven white dwarf daughters who surrounded the system in a fiery display of blue and white diamonds set in a haze of mutable vitality: the great reflecting nebula... a dusty cloud of interstellar matter shrouding the scorching ultraviolet rays of the brightly lit system to a warm blue glow and holding back the fury and brilliance of their master. Nestled in the middle of the haze, unseen by the naked eye at this distance was Cheops, a hostile world of stormy oceans and barely breathable air, turbulent seasons and unpredictable weather changes; an oddly evolved planet of spirits in the mist that once nearly became home to an exhausted human race.

Though Bjorn and Sky both were very young when the Fleet came through here nearly 20 years ago, they distinctly remembered the nebula being a distant anomaly shrouding most of the fury of the outer three suns, the sisters to the southwest, Merope, Elektra, and Maia. With no real "night-time" to intermittently cool the surface of the planet, it was widely speculated that as the system passed through the nebula, Cheops would slowly become uninhabitable due to extremes in solar radiation leading to the extinction of all plant life, but to some, it was a promise of some reprieve from the intensely cold and shifting weather conditions they usually endured here, and its passing was something to look forward to. In either case, its anticipated passing was the basis for the type of accelerated terraforming the Fleet focused on for the first couple weeks or so, but abandoned as the politics made settlement next to impossible.

Bjorn shifted the holographic view of the system another 90 degrees, turned it on its side so they could see straight down, then zoomed in on just the nebula and some of the surrounding quadrant. The nebula clearly shrouded not only the three outer suns, but the three closest sisters, Asterope, Taygeta, and Celaeno as well as Atlas, Pleione, and about half of Cheops itself! Bjorn typed a few commands into the computer and the view shifted to show the nebula's last recorded position... the day the Fleet embarked on its voyage to the Algol system, clearly showing the nebula on the outer rim of the system, engulfing only those three stars and their orbiting planets. Bjorn looked up at Sky to get her reaction.

"Isn't that about right...? Given the 20 years that have passed?"

"It moved in the wrong direction, Sky!" Bjorn stated melodramatically, squinting his eyes at her, though only a few feet away. "I've run multiple scans of this in the last several minutes, and, well... this seals it. The cloud is moving from the *other* direction... *toward* the position I just showed you... when we were here before."

"So what are you saying, Bjorn?"

"We *are* in the past! This proves it!"

"Proves what?" Thor spoke out, coming through the open doorway with Erük right behind him. They approached the hologram and Thor paused by Sky's side, leaning forward to kiss her gently on the forehead. He stood up with one hand on her shoulder and stared at Bjorn, waiting for a reply.

"Watch," Bjorn said to everyone, hitting a couple keys. "The image flows through a period of twenty minutes time-lapsed in a few seconds, showing by reference coordinates below that the nebula is moving away from the planet, uncovering it, so to speak, however slowly, but toward the southern hemisphere. "

"And the problem is...?"

"Here's the shot of the planet from the same vantage point on the day we set sail for Algol 20 years ago," he said, hitting a few keys. "The nebula was already nearing the southern edge of the planet, but thick around the three suns in the outer quadrant to the southwest. It is nearly clear over the entire rest of the planet."

"Couldn't it have changed directions for some reason?" Thor asked.

"The nebula isn't even really what's moving, the solar system is what's moving... through space. Believe me, we _are_ in the past! It had to have happened during the tachyon storm."

"How far back are we?" Thor asked, closing his eyes and trying hard to wrap his mind around the events of this day.

"I can't tell from here... I need a point of reference. There are too many variables. Could be just a few hours... could be significantly more."

"If I read the reports in the computer right, there should be a small settlement down there, right?" Thor asked Bjorn and Sky.

"Not anymore. I'm pretty sure everyone left when they firebombed the surface. It destroyed their terraforming cultures. I was pretty young, though," Sky answered.

"Not settlers.... The report says it's an abandoned *penal* colony. The rebels who turned on the Fleet after the firebombing... aren't they still down there? Exiled and left unlocked to fend for themselves...?" Bjorn shrugged, probably being but a child at the time, but Sky sat with an intense stare. It was starting to come back to her.

"I think... You know, it seems like there was a lot of talk about a group of separatists from one ship, in particular... I can't remember the name, but that's probably what you read about. Bjorn, bring up the close up of the pyramid mountain, turned 180 degrees upside down... I want to see it again. If there is still a colony, that's where it should be.... They wouldn't have had the equipment to move building materials very far." He hit a few keys and the image of Cheops grew to about the size of a basketball again, dominating the entire view, then shifted upside down, revealing the pyramid mountain, shrouded in a vortex of bad weather. As it moved visibly fast around the great landmark, a small group of what looked like could be buildings were visible near the base. She leapt from her seat, pointing at the globe. "There! At the base of the mountain! Look!"

"Yep... I think I see it too. Are these people we would want to contact, though?" Thor asked.

"They were separatists, not murderers. Aren't we as well?" Sky posed softly.

"How many are there?" asked Bjorn, scrolling through the Fleet record on the subject, but not finding any definitive information.

"I don't remember. It seems like quite a few families, but there was also talk of Fleet prisoners being marooned on some planet... Maybe it was this one. I'm not really sure. What I do know is that we were following a beacon from some kind of civilized source when we made the decision to land here in the first place... It was actually the only reason we even found the place to begin with, having entered the system from the nebula side. It was sort of like a lighthouse beacon in the fog to us. Searches were conducted all over the planet... searches that cost many lives and a fortune in resources in the end, and we never found the source. We lost... we lost-"

"What? What's wrong, Sky?" Thor leaned in to comfort her with one hand on her back. She was starting to get choked up, her eyes tearing up and her breathing getting a little shallower. She looked up at him with a look of grim revelation on her face.

"I think that was when I lost my parents." She was slowly recalling things she had somehow forgotten, or rather buried deep down in defense and blocked herself from remembering. Her eyes were miles away as her voice quietly emerged, melancholy and entranced. "They went out looking for me during a bad storm shortly before we were supposed to leave the planet. I was... exploring the mines. I was looking for the spirits the workers kept encountering and got stuck inside until the storm passed. Their skiff never made it back to the compound. The last transmission they sent, they were following some kind of signal coming from within the eye of the storm. They... they thought it was me," she sobbed, leaning forward with her head in her hand, "When I returned the next morning, they were gone, along with three others who went out looking for them. I guess I never really let myself grieve... hell, I didn't even accept that they were gone for quite a while afterward... kept expecting them to come around the corner at any moment with some bizarre story of where they had been. I guess I blamed myself."

"I'm so sorry," he said, gently rubbing the back of her neck and shoulders. "I'm sorry for the timing, as well, but we need to go down there. We need to take star chart readings from a point near the mines where their old readings correspond, then cross reference them to find out just how far we traveled… but you don't need to come. In fact, it might be wiser if you didn't," he said in a fatherly way, placing his hand gently on her stomach and looking thoughtfully into her eyes.

She mustered up a smile, then playfully pushed him back a few feet. "You can kindly fuck off, *Captain* Krey! Nobody knows that place like I do, and I am *definitely* going with you, thank you very much."

"That's what I wanted to hear," he said with a smile, then scruffled her hair on his way to the front bridge controls. "Plot us a course for atmospheric re-entry and download it to the shuttle, Bjorn, I think it's probably best to leave the Phoenix in orbit to conserve fuel and limit the chances of any kind of enemy incursion by the so-called settlers." Thor pulled his katana from its sheath and pointed with the tip at the small cluster next to the pyramid on the hologram, itself, causing light distortion to sketch out and shine in random directions as the shiny steel blade penetrated the image. He skillfully moved it just slightly, over to the right behind the corner of the mountain outcropping. "Put us down right next to the settlement on their blind side, around the southwest corner of the pyramid mountain. Sky, you know the terrain... help me stock the shuttle. We leave as soon as that storm down there breaks." He slashed out and to the right, fanning down, then returning overhand to the left, pulling the blade back along his left hand, then returning it to his sheath with a quick slap on the hilt.

CHAPTER 8: AT NEBULA'S EDGE

Admiral Reid looked proudly back at the widescreen monitor to his right, feeling a mostly undeserved sense of fatherhood for the Fleet he stared at who were now following his giant flagship Carrier, the Helios, toward what appeared to be a beacon of hope for mankind. A signal that, until a few hours ago, didn't exist, even on the long range deep space scanners of their reconnaissance ship, H.O.R.U.S., which was fitted with the most advanced telemetric and observatory equipment mankind could salvage and unite onto one vessel. The crown jewel on H.O.R.U.S. was the Hubble Telescope itself, fitted into an underside observatory used mainly for deep space mapping and topographic surveying cartography of planetary surfaces from orbit.

Admiral T. Alexander Reid commanded 14 Carriers: large ships that could be fitted while in-flight for use in battle and as mining vessels, or Harvesters, as they were called, like the Phoenix. The only difference was the in-flight attachment and fitting of the Harvester unit, a large barge-like vessel capable of limited flight by itself, but at much slower speeds, due to its simplified construction and structurally reinforced hull. This unit detached, and the Carrier unit in its place, the ship then became the equivalent of an Aircraft Carrier of old, holding in its bays hundreds of manned and unmanned fighters, bombers, and munitions magazines. Though fully intended as an exodus of peace for the survival of all mankind, the Fleet moved as a highly efficient, highly trained military operation, and was bound by strict martial law for the protection of its citizens and its cause.

The Fleet was ominous to behold, stretching for as far as the eye could see, and was led, trailed, and flanked by fully rigged Carriers and Battleships; and Admiral Reid wore his rank and command on his sleeve, both literally and metaphorically. His elevated sense of pride in this armada was apparent in his every mannerism as he strutted around the bridge of the Helios like a lone rooster among hens. He punched up the front viewer and fearlessly stood back, looking for conquest amongst the blue clouds stretching out in all directions as they started into the nebula.

It was vast. The entire phenomenon seemed to stretch across the horizon from star to star, nearly shrouding the deeper parts of the constellation from view altogether. From Earth, it was the constellation "Taurus," but from here, it was something far more vast and wonderful, bringing into long-range view a myriad of uncharted stars and whole galaxies never before visible to the human eye.

"Any signs of solid matter?" the Admiral asked.

"Too hard to tell.... Our scans seem to bounce back in fragments from the particle matter, but it looks like mostly dust and gasses," responded one of his helmsmen.

"Cut speed to One-Third, inform the rest of the Fleet."

"Aye, sir. Ahead One-Third!"

"Ahead One-Third!" a voice shouted back over the com.

"Helm, see if you can find a way around this that still offers scanning of the outer rim planets. I'm still not convinced this is worth the risk. It could be nothing but a fragmented radio signal bouncing back at us, years later.... We'll probably reconstruct it and find out it's an episode of South Park, or a 20th century newscast or something!" The Admiral scratched his head, standing in one place and staring at the sparkling haze of clouds before him. One of the officers to his right anxiously turned to him, listening earnestly while holding his headset and boom tight to his head.

"Sir, Horus reports it's a beacon of some magnitude in the center of the system, near Alcyone!" He strained to hear further.

"A beacon?"

"Aye, sir! They're reporting it as a complex signal... distorted from the system's energy fields and the extreme rotation speed of the class B7 blue giant, but definitely intelligent in origin."

"Set course for Alcyone. Ahead One-Third power! Keep your eyes open, ladies and gentlemen; this place could hide just about anything.... I don't want *any* surprises! Keep all focus on frontal scans. Be on the lookout for anything bigger than a golf ball!" The Admiral smiled, feeling a renewed sense of purpose he had not felt since taking command of the Fleet.

CHAPTER 9: THE ASTRAL WINDOW

Thor lay sprawled on his back next to Sky, unable to sleep. She was mumbling something repeatedly, and he was debating on whether to wake her up, but she didn't seem too distressed, and he figured she needed the sleep worse than the relief from her dream. He reached over and put his hand on her stomach, unable to wrap his mind around the events of the last few days, the most intense of which, at least insofar as he was concerned, was his own transformation into the semblance of McGinn. Something was changing within them all... something well outside their realm of understanding.

He wished like hell he still had Ragnar to talk to. Since his father's disappearance during the government raids of his childhood, Ragnar was his only real link to the family that once was; the family that he vowed would live on, so long as he still drew breath. It was during times like these that the counsel provided by a simple family gathering around a campfire would set into a state of clarity even the most confusing of events, and set into motion even the largest of collaborative endeavors. He had memory, however vague, of his family's elders speaking of shape shifters and plane shifting, but other than his own delving into the manipulation of energy, he had never before seen any of it first-hand.

Thinking about it rationally, it seemed to him to work on the exact same premise. *It might be nothing more than the manipulation of one's own pitch of energy to match the energy of the target,* he thought to himself, *just on a much more evolved and encompassing scale.* He took a moment, then a deep breath, clearing his mind and centering himself. *Clean energy in through the nose... let all impurities break loose, then exhale, releasing it all... letting everything go... out of the mouth. No attachments.* He repeated this several times, finally putting himself in the space he needed to be in: *Mushin No Shin.* Mind of no mind.

He focused on Ar'Jvikkah, using his connection with Sky to home in on his energy, pulling it through his hand and arm. Even though the young dragon had regressed into her womb somehow during the tachyon storm, his energy was well defined and felt advanced... like that of a young adult, or someone with very keen powers of observation. Thor could sense that the young one was aware of what he was doing even now, somehow.

He became very relaxed and then started to drift off into something similar to a dream, but different. He had spent years conditioning himself not to fall asleep during meditation, no matter how relaxed it made him, or how fatigued he was while he was doing it, but somehow this was different. This was not sleep, but rather, the relinquishment of consciousness; and it was not him that was causing it to happen!

He opened his eyes and found himself walking up the same hillside he had visited many times in his dreams. He was focusing on the house: a small cabin standing alone on a rocky hill covered with tundra. It was cold outside, but not enough to bother him. As he hiked diligently toward the lone building, he suddenly became aware of someone behind him. He turned and saw Sky walking quickly up the hill toward him. She was smiling and obviously glad to see him, yet apparently a little surprised to see him *here*. He stopped and faced her.

As he opened his mouth to speak, he became acutely aware of another presence coming from what seemed like behind her. He tried to lean sideways as she drew closer in an effort to see who, or what, was there, but he started to lose his balance and something else took over. He realized his feet were no longer touching the ground.... *He was flying!* He rose a few feet up off the ground and hovered, waiting for her with his arms out to the sides, palms up, as if to say, *"Check me out, what do you think?"*

He felt the other presence again, only this time it was much stronger, and behind *him*.... He spun around in midair, revealing nothing. He quickly scanned the hillside with his eyes, and finally spotted the source. A lone figure, cloaked beneath some kind of hooded robe, was standing in front of the front door to the cabin, staring at them both. He spun back around to warn Sky to be on her guard, but as he turned to face her, his heart suddenly skipped a beat.... She was gone, and the cloaked figure was now standing in her place, not two feet away! Startled, and unable to get an energy read or even see the man's face for some reason, his heart jumped and he quickly prepared to defend himself.

Thor quickly reached across with his right hand, preparing to draw his sword, but the man blocked his action in the blink of an eye by grabbing his wrist, rendering him unable to pull it out. Thor countered by putting his left hand tightly over the man's fingers and preempted with his sword hand around to the right, clockwise, then pointed straight down with the man's hand still trapped by the fingers, putting tremendous strain on his wrist.

As if being aided by some extreme source of energy, the man somehow overpowered Thor, despite his leverage and technical advantage, and reversed the motion back the other way. Having been trained to anticipate this, and using the momentum he created, Thor spun quickly around the other way with his knees bent deep and turned his back to the man while bracing his arm in a painful bar over his shoulder. Holding his wrist tight to keep his arm straight and palm up, he then stood up tall to the sound of the man's elbow crackling and snapping apart.

Once again, as if driven by Odin himself, the man curled his arm at the bicep, somehow breaking his maimed arm free of the arm lock with nothing but sheer strength. As his arm came up into an "L" shape, Thor grabbed his wrist and spun 180 degrees around underneath the man, and using his elbow to assist in curling his arm up the rest of the way, he took the man quickly in the direction he was trying to go in the first place; exaggerating his efforts and using his great strength against him. As soon as he had the man off balance and his arm tied up like a pretzel, Thor stepped through and swept his legs with his right leg, adding a "pop" with his hip in an inner throwing technique known to the Japanese as "Irimi nagi." The man went straight down on his back with his arm still trapped in a tight curl, and Thor, keeping him pinned down effortlessly with just a little pressure on his elbow, struck him hard in the lower rib cage with his right fist to stun him, then pulled back his arm with his two strong fingers poised for a lethal pressure point attack to the throat.

"Who the hell are you?!?" Thor demanded, still unable to see through the man's hood for some reason that made no obvious sense. There was a slight grunt of pain from within the dark cloak, but still no reply. Thor leaned in on him with all his weight, applying painful pressure to the arm lock, and yelled even louder. "I said, who the fuck are you?!? ANSWER

ME!" Spit shot randomly from his mouth, and he started to become outraged and uncharacteristically hostile as the figure not only refused to answer, but actually started to laugh. It was just a windy, wheezing laugh, at first, but quickly escalated into full blown, guttural laughter, mocking him profusely.

Conditioned for years not to ever lose his cool in a conflict, for fear of becoming disbalanced and handing your opponent the advantage, Thor took a deep breath, then reached up with his free hand and grabbed the hood on top of the man's head. Pulling it back and forcing it down between his head and the ground awkwardly, yanking on the man's hair as it came off, he was absolutely shocked to see the familiar face of Kieran McGinn, staring at him with all the cold definition he had in his eyes in their final moments on the bridge during the tachyon storm.

Momentarily shocked by the surprise, Thor relaxed his grip on McGinn's elbow, if only for a moment, and suddenly felt a powerful blast to the solar plexus by some kind of focused energy, sending him flying backward through the air about ten feet uphill toward the cabin, where he flopped onto the cold ground like a ragdoll, momentarily unable to breathe. As he lay there gasping for air, the wind utterly knocked out of him, he rolled to his side to see Kieran get slowly up to his feet, pull off his cloak and throw it on the ground, then start slowly walking toward him. As he was quickly regaining the ability to breathe, he started clambering to his feet, never taking his eyes off of McGinn as he drew closer, then, when he was just a few feet away, he actually smiled at Thor, then began to speak.

"You know, back on Earth, before this all happened, I kinda had it made.... I had plenty of money... the respect of my peers... Hell, Mr. Krey, I guess you could say I truly had a sense of purpose!" He closed his eyes and took a deep breath, exhaling out loud. He was obviously caught up in some kind of deep thought that he was having trouble finding words for. "Shit, man, they told me you would do this if I let you," he chuckled, a little frustrated.

"Do what?" Thor grunted, almost totally back on his feet. "_Who_ told you?"

McGinn stopped advancing and stood directly before him, face to face. "They told me you would try to return... that the prospect of a life of servitude would never pacify you. They told me to stop you before you had the chance. I've got to admit, after seeing what you're capable of, I can see why they're running scared! It's almost worth letting you go, just to see what happens," Kieran laughed, "I truly wish I would have known you in another life, my brother..." His charming gaze changed to pure focus and he took an advancing step toward Thor.

Thor turned to the right as if he was going to run, just far enough to shroud Kieran's view of his sword handle at his hip. As he was turning to the right, McGinn quickly stepped forward to give chase, over-committing himself. Thor silently drew his sword with a spiral downward and finished his turn to the right, 270 degrees backwards, coming all the way back around and attacking McGinn's legs as he was stepping with his right foot out in full stride. Before he could even fall over from the severed arteries and tendons exposed during the surgically precise, bone-deep slice, Thor pulled a lightning fast reversal, rising up and using the power and momentum gained from turning back the opposite direction for the full 270 degrees to completely decapitate the man right where he stood.

He wiped the blood from the blade, re-sheathed his katana and bowed as McGinn's dismembered body collapsed to the ground before him in pieces; extending honor to a worthy opponent, even in defeat... _even in death_. He turned to start back uphill toward the cabin and nearly jumped right out of his skin in complete gut-wrenching surprise as he almost stepped right into the man, who was now standing directly in front of him again, cloaked and hooded as before, as if absolutely nothing had ever happened. Thor gasped for air, feeling suddenly as if he had just jumped into a pool of freezing cold water and could only breathe in short, frantic bursts.

McGinn's voice was now booming and sinister as he spoke to every fiber of Thor's being. *"You didn't really think it would be that easy, did you?!?"* Thor reached for his sword again and was sent flying as before, but this time it was much worse. He was flying through the air backwards with the wind completely knocked out of him, dumbfounded at how he could have cut this man in half, twice, and still not defeated him.

He instinctively stretched out his awareness to "feel" for the ground before the moment of impact so that he could slap with his hand to break his fall for damage control, when he was blindsided from above and off to the side, then carried off to the right with talons digging into his rib cage and thigh. He smiled, in spite of the pain, remembering how he and Erük first met. He reached up to thank him for the bailout, unsure how this fight would have turned out, when he suddenly realized this was not Erük at all! "Ar'Jvikkah?" he asked, bewildered at the sheer size of the young dragon.

"Yes."

"What the hell is going on...?"

"I'll explain later... right now, you need to go somewhere safe. Somewhere he can't follow!" Thor looked back, realizing that McGinn was hovering in the air, and no matter how far or fast they fled, they never seeming to get any further away from him. He was preparing to launch something big at them, Thor could sense it. He conveyed the intention to Ar'Jvikkah, who glanced back, then closed his eyes and grasped Thor tighter. There was an overwhelming flash of light, sound, smell, and emotion; a complete sensory overload,

then the feeling of being yanked out of a dream by a giant rubber band, and Thor opened up his eyes to see that he was still in bed next to Sky, drenched in sweat with his hand still on her belly over Ar'Jvikkah, but he was quite sure that what he just experienced was absolutely no ordinary dream!

"It was no different than that which you have called 'dreams' your whole life... and in fact was quite real! The only real difference lies in your ability to control it, and to remember it. It is in your ability to navigate this plane now, just as you navigate within our own prime material plane...." He jumped up to see Erük standing just off the side of his bed, staring at him.

"Jesus Christ, brother! You almost gave me a heart attack! Have you ever heard of knocking? No... I guess you haven't. Shit!"

"I am sorry... I heard you yell and I wanted to make sure you were unharmed." Erük leaned in toward him, staring deep into his eyes.

"Thank you, my friend."

"You saw Ar'Jvikkah, did you not?" he said aloud, holding a talon over Sky's belly with his eyes closed and a warm smile playing at the edge of his reptilian mouth.

"Yes! I did! He was older. I think he may have just saved my life. Erük, could I have died in this *'dream-plane'* if my body was out here?"

"That is definitely a very real possibility! It depends on <u>how</u> you are killed. If the wrong circumstances occur, one <u>definitely</u> <u>can</u> lose their life energy in an irretrievable manner in their sleep.... Why? What happened?"

"*McGinn* happened! Apparently he's <u>not</u> dead... and it was Ar'Jvikkah who saved me."

"He's doing it," Erük exclaimed proudly, *"he's mastered his power already! He's traveling!"*

"I don't understand... Aren't dreams basically just visions to show you what *may* happen, however symbolic... or visions based on unresolved emotional issues?"

"Not really. The dream state is more or less a window to the astral plane. There are those who have learned how to navigate it with much control, but for most people it is a confusing third-person spectacle in which they are nothing but a hapless participant in a seemingly random and unpredictable chain of events. Some meaning or coincidence can be sought, but is usually contrived, and makes us lose sight of the real truth."

"What truth?"

"That our existence on that plane, however fleeting and chaotic, is as real and relevant as our existence within this prime material plane, and that we are psychologically affected, for better or worse, by the events and relationships of that plane... sometimes more intensely than by our so called 'real' experiences. The only real difference between the two realms is that in the astral plane, time doesn't exist as it does here... at least it isn't reckoned in the same manner. This is why it is so hard to quantify and record the events of your dreams with any tangible accuracy. You can visit any time, from any point in your life. This is why sometimes things seem so familiar... like you've done them before-"

"Déjà vu!"

"Gesundheit! Anyway, it happens when you reach a point or event that you have already visited or witnessed astrally. You can literally travel time in this manner."

"Through the control of the dream state... damn, Erük! Is it possible to travel between planes in either direction... also disregarding the timeline in the material plane?"

Erük laughed mischievously, "Not so long as you remain rooted in the material plane's timeline," he said aloud, leaning toward Thor intensely. "The discipline to do so has been the quest of many sects of our Jvikkahn elders. It was said that at one time, in another world, we had such an ability. To do so not only enables one to transcend time, but space as well, and was said to be the ultimate downfall of an entire earlier version of our culture. To do so rips the very fabric of the time-space continuum in much the same manner as the paradox created by being in contact with two times at once."

Thor looked puzzled. "What do you mean, two times at once..."

"The same matter from two different times cannot occupy the same space. If you were able to actually put into contact with each other the same matter from two different times, in that moment no natural 'displacement' is possible... The universe cannot accommodate it, balance is lost, and it is repelled through the path of least resistance, tearing a hole in the very fabric of the universe itself. Since energy cannot be created or destroyed, and can only change forms, as the universe seeks to rebalance itself, the surplus energy will change, at the molecular level, into a balanced version of itself... a sort of 'half-life,' split between planes of existence... a *convergence,* if you will. These paradoxes are why it was forbidden for our kind to pursue such practices outside of the counsel of our elders. Such a being would become immortal, and would be an abomination of the natural laws of the universe."

"McGinn!"

"What about him?"

"We all watched him die... Now he comes back in my dream and is virtually unstoppable! I killed him outright... took his head! Why else would he have survived that... or even been there in the first place after what happened on the bridge? How is this possible?"

"OK... Let us consider, for a moment, what actually happened on the bridge.... You killed McGinn while traveling backwards *physically* through time…. When you die in this plane, you shift automatically, but not before time stops for you… His sudden death *caused* his transformation! Leaving his body, he would have run unwillingly into himself because of the reversed time flow… We weren't traveling by jumping to a point from outside this plane; we were sliding backwards *within it*. Essentially, you *made* him what he is!"

"Great… so how do I make him dead?"

"You can't." Erük contemplated for a moment, then jumped back in Thor's face with a sudden epiphany, making him jump as well. "Unless you kill him on every single plane he exists on, either simultaneously, or at least collectively before he can regenerate each of these other states," he exclaimed, eyes zeroed in on Thor's, "including, at this point, his eternal spirit in the ethereal plane… after he dies. He has become capable of returning from there, where most cannot."

"Oh, is that all…?" Thor rolled his eyes and flopped back into the bed. "Outstanding." Thor breathed a heavy sigh and drew his hand through his hair, suddenly noticing that Sky was awake… listening intently to every word. "How long have you been awake, gorgeous?" he smiled.

"Long enough to realize that a great many things are not as they seemed a week ago," she joked, laughing nervously, but strangely relieved. "Has anyone ever done it?" Sky asked Erük, awake and wide eyed, "Has anyone ever achieved this sort of immortality before?"

"Not any individual that we know of, but…" Erük paused and lowered his head, holding back as if there was something he didn't really want to say.

"What is it, my friend?" Thor asked quietly, leaning toward him.

"There is a reason we have the same DNA." Thor's eyes got wider as Erük lifted his head up and looked deep into his eyes. "We lived, long ago, on the same planet you came from." Thor's jaw popped open and he stared at Erük blankly. "We were an advanced society of mathematicians, scholars, scientists, and artisans. Your people were fairly primitive, and for the most part, we were considered to be gods. We stumbled onto this truth, and through our own vanity and carelessness, it consumed us. Our great city and everyone in it was transformed in a violent cataclysm that swallowed our civilization into the sea and left us scattered and leaderless for centuries.

"Transformed, and rendered incapable of speech, we became deeply feared by mankind... *and hunted*. Befriended by a telepathic race of 'travelers' from the stars who had been tracking our progress through the millennia, we left the planet long before your civilization grew to the point you spoke of, and didn't get back to our quest for harmony until we found ourselves on the Twin Planets of Algol, where we met. There, a simpler life caused a great re-shuffling of our priorities, after which, only truth and efficiency remained. We found balance through primitive, intuitive living, and adapted to our new home physically and spiritually."

"How did your people become... well..." Thor stumbled.

"Dragons?"

"Yes."

"Nobody knows for sure... In the process of unraveling and losing ourselves to the wake created by our rift, we were rearranged by the universe in exactly the manner that was needed to rebalance it. Apparently this included an advanced evolutionary 'kick' that still affects us deeply. This adaptive defense mechanism is the root of our 'Jvikkahn' skills... the source of our power over our environment. Wherever we find ourselves, in whatever situation, we very quickly adapt, even on the most energy-based, primitive, or physical level. Our bodies transformed within a generation to mesh with our new friends, then again to adapt to the extreme conditions of extended space travel, and still again to the environment of our first new planet. We changed dramatically in the generations that followed, and even more as we effected our move to the Algol system. Now, on the brink of extinction, we seem to have come full circle, evolving into something else entirely..." He placed his hand carefully on Sky's stomach and sighed deeply, closing his inner eyelids, then the thicker outer ones.

CHAPTER 10: A MIRROR FOR MADNESS

The small shuttles onboard all the Carriers and Harvesters of the Fleet were truly a masterpiece of modern art. Designed for both peak aerodynamic performance within atmospheric parameters, as well as extended solitary space flight, while accommodating up to 20 passengers in extended cryostasis bunks; every square inch of the lightweight craft was a display of pure scientific efficiency and state of the art engineering. They were stocked, by default, with all the tools, spare parts, and material, stored deep within the hull structure of the ship, to repair, and if necessary, rebuild practically the entire ship once over. It had a huge cargo hold, complete with side, floor, and ceiling compartment storage, utilizing nearly every void of any substantial size, while still accommodating its passengers safely and comfortably.

Sky pushed the envelope as they found their approach trajectory, hitting the throttle lever forward with an attitude as the entry flames started to billow off of the nose of the craft, momentarily consuming it in fire like a meteor rushing in from the heavens. The flames shined an orange hue onto the surrounding dark storm clouds as the small ship cut its way down through the pseudo-night sky. The flames subsided as the nitrogen rich air that engulfed them combined with the hard rain of the lower atmosphere, cooling the ship quickly. Sky hit the button to reopen the front cockpit shield and backed off her descent speed, straining to see out over the wind-torn black plains that were being lit up randomly by increasingly frequent bursts of lightning.

"Isn't *that* intense..." Thor commented.

"Yeah, intense is right," Sky yelled back over the sound of the repulsion engines winding up as the combustion thrusters cut off. "If you're caught out in the plains when the wind picks up, it'll strip the flesh from your bones in under 10 seconds. There's a naturally occurring graphite in the dust here that has a barb on the end of each fiber when you magnify it.... During weather like this, it permeates the air because of the static electricity and wind. When the wind hits, this stuff impregnates your gear, your clothes, and eventually your skin. Your body will try to reject it and push it back out, but when it does, the barb sets it in place like a fishhook! You can reach fatal toxicity from one hour of exposure! Don't fall in love with the scenery boys, this place is no picnic! Let's just get what we came here for and get the hell out in one piece! This planet has cost me enough already...."

Thor reached over and stroked the back of her hair, knowing full well to which loss she was referring. Erük stood close to the front window, staring intently at a major storm center hanging over the highest ridge of mountains in the distance. The clouds were moving fast, swirling around the tallest peaks like a giant tornado. Thor hit the com switch on the console.

"Bjorn!"

"Eriksson here... How are you guys doing?"

"So far, so good... Hey, Mr. Wizard, can you see what direction this large storm to our northeast is heading? I thought we were in the clear for a while, buddy," Thor asked, a little disturbed by what he was seeing.

"Well, 'a while' on Cheops is sometimes all you get... It looks like it's not moving at all, but rather, growing at a pretty alarming rate. I think we may want to consider pulling the plug on this one, guys.... The class five we observed before you left will collide with this center in about an hour! How's the weather on the ground, right now?"

"Wet."

"Wet is nice.... Keeps the dust down! How long will it take you to get the equipment up?" Thor looked at Sky inquisitively, his eyes becoming more and more serious as he glanced at the storm. Sky looked up at him with a purpose he had not seen in her since the day of the attack on the Phoenix. He could tell she needed this. She needed to face her demons.

"Give us about 30 minutes... and keep your eyes open for us!"

"Roger that. Eriksson out."

Thor stared straight out to the front as they sped across the plains at a progressively lower altitude, finally flying so low before they balanced out that the ship was actually ripping a wake into the mud and water pooled up in the blackened swamp fields and throwing a rooster tail 50 feet into the air. Thor remembered this effect from the sandy plains on Erük's home planet. The technology of their repulsion thrusters worked on this premise... the faster the forward momentum, the closer to the ground the ship would travel. Not a huge inconvenience on flat ground or shallow hills, but when flying through mountains or canyons, it forced them to slow down considerably for fear of high centering on rocks or other outcroppings. This was its one limitation, and the cost of its tremendous fuel economy... a small price to pay for an almost perpetual energy source on a craft of this size.

Sky was obviously starting to genuinely enjoy herself; slaloming back and forth casually between the large boulders that were starting to increase in frequency as they sped towards the foothills of the mountains. Judging by the surrounding topography and the shape and frequency of the boulders, it was obvious that this field had been bombarded at some time by a meteor shower. These rocks were asteroids... probably deposited fairly recently, judging by the extreme level of visible erosion on nearly everything else, as well as the freshness of some of the craters. What effect they may have had on the volatile ecosystem of this small world was still a mystery. They may have been at least partially responsible for all the erratic weather patterns tearing at the face of this hostile world, but the abnormal and extreme magnetic fields generated by the high rate of rotation of the blue giant that it orbited was undoubtedly a major factor as well. Sky looked over at Thor out of the corner of her eye. "Run a heat signature scan, we're closing in on our destination. The pyramid mountain should be right over those hills and just off to the northwest. The old colony was right at its base, near the entrance to the mineshafts."

"Gotcha." Thor started pushing buttons and then paused, looking confused. "I'm not getting a damn thing! Are you sure the area is right?"

"Yeah... I stayed here myself for quite a while. Expand the search to include the nearby mountains... and increase power to maximum; they very well might be holed up in the mines because of the storms!"

"Good thinking." He hit a few keys then started tapping the console with his fingers as he waited for the results of the scan.

"I feel a presence here... but it's not human," Erük said.

"Where?" Sky asked, starting to gear down as they entered a small canyon with rock formations growing taller on both sides.

"Everywhere..."

Thor looked up from his console. "I don't see a thing... It's as if we are the only life on this entire planet! I even linked up to the Phoenix and ran an aerial infrared scan on this whole area.... If they were here, they're gone now."

"Dead," Sky corrected.

"What?"

"You mean _dead_. They had no way off this rock... Fleet Command saw to that! They're all dead. Men, women, and children.... All dead!" She started to get choked up, then swallowed it and continued through the winding valley. The canyon walls seemed to get taller and closer as they made their way up the maze toward the base of the mountain.

Thor looked at Erük again to see if he was sensing anything new. "Keep your eyes open, brother, we're like fish in a barrel down here."

"Thor, I'm going to put down right at the old colony, so long as there's no sign of life. We may as well see for ourselves what happened, plus the mountain will shield us from the weather for a little while."

"Sounds good. I'll prepare the equipment. If we hurry, Bjorn will get all the data he needs to get an accurate read on the horizon, with or without the weather blocking our view... he'll just use us as a fixed point of reference, then do a radial survey from orbit of the entire sky, closing the horizon. We just need to know exactly where they were set up when you were here, Sky."

"The concrete base of our old tower should still be here... that part will be easy, especially since we can walk right into the old camp. I thought we were going to have to use laser EDM's to paint it from the hillside nearby without being seen."

"Where do you want me?" Erük asked.

"Right by my side!" Thor joked, patting Erük on the back. "No, seriously, just keep those keen eyes of yours open and watch our backs! We don't have time for any complications."

The shuttle coasted through a series of natural arches and was suddenly out in the open, wind and rain slamming into the front shield as she piloted it straight toward the base of the giant pyramid mountain, now plainly in view. A bolt of lightning shot nearly sideways across the upper half of the massive landmark, forking in two and illuminating everything on their side of the pyramid. Sky hit the landing lights and hooked around to the left near a set of tall rock formations before setting down with a soft bounce. "I don't understand it," she said, clearly surprised by what she was seeing, "it's not here!"

"What's not here?"

"None of it! The colony... the whole fucking village is gone!"

"Maybe they moved... or were wiped out by a storm. Hell, I don't know."

"They weren't wiped out by a storm," she contemplated, searching her memories for pictures of the outpost... its buildings, makeshift roads and infrastructure, hell, even its imprint on the land. It was as if it had been completely erased. "The buildings were too strong. Too stable. We even came up with a mix for a type of concrete made from the minerals in the mines to use as foundation pads for the buildings to control erosional instability.... Where the hell are those? You can't tell me they moved a bunch of concrete foundation pads! They were over six inches thick, and most of the buildings were 10 foot wide by 30 foot long cabins with steel reinforced domes designed specifically for high wind shear! These people were left with almost no equipment, just basic hand tools!"

Thor popped the clasp on his harness and started grabbing their equipment bags from the cargo hold. "I don't know. It doesn't make any sense. All I know is we better hurry before someone has to come down here to figure out what happened to *us!*"

Sky hit the com switch and typed some commands into the console. "Bjorn, we've landed right on top of the old colony site. It appears to be completely gone. Keep running subsurface scans near the base of the pyramid for heat signatures and keep us posted on the storm."

"Roger that. Upload that data as soon as you can. There is bound to be some major interference from the storm... getting worse as it grows. I don't know how long we'll have communication."

"All right guys, let's get this thing up and running as quick as we can! The old observation tower was set up directly on top of that formation," Sky said, pointing one of the outer spotlights from the shuttle directly at the tall rock formation with the use of a small stick controller on the dashboard console. "Now, I'm not sure if we'll be able to get back on top of it and get a strong base for the unit established in this weather, but right next to it should be close enough for Bjorn to run his calculations. Erük, can you get up top and check it out?"

"Sure can. Thor, let me see the base of the unit." Thor handed Erük the base: a solid steel square with holes around the outside and a series of threaded outcroppings and booms sticking up on the top side. The 7 foot tall dragon had no problem hoisting the apparatus in one hand as he picked the impact gun up off the floor and stepped toward the cargo door.

"Hold on, Erük... I need to double check the atmosphere before we open up," she said as she punched some keys on the main computer console. "That's odd," she mumbled, scratching her head.

"What?" Thor asked, still grabbing up supplies.

"The air's a lot like it was when we first arrived... 20 years ago!" She kept typing in commands, looking more and more puzzled. "I don't get it. The advanced terraforming wasn't finished, but it definitely should have, at the very least, succeeded in significantly raising the O2 levels in the air.... It seems like it's gone completely back to the way it was!"

"Well, is it breathable? Is it safe? I mean, we're not really geared up for zero atmosphere... please tell me we at least have breathable air!" Thor asked, frustrated.

She looked close at the figures on the screen in front of her. "Yes... It is breathable. Take your time, though. *Don't* get over excited or allow your heart rate to get too high! The nitrogen level is extremely high for humans... Erük, I don't know how this will affect you, but we need to breathe in shallow, slow breaths, otherwise we run the risk of getting 'the bends' exactly as if you came up too fast from deep sea diving without taking the time to decompress. Thor, be careful! We didn't have too many problems last time, except with a few of the elderly and a couple asthmatics. No longer than we're going to be here, it shouldn't be a problem. Mostly, you'll just feel a little out of breath... like you just got finished running laps. The rain will eliminate the need for EP suits to protect your skin from graphite impregnation, just don't overdo it... and for God's sake, let's *stick together!*"

"Aye," Thor shouted, hitting the panel and releasing the door lock. The large door popped open to the outside and lifted up as a wide ramp lowered subsequently below their feet and the wind fiercely howled in, blowing Thor's hair and loose jacket straight back as he fought to keep his stance. He started to lead the way, then Erük put his large taloned hand on his shoulder, stopping him.

"Like I said, we are not alone... please let me go first, my brother," Erük said silently, not wanting to alarm anyone, as he still wasn't sure they were any threat.

"Who do you take me for?" Thor said out loud, grinning playfully up at him, then slapped him on the back and proceeded down the ramp, squinting to see in the dark and howling tempest. Erük took two steps out of the small craft, then took to the air, circling high above the rock formation, then spiraling down to the flattest part of the top of it. He stood perched like an eagle, looking off in the direction of the storm for a moment, then down at Thor and Sky, who had joined them and was now walking toward the base of the tower with a large coil of some kind of shielded cable.

"We'll run this to the base of the scope and use the ship for a power supply and uplink," Sky yelled through her belt com over the howling interference of the wind and rain. Erük nodded and set the base unit down on the flattest part of the rock, then lifted up the giant, 2 man impulse nailer, and shot several nails around the perimeter, pinning the steel base to the rock formation as if he'd been doing this all his life.

"Damn, Brother! Where the hell did you learn how to use that?" Thor laughed, duly impressed.

"It just seemed proper..."

"Proper, my ass... you kick beak! Too bad we didn't know each other back in the day, we'd be rolling in dough!"

"Dough...?"

"Nevermind… catch!" Thor threw the second part of the base, a leveling disc with built-in bull's-eye leveling windows that threaded onto the base, providing a calibrated interface for the scope to mount to. Sky cringed as she watched the high-dollar, precision instrument component fly through the air toward the top of the rock formation in the high wind, but breathed a little easier as Erük reached down effortlessly with one arm and caught it.

"Thor! Goddammit! What the hell are you thinking? *Please* don't do that again!" She half smiled, half yelled in anger, not truly realizing why Thor was so confident in Erük's abilities or in his own.

He smiled back at her. "Sorry."

She approached the column, then started scaling the side of it with the roll of cable over her shoulder and a large apparatus on her back in a sling. Thor watched in amazement as she seemed to know right where every foothold and ledge was, and instinctively reached the top next to Erük as if she had done this a hundred times before. She placed the scope in its proper position, using the bull's-eye levels on the interface to calibrate it for plumb and level, then tightened it down, hooked it up to the power cord and the data cable, and threw the roll of cable down to Thor, who was staring off in the direction of the mountain and almost got hit with it as it came down right next to him.

He grabbed the coil, unraveling it as he walked slowly over to the open cargo door on the shuttle, never taking his eyes off the mountain's base. *"What's on your mind?"* Erük asked.

"I'm not sure... I just-" Thor suddenly spun back around with a terrified look in his eyes, retracting the slack from the cable by wrapping it around his right arm once, then, in one quick motion, he yanked hard on it with his whole body, pulling Sky, who was busy trying to hook the other end of it to the scope, off balance and right over the side of the ledge she was kneeling on. As she fell off the side of the rock formation, Erük took flight, straight up and out, toward her side, in an attempt to arrest her fall. Thor had already sprinted toward the base and was one step away from where he needed to be to catch her.

With a blinding flash, and a sound that shook the very ground beneath them, a huge bolt of lightning slammed into the steel base and rock formation, right where Sky was kneeling. Temporarily blinded from the flash, Thor trusted his instincts and braced himself to catch her. He flinched from what would be the shock of her landing, but to his surprise, she never came down! *"Nice catch, my brother! How the hell did you get to her that fast?"* Thor asked Erük telepathically, still unable to see from the flash-blindness.

"I don't have her!" Erük yelled aloud, more frantic than Thor had ever heard him before. Thor panicked! He struggled to regain his vision, feeling all around himself in case somehow he missed her and she fell all the way down.

"Sky!" He yelled at the top of his lungs, starting to fear the worst.

"Over here!" Erük called out again, this time from the direction of the shuttle. Thor dropped the cable and b-lined for the sound of Erük's voice, leaping up the ramp in two huge steps, then sliding to a stop just inside the cargo hold. He looked up toward the cockpit and saw her, cradled in Erük's massive arms, awake and in one piece! Thor rushed over to her and held her tight, not knowing what to say.

"Y-you saved my life," she said shakily. "How did you know?"

"Old habits die hard... I'm just glad you're all right! But.... How the hell did you-"

"I'm not sure. The other day... in the dome, I-"

"It was Ar'Jvikkah. He caused you to shift," Erük told her, placing his hand across her stomach as if to make sure he was okay. She looked at him, finally starting to understand what was happening to her a little bit better. *"This was not the first time?"*

"No."

"He is projecting his power through you, somehow. Have you been able to control it?"

"No."

"You will."

Thor exhaled loudly, trying to get a grip on this new turn of events. "So... what now? The scope's fried, I'm sure of it." Just then, another flash, much larger than the first, erupted just outside the shuttle, catching them off their guard and causing all three of them to jump. "Holy shit!" Thor exclaimed, "Okay, this is getting a little bit hairy... what say we blow this popsicle stand!"

"What?" Sky laughed, looking at Thor strangely. Erük nodded, understanding the context more than the words. Thor hit the switch to hail the Phoenix.

"Hey, Bjorn! We're going to have to try this another time... We're taking a beating down here! We've got to abort! The scope got hit by lightning. It's toast!" Thor looked at Sky and smiled, rubbing her back to console her.

"Copy... Look, Captain, I think we can do this another way. I'm going to use the shuttle's beacon as the reference point since you guys are so close to the old tower. Just stay put and give me a few minutes... I should be able to get all the information we need fairly quickly."

"Alright. Just make it quick... I'm not shitting, Bjorn, we almost lost Sky! Double time!"

"Copy that. Hang in there; I'll have you out of there in no time. Eriksson out."

Thor stood up and looked precariously out the front windshield of the cockpit, amazed at the power of the storm that was building. "I'm going to grab the rest of our gear before it disappears into the mud!" Sky held onto his hand as he started for the door, not wanting to let him go back out there. "No worries... I'll be fine. I have a way with electricity... *trust me.*"

"I fucking hate it when people say that," Sky mumbled as Thor started for the door again. He spun around like he just saw a ghost, staring at her.

"What did you just say?" He asked, looking at her quizzically.

"I said, I fucking hate it when people say, *trust me*," she repeated, looking at him with a coy smile, just as Kait always had. He stared back at her, smiling, but unsure whether to try to explain it or not. "*What?*" she insisted.

"I'll explain later." Thor walked outside in the wind and rain, smiling from ear to ear. He started winding up the cable and pulling it inside when something strange caught his eye. From the edge of the rock formation, near the side where Sky had climbed up, he could see movement. It was as if something or someone was trying to emerge from the rock itself. There was water cascading down the rock face, and from where he was standing, in the dark, it could easily have been his eyes playing tricks on him, but there was something about the timing....

He started to walk cautiously over toward the rock formation, holding his right hand up to shield his eyes from the increasing wind, now blowing straight sideways and sometimes even straight up. He froze in his tracks. Standing not ten feet away from him, dressed exactly as she was the last time he saw her on her way to the Border District, was Kait, staring back at him with a blank stare. He dropped the cable and glanced behind himself at the shuttle, now a good twenty feet away. Sensing movement, he quickly looked back in her direction, and barely caught her stepping behind the lower outcroppings of the large rock tower.

Something wasn't right, and though all common sense and reasoning told him this couldn't be real, he was inexplicably drawn to resolution... to closure. He *had* to see her face close up. She disappeared behind the tower into the dark, just as she had that fateful morning, and though his mind allowed him to let her go then, despite the warning of his heart, this time he followed.

Sky was just starting to doze off when the com began to crackle, and a message from Bjorn started coming through in fragmented syllables and broken sentences:

"Get----a-safe---ace! Fleet-----we--ren't---we should be!-Do you co---Get to----fe place! ------ incoming! Leaving orbit--- for -- eye of sto--- I repeat---" ...and then it was silent, save for the droning static and white noise of the storm's interference. Sky turned to Erük with her jaw wide open.

"Did he say, *Leaving orbit?* We have to get clear of this interference and get him back on the com!" She looked toward the shuttle door, impatiently. "Christ, I hope this isn't another crazy dream!" She made a quick attempt to hail Thor on his belt com, then waited, nervously.

"I'll get him," Erük said aloud with one hand lightly on her shoulder. He bolted out the shuttle door, protectively sealing it behind himself.

Thor was walking faster now, through every manner of sharp rock, pool of water, strange plant and scraggly bush. He was trying very hard to stay mindful of his surroundings in the bluish dark, but he didn't want to lose sight of her. It seemed no matter how close he got, she was always the same distance away, never turning back to look at him, regardless of his cries. Then, as he climbed over a small hill made almost entirely of debris from some sort of landslide, he lost her completely.

He knew he had to be getting very close to the base of the pyramid mountain, due to the direction he was traveling and the fact that he had been going steadily uphill for some time. He heard a crackle on his belt com and realized he was getting pretty far from the shuttle, given the increasing interference, but just as he was coming to his senses, and about to make the decision to turn around and head back, he got another sign.

The lightning crashed all around him, lighting up everything, and confirming his instincts. The mountain was magnificent! It rose up into the night sky so far and vast that the top could not be seen through the swirling black clouds. Though obviously not manmade, the dimensions were nearly perfect, leaving only the inconsistencies that would be expected from the centuries of advanced erosion that would undoubtedly be a factor on this tempestuous planet.

Squinting hard at a group of openings along the base that looked like natural cave mouths, he caught sight of her again. She was standing in the opening of one of the caves with her arms at her sides, just staring at him. As soon as he advanced up the debris slide and steady stream of muddy water coming down from the caves, she backed up, never taking her eyes off of him as she was slowly engulfed in the darkness of the pitch black opening.

Erük searched frantically, unable to pick up any tracks, or even the faintest scent, anywhere in this dark, stormy landscape. He concentrated all of his thoughts on Thor's energy, trying hard to hail him telepathically. As sure as this violent cataclysm brewing all around them was preventing any radio communication, it seemed to be interfering with Erük's abilities as well, leaving him in a primitive state of silence that rendered him almost defenseless. He was having trouble even sensing his very surroundings, when he came out of the thick into a clearing and nearly walked right up on him. Erük was relieved to see him and paused for a moment, then Thor started motioning to him frantically with his arms. His motions seemed random and aimless, leaving Erük more and more confused.

He was standing on top of a small group of rocks and bushes about thirty feet away, waving for him to follow, but also making some other sort of wild hand motion that Erük couldn't make heads or tails of. Erük bounded to catch up, and Thor continued uphill as they ran for what looked like the base of the pyramid mountain, closing his inner lids to shield his large eyes from the onslaught of particle matter blowing down from the vast darkness above them.

Erük took flight for just a moment to catch up, despite the growing concern for safety as the lightning strikes continued randomly overhead. He caught sight of Thor bolting into one of the dark cave mouths at the base of the pyramid, and he quickly followed, widening his gaze and opening his inner lids he had shut outside for protection, so he could see in the darkness. Absolutely at home in this natural subterranean setting, so very similar to the cave network of his home planet, Erük looked all around immediately inside the natural cave, knowing Thor couldn't have been but seconds ahead of him, yet he was nowhere to be found.

CHAPTER 11: TEMPORAL CAUSALITY

Bjorn was in a state of utter panic, not doing too well with the notion that at this moment, he was the sole crew member on the bridge of a world class deep space exploration vessel, despite the fact that he had been trained for this function and no other from the time he was first able to read. The giant Harvester was actually designed to be capable of single man operation when necessary, but as far as manual maneuvering and atmospheric reentry, it was always nice to have a committed navigator, helmsman and co-pilot by your side. Seeing the large Fleet's unmistakable signature show up on the first deep space scan of the known star positions from the planet's horizon changed his situation from one of convenience to one of necessity, and most likely, of survival, in the blink of an eye.

The only reason the Fleet would have bothered to follow them back in this direction, and be here right on their heels following the tachyon blast, was if they were inadvertently carrying something that Fleet Command needed *very* badly. As pompous as he could be, even Admiral Reid, whose beloved flagship was burned to the ground back on

Erük's home planet just before they fled the system, wouldn't be doing this simply out of the need for revenge. This move made no sense... and yet here they were.

Bjorn quickly shut down all inessential systems to lower the strength of their own signature, praying that the nebula's interference, combined with the ambient static from the high gravity field of the blue giant would cover his tracks long enough for him to think of something. He grabbed the controls with confidence, manually pulling the Phoenix into a decaying ellipse toward the blind side of the small planet to buy more time.

Not wanting to risk any further radio use for an attempt at contacting the shuttle crew that would most likely be an exercise in futility, Bjorn simply hoped that they had somehow received his last transmission. He stared at the viewers of the surface near the quadrant where the shuttle landed, then took a huge breath, crunching a few numbers in his head. He knew that almost every possible scenario would result in Fleet Command becoming aware of their presence, and now that they basically got caught with their pants down, separated and unable to communicate with each other, they didn't even have the option of trying to outrun them. There was only one thing that the young genius-level Ensign could come up with, and it was an extremely risky proposition, but still better than spending the rest of his life in cryo onboard the prison barge or being shot for treason.

He waited until the very last possible moment, so that the angle of decent was as shallow as possible, then broke through the atmosphere, hoping the intense light from Atlas at this angle would cloak the large ship from the view of the first Fleet ships, just breaking through the thick blue debris cloud, as the Phoenix sped toward the surface like a flaming meteor. Knowing full well that there wasn't a cave or natural structure on the entire planet that could hide this large of a vessel from the scanners of H.O.R.U.S. once the Fleet was in orbit, Bjorn did the only thing any sane person would do in a time of intense crisis such as this... head straight toward the very eye of the giant storm! The way he figured, they at least wouldn't be able to use their scanners to find them, and if they were fortunate enough to have not been detected already, they might, by the grace of God, be overlooked entirely.... *"Are you out of your fucking mind?"* the voice, most likely his own, boomed in his head like an echoing loudspeaker.

"Absofuckinlutely," he replied out loud, as dignified as possible, given his current situation and the fact that he was, in fact, the only one on the bridge. He started his decent into the mouth of Hell itself, an ominous blue vortex of sheer violence surrounding a relatively calm circle in the center that seemed to get larger by the moment as he moved towards it. It was socked in with a thick haze and was calm enough right in the center, but his concern was mainly for the small shuttle with his friends onboard. Even if they had received his warning message on the com, there was still grave concern as to whether or not the puny shuttle craft would be able to handle penetrating the walls of the storm, now grown well beyond any of mankind's known classifications for measuring the magnitude of violent windstorms, hurricanes and tornados. There was still the prospect of them flying up and over, but if they hadn't started the maneuver already, it would likely get them spotted by H.O.R.U.S. and the Fleet as they ascended above the interference and popped up on their screens.

He said a quick prayer, making the sign of the cross on his forehead and chest, then opened his eyes and focused bravely on the screen in front of him as he held his course, swooping down into the eye of the storm from above and starting to adjust his course manually across the wind-stripped mud field and straight at the giant pyramid that was getting hit just above the thick cloud canopy by the giant sun's morning blast of blue light. Looking up at the mountain's shining crown winking at them through the walls of solid destruction and the thick blue haze of the storm center, the very young officer was suddenly overcome with a profound sense of loneliness that he hadn't felt since they separated from the Fleet. For the first time since that fateful day, especially as they drew ever closer above him, he actually started to regret his decision to remain onboard the Phoenix.

Reid was staring intently at some files on the computer screen regarding mineral contents and weight ratios when the call came in from the H.O.R.U.S..

"Admiral Reid! We're picking up something on the surface... near the great pyramid mountain! It looks like the heat signatures from several life forms! There's also a very faint signal. This could be first contact with intelligent extraterrestrial life, Sir! I repeat, this could be first contact! Requesting permission to try to establish communication."

"By any and all means, Captain Levitt. Patch us through the moment you get any response. Increase scan to include entire surface. We're preparing a landing party right now... I want to know *exactly* what we're jumping into. Reid out." The Admiral stared at himself in the reflective glass of the radar screen, picked at his neatly trimmed moustache, then cleared his throat multiple times, preparing to give a speech to the entire fleet he had undoubtedly given in his berth dozens of times in front of the mirror over the years. He took a deep breath, serious on the surface, but having noticeable difficulty containing his giddiness as he reached for the button to switch on the com and proceed with the writing of history. Just before his finger found its target, he was interrupted by the com beeping on his end, making him flinch and completely lose his focus.

"Admiral... it's gone. The signal is completely gone! So are the signs of infrared heat. It's as if they just... vanished!"

"Get them back, dammit," Reid insisted, "I don't care how long you have to look! They didn't just vanish! Figure it out and *find them*!"

"Aye, Sir! We're turning the Hubble down now, it'll be up and working within 20 minutes, but visibility is almost zero... there seems to be a giant storm centered almost right where the signal was coming from, and it's growing by the hour! I don't advise sending a ground crew until it passes, Sir, with all due respect."

"Yeah, I see it. We've worked in worse. We *are* sending a ground crew, and we could sure use that intel, Captain, so keep on it and inform me when you've got news! Reid out."

"Aye, aye, Sir! Captain Levitt out."

The Admiral exhaled loudly, paused a moment, then slammed the console half-assed, but angrily with his fist. "Dammit!" he yelled, causing the previously joyous atmosphere on the bridge to falter into a sort of nervous business, as if the entire team was holding its breath and waiting for Reid's next reaction. He walked with the malignant aire of unearned royalty back to his throne in the center of the bridge, seated himself, and placed his elbow on the armrest while holding his chin in a most presumptuous pose; childishly naive as to the true regard of his subordinates: a pillar of humanity, a leader, a usurper... a douche bag.

CHAPTER 10.5: THE OTHER SIDE OF THE MIRROR

Sky sat alone in the shuttle, feeling the additional strain of her unexpected pregnancy in a way that her body had never been given the time to adjust to. She was beyond fatigued, hanging on to consciousness by a thin thread composed solely of concern for her friends. As she stared out the hazy, rain soaked front window at the darkness beyond the small craft's landing lights, the water running across the glass distorting what small detail she could make out in the first place, she became hypnotized; relaxing from a point deep inside her mind, then followed, in turn, by each and every part of her being until she finally surrendered to it, fading into an instant and deep sleep.

She was floating high above the alley where she had witnessed what she believed, at first, to be her own death. A man she did not know stood above her body as it shook violently from some sort of electric weapon used on her by the man with the hat that she mistook for Dagaz, now laying almost on top of her, dead from a single gunshot wound to the forehead. He had just been shot by another man... this man in black who now stood before her, leveling his single shot pistol calmly at her head. She strained to break free of her astral window and rejoin her former self on the ground in order to help somehow... to see his face.

Gunfire erupted from the side alley across from the bar just as he was about to shoot her too, and she started to feel the pull of being yanked from this plane, back into consciousness. She focused hard on the man, not wanting to leave this place. *Too many unanswered questions.... Got to warn the others!* She was pulled, instead, back into her body on the ground, where she was suddenly stricken with pain, stricken with fear, and convulsing madly as the device on her wrist shook her to the core. She focused hard on not passing out this time, as the man who was just about to finish her was sent straight backward, losing his gun instantly as huge wounds opened up in several places on his chest, abdomen and neck. She completely lost her focus on the pitch of the device and was taken over violently by the stunner's charge. She started fading out of consciousness and forced herself with all the will she could muster to remain where she was.

She tuned into the things that kept her rooted to this time and place: Thor... Dagaz... Tyr.... She even smiled as she remembered Uruz, with all of his belligerent, boorish charm. Another presence entered the picture. A few men in tactical gear descended on the bloody scene with military precision, but apparently were uninterested in preserving the incidental integrity of the crime scene. These men were not cops, but instead, it seemed, driven by some other agenda focused on covering up the entire incident. The two smaller men started lifting the man in black by his legs and wrists up off of the ground, and the larger man bent down toward her on one knee, analyzing the device without touching her.

He found the control lying in the dirt next to her knee where Stanton fumbled it and shut it down. She relaxed so much that she actually felt the sensation of pissing herself. She half smiled from the irony, half from the pure relief, realizing this was the absolute least of her concerns at the moment. The huge man tested her joints quickly, making sure nothing was broken, then hoisted her onto his shoulder, fireman style, and started walking off into the adjacent alley.

The other two men were having tremendous difficulty with the assassin; fumbling and pulling as if he was rooted to the earth with some sort of immoveable anchor of energy. Struggling with him repeatedly, they finally made the choice to give up when some commotion started from around the corner by the bar. It sounded as if half the bar was coming out to see what happened. They dropped the man randomly onto the ground where he crumbled into a contorted pile, face down, almost in fetal position, away from her line of sight.

She could make out some sort of tattoo on the back of his neck, and realized she had seen this before! She struggled with all her remaining strength to see clearly, and somehow, her eyes were able to not only focus, but zoom in like a predatory animal. She could clearly make out the pattern and numbers, very similar to a late 20th century retail barcode, but something she had recently stared at with some serious concern... *concern for Thor!*

She had a sudden epiphany. Two lives separated by the natural boundary of death and rebirth suddenly collided; memories spilling over the natural walls of the psyche like a levy exploded, filling her mind with a raging river of thought, and as usual, more questions than answers. *McGinn!* She could now see the resemblance. It was him, but when he leveled his gun at her a moment ago, she recognized him no more than he did her... He was simply going to kill her because she was there... just a loose end, nothing more. She started to fade off again as the large man carrying her walked quickly into the dark alley, and was slowly losing sight of McGinn's body lying there, close to the intersection, when she suddenly noticed him twitch, then start to get up; bleeding profusely.

Sky tried hard to get the attention of her savior, fearing McGinn would rise up and shoot him in the back, but for some reason, she couldn't influence anything... she seemed unable to do anything but observe. McGinn looked around himself, now up on one knee, struggling to rise. He looked in their direction and her heart missed a beat. She seemed suddenly able to focus to an outstanding degree of clarity, and not just her eyesight, but her thoughts as well! Her animal-like vision zoomed in on his cold stare as if he was right in front of her, close enough to reach out and touch.

Her eyes focused in on his, looking deep into the windows of his soul and seeing something not entirely human, and not entirely sane.... There was something to this man that couldn't be easily qualified, quantified or explained. It was almost like looking into the eyes of someone who knew you better than you knew yourself, knew your thoughts before you did, and then suddenly realizing they didn't like you at all. She felt vulnerable in a whole new way.

He was still struggling, but almost on his feet, never taking his eyes off of her. She was growing increasingly worried, not so much for herself, but for Thor and the North Clan family. A vision of her childhood home flashed through her mind, mixed with thoughts of the attack on her own family in the underground... then of Thor, and how he took her in without question or expectation. She had a flood of thoughts spilling over from her life now, backward into the past. Her parents searching for her on Cheops... the Fleet... Erük and Ar'Jvikkah and her new abilities... Thor and McGinn fighting on the bridge. *Thor! He was the one constant.*

Suddenly she had the sensation of being "read" and she realized her thoughts had betrayed her... probably betrayed them all! McGinn was staring deep into her eyes, from all the way down the dark alley, reading her like a book! A devilish grin started on the edge of his mouth and he winked at her just as the man who was carrying her rounded a corner and took her out of his line of sight. As he kicked a door open to an abandoned building and started up some stairs with her, she pulled away with all her will, needing to warn them. She was floating again, watching the man proceed up the stairs with her body slung over his shoulder and then became aware of a droning noise; a low vibration becoming louder and louder, until it was almost deafening.

She awoke suddenly to the tail end of what almost felt like an earthquake. She saw the reflection in one of the console's dead screens of movement behind her, and she jumped a little, releasing the swivel lock on her cockpit chair and spinning around to see Erük, standing alone by the closed cargo door. Something was a little "off" about him, and she glanced around quickly, looking for Thor, still groggy and disoriented from her deep dream-state experience. "Wow," she said to Erük, wiping a little sweat from her brow, "I didn't even hear the hatch open when you came in! Where's Thor?"

All at once, as if they were standing on the deck of a Carrier, the intense sound and low, earthshaking vibration of a ship passing directly overhead rocked the little ship to the core. It was nearly pitch black outside, save for the increasing flashes of lightning, and the ship was at least high enough into the thick storm clouds that it couldn't have seen their dim, downward pointed landing lights, but they were obviously tuned into this spot for some reason, and most likely it was the small ship's ambient electronic signal emission. It didn't sound familiar, and she didn't want to stick around to find out if it was friendly, nor break radio silence to find out what Bjorn knew. "Where's Thor!?" she yelled at Erük, knowing they had only moments before it came back and landed, after reading sonar information on the topography.

There was no reply, and she spun around, starting to get frustrated, and saw no one! There was nowhere on the small craft he could have gone, and the door never opened. He was simply *not here*. She hesitated for a moment, then figured they would have to follow on foot. She switched on the repulsion engines, but not the spotlights, and took off toward the base of the mountain as low and fast as she could maneuver with almost no lights.

Remembering a particularly large cave-opening-turned-hangar bay by the Fleet, she piloted in close, scanning the row of mouths across the base. They looked so much different than she remembered as a teenager. They seemed smaller, in general, and seemed to have been left without the shoring built in to them to reinforce them against cave-ins for the miners. At first, she couldn't tell what the noise was... it sounded like some kind of oscillation error in her engines. She got a little distracted checking her gauges when the light started to get brighter and brighter overhead, coming from the blind side of the mountain. Her heart missed a beat as she madly flipped off the landing lights and cut hard directly at the largest opening she could see. It was right where she remembered the old hangar being, but looked like it was about half the size. She didn't care... it was either take her chances with the opening, or stay outside and be caught for sure!

The shuttle craft sped toward the hole, banking hard right, then leveling out just before the breach. It wasn't quite large enough, and she cringed as the right wing, despite a last minute hook to port, slammed into the cave opening wall, causing the collapse of the opening all the way across the mouth of the cave. She skidded sideways to a stop less than 30 feet in and immediately killed all systems on the ship so as to leave no traceable signal, as a huge pile of rubble and mud slammed in behind her, completely sealing her in. There was the sound of rock falling on top of the shuttle and behind her, but it didn't sound like enough to worry about, so for the moment, she sat in the darkness and listened... just listened.

The sound of the other ship got louder for a moment, then leveled off at a steady rumble. She started to panic, fearing they had seen the collapse and were investigating, then, all at once, it faded off. They were leaving... at least for now. She breathed a heavy sigh of relief, and sat back in her chair with one hand on her stomach and closed her eyes, concentrating. *"Erük, can you hear me? I need your help! We have company."*

———————

Not wanting to give up his position as he explored deeper into the opening maze of natural corridors, Thor had been using his instinctive sense of his surroundings only, keeping his eyes closed and just listening calmly to the expanse of the many rooms and tunnels; but just as the darkness started to effectively swallow him entirely, he heard the loud hum of another ship coming from back in the direction he came, and he realized the system of tunnels was far more vast than he originally thought. He also realized he had been operating with a clouded mind. Starting to worry about Sky and Erük, he cursed himself under his breath for veering so far away from his mission and leaving the shuttle alone. It was then that he heard the crash. It seemed to be coming partly from back the way he came, and more clearly from off into the depths of the cave. *The tunnel looped back around!*

Deciding at this point that it was better to give up his ambiguity than to remain in this kind of darkness, he reached down to his belt to turn on the small, shoulder mounted light attached to his harness system. It didn't work. He tapped it a couple times, not sure about the possibility of water damage. Still nothing.... He reached into his front pocket for the old style trench lighter he had been carrying since he took command of the Phoenix; one of the many old school treasures he and Sky had stumbled onto in Captain Parnell's berth.

The Captain, apparently an avid history buff, kept a large footlocker-style container in his cabin, literally full to the top with every manner of paraphernalia, news clipping, post card, music, money, and small device from pre-Exodus, 21st century Earth he could get his hands on. Thor's guess was that he most likely pilfered the items from people's cryo tubes whenever their rehabilitation took an ugly turn. For the most part, he and Sky were either uninterested in the contents, or didn't want anything to do with them, mainly out of sympathetic respect for the fallen. This was one of the few exceptions. It was an actual brass trench lighter from WW2 with more patina than shine; a relic even in *his* day! This was an object of extreme rarity in the Fleet due mostly to the fact that because of the enclosed environment and recycled oxygen, smoking was militantly banned upon departure, as was any kind of open flame, including candles, and all forms of incendiary tool were to be relinquished upon boarding, to be used only at the discretion of Fleet's senior officers.

He had found a type of highly flammable solvent on board in maintenance, normally used for cleaning dirty mechanical parts, which turned out to work great as lighter fuel. Luckily the flint was still in great shape, and had seen very little use. He instinctively blew hard into the end of it to clear any lint from the mechanism, and held it up about neck level and out in front of himself. He was just about to strike the top to produce flame, when he caught the scent of something familiar.... *It was ether!* He suddenly became worried as he

108

remembered the story Sky told back on the Phoenix about the miners. He tapped on the waist switch for his shoulder light again and this time it flickered, just barely sending a flash of light out into the large room.

He gasped, retaining the mental image of what he just saw as he was cast back into darkness. The entire cavern was absolutely *crawling* with movement! It seemed, in that strobe-like flash of sudden revelation, that almost every square inch of the room's walls and formations, including the large stalagmites and stalactites forming columns in the middle of the huge chamber, were literally changing form from one thing to the next while more forms were swirling around him in a circular pattern like Indians circling a covered wagon full of settlers right before they massacred everyone! He swatted the light controls over and over with his other hand out in front of his face a few feet in anticipation of an attack.

Sky had been sitting long enough. After hearing a few thunder bolts but realizing that she couldn't see a shred of light from the outside through the rubble, she made the calculated decision to turn on the ship's external floodlights and see where she was. She had been sitting in the dark for so long that the light hurt her eyes. The first thing on her mind as she adjusted to her new surroundings was that this wasn't the old hangar. It was about the same size after you got past the opening, which no longer existed, but this chamber looked as if it had never been touched by human hands! This was all starting to piece itself together in a certain light, but she temporarily dismissed the entire subject, knowing full well that she wasn't out of danger... they *would* be back!

She was relieved to note that there wasn't any dust in the air from the cave in, which was probably the only real reason that the other ship, having come around the corner just after the cave in happened, didn't notice anything. The only real questions now were how bad was the cave-in, did the ship get damaged, and where the hell were Erük and Thor? Obviously the other small ship didn't cross deep space all by itself, so she had to assume, for now, that Bjorn saw its mother ship coming, and hopefully took appropriate action before it saw him. In any case, she had more immediate concerns. She tried to communicate with Erük one more time, trying *very* hard to focus all of her strength and energy, then suited up with a rifle to go with her already harnessed weapons ensemble.

The particular rifle she brought, given the Fleet's last encounter with the indigenous of Cheops, was the perfect choice. It was a miniature flame-thrower, capable of firing conventional bullets by itself, or at the same time as it spit a 40 foot long, tight stream of concentrated liquid incendiary fuel, then lit it upon the release of the trigger or at the beginning of the burst. They used these mainly as a tool for deep space maintenance and in-flight salvage operations, for the precise, controlled thawing of small components and short burst breaking of ice on satellites and small craft pulled into the hangars by Fleet after contact with particularly corrosive freezing gas clouds near the particle rings of certain planets and moons. In this particular case, though, it kind of made her feel warm and fuzzy as she locked and loaded, preparing to open the cargo hatch.

She waited for a moment for some kind of a sign from Erük or Thor, cleared her mind and got herself centered, then hit the panel to release the locks on the heavy cargo door. It let out a sigh of pent up air pressure and slowly rose up, as the ramp lowered down simultaneously to the ground. She stood defensively, looking around for a moment and remembering the stories of her childhood. Though she had never actually witnessed one of the creatures that caused all the mayhem while they were here before, she definitely spent her share of time in the caverns and mine shafts. This was not how she remembered them looking at all.

The Fleet had all but butchered the entire population of whatever they were, and reconstructed what was, essentially, a complex matrix of natural caves, as they followed several veins of different ores, the most prominent of which was the vein of an unusual variation of iron pyrite that ran from the west end of the mountain almost straight through the base, and down toward its core. They never found the source of the deposit, but the vein got larger and considerably more pure as they started mining straight down, following it into the depths of the mountain.

The ferrous crystalline metal was the primary catalyst for a type of repulsion reactor in the larger ships responsible for everything from the generation of their shields, to artificial gravity, to the very technology allowing them to approach light speed in the first place. Due to its highly magnetic properties only when in the presence of other metals, there was always a field around the mountain of magnetic interference and anomaly, very similar to the ultra-pure version they found later in the crystal sand of Erük's home planet.

This was the reason why closed cell power sources didn't work within the mountain. Something would simply cause them to discharge as fast as they could be charged up. Radio communication was almost useless, and their plasma-based weaponry wouldn't work within the pyramid, neither ship mounted for construction blasting, nor hand held guns for defense. They used torches for light within the mines for a while, but the revelation of the ethereal life forms' high degree of volatility left them only the old-school light-stick as an option after the mining accident they experienced.

Very small supplies of these outdated, disposable tools existed within the Fleet, as they lacked the facilities to produce most plastic and chemical compounds, and halted the production of anything that wasn't 100% recyclable or reusable due to the pivotal importance of self-sustaining practices for the very survival of the species. It was mandated that they divide among the mining vessels the last of the reserves kept in stock from Earth, to be used sparingly at the discretion of the individual ship Commanders.

Sky was aware of their existence and usage, so she had already included them on the shuttle before they left. What she hadn't counted on was getting separated. She broke one, shook it a few times, then shut the door behind her and started for the one opening she could see: a small cave in the northwest corner, no more than a few feet in diameter. She looked back at the shuttle as if worried that she wasn't going to see it again and punched a code into a small, flip-open touch screen control pad on her utility belt. "Switch to voice command only," she spoke clearly and loud enough to produce a small echo in the quiet chamber, "Commander Davies, enter. Captain Krey, enter. All power down." The ship lights shut immediately off and she turned toward the small opening, light-stick out in front of her.

Thor widened his benign energy, becoming instinctively aware that they had no desire to attack him. He could feel them all around him, and they were not just in the walls anymore... they were close! Standing alone in the dark, he reached out with his arms, closed his eyes, and tuned in to their energy. He pulled it to his center, accepting it and attempting to raise his pitch to match it. He could feel himself changing. He had never experienced an energy so pure... so elevated. They seemed to exist on a plane altogether different than humans. It was as if they transcended physical manifestation entirely. They were here, and yet they were somewhere else simultaneously. To see them at all, or to be seen by them was like looking into a mirror hard enough to see past the reflection and into the world beyond.

His body, mind and spirit were vibrating faster and faster. He felt himself change physically, several times, into this or that, unable to control or identify the result. He sensed that they were still worlds apart, and he changed his method, relinquishing his very grip on what he had perceived from birth to be "reality." It was then that he felt actually free of his body in a very literal sense. This was not the stuff of dreams, but simply a fusion between himself and the earth beneath his feet... the walls... the very air in his lungs, until at last he felt it....

There was a liberating "pop," as if a ball of liquid had broken membranes to fuse with another one. Quite simply, he was sound. Low at first, like the lowest pitch of bass vibrating your stomach. He rose further up the scale, slowly at first, then he quickly escalated through the entire audible range of sound, hitting a supersonic pitch heard only by the keenest of animals, and then things started to change dramatically.

His vision became surreal, at first, matching the colors of his tone, straight through the spectrum of color on any prismatic array. Upon reaching the highest pitch of light, he saw the room in a different way. It was as if he could see many places at once, depending on where his attention lay. The beings around him were now standing still, staring at him through eyes like his; spawning black holes in the middle of a being of pure light. He became aware again of the scent of ether, and was able to "hear" voices from all points of the universal collective, aware of everything, yet focused on nothing. He seemed to be in a place between places; alive, but not living... a distorted reflection of life unable and unwilling to turn away from the mirror.

Sky had to struggle to reach the end of the small tunnel, as it just kept getting smaller and smaller. At one point, she was down on her hands and knees, crawling through some kind of mud and mire that was flowing though the almost perfect cylinder. She breathed in and smelled something foul... something familiar. She closed her eyes for a moment, trying to place it. When she opened them, she was no longer in the small cave, but in a concrete tunnel, full of mire. She was following Thor, and they were both laughing about something. She blinked again and was back in the cave, surrounded by the cool, blue light from the stick in her hand. She paused; breathing a little heavier. Something about this place was bringing down the barrier between life and death, past and present.

She was nearing the point of being able to stand straight up again as the cave widened and curved around to the left. The opening in front of her split off once, then again, joining with a couple other caves. This part, she recognized! It was the junction to the hangar and the vertical shaft, following the pyrite vein... the only problem was this would mean she just came from the hangar! *How could it have gotten this much smaller?* She looked back from the junction toward the old hangar tunnel, unable to believe her eyes. There wasn't a single trace that anyone had ever even set foot in this place! Even the layer lines formed on the stalactites over centuries of slow formation remained.

She placed her hand on the cold, damp wall, as if contacting the surface with her physical skin would somehow validate the impossible. Caught up in the strangeness of the moment, she fumbled the light-stick, sending it flipping out of her hand and into the small pool of water at her feet. The light was dimmed dramatically by the muddy water, and as she leaned over to retrieve it, she noticed another, considerably brighter glow of light, coming from down one of the tunnels to her left that she was about to pass up. She left the light right where it was, raising her rifle slowly and stepping quietly out of the water. She paused for a moment, just listening. It was almost as if she could hear the sound of someone mumbling under their breath, but it seemed to be coming from all around her. She pressed on, keeping silently out of the narrow stream of water flowing down the tunnel toward her.

As she got closer to the source of light, nearing another junction in the caverns, she became aware that the voice in her head was Thor's! It was the same *"sound"* as when he spoke to her telepathically, but for some reason things were disjointed and confusing. It sounded like him, but like *many versions* of him, all talking at the same time about different things. Some of the conversation threads she even recognized… others she did not. She became frightened to the very core. Something was very wrong about this, she could feel it. She was having severe difficulty conducting herself with her usual degree of military equanimity.

Taking a deep breath and trying very hard to block out the voices in her head, she calmed herself, regaining her center as she focused on keeping the little red dot from her rifle's laser sighting system from shaking about on the cave wall in front of her. She focused her energies on Thor, sensing that he needed her help. *"Hold on, I'm coming!"* she said back, concentrating her signal to include only him.

The light seemed to be emanating from a large side room, one that they turned into a magazine for mining explosives due mostly to its structural stability and "blowable" cap, being so very close to the openings with only a thin membrane of earth between the chamber and the outside. The premise, of course, was that if there was an accident resulting in the explosion of the magazine, being the path of least resistance, the side would blow out easily, leaving the rest of the shaft network as undamaged as possible. Given the sheer amounts of high explosives stored at any given time, this was a theory they hoped they would never have to test.

She could clearly make out the ominous glow now. It was definitely coming from within the magazine, and was flickering, as if being filtered through many translucent moving screens, shifting randomly about the room with the fluidity of flowing water. It seemed at first to be going faster and faster, but after a moment of observation, she realized it was not a linear transgression, but rather, an ebb and flow, oscillating with a vibration within a vibration... a pitch within a pitch. Thor had spoken to her of this concept, mainly with regard to the higher vibrational properties of the universe's more complex phenomena: the human body, planets, even the universe itself, all composed of myriads of smaller vibrations of energy combining to lend pulse to a greater vibration... the ebb and flow of a life!

This concept explained, rearranged and consolidated the convoluted theories of the linear thinking scientists and religious leaders who came before them to leave them with a universal truth that could be witnessed *everywhere*. This *was* eternity, as it was also the only viable explanation of infinity. The universe was not *just* expanding... it was contracting! And now, it seemed, as she grasped at the concepts of different planes of existence, it seemed it was doing both, simultaneously, as was literally everything in it; from the crudest form of cold, dense matter floating seemingly lifelessly through space, to the pulsating, blinding white light from a quasar, and literally everything in between.

As above: so below. She realized she was witnessing this universal truth firsthand, and save for the terror and uncertainty before her, should be basking in the experience. She steadied the rifle, rearranging her grip by wrapping the sling around her forearm once, then grabbing the stock tightly with her left hand, she walked bravely forward. Rounding the corner into the lit up chamber, she walked into a scene that couldn't easily be described.

There was a figure in the center of the room, hovering a few feet off of the floor, with its arms out to the sides, palms out. It was changing from form to form, being to being, color to color, as a hoard of apparitions swirled through the air around it in a spiral, flying right through it from time to time as they meshed with everything else in the room as well, even the walls and floor. It seemed malleable, made up of any number of the others at any given point in time, yet still retaining some pattern of unique energy, a root, or core from which the others branched.

She instinctively raised her weapon, staring deep into the black voids where its eyes should be. Becoming entranced, she slowly lowered it back down from its weight alone, not even thinking conscious thought at this point, but rather joining in the outskirts of some kind of ritualistic orgy of energy, requiring her presence... requiring her union. Requiring *her*.

Staring deeper into the eyes of this ethereal compound of souls, she noticed a familiarity she hadn't picked up on before. *The voices... the thoughts shared between us.* She knew them! She knew *him*.... Still caught up in the powerful energy trance these things were manifesting, she tried hard to focus enough to isolate him from the group collective. He sensed what she was doing for just a moment, and collapsed, looking up at her with his own eyes from behind a sea of shapeless energy. *Thor!*

Sky snapped out of it and rose to her feet, rifle drawn. She flipped the lever to charge the pressure tank with a shot of flammable gas and trotted out to the center of the room, intending to fend them away from him from there with the flamethrower. As she approached him, many of the beings shot out of him and started flying through her to her womb, apparently trying to control her through Ar'Jvikkah, as she suddenly found herself stepping wildly backward, against her own will. It felt as it did when she teleported in the bio-dome, and she knew they were affecting Ar'Jvikkah directly. Mistaking their involvement for an outright attack, her protective nature kicked in and she quickly raised the weapon at a large cluster of them in the wall to her right and pulled the trigger, releasing a very thin stream of incredibly hot blue and orange flame.

As if pulled by a powerful magnet, the flame bent in midair and started spiraling around Thor, getting closer and closer each revolution, as he pulled his right arm over toward the left in a blocking motion, preparing to redirect it into a harmless direction. He shifted his stance slightly and rolled his wrist upward again, splitting the fire in two directions with a manipulation of energy from his Tai Chi training known as *"parting the wild horse's mane."* The blast of fire shot toward the nearest wall, split into two smaller, cooler streams and Thor looked almost relieved, when he suddenly noticed the entire wall seem to come to life. Energy seemed to flow in every direction away from the path of the oncoming fire, but not fast enough.

The smell of ether permeated the air as a giant blue fireball erupted from the proximity of the wall's closest outcropping. Ear piercing shrieks and screams filled the air and smaller fires shot out from it randomly, spreading the destruction from creature to creature as they abandoned their dance and fled the circle by any means possible. Thor doubled over in excruciating pain, obviously still very much in some sort of communion with them. Sky let loose another round right into the thickest part of the cluster of light, madly intending to protect Thor and Ar'Jvikkah, no matter what the cost.

The intense burst of flame shot out almost ten feet from the end of her barrel when she jumped back, nearly dropping to the ground from surprise. Erük came into sight out of nowhere, directly in front of her fire, wings outstretched and mouth wide open in an intense, bone-chilling roar that caused her knees to buckle, nearly knocking her down. He breathed inward so loudly that the hiss from it hurt their ears, then blew all his air into the room, displacing the oxygen that was causing the fires to burn, with nothing but thick CO_2, sucking the life from the fires and extinguishing most of them instantly. The shrieks continued as the acrid smoke filled the air, adding to the effect, and the two humans, gasping for breath, slowly rose to their feet.

Thor, still pulsing with light from the ethereal fire, rose back up, pulling most of the remaining beings with him. They started swirling back around him, spreading flame from one to the next as he wound up in pitch, running right through the entire gamut in an instant, then dropping off, slowing more and more until he homed in on one particular sound wave and frequency, his color and appearance returning to normal as he finally isolated himself from them.

Sky covered her ears, kneeling in pain, as he continued for a moment, quickly reaching a crescendo in magnitude and harmonic oscillation that started vibrating the entire room, even the air inside! The low hum reached a terrible volume as Thor layered voice on top of voice to this effect, each one louder and clearer than the last, until finally, a deafening culmination, like every word in every language, uttered at once, sent a shockwave out in the shape of a perfect sphere, taking every one of them right through the walls, floor and ceiling as it passed into entropy.

Thor collapsed in the center of the room as the last bit of light faded and the three of them were in the dark again. Sitting in the pitch black chamber, listening to each other breathe, the trio had no need to speak. There was a closeness between them that transcended any language and simply didn't need to be expressed. All at once, the sound of Sky throwing up echoed through the chamber. There was a moment of awkward silence, then a small cough.

"Gross!" Thor mumbled facetiously, smiling slightly as he passed out on the ground.

Sky was the first to awaken, and for a moment, as she stared blankly at the console of the small craft from her pilot's chair, wondered if it wasn't all just another crazy dream. As her eyes adjusted to the soft blue light from one of her own light-sticks, she heard the faint sound of breathing coming from behind her. She turned slowly and saw Erük, curled up on the floor like a giant wolf, sleeping peacefully. Thor was next to her in the copilot's chair sleeping with a child-like innocent smile on his lips. He was starting to stir.

She smiled broadly, taking note first that despite what they had just experienced, he seemed none the worse for wear. She had to admit that it also made her feel just a little bit refreshed to see him in this vulnerable state. Reaching down to her left forearm, she pulled up her sleeve and pinched herself hard, wincing.

"No, you're not dreaming," Thor said softly, causing her to jump. She looked up at him, smiling broadly. "At least, I don't think you are...."

"No, you're not." They both turned around, smiling, to see Erük, awake from his slumber behind them.

"How did we-" Sky gestured around herself quizzically at the ship... at themselves.

"I brought you both inside," Erük answered. Sky glanced at him with a puzzled look on her face. Erük smiled. "Cargo door open," he said, imitating Sky's voice perfectly.

The door unlocked and hissed, then popped open, bringing the internal lights and the computer online.

"Well you're just *full* of surprises," Thor joked, smiling at him and giving him a nudge on the shoulder.

"It's nothing, really. Our vocal cords can articulate anything we perceive as sound. For us, it's no different than the way we learn your language simply by communicating with you telepathically a few times. We just tune in to your energy, and the rest is pretty much involuntary."

"Cargo door close! All power down. End voice command only," Sky said quickly, remembering that they were still most likely being searched for. "Neat trick... That ship is still out there though, guys, make no mistake." She sighed, pulling one hand over her forehead through her black hair. "What the hell happened to you last night, Thor?"

"Where do I begin?"

"At the end."

Thor chuckled, "At the end, huh? Well, who says it's over?" He smiled at Erük.

"What the hell were those things?" Sky asked.

"It's very hard to describe... Think of them as pure energy with a collective subconscious. I think they are all actual spirits from fallen races throughout time. They've been drawn to this place like a magnet! I think it has something to do with the pyrite core you spoke of in the center of the pyramid mountain... it is the air they breathe. There was a point when I couldn't escape its pull myself. When I was completely in tune with this place, with them, I could almost see their world through their scattered memories! I think some of them were from a rogue moon that couldn't escape the pull of the blue giant... It took their mother planet, then them. Others seemed infinitely more familiar to me... They were already ethereal in nature, so fleeing their doomed world wasn't hard, they simply wandered space between planes until a power source pulled them in."

"A power source?"

"Crystal," Erük responded. *"It acts like a battery for spiritual energy... They are attracted to it and pulled in."*

"Like the V'eíshnioü Larva on your world... the way they migrated from your world to the rings of Sigyn after their metamorphosis into those manta-ray-looking creatures," Sky added.

"Exactly." Erük became silent, lost in thought.

"They were able to fly between planets with no air, through the cold of space! We tried on several instances to capture one to study it, but we never could... It never occurred to our scientists that they could have actually been in existence on another plane!"

"The unfortunate thing about killing these things, is that they seem to be in some sort of Limbo already; a pseudo-existence between planes, having already been trapped outside of their natural course of life and death. I think their actual afterlife has been arrested, and I'm not so sure that killing them from here results in anything other than consigning them, as well as their very essence, to oblivion! They are unable to pass on either way." Thor scratched his head, obviously taking a great deal of the weight of these beings' plight onto his own shoulders after coming to understand them in such an intimate way.

Sky rubbed his back, feeling for him. "Aren't we basically doing them a favor, then, by at least ending their entrapment?" she offered.

"Did you not see them struggling for survival? So long as any creature puts up a fight to save its own life, intentionally or instinctively, it is not truly ready to die. It places some value on its own life, and given the choice, would prefer to keep it, no matter how pitiful of an existence it has been reduced to. Hope exists, even on the most primitive, subconscious level... Who are we to play God and take that away from anyone?"

"I think you are correct... It's too bad much of the rest of humanity doesn't share your sentiment toward what they consider to be 'lesser' beings. Their inability to understand another's culture seems all the excuse they need to wage war under the flag of 'self-defense.' I think we would do well to simply let them be. Though it would seem most unfortunate, even their grim fate may have some sort of universal role still to play...."

There was an awkward silence for a moment, followed by a strange vibration. They all started to look at each other, then around the ship, trying to figure out what was happening. Even Erük seemed unable to sense what it was. Suddenly they heard a tremendous banging that was coming from *outside* the ship. Sky hit a switch on the console, bringing the outside flood lights up to full intensity immediately. Looking out the front windshield, they couldn't see anything moving, but the vibration started to feel more and more like an earthquake. She hit another switch and the ship immediately started powering up, console lights flashing and all monitors and view screens coming online.

"What about the other ship? Are you sure we should go hot?" Thor asked her, a little unsure of the wisdom of her thinking. She said nothing, but instead pointed at the rear-starboard viewer. Thor squinted, noticing a small amount of rubble sliding down the muck pile where the cave opening used to be. The vibration started to increase in magnitude and began happening in rhythmic pulses, causing more and more of the rubble to loosen, falling down from the top to the bottom. Suddenly, a small beam of bright light shot through a tiny opening in the rockslide, and they became acutely aware that this was being done by someone on the outside!

"Strap yourselves in!" Sky yelled, pulling her five-point harness over her very pregnant belly and madly hitting the sequence of buttons necessary to power up the repulsion engines, while keeping the main thrusters primed for a lightning fast take off, if necessary. She was very much hoping to not have to use them, as it would burn up the fuel that they still needed to break free of the planet's gravity and return to the Phoenix.

Thor and Erük took their places and prepared for whatever came next. Thor began charging the small, front firing plasma gun turrets, knowing they wouldn't fire within the cave, because of the magnetic anomaly around this mountain, but just in case they needed to fight their way back to the Phoenix, wherever it was. Bjorn had not broken radio silence in the nearly 24 hours that had transpired, though they wouldn't have been able to make out a transmission from in here if he had, so they pretty much assumed that he was also in hiding. They *prayed* that he was also in hiding....

There was now a growing hole at the top of the cave-in with more and more light pouring into the chamber. Looking closely at the growing gap, Sky killed the floodlights, revealing to all of their amazement that the light was natural blue sunlight from Atlas, and not spotlights from the workers outside. It was extremely bright considering the thick black clouds from the intense storm that had been directly over them this entire time!

All of the planets in this system, including the largest sun, Alcyone, or "Atlas," as it was otherwise known in mythology, were spinning much faster than the Earth, so weather usually moved much more quickly across the surface of the planet, in some cases causing entire worlds to become uninhabitable, wind-stripped planets, sandblasted to the point of utter lifelessness. Even so, there was absolutely no possible way a storm such as this one could have passed already. It was just starting to hit their location head-on when they fled into the mountain, and according to Bjorn, it was doing nothing but growing, arrested from lateral movement by some kind of geographic variable none of them could predict.

Sky put all available energy into the shuttle's front shields and nervously focused her attention on the opening, getting ready to gun it for the gap the very moment it was large or loose enough. They suddenly caught sight of a robotic vise-like claw reaching through part of the top hole and grabbing a particularly large piece of rubble, crushing it with sheer strength, then pushing aside a large portion of the loose dirt across the top of the slide, exposing them further. Still not visible from the outside, she cringed, recognizing the device as one of the Fleet's "Unmanned Remote Controllable Robotic Assistance Mining Machines," or URCRAMM, known to the operators and workers simply as a "RAM."

They bore a sensor device at the helm, capable of "seeing" for the operator, in normal mode, infrared, X-ray or radiation arrays, and a myriad of other programmable variations relating to mining and hazardous excavation by the advanced use of material scopes, radar, fracture detection, ultrasound, etc.... What this unfortunately meant, is that someone was on the other end, at a mobile terminal or onboard a ship, jockeying this thing, and that this person was from the Fleet. This answered her question as to whether they made it away from Algol alive during the supernova, but it left many more unanswered, and though she was at least relieved that they survived, she knew full well what this meant.... They were pursuing them!

They had either sacrificed all progress toward their new destination just to catch and punish them all and retrieve the stolen Carrier and all of its fuel, or they simply lacked the fuel necessary after the destruction of the three Carriers, including the Flagship, Helios, to even make the trip, and were doubled back to rape Cheops some more. In either case, it seemed, here they were, and this couldn't be good. All three of them stared intently at the screen, totally silent, waiting for the moment of truth.

CHAPTER 12: AS ABOVE: SO BELOW

Kieran sat at the rickety table in the candle lit dining room of the cabin and took a long, slow drag of his cigarette, looking around the room for something to use; some angle that might bring them back here, preferably one at a time, as they seemed to be gaining power very rapidly. He was finally starting to get used to the parameters by which navigation outside of the material plane was possible. It seemed to work on the same premise as a *living* combination lock, like the way a key group of known doorways in an otherwise obscure wall full of blank doors might be understood.... If one knows, or more specifically, is shown, the right series of doors, or combination of a lock, remembering it and repeating it becomes no more complicated than tuning into that specific memory set.

In this case, as it pertained to individuals, the memory set he needed to tune into was the dream energy of his quarry; the specific combination of the individual life energy of the person, combined with the energy of the place or situation specific to that particular dream. What he hadn't figured out, just yet, was how to "summon" them to the place, or a particular dream. So far, waiting for them in recurring dreams seemed like it might work, but he was a predator, and he needed a more proactive approach.... A predator needs to hunt.

Many people have recurring dreams, but what they seldom realize is that this is not a random occurrence, nor is it usually a "message from God," the universe, or anyone else. In fact, these dreams *usually* tend to lack any real cosmic significance at all. When you do the same combination of things in life, you tend to get the same results... over and over again. Sometimes there will be small environmental variances depending on the subtle differences in input, such as mood, vagueness in memory, emotional stress or fatigue, and even changes in the relationships one has with other people featured in the dream. As the unique aspects of a relationship with someone progress, the energy of the whole thing evolves as well, combining to become one tangible "feeling," and making the once tremendous variables of the astral event something very predictable and malleable.

Since time doesn't exist in the same way on this plane, one of the hardest factors to work with in any astral collaboration between people is timing. Quite simply, the slightest non-synchronicity in the field will result in a complete miss. Conversely, since time is not reckoned linearly in the astral plane, simply "showing up early and waiting" for someone isn't effective either. One could literally end up waiting for an eternity without the correct combination ever having been reached to provide the conditions necessary for a "shared dream."

The only viable method is direct contact between two people on one plane, prior to shifting. On multiple occasions Thor and Sky had shared at least part of the same dream, then awoke holding hands, laying with one leg over the other's, or whatever. It seemed Thor was even able to unknowingly and involuntarily pull Ar'Jvikkah into his last encounter with Kieran due to physical contact on the material plane, which most likely saved his life.

This was a bit of a problem for McGinn, who was now no longer physically in existence on the material plane, after his botched assassination attempt on Krey during the tachyon storm. He was, however, still very much alive, and incredibly powerful in *this* place... much stronger than he was in his material life. It appeared as if he had received some sort of training as well, not only in combat, but also in the specific navigational technique and "physics" of this place. This inherited knowledge was almost certainly where his seemingly natural ability to stay right on top of an enemy was coming from, and thusly, began posing many other questions about his origin and purpose.

McGinn squinted as a ray of light shining through the top half of an open Dutch door cut through the haze of smoke and dust in the air rejuvenating the kitchen in a wash of color and motion. He took a long drag off of his cigarette, then exhaled directly at the sunbeam, smiling slightly as the smoke billowed within the confines of the beam like a blast from some sort of ray gun. He dropped the cigarette on the dusty, misshapen hardwood floor in front of himself and quickly repositioned his boot to crush it out with the tip of his toe.

As he leaned forward to finish the job, he became keenly aware that he wasn't alone. Standing quietly in the living room, staring at him with huge, yellow eyes, eerily reflecting the sunlight through the darkness of the room, was a giant black wolf. He felt a very real tingle of fear for just a moment, not being able to discern how long the beast had been standing there. These were among the humbling few moments in a warrior's life when he pauses to question his own skills... and his own mortality. He took a deep breath and then stood to face his foe.

As he arose, his body seemed to block the ray of light from the doorway, making it hard to see the wolf through the shelves and partition knee-wall dividing the two rooms. The only access was the open threshold off to the right connecting both rooms to a hallway that led back to the front door and the bedrooms. He studied this for a moment, then glanced back into the living room. He couldn't seem to focus on the wolf. It was as if it was in one place, one moment, then in another, the next; always staring at him... always silent. He tried hard to keep his focus on it as it made its way around the various dark corners of the house, never taking its eyes off of him.

His heart jumped as he heard a sudden flutter behind him, and he spun around to see what it was. Sitting in the open half of the Dutch door was a large bald eagle. He had only seen them in pictures, and was quite amazed at the size and presence of the mighty bird. It stared at him for just a moment, then suddenly flew off out over the tundra, letting loose a loud squawk that echoed across the highlands, as if inviting him to follow. He turned back around, instead, somehow not even the least bit surprised to see the giant wolf standing directly behind him. He grinned devilishly, his eyes starting to glow from somewhere deep beneath the surface.

CHAPTER 13: SOLACE IN THE EYE OF THE STORM

Sky had one hand on the throttle lever, and the other gripping Thor's leg nervously. The light beam coming in from outside the cave at the top of the muck slide had illuminated the walls and ceiling, but had not yet given away their position down low in the shadows, among the pools of water and stalagmites. They silently waited, knowing full well that very soon the efforts being made from outside would expose them in their cornered state and leave them no option but to attempt to blast their way through what would undoubtedly be a well-conceived blockade.

Thor closed his eyes, trying to get some kind of read on how many they were up against. It remained silent outside long enough that he was able to enter into full meditation. As sudden as a gunshot going off, a large crash echoed through the chamber, jarring him back from his trance. His eyes popped open, and Sky actually noted, in the confusion, that he was smiling broadly.

The RAM had smashed through a critical area of the cave-in, causing the bulk of the obstruction to fall outward, free of the natural mouth of the cave. It paused, then stood fast in the large opening it created, obviously noticing them, and conducting a scan of the life forms within the small craft.

"Oh, shit! Here we go," Sky complained nervously, watching her screen for any indication of a weapons lock, while training her own tail guns manually on the RAM so as not to trigger a lock response in return. It was a standoff, and though she was relieved that there weren't troops standing immediately behind the RAM, for all she knew there would be a gunship waiting in ambush somewhere just out of sight for them to flee. She maintained her calm demeanor and waited for the situation to unfold before reacting. "You mind telling me what the shit-eating grin is for?" She asked Thor quietly after realizing he was sitting there, not worried, but smiling for some reason. She asked again without taking her eyes off her screens for even a second.

Before he could say a word to explain, it took a step back. She came one twitch away from blowing the large piece of sophisticated hardware straight to Hell in pieces when it moved its right arm down to its waist, lifted its left arm out toward them and off to the side, then bowed at the hip sarcastically, but as proper as a machine was capable; a maneuver they had all witnessed Bjorn making in jest numerous times on the Phoenix. Through the hull of the ship, as well as the audio sensors tied into the viewing screens, they could clearly make out the sound of Bjorn's voice booming over the loudspeaker in the RAM.

"So, what are you guys waiting for, a formal invitation?" All three of them started laughing uncontrollably, instantly relieved from an almost unbearable level of tension. She glanced at Thor, returning his smile, then flashed the floodlights on and off a couple of times, knowing better than to break radio silence by trying to hail Bjorn directly, despite the many questions they had for him.

"Follow me!" he added, waving one of the RAM's mechanical arms for them to follow, then turned away from them toward the opening and cleared a path for the shuttle to escape through.

The giant, almost humanoid shaped robot rose off the ground, powered by the same repulsion technology as their ships, then transformed slightly; folding its arms and guns in on itself like wings, providing lateral stabilization as it hovered in the air facing them. It spun around quickly and started out over the landing area toward the rock canyon they traversed to get here. Sky fired up the ship's engines and quickly followed, very narrowly slipping through the newly expanded cave mouth with only inches to spare on either side.

Upon reaching the outside of the mountain, they were instantly astonished at how much the weather had changed. It was absolutely stunning! The saturating blue light from Alcyone could be seen upon everything. There was much devastation from the storm, but in this moment, it almost seemed unseasonably calm outside as they sped through the rock formations and arches to catch up to Bjorn's RAM.

As a seasoned veteran of the Fleet's first tour on Cheops, Sky understood the erratic weather patterns here and didn't trust it, looking incessantly upward through the window and trying very hard to see more and more of the horizon as they made their way back toward the coordinates where they first made atmospheric entry. As the canyon grew shallower, making the transformation into foothills and winding erosional stream valleys, the look on her face started to change for the worse. Thor started to notice something too....

Out over the wind-whipped plains of short grasses and weeds that were being baked dry in the aftermath of the massive storm by the combined light from the blue giant and two of the other smaller suns was a wall of tumultuous haze; billowing in its contained fury from ground to sky in a controlled arc that seemed to be kept at bay only by the centrifugal force created by its own inertial mass. At first it seemed that they might be headed straight for it for some insane reason, but as they looked to the left, to the right, and finally all the way around behind themselves only to realize that they were completely surrounded, they finally understood the only possible reason for this.... They were directly inside the eye of the largest storm any of them had ever seen in their lives!

Sky appeared to be lost very deep in thought, and Thor could sense she was flashing back to some memory of this place from her childhood, giving way to the momentum of the daydream. He placed his hand gently on her shoulder to try and pull her out of it, as he seemed to be having difficulty seeing where the RAM went, and couldn't get an accurate read on any of the sensors. She looked at him, a tear dripping down her cheek as she forced a half-assed smile. She put her hand over his, stopping him from all the senseless typing he was doing on the control panel. Instead, she merely pointed at the compass needle on the top of the instrument panel. It was literally spinning in clockwise circles, never stopping or even slowing down.

"Don't worry, I think I know where he went," she said with an almost frightening equanimity as she wiped her eyes and sped up the shuttle, zeroing in on what appeared to be a labyrinth of deep cracks in the surface of the planet... the very labyrinth where her parents disappeared while searching for her in the storm all those years ago.

"Why aren't the scanners working?" Thor asked. "Is it the storm? I mean, it's so calm right now, here in the eye. It just seems strange to me to experience this much flux."

"Yeah, I know what you mean, but yes, it's almost entirely the storm's disruption of the magnetic field of this planet. Bjorn must be using it to hide from the Fleet. I only hope he made it into the void before they turned his signal into anything definitive!"

"The void?" Erük pondered.

"That's what we called the area inside the eye of these super-cell storms that have literally no discernable radio waves. It's as if all the normal physical and energetic parameters simply cease to exist, then reappear in a frenzied mass along the threshold of the inner wall." She gestured with her hand toward the dark, billowing wall of clouds and violent flashes of light just out on the horizon. "While studying this phenomena last time we were here, we observed the same radio transmissions being thrown around, over and over without degradation, just *within* the eye... all along the inside diameter. It was almost as if the energy from the radio waves themselves were being 'bent' rather than flowing out spherically in their usual wave pattern.

Save for the natural laws of entropy governing the entire universe, this point of critical mass within most of the major storms taking place here is probably the only example of true perpetual motion mankind has ever recorded! This could very well even be the very same storm we experienced 20 years ago!" She smiled slightly, realizing how preposterous that must actually sound, even given the rarity of the weather occurring here.

Thor scratched his chin, suddenly as giddy as a professor on the verge of a major discovery. "Rather than exhausting their energy through entropy and slowly winding down, it is built up and stored through the cylindrical field and held fast by its own centripetal grip on the heavily ferrous, mineral rich soil it unearths in layers as it passes over the same surface, over and over again, building up an immense static charge as it goes."

"Yeah, that's basically what I just said," she joked, "but if you feel the need to upstage me and make me sound like an idiot, Einstein, by all means, go right ahead!" She facetiously waved her hand out in front of herself in an animated gesture, twirling it around as she spoke, then backhand slapped him in the stomach, laughing. Erük stared with a puzzled look at Sky, then Thor... then back at Sky, making her laugh even more. She finally gained her composure just as the outer fingers of deeply cut fissures and valleys started to appear across the vast landscape beneath the tiny ship.

The drop-offs were becoming absolutely dramatic! From above, the entire labyrinth almost took on the appearance of a giant spider web, with a huge lake in the center crater that seemed to go down forever. It was ice blue for as deep as one could see, with no immediate signs of life at the surface. As they flew in low and passed overhead, Thor noticed that not only were there no wind waves from the storm, but the surface was not even responding to their repulsion engines or the wind shear from the craft itself, as it sped across the lake, less than 10 feet above the surface at speeds in excess of 500mph, without leaving even the slightest wake behind them!

The entire surface was like glass, save for a very slight, almost undetectable vibration across the entire plane of water that they almost certainly would have passed right over without a second glance, but for the keenness of Erük's amazing vision. Sky smiled as she circled around the large body of water, rising upward in altitude in a spiral until they could see the entire lake in one view, then went nose down, straight at the water. Sky glanced over at Thor and Erük to explain as she accelerated into her nosedive.

"I've seen this effect before," she practically yelled over the repulsion engines, now groaning loudly in reverse compression as she geared down and slowed their descent. "It's what happens to a body of liquid when in full contact with our shields! It happens because the liquid is a conductor, albeit a poor one, and our shields are basically electric, in nature. We first witnessed this on Titan, one of Saturn's moons, while we were harvesting gasoline from one of the smaller fossil fuel seas on that hellhole! We had to modify our shields to allow for the complete submersion of a Harvester without succumbing to the extreme pressure or igniting the fuel source in the process. Bjorn is down here... The Phoenix is down here, I guarantee it!"

"That wily little fox... what a fucking genius! That's how he avoided capture! He hid from the scanners in the eye of the storm, and from sight altogether by turning the Phoenix into a bloody submarine!" Thor smiled broadly, obviously more than a little relieved that he had managed to keep the Phoenix out of the sight and clutches of the Fleet. He was careful not to give in to the moment, however, as there were still many risks involved with piloting a manned craft into a deep lake of uncharted water on a hostile planet without the use of any sort of scanners.... He strapped himself into the copilot's chair and leaned forward a little, eyes wide open and on watch with Erük. "Remind me to promote him!"

They hit the surface of the water and lunged forward, even despite Sky's last minute approach angle reduction maneuvering to relieve some of the impact, but no one was injured. Much to the surprise of even Sky herself, all the sensors were instantaneously back online, and appeared to be working perfectly. Something about the augmentation of the water's normal properties, now saturated with stabilizing energy waves, was causing the dramatic lessening of the storm's disruption of the magnetic field, at least in this environment. Sky tried numerous times to get a read on the topside situation from where they were, and still could not. She still had no idea how many they were, or where, exactly, they were positioned, but there was absolutely no doubt in any of their minds that for the time being, at least, there was no safer place for them to hide until this blew over and the Fleet decided to press on.

Outside the shuttle was a mystical world, the likes of which none of them had ever witnessed. Within the confines of this secluded underwater universe was an entire ecosystem, operating completely independent of the topside's hostile changes. The first thing they noticed was that there was another reason aside from their shields why the surface barely moved. The first layer of life in the water was an almost 30 foot thick reef of living plankton, algae and every manner of water-borne plant and fish imaginable, thriving on the abundant photosynthesis chain created from the penetrating blue glow and the solar radiation being emitted from the planet's many suns. As this small planet's surface was covered by more than its share of water, this explained the roughly breathable air, despite the shortage of oxygen producing trees and plants growing on its wind torn surface.

Thriving in symbiosis throughout this floating canopy was a myriad of smallish creatures, some more intelligent and capable than others, but each busy carrying out their daily business, blissfully unaffected by the tremendous hole the shuttle just punched right through their world on its way to the darker places beneath them. Absolutely fascinated with the diversity of some of the creatures they were seeing close up, they all stared out the front window at the silent, graceful world before them, completely oblivious to the chaos and harsh natural violence transpiring just overhead. One could spend an entire lifetime studying just the different life forms they witnessed dodging the shuttle on its way down. Most resembled the fish of Earth in one way or another, but there were definite and wondrous exceptions.

One such deviant was a strange, sucker-like being, about the size of a small monkey, stuck to the windshield by its mouth. It had characteristics of a bottom feeder, yet its eyes seemed vastly more intelligent... and it seemed to be studying them through the glass. Erük stepped over to the small creature and leaned forward, looking deep into its eyes. At first it jumped back, peeling its mouth off of the glass as if it was going to flee, but after a quick reckoning between the two of them, it decided to remain where it was, and even reattached itself to the glass, resting its four arms and two legs by letting them dangle carelessly in the water's currents. It seemed to have some sort of retractable wings on its back that pulled in close like dorsal fins when not in active use.

Though not as well lit as the seaweed canopy, there were many small oases scattered here and there with light producing plants and phosphorescent algae keeping the entire place in an eerie glow and revealing many other creatures abound throughout depths of the lake, seemingly growing larger and stranger as they descended. The little guy on the windshield turned his head quickly as a small flock of what must have been his species fluttered by in the darkest part of one of the lake's many underwater channels; subterranean caves descending deep into God only knows where and home to all manner of reclusive nightmare from the depths of the imagination. He opted not to follow, and instead turned his attention back to Erük, who seemed unusually intrigued with him.

"It looks like you've got a new friend!" Thor said, punching Erük on the shoulder. The little creature suddenly glared at Thor through the glass, his dark eyes turning almost jet black and growing to over twice their normal size. He lifted his tail up like a whip, the tip of it flickering with some kind of blue electrical charge, and thrust it straight toward Thor, who didn't flinch or really react at all, as there was a protective layer of three inch plasticized carbon glass between them.

To his complete surprise, the tail came straight through the glass without breaking it and hit him right on the nose, shocking him and sending him back about five feet on top of Sky's lap, utterly stunned and speechless. Before he had even landed, the creature was back to normal, looking at Erük again with a nod and a look of smug satisfaction on his face, now entirely on the other side of the glass. Thor started to say something, but only blubbering came out as he felt his whole mouth go numb like he had received a large dose of Novocain. He started laughing and Erük joined in as well, nearly doubling over in front of him.

"It looks like *you* have a new friend as well!" Sky taunted, petting the back of his head to comfort him sarcastically. She suddenly jumped and pointed at the center console while pushing Thor off of her and back up to his feet. "Hey! I've got him!" she exclaimed, bringing up a holographic image of the Phoenix over the center of the instrument panel between the pilot chairs. The entire starship was nestled neatly in between what appeared to be an enormous overhang and a sturdy underwater plateau sticking out from the cliff wall, and was virtually invisible from above at any possible angle as it remained absolutely still directly above a seemingly bottomless pit of a chasm... so deep they could see no end reading on any of the instruments. Sky started piloting the shuttle directly towards them and flashed the front lights to say hello.

"Good to see you... We were starting to get lonely down here!" Astrydd's voice came over the speaker on the console first, confident at this point that no radio wave interception from above the lake was possible. *"Not to mention more than a little worried!"*

"Good to see you too!" Sky replied, while releasing her harness and punching in the docking sequence on the console. She let the control of the shuttle switch over to automatic pilot and turned around to Thor, wrapping her arms around him and closing her eyes. For the first time since they arrived here, it seemed as if things might just work out alright. For the first time since they arrived here, she was thinking about the future again, instead of the past.

CHAPTER 14: THE EYE OF H.O.R.U.S.

Admiral Reid had been pacing the floor of his quarters for nearly an hour trying to make sense of all of this. The signal they had been following turned out to be inconclusive, yet for several hours *before* entering the system, it shone like a beacon in the dark for all to see. Then there was the intense feeling of déjà vu... something much deeper than meets the eye was going on here.

There was a slight crackle on his room's intercom, then he could clearly make out the voice of one of his helmsmen. *"Bridge to Admiral Reid."*

"Go ahead, Ensign."

"Admiral... We just spoke with a messenger from Ground Ops-1. They say that the storm is preventing any radio or signal transmission, so they can't pinpoint the source of the signal yet... but, Admiral... "

"Yes, bridge, what is it?"

"They say they've found something manmade at the site."

"An artifact of some kind? Alien tech...? What!?"

"A base plate."

"Come again…?"

"Sir, they found what appears to be a transmitter base plate… the kind we use as an interface for attaching transmitter/ receiver towers and surveying scopes to solid ground…. It was nailed to the rocks with some of our own impulse driven concrete anchors! And Sir… the lack of corrosion on the alloy suggests that it had only been there for a very short time… days, perhaps… maybe even less!" Reid started pacing again, unable to formulate words that would make this new development add up to anything resembling a sensible observation. *"Sir, did you hear me? I said it was pinned with OUR tools!"*

"I heard you, Ensign. Is there any chance it was set up by someone on their own team… before they found it? Before the storm hit and they all evacuated?" he fished, assuming this *must* be a coincidence, or simply a matter of miscommunication. "I mean, what else could it have been?"

"Negative, Sir. With all due respect, the officer who reported this was Commander Parnell from CSE. He wouldn't have made the report without checking that possibility out first. Sir, we have a rogue… that's the only explanation! They must have gotten here just before us somehow!"

"Yes… the question is, why? Have a security detail comb the site. If there are dissidents, they are still down there… there have been no shuttles or off-world flights since our arrival besides Ground Ops-1 and Colony Setup and Engineering. We are about to start mining and colonization protocol on CSE's command, so let's get this wrapped up quick! We don't need any more rumors about separatists feeding into paranoia…. If this leaks, let's spread the word that it was something very old left behind by some unknown party, and leave it at that. Now put me through to H.O.R.U.S.! If that storm won't let up, then at least we can use our eye in the sky to try and find them from up here!"

"Copy that. Patching through to Hubble Observatory Reconnaissance Ship."

"H.O.R.U.S. here... Commander Lewis speaking."

"Commander Lewis, this is Admiral T. Alexander Reid, ordering all use of the Hubble Observatory to be focused on my mark to the coordinates my helmsman will be sending you. You are to postpone all mapping and chart work, as well as deep space scans and cartography, and exercise Recon Protocol 5 until I specifically give further orders. Authorization code: 3942871-Tango-Alpha-Radar... Over."

"Copy, Sir... 3942871 Tango-Alpha-Radar Authorization code: T. Alexander Reid H.O.R.U.S. ceasing all activity and commencing with Recon Protocol 5... Commander Lewis Out."

"Bridge, this is Admiral Reid."

"Copy, Admiral, I'm sending H.O.R.U.S. the coordinates of the pyramid mountain. Sir, you are aware that Recon 6 is a general sweep for unidentified intruders, right, not 5?"

"I said, Recon Protocol 5, and that's what I meant..."

"But sir, that's Search and Rescue! Many more resources will be-"

"I said 5, and that's an order! If we have a dissident problem or a rebellion brewing, I want it shut down IMMEDIATELY, and by any means necessary! Is that absolutely clear?"

"Yes, Sir! Increasing the coordinate field radius and sweep frequency to Emergency Protocol 5! Bridge out." Reid stared vainly into the mirror next to a portrait of the men on his side of his family; each in uniform... each a higher rank than the last. He not only carried the burden of being a successor to their legacy, but also the burden of being but a mere product of his times. In mankind's most desperate hour, on its somber exodus through space, he climbed the ranks he ruled almost

entirely by default, and would likely never have the opportunity to prove his valor on the battlefield the way every single one of his forefathers did. This was the silent weight he had always carried... the silent weight he was ever on the lookout for a way to offload, even to the detriment of righteousness, or the cost of true honor.

CHAPTER 15: THE ARCHITECTURE OF DESTINY

Bjorn had been listening in amazement to the story the three of them had to tell, while Astrydd checked them over medically from head to toe; and nearly forgot that he had some serious news, himself. "Guys, I don't mean to cut you off, but there's something you need to know!" he started in, wide eyed and obnoxiously flamboyant.

"You're gay?" Sky joked, causing all of them to laugh hysterically. Thor raised his hand, smiling, and she "high-five'd" it without looking away from what she was doing.

"Fuck you both! Seriously," Bjorn laughed, playing along, "just before I fled orbit... before the Fleet could have seen me, I was scanning backward with our long-range, deep space scopes toward Earth, in the hopes of finding a close enough starting point that has already been charted to use as a point of reference for our survey, when *there they were!*"

"What?"

"The Fleet! Coming from *in front* of us! From the direction of Earth!"

"How is that possible? They came from the direction of the Algol supernova, just like we did... you know that! There's no way they could have passed us and hooked back around, is there?"

"I was willing to entertain that option... at least until I looked a little closer at this," Bjorn punched a few keys, and brought up a ship on the holographic viewer in front of them. He started turning it around slowly, 360 degrees, then top to bottom until finally Thor stood straight up, wide eyed, and pointed at the image, shouting proudly.

"Yeah, I know that ship anywhere! That's the old Flagship, the Helios, Admiral Reid's pride and joy! I watched it burn to the ground with him in it back on the sandy plains, right in front of Erük's lair! We all did! That son of a bitch was the one directly responsible for the death of Erük's entire race!"

"Well... how do I say this, exactly...? *It's leading the Fleet again!*" Bjorn said dramatically, leaning toward them as he spoke and almost whispering as if it was some kind of conspiracy. He paused, looking down. It was obvious to all of them that there was much more to this, so they just waited for him to collect his thoughts and proceed. "There's also the fact that the planet doesn't carry signs of our presence from 20 years ago... then the location of the storms and the nebula... and now there's also this..." He hit another set of keys, and a star chart from orbit around Cheops appeared. He put the chart program into a reverse search mode for rough comparative analysis, and after about 10 seconds of whipping through thousands of "days" in real time, it finally stopped, fixed on one set that was as close as could be matched; the surrounding constellations lining up nearly *exactly* with reference to the surface of Cheops. They all stared at the screen, thinking the same thing, but afraid to ask.

Bjorn breathed deeply inward, held his breath for a moment, then exhaled, slowly lifting his gaze from the floor to their eyes. "According to all of the available data, we have traveled back in time *almost 20 years*... until *just before* the Fleet's landing on Cheops during my childhood and Sky's late teens. This isn't *our* Fleet, following us from the solar explosion... hell, there's a good chance none of them even made it out! These guys are from *our past!*" There was an awkward moment of silence that seemed to last a little bit too long, then it was Sky who finally broke the ice. She took a long, deep breath, then looked up at everyone, pulling her hand through her dark, medium length hair.

"Well, friends... that certainly answers more than a few questions in *my* mind!" She turned her attention more specifically to Bjorn with a puzzled look brewing on her face. "I assume this means that there are other versions of ourselves onboard, and that we better *seriously* watch what we do from here on out, right? I mean, I was only a teenager at the time... hell, Bjorn, you were probably just a kid, but we are out there right now, doing whatever we were doing then, right? What a mindbender!"

"Yeah, and I'm probably still in the freezer with the fish sticks!" Thor joked sarcastically, apparently not very excited, nor really all that surprised by any of this. "Not much chance for a face to face paradox there, eh, Doc?" he grinned, getting very little back from the preoccupied helmsman.

"Well, guys," Bjorn added, "as far as paradoxes go, there is one thing that concerns me." He stepped away from the console and looked at Sky, in particular. "You said you managed to get the mounting plate down for the instruments before all hell broke loose, right?"

"Yeah... and it was still there, attached with modern impulse nails straight into the rock when we took off," Sky pondered, starting to get a little worried, herself.

"That may not have been such a great idea..."

"Yeah, well, we didn't exactly have time to stop and discuss our options," Sky laughed. She thought for a moment, trying to remember back to their arrival on Cheops all those years ago. "You know... it seems to me that there was talk of something being discovered by the pyramid upon our arrival.... It just seems like they were all saying it was some kind of alien tech that had been there for a long time." She stared off into space, trying to remember more. Bjorn looked even more blank on the subject, as he was really too young to remember any of it clearly. "It does seem like there was some talk of the whole thing being a cover up for some kind of separatist movement, but there were *always* such rumors." Sky glanced up at Astrydd, being careful with her wording so as not to offend her. "I guess this time the rumors will work in our favor. It doesn't matter anyway, we'd never get in there undetected to get it back... *would we?* Astrydd, didn't you tell me before that some of your family were among those who *stayed behind* when the Fleet left?"

Astrydd sighed, never looking up as she finished the last of a quick diagnostic scan on Thor. She quickly scribbled down a couple notes on a small device in her hand, then switched it off, deactivating the personal quarantine shield from around his body, then looked up at Sky, reluctantly. "Both of my uncles, my aunt, and my only cousin... pretty much the only family I had left, were among those that the Fleet banished here without the resources to finish terraforming, or to defend themselves from the extreme weather. They all wished to separate from the Fleet's insane agenda and give Cheops a chance at being a home, but not under those terms! It was practically-" She cleared her throat, getting noticeably choked up; "It was practically suicide. They wouldn't have done it willingly. I know they wouldn't have. Admiral Reid and his so-called *Military Justice Tribunal* did nothing more than strand a number of outspoken radicals on a ready-made penal colony when they left them here with nothing but the clothes on their backs!"

"I'm so sorry... I never knew the whole truth, and as you know, we sort of grew up in different circles. I meant no offense, Astrydd, I was just asking if you might have heard anything a little more specific about the alien tech they supposedly found... given who your family ran with." She offered Astrydd a hug, which the slightly older woman accepted, in and of itself, but remained somewhat distanced from her as she elaborated.

"Sorry, it's still a very sore subject for me... I wasn't much older than you were at the time, but I do remember that the debate over what was found was a large factor in the Fleet's decision to deal with them as they did."

"Meaning?"

"They were all but *blamed* for it! Fleet knew goddamn well it wasn't *alien tech*! And there was *definitely* a debate over what was found! I remember overhearing a very edgy conversation between my uncle, who had been a major factor in the separatist movement, and who was actually going to be the unofficial leader of the new colony, and Admiral Reid, himself. They did spread the rumor that something very old was found at the site, but Reid blamed *them!* He never trusted them, and did all he could do to discredit the lot of them, until this happened... then I guess he believed he had all the reason he needed to get rid of them without any further resistance or debate. The reason he hated them so much in the first place was that they challenged his authority and proposed new governing ideals that would undermine his supreme dictatorship over the Fleet and change the future of our government!"

"That makes a lot of sense, given the Admiral Reid I came to know over the last 10 or so years serving under

Captain Parnell. He was always a shady, self-serving, ego-maniacal douche bag, but to leave them without proper supplies on a turbulent rock like this... that was nothing short of homicide! Without advanced terraforming, this planet would scarcely provide sustenance for *any* land animal, much less human beings! The only chance they would've had would have been to grow gills and live down here, underwater, or else-"

"Or else get rescued by someone from *outside* the Fleet... " Thor interjected, a cunning smile on the edge of his lips, and a devious twinkle in his eyes. Astrydd was dabbing at the tears welling up in her eyes with the edge of her sleeve, when she suddenly stopped, staring at Thor with a look of hope, tempered with the reservation of their times. They all looked at him, then at each other, and ultimately at Bjorn; awaiting confirmation of the plausibility of this profound suggestion.

"Could this actually work? Wouldn't we be facing some sort of quasi-paradox, or something?" Sky asked, not wanting to be a buzz-kill, but always looking out for the safety of the group.

Bjorn scratched his head, glancing at Astrydd quickly, but trying to avoid direct eye contact with her until he thought this through a little bit further. "I don't know... I mean interference of *any* kind is potentially disastrous, but they were never heard from again after they were stranded... so who's to say someone didn't come by and scoop them up anyway?" He looked over at Astrydd again, this time giving her a quick wink and a smile. She smiled back in a sort of half-assed way, then cleared her throat and finished wiping her eyes as he finished his train of thought. "This means, of course, that we would have to lay low until the Fleet finished its business here and left for Algol before we could act on this, or we'd be risking *everything....*"

"Yeah, I think that's probably in the cards anyway, boys and girls," Thor said quietly, gesturing at the rotating holographic image of the Helios, still up in front of them in the center of the bridge console. He looked at Sky, who seemed extremely preoccupied all of a sudden, as if lost in deep thought. "How long did the Fleet continue mining here before leaving for Algol?" he asked. She hesitated, still very much distracted. He reached over and put a comforting hand gently on her shoulder, massaging it skillfully between his thumb and fingers. "Are you alright?" he asked softly, directing the question straight at her.

"Y-yeah... I'm sorry, what was your question?"

"How long did the Fleet remain here before they left for the Algol system?"

"It was a matter of recorded Fleet history, so the exact time and dates will be in the computer archives, but if my memory serves me correctly, it was about a two week campaign, start to finish. We left just as the giant storm cells collided; causing the eye to start collapsing on itself, and conditions became too unpredictable and violent for a safe departure. That's when they called off the search for-" She stopped in mid-sentence, eyes a million miles away. "For-" Her eyes rolled back slightly, then closed all the way, where she sat still, trying to keep her composure, but unable to finish conveying her thought. Her chin quivered slightly, and a tear forced its way out from under her closed eyelid as her friends realized she was talking about the event that cost her both of her parents. Thor took a knee in front of her and gave her a long quiet hug, both of them knowing that any intervention by them in an attempt to save them would undoubtedly result in extreme complication, if not complete temporal paradox.

Erük had been unusually quiet throughout the entire conversation, even for him. Truly, it was apparent from his demeanor that something had been weighing heavily on his mind ever since their arrival. He slowly lumbered over to the main deck entry door from the side of the bridge and opened it, wandering out on deck, protected from the tremendous mass above them by the energy shield overhead that was creating a dome of airspace between the ship and the underwater world that engulfed and concealed them.

He stood next to the outer knee wall, staring somberly as a school of strange winged fish gracefully swam by, trying to catch up with a much larger population just a short distance away as it headed back into one of the tunnels on its way home from a routine daily feeding trip. Though he had always been one of the very few *true* individuals among a mass of hive dwelling, collectively conscious creatures, and was never truly understood, even by those closest to him, he looked outward now with a very distorted sense of purpose, and realized that in all of his very long life, he had never felt so utterly alone.... Though he couldn't begin to completely understand the possible ramifications of what he was contemplating, he knew now exactly what he needed to do.

CHAPTER 16: A CROSSROADS IN TIME

"Get those supports as plumb as possible! They're going to be supporting tremendous weight and even worse wind shear when that storm starts moving through here again!" the young Commander yelled over the sounds of the RAM machinery from his CSE unit digging into the face of the mountain nearby.

"Sir, our leveling instruments and laser EDM's don't seem to be producing accurate results... something to do with the messed up electromagnetic field from that giant storm! We can't trust our own calibrations! This place is going to look like it was built by monkeys!"

"Lieutenant, let me show you a trick," the Commander said without any condescension as he pulled a long section of fluid line out of a large reel onboard one of the CSE flatbed transports parked nearby and began filling it up with water. He kept his thumb over both ends, handing one to the young Lieutenant who stared at him with a very confused and frustrated manner about him, yet a bit of a gleam in his eye that only comes from a student's trust and wonder. Commander Parnell grabbed the man's wrist, pinning it against the side of the flatbed and handed the man a small marker. "Keep your thumb on the line until I say!"

He started walking toward a large pile of boulders, just outside of the proposed foundation perimeter for the new tower they were constructing to hold purified water for the small mining colony that was to be located at the base of the new pyramid mountain mine entrance. When he reached the other side of the site, he held up his line and pinned it against the rocks with his hand, lifting his thumb off of the end of the tube.

"Okay! Let off your thumb," he yelled. The water inside the clear tube immediately started moving up and down, then quickly settled on a spot perfectly level with the top of the water level on the other side. He waited until it completely stopped, then marked the spot with a small crow's foot on the rock, nodding for the other man to do the same. The man smiled broadly. "Physics 101.... Water will always seek its own level. Cut a 50 foot length for each one of your men and fit them with end-caps." Parnell gave him a wink then nodded, gesturing toward the row of flatbeds in front of them. "When technology fails you, and it *will* fail you, The Old School is always the best!"

"Holy shit, I can't believe I didn't think of that! It just never occurred to me!" The young man started walking toward the flatbed, smiling as he rolled up the tube while water slopped out of the downhill side. Suddenly he got a disturbed look on his face, paused in his tracks, then turned back around to face the Commander, who was still watching him, smiling as if he had anticipated this and knew what the younger man was about to ask. "Commander.... What about plumb? This is great, but it obviously won't work for vertical measurement... only horizontal!"

Parnell looked around quickly, scanning the ground for something useful, then smiled and opened the top of his uniform and removed the dog tags he had hanging on a long, thin chain around his neck. He disconnected the chain to make it hang even longer, then hooked his marker point down onto the end of the chain. To demonstrate the technique, he held a small stick as horizontally as possible, then carefully lowered the small makeshift plumb bob from a spot he marked on the stick toward the ground and patiently waited for it to stop swaying like a pendulum. Once still, he marked the spot the tip pointed to directly beneath the top mark and smiled at the Lieutenant, patting him on the back as he stood there with a blank expression on his face, once again shocked by the apparent obviousness of this nearly forgotten construction technique.

"Our entire race has been spoiled stupid by technology, that's all there is to it!" he said, walking with him back toward the communications station and smiling broadly. "Twenty foot rolls of string on a spool with just about anything sharp and heavy as a plumb bob on the end should do it," he added as he removed the marker from his chain and reconstructed the necklace. "Keep me posted, Lieutenant, we're already a little behind schedule. Ground Ops-1 is almost finished reinforcing the cave mouths and shafts and tunneling down to the largest vein, so they're wanting to send full mining crews down by this time tomorrow.... Their families will follow in about three days."

"Where does that leave us?"

"It leaves us working right through lunch, I can tell you that much!" Parnell laughed, slapping his naïve friend on the back one last time and giving him a friendly but authoritative shove toward the direction of his crew, who were already starting to gather around idly as if needing more direction.

Commander Parnell had reluctantly requested his foreman position with CSE, Colony Setup and Engineering, for which he seemed to have been born, in spite of his inane desire to be in the middle of the action, so to speak, that pushed his pen through the many applications he submitted to Ground Ops and Special Forces Units in the last couple of years. The truth of the matter was that he was next in line for command of the Phoenix, one of their largest and most advanced Carriers, and everyone knew that the neurotic Captain Ming Chen didn't have too many more years at the wheel. The Fleet simply couldn't afford to misuse an investment like someone of Parnell's training level and experience; but he had a very personal reason for the unusual career move, and even those who knew him best knew very little about her.

He descended from a long line of Carrier Captains and Engineers, and was a born leader and a very crafty Engineer, himself. This was probably the only off-ship job for which he was truly suited, but for all his strengths, what he had always lacked was patience. He felt stifled, like there should be so much more for him in this life. No matter what new level of accomplishment he achieved, it was never enough. Sometimes he wondered if this feeling would ever go away... ever be *truly* satisfied. For the time being he conditioned himself, as did everyone in the Fleet, to accept their small part in the grand scheme of things and keep pushing forward, hoping soon to find their Garden of Eden... *their new Earth*, just over the horizon.

He started to walk toward the mountain, noticing that the noise had stopped. The RAM drivers were apparently on lunch break, so he decided to check out their progress while he still could. Being remotely operated and blind to the rear on top of that, approaching them during operation was both dangerous and foolhardy. He pulled out his flask from his belt and poured a cup of coffee from a large, multi-drink dispensary on the side of the electronic equipment van, then started off toward the row of haphazardly parked RAM machines. He took a few steps while whistling an improvised little tune and swirling his coffee around inside its new container. Despite the ominous wall of impending violent weather surrounding them out on the horizon in every direction, it was an absolutely gorgeous day. He was taken aback by the beauty above... the hugeness of the ever expanding sky, stretching out as far as the eye could see, when - WHAM!

He looked down, nearly falling over from the impact, and noticed the young Davies girl, teenage daughter of two of his old crewmates from onboard the Phoenix, whom he had followed in transferring here. She was covered with coffee stains and was holding her head in pain, her nearly jet-black hair shiny with liquid on that side as if his cup hit her directly on the side of her head. She started to topple over, dazed from the impact, but caught herself as Parnell grabbed hold of her arm to steady her, trying not to spill any more coffee. She shook her head to get her bearings, then looked at Parnell, forcing herself to smile through her obviously disconcerted look, as she quickly wiped the coffee off of her arms and face, wherever it was able to touch her skin. "God, I'm sorry, Commander Parnell," she offered.

"*John*... please! Anyway, *you're* sorry? Miss Davies... *Kaitlyn*... I'm the one who should be apologizing! I wasn't watching where I was going.... Are you alright?"

"Yeah... I'll live. I wasn't paying attention where I was going, either. It's just this incredible sky! I've never seen anything like it! Only in video and in books.... It's *so* beautiful!" She had a refreshing smile on her face beaming through her ice-blue eyes from somewhere deep inside that Commander Parnell found utterly intoxicating. Despite the fact that she was but half his age, he couldn't help but be attracted to her in a very unique and powerful way that he had a bit of trouble concealing. Only one other person knew of their connection, and it was most likely in everyone's best interest that it stay that way. The older Kaitlyn got, the more he realized, she had her eyes... her hair... her energy. In fact, he really didn't see any of her father in her at all, save for maybe higher level traits still remaining to be seen.

"Look, just be careful.... These drivers don't mess around, and they don't give warnings when they are about to fire those things back up! In fact, I'd stay clear of the mines all together while the RAMs are in there! Their accident rate is off the charts! They're run by video game junkies who are used to having extra lives, not mature machine operators used to operating hundreds of thousands of dollars' worth of heavy military tech!"

"Okay, *Dad*," she said sarcastically, not even realizing what a sharp blow from the ironic fist of reality she had just socked him straight in the beak with. She winked, teasing him with a coy, almost flirtatious look in her eye; and he forced a fake smile in return to camouflage his bruised ego, then proceeded back toward his mobile office to do some administrative work... a man become a boy, become a man.

Onboard the Phoenix, Thor broke off a conversation with Bjorn, noticing out of the corner of his eye as Sky tipped over sideways in her chair, then recovered, holding the side of her head in obvious pain. He rushed to her side, noticing as he approached that she had a very distant look in her eye, almost as if she was asleep. She smiled... lips moving slightly to mouth out something unintelligible. He slowed down as he got close to her, watching her intently. "Okay, *Dad*," she said sarcastically out loud, her eyes seeming to come back into focus. She shook her head, confused.

"Are you alright?" Thor stepped out in front of her, demanding her eye contact while gently holding onto her shoulders.

"Yeah... I told you, I'll live. I wasn't paying attention where I was going, either," she mumbled, still not entirely with it. Thor smiled at her, chuckling a little, then became very serious as her body became limp and lifeless and her eyes rolled back in her head. Thor leaned in and listened closely to her breathing to make sure she was still alive, and she slid right out of her chair toward him, literally ending up in his arms, unconscious. He scooped her up quickly and ran toward the main door, yelling back at the bridge as he went, but never taking his attention off of her for even a second!

"Bjorn! Get Astrydd to meet me in the Medical Bay immediately! Tell her to have a bed prepped for Sky before I get there!"

"Aye, sir, immediately!"

Finished with their awkward exchange that left the Commander somewhat distracted, Miss Davies strutted off, glancing quickly behind her at the last second just to make sure she was out of the view of Commander Parnell, then ducked into the last opening in the mountainside to her right, safely past the fleet of RAMs and all the other heavy equipment. Lunch break was about the only time she could get past them unnoticed, and she had been doing so, without incident, for the last two days. Today, things were different. She had overheard several of the deep mine workers talking about some "spirits" they had seen deep within the mountain, and given her inquisitive nature and sense of adventure, this was just too much for her to bear!

She pulled the slender supply pack she had concealed beneath her cloak off of her back and refitted it in its waist-belt position, pulling out a light stick from among the scant provisions she had prepared in a hurry while her parents were getting ready for work. She marched bravely forward into the darkness, unnoticed and pretty much oblivious to the very real dangers that lie ahead; oblivious also to the encroaching wall of turbulent weather approaching from behind the mountain as the storm center began to shift for the first time in days!

———————

"I don't understand, there doesn't appear to be anything wrong with her," Astrydd spoke out as Sky lay before her on the examination bed, now utterly catatonic, "in fact, the only thing even the least bit unusual is the extreme level of activity of the fetus! It seems like he can't hold still, even for a second. I think I'm going to give her a sedative to help with that part, at least... I'd hate for this to induce a state of false labor in her present condition." She started to shuffle through the medicine cabinet to her side. "That would be *most* unfortunate and untimely for the baby...."

"Astrydd," Thor interrupted hastily, "please hold the phone on that.... Just keep a close eye on the situation and do it only when you have no choice," he offered skeptically. "It's just... there's something unusual about this whole thing... and I don't want to second guess Ar'Jvikkah's role in whatever she's going through. There's something maternally symbiotic between them, as I'm sure you've noticed... then there's all the weird shit going on with *all* of us. Let's just give this a few minutes... It doesn't appear dangerous, yet..."

"Famous last words." She nodded and put down the syringe she had prepared, but left it nearby, within arm's reach on the counter top. "There's *definitely* something weird about this whole thing, Captain Krey, and you have a talent for understatement!"

———————

He had reluctantly given the order to cease all mining and construction activities until further notice due to the sudden shift of the massive storm, bringing the outer edge of its eye into contact with their site perimeter. Back aboard the small CSE vessel, Parnell sat in his berth and poured himself a glass of cognac, then lit a candle on his desk and set the snifter on top of the flame in its stand. Generally, he waited until nightfall to pour his favorite load-leveler and shake off the stress of the day, but given the ominous darkness looming above them now, combined with the almost comical slow start they had already succumbed to, he knew the work day was already utterly spent before it could even get into full swing!

It was getting unnaturally dark and hostile outside his large circular window as he watched the last of the workers tying down their various projects and gear with a purpose, and packing it in for a long break. The clouds had descended fast, and now the meteorologists onboard the Horus were predicting several days of down time, if not more. The only crews that would be able to work tonight and in the predictable future were the "Tunnel Rats," as they were called, or Subterranean Mining Ops and Subterranean Structural Reinforcement crews, neither of which were directly under his chain of command, so he predicted that this would most certainly not be a one drink evening.

Knowing intuitively that his cognac was at its perfect temperature, he pulled it off the small stand, swirling the small brandy snifter around and around, as he inhaled the sweet aroma of the finest cognac ever to come out of France... a bottle of King Louis the 13th he had won from Admiral Reid in a game of poker onboard the Helios during an extended internship when he was younger. Where the Admiral had managed to get his hands on such an old and expensive bottle, he hadn't the slightest clue; but he speculated that Reid had even more in his possession by the way he so graciously delivered it to him. Parnell had always been a bit of a prodigy, as well as a "pet project" to the Admiral, and it was the subject of much Fleet gossip that he would one day be his successor, spoken of as if it were an hierarchy of divine royalty in question, not a chain of military command. For as much as it displeased nearly everyone else, this was certainly the aire that the Admiral seemed to go to great lengths to maintain.

Parnell took a long, thin pull off of his glass, savoring the taste before finally swallowing it, then reached for a book on his shelf. He was leaning nearly all the way over the arm of his antique desk chair, half full snifter still in hand and stretching closer and closer to his target when the chirp of his small hand communicator went off, signaling an incoming call from an anonymous party. Annoyed, he exhaled, temporarily abandoning the book, and picked the small device up off of his desk, pressing the center in with his thumb. "Parnell."

"Commander?" He looked around, puzzled, not recognizing the voice of the woman on the other end.

"Yes," he responded apprehensively, "Parnell here... How can I help you?"

"Commander, this is Regina Davies, from Engineering."

"Yes, hi, Mrs. Davies! What can I do for you?"

"Commander-"

"John, please, Gina," he laughed, "*you know me....*"

"John... have you seen Kaitlyn? She hasn't returned to our rig, and it's getting pretty nasty outside."

"Yeah, Gina, I saw her just a little while ago. Well... I guess it's been a few hours, now. I bumped into her outside while it was still nice out. We were both staring at the sky and walked right into each other."

Her mother chuckled on the other end, sounding a tiny bit relieved. *"Yeah, that sounds like our little Kaitlyn. She's *been staring at the sky since we arrived. She's absolutely obsessed with it! Can't blame her after being raised indoors, never seeing the real thing above you... Anyway, where was this?"*

"In front of the transports, near the RAM corral. I'm not sure where she was going... she looked like she was just taking a breather and enjoying what was left of our small window of nice weather. I'm sure she's just hanging out with her friends or something...."

"Sure... We're just getting a little concerned. This weather came up suddenly, and you know how adventurous she is! She keeps asking us to take her in a flatbed out on the plains... I keep telling her we don't do things that way. We have to get established as a colony before any exploration or R&R can happen, and even then, there's a procedure for the surveying of unknown territory on a new planet... She has no patience! Never has!"

Parnell laughed. "Yeah... I've noticed! Well, let me know if you can't find her, OK?"

"Oh, we will! Thanks John... I appreciate it. Please call me if you happen to see her, OK?"

"Absolutely, Gina. Don't stress. She'll show up. There are workers everywhere, cleaning up and preparing for the storm... They'll spot her if she's still outside and get her indoors! There's a grounding on all shuttle flights and flatbed runs, as well as a general curfew in effect from dark until the storm clears, so she won't be gone long."

"Great, thanks again."

"Talk to you later... tell Connor I said, 'Good job on the Entryway and Shoring drawings,' OK?" he said with just the slightest disingenuous after-tone; a minute transparency revealing his long hidden feelings for her through a tiny bit of jealousy toward her devout relationship to someone he otherwise respected very deeply.

"Will do... Goodbye John." She hung up, smiling in a coy, yet semi-innocent manner, hiding behind it just a bit, in a way she couldn't justify or speak of to anyone.

Parnell swirled his cognac around, noticing it had gone cold. He took no pretense as he knocked it back and began pouring a larger one, still staring out the window. The reflection of his antique trench lighter flickering as he lit the small teacup candle shone brilliant against the darkness beyond the uncovered window and he squinted as he set the glass down again, straining to see at all as the last bit of light outside disappeared completely from his view in the contrast. Despite his subliminal intention to reach an invigorating tier of inebriation alone in his berth, he grabbed a selection of high level reading: an old philosophical tome that his father passed down to him written by J. Krishnamurti, a book so heavy that he usually read one page or paragraph, then contemplated it for the rest of the day just to get a firm grasp on the concepts being discussed.

He literally had no chance whatsoever of digesting anything but liquor in his present state, but as much as some devout Christians keep a bible near them at all times, yet never *really* read it, it made him feel like he was onto something larger than himself... *On the right track... Going places... One step... ahead... of the...* He was asleep in his chair before he could focus on the first page. He slowly slumped forward, his head landing across his forearm and the desk top, nearly spilling his drink as it continued to heat up in front of him, still sitting on the stand with the small candle burning away.

Suddenly Commander Parnell found himself onboard the Phoenix, walking away from the bridge with a very hazy sense of what was going on. Passing crewmembers were addressing him as "Captain" and he had no real thoughts or memory of Captain Chen. He felt older... more weathered...

somewhat bitter. He couldn't remember what he was doing, or where he was going, but for whatever reason, nothing felt out of the ordinary at all. Even people he knew, who were his friends and colleagues, had aged considerably, yet nothing seemed out of place.

He had a name he did not know on his mind, being repeated over and over as if it were being whispered in his ear. *McGinn*.... He *seemed* to know exactly where he was going and *seemed* to be in control of things, yet a series of movements and events were being executed without any thought at all; no more voluntary than the beating of one's own heart. It felt as if he was simply an observer in a movie, using his body as a vessel and seeing what was happening through his own eyes.

He walked directly past the Medical Bay doorway, then hooked quickly through the next opening into the security clearance room just before the entryway to the storeroom for the cryostasis tubes and gear, where all of the cryos were stored intermittently while in solo flight or on planet during mining ops, to prepare them for quick and easy regeneration and utilization. At any given time, there could potentially be as many as 30 of them, awaiting thaw out and implementation next door. He placed his open palm over the security pad and the double doors whisked open quickly and quietly. Upon removing it, he caught a glimpse of the reflection of a man he did not recognize standing just behind him, practically looming over his shoulder with an unusually serious look on his face.

He spun around, defensively, but to his unnerving surprise, there was no one present at all! He felt as if he couldn't catch his breath and his heart was pounding madly. He stepped back from the door and it slid closed as he shook his head, thrashing about madly in an attempt to shake off the overpowering feeling he was experiencing. It seemed as if he was losing control over his own body.... He felt a great pull back toward the door and literally had to force his eyes open again, as if his eyelids weighed 1,000 lbs. each. As things finally came back into focus he realized, to his very sincere astonishment, that he was still sitting at his desk; cognac, broken glass, and melted wax strewn across its meticulously polished surface.

CHAPTER 17: DESTINY'S CONSTRUCT

Nearly a full 24 hours had passed since Sky lost consciousness and Thor still remained right by her side, growing increasingly concerned for her safety. He was starting to nod off when he remembered his contact with Ar'Jvikkah through his dreams and decided to try to reach out to them both again in this manner. He made room and literally crawled into bed with her, once again placing his hand over her womb and homing in on Ar'Jvikkah's energy. He had no trouble dozing off this time, and very soon found himself on familiar ground.

He looked around at the vast landscape and expansive sky above, smiling, because for the first time that he could recall, he was completely and consciously aware, and in control of his dream... *or so it seemed.* He took a moment to simply bask in the glowing sun and fresh air of a fine summer day, already missing such simple pleasures after several weeks onboard a starship, and living entirely within an artificial environment. He closed his eyes and breathed... *just breathed.* Upon opening them, he half expected to see Sky, or

Ar'Jvikkah, or maybe even McGinn, standing right there, or maybe right behind him; but to his surprise, and partial relief, he was still very much alone... at least for the time being.

Looking uphill he could spot the cabin, but still did not see Sky or Ar'Jvikkah, so he proceeded with caution, remembering full well the power Kieran seemed to possess in this plane. As he got closer and closer, certain aspects of the dream that he had never stopped to notice before began to pop out in vivid contrast to the smooth, almost surreal hue of most dreams. The softness of the ground. The dampness of the air on his skin. The subtle aromas in the air, changing slightly as he approached the front door. From a bouquet of earthy grasses and flowers, to the slow decay of wood and antique hardware emitting a bit of mildew smell into the air as he reached for the door knob; things were crisper and infinitely more vivid... much more detailed... more *real.*

As he entered the cabin, these phenomena continued to astonish him. There was literally no difference between this dream state and the *real* world. He was beginning to understand the source of McGinn's strength. To have been deprived of his material plane existence had actually served to augment his presence in the other planes of existence in much the same way as a blind man finds his other senses growing unusually strong to compensate for his lack of sight.

He actually took the time to shut the door behind himself for the first time he could truly remember. It became very dark in the foyer, and he was about to reopen the door when his eyes started to adjust to the small house around him. There was light coming from the kitchen area, around the corner and down the hallway, and due to the openness of the floor plan, that seemed to be sufficient to see around the house, as it usually was. The smell of mildew was getting stronger, and as he crinkled his nose in malcontent at the foul stench,

Thor kind of smiled, realizing how blissful the obscurity of dreams can be.

Walking slowly down the hallway he started getting the feeling that things weren't just more vivid, they were actually entirely different. He could see into the corner of the family room at the bookshelves he had glanced at a hundred times since his childhood, and now noticed that they had all been knocked about, or gone through one by one and replaced carelessly, a few even ending up on the floor. He widened his gaze into the living room as he approached the opening to the kitchen on his left. The dream usually felt as though he was just a spectator, but this time something was definitely different. *There was usually another presence in the room...*

He rounded the corner into the well-lit kitchen, brightened from the windows wrapping around the two outer walls of the house, as well as the rustic style Dutch door; top half left wide open as the sun peered through a hazy, high altitude cloud bank and sent a broad beam directly down into the center of the room, dust particles swirling slowly around within it, giving it a life of its own. Thor actually gagged as he stepped into the room and the overpowering stench hit his nose for the first time. It was not mildew that his nose had detected from afar... it was the smell of rotting flesh! *The unmistakable smell of death.* A cool breeze coming through the open doorway was carrying its pungent malevolence through the entire house now, but in the kitchen it was nearly unbearable.

Looking about the room, he could tell there had been a struggle. The table was turned on its side and the chairs were knocked about the room, one of them broken in half. There were fresh scrapes and scuff marks everywhere on the dusty old hardwood floor, and he found a very coagulated blood trail leading toward the Dutch door. He started toward the doorway, realizing that because the solid wooden table had become wedged between a corner cabinet and an old, 500 lb. stove, he would have to hop over it to get to the door. He took a couple preemptive steps, trotting up to the overturned table, then put one hand on its edge and hurdled it sideways, both legs gracefully clearing it on his left side.

Unable to stop his descent on the other side, he gasped as he came down right on top of a rotting, putrid mass of matted, blood-soaked black fur that could have only been the giant wolf from his dreams! He gagged, trying desperately to hold back vomiting long enough to examine the corpse a little closer. Through all of the thick, tangled fur, crawling with maggots, flies, and other insects, he could clearly see cuts on its face, nose and neck that could have only been caused by a knife or a sword.

In all of his many dreams of this place, dating all the way back to his childhood, this shape-shifting being had never attacked him, nor he, it. The huge wolf, stalking him from amidst the darkness of the house, then baring its teeth right in front of him, had always struck him as being an omen linked very directly to his personal fears, and then future freedom in the form of a giant eagle. Though he was fully awake in his mind, and completely aware that this was just a dream or some other type of astral projection, he was still deeply saddened by the sight of this. Whatever it represented could not be good.

As his mind raced through all of the possible causes he could conceive, and what this obvious violation of his inner sanctum could possibly mean, he felt another presence directly behind him. Knowing instinctively that a fight from where he was standing would be extremely disadvantageous, Thor quickly dove through the open top-half of the doorway, coming out of his chugari facing 180 degrees back, toward the house, with his sword already drawn. He squinted hard, straining to see back into the cabin from where he was standing. He could see movement from just within the door, and the hair on the back of his neck stood up as he heard the unmistakable ear piercing shriek of a child's scream.

Mr. and Mrs. Davies entered the small, dimly lit pub late in the night after calling everyone they knew in a fruitless effort to locate their daughter. She was still missing, and though she disappeared rather frequently, only to return the next day from another ship or party with friends, something felt different about this. Their parental intuition was warning them that she was in grave danger and needed their help.

They rarely frequented these Fleet-wide liquor dens this late after work; but aside from recreation, these social gathering spots onboard almost every ship were coincidentally also the hives for almost all the Fleet gossip. If anyone knew anything at all, it was likely that it was talked about here at some point in the evening.

They meandered through the relatively small barroom, carefully avoiding any conversation that might steal precious time from them in a vortex of intoxicated obscurity. Though just a simple watering hole for CSE and mining folk housed on a ship about one third the size of a Carrier with an even smaller fraction of a crew, it still had the vibrancy and drunken candor of a galleon full of rum soaked pirates. These people worked hard, and played even harder.

They had made their rounds and were about to call it a night, when Mr. Davies overheard a particularly drunk gentleman who was sitting all by himself mumble something interesting. He reached out and grabbed hold of his wife's wrist, pulling her back a couple steps. She looked at him kind of surprised, then got the picture as he rolled his eyes over toward the young officer. He was sitting by himself at a small booth, so they quickly sat down next to him.

"By all means, make you-selves at..." He hiccupped, eyes never really focusing on them.

"My apologies, *Commander*, is it?"

"Admiral. General Admiral Major Pain...." He hiccupped again, bursting into laughter at his own joke as his eyes nearly rolled back in his head. "Pain in my ass... ha! How do ya like me now?" His eyes drooped almost closed and his head started to weave back and forth. Connor reached out and braced the man up by his shoulder, giving him a little shake.

"Whoa! Easy, partner, we almost lost you there!"

"Lost... there. Lost- Search and rrrssss-cue protocol."

"That's what we need to talk to you about! Sir, what do you know about a search and rescue mission? Who's lost?" The young officer started to nod off again. "Sir!"

"Whu-what?" He perked up a little.

"What do you know about a search and rescue? Our daughter is missing!"

"Don't worry. We're running Search and Rescue Protocol-" He started fading again. "Protocol... searching eye... for signal... H.O.R.U.S.," he mumbled as he finally gave in and collapsed in a dramatic face-plant on the table right in front of them. Mr. Davies stared at his wife for a moment.

"He said H.O.R.U.S.! Something about searching the eye for a signal..."

"He's a drunk, Connor.... He's probably just making shit up out of nowhere based on what you said to him!" Mrs. Davies shouted a little too loudly. A man in the booth next to them turned to her, holding his finger over his mouth to get her to lower her voice.

"That's Commander Lewis from the H.O.R.U.S.! He's been bitching about that shit most of the night. Something about Reid ordering immediate Search and Rescue Emergency Protocol... Wasting resources because of total cloud cover...

Something about a signal within the eye... I don't know, but he ain't no drunk! He's just in his cups at the moment, and a little pissed off at Reid! He's a good soldier and he knows what he's talking about... Hell, he practically runs the Hubble by himself!" The man instinctively lowered his volume and glanced around the room as his statement started to include Admiral Reid, more out of fear than respect, in case the wrong ears were listening in. "If he says there's a search on, then there is!" Connor took one long look at Regina and they both got up and quickly exited the bar, heading directly for the shuttle and flatbed hangar.

Young Kaitlyn had been wandering through the same few familiar corridors over and over, unsure what to do. She could hear the wind outside, howling so hard it would rip the skin off a full grown man in a matter of seconds. No one went outside under these conditions without at least a Level 3 EP suit with air. They had all been educated for weeks prior to landing about the presence of graphite in the soil, brought to the surface during storms due to the static electricity in the air. Even being in a mild windstorm on this planet will cause fatal levels of toxicity in the skin and eyes unless the body is covered from head to toe. She was not.

When she left on this outing, nearly 8 hours ago, there wasn't a cloud in the sky. No sooner had she gotten herself lost the first time in the lower catacombs, when she started to hear the first sounds of thunder and wind as the giant storm shifted, pulling the relatively serene eye along with it. It must be shifting toward the northeast, she thought, remembering with a sickly, ironic smile how that would put the longest part of the elongated ellipse directly in her path before it could possibly blow over... not that a polar storm of this magnitude was predicted to exhaust itself or move significantly from its centripetal center in their lifetime.

The absolute best part was that she didn't tell another living soul where she was headed. She started laughing deliriously, compounding her mental breakdown by hearing her own laughter echo through the pitch black caverns. Slowly, steadily, her laughter turned into crying, then into sobbing, and finally, into tears with no noise at all but intermittent sniffling. She leaned up against the cold, damp wall, wrapping her arms around herself for comfort, and slowly nodded off to sleep, giving in to the stress of the day and conceding, finally, that this was now a situation in which she was a hapless participant in need of the help of others, rather than its master.

She suddenly found herself where she often did… alone in a cabin somewhere high in the mountains above timberline. She had visited this place in her dreams off and on since she was very young, but it seemed much more vivid today. There was a mess in the kitchen and a horrible smell. She looked down and noticed that the giant beast that had plagued her childhood with fear was slain, lying on the floor in a pool of blood. The very sight sickened her, yet she couldn't help but be excited and relieved about it.

Looking out the door in the direction she used to always run to escape this monster, she saw a man with a startled look on his face standing in the tundra, holding a Japanese sword. She screamed bloody murder, more out of surprise and pent up tension than out of real fear, though he did seem quite intimidating to her, and judging by the mess in the kitchen, was apparently more dangerous than the beast.

Thor stood in amazement, forgetting for a moment that he was holding his katana in a very threatening manner, as the young girl bravely reached over the top half of the door and bumped the latch from the outside, opening it with a low kick as if she had done it a thousand times, despite the fact that this was *his* dream. He was even more astonished when, after locking eyes with her for just a moment, he immediately knew exactly who she was. "Sky?" he asked, absolutely sure it was her, despite her apparent age.

"No, my name is Kaitlyn." She smiled, definitely exerting the same energy and personality, yet clueless as to who *he* really was. She simply did not know him.

"Kaitlyn Davies, right?" he smiled, sarcastically, remembering that she didn't take the nickname "Sky" until later....

"Yeah!... How did you know? Do I know you?" she asked, still smiling broadly, her nervous energy fading fast and being replaced by honest curiosity.

Thor was suddenly very unsure as to whether or not he should be talking to her at all, yet, here she was. "You will... you will. And you did! *A very long time ago*... How's that for an answer?" he scoffed, with a friendly smirk on one half of his mouth. "Do I look familiar to you?" He was absolutely mystified with her... seeing so much of Kait in her young eyes. He knew now, there was no mistaking it. *They were definitely the same person! ...And by the Gods, fate had somehow brought them back together!* Wanting to be with her in the flesh, he actually shook his head and tried to pull himself out of this dream, temporarily feeling a shake and seeing his periphery quiver and distort, then go right back to normal.

"What the hell was that?" she asked, wide eyed, having experienced it herself.

"I'm not sure... I'm not sure," he mumbled, not wanting to tell her too much, as he was starting to understand that she was much more than just a projection of her by his own mind. He glanced around, still amazed... *So vivid... so utterly real!* Not only was it more realistic, but his awareness was as keen as in real life. It lacked the haze that buffered his dreams and always kept him from asking too many questions, or being too overly concerned with the validity of their answers. There literally seemed to be no difference between this plane and the material plane. He couldn't help but wonder if this was just a function of his growth as a planeshifter, or if maybe this was actually much more than a dream in the first place! He decided, for better or worse, to let it play out. "Let me try something," he said out loud, even though she was now just beyond earshot, running through the tundra, staring at the sky and pretending to be a bird.

He closed his eyes and focused hard on Ar'Jvikkah's energy, trying to summon him. He pulled hard through his right arm, remembering that his arm was still across Sky's womb, just over Ar'Jvikkah's body, in the material plane. He started to feel his energy… then he started to see it. First in the form of a prismatic array of light and colors, then it slowed to sound waves, becoming louder and louder as together they bridged the gap between the audible and inaudible... the seen and the unseen. Kaitlyn had already dropped what she was doing and was staring at Thor, obviously a little scared. Thor focused hard on Ar'Jvikkah, exactly as he last remembered him, in every regard. The sound vibration gave way to a distortion in his field of vision, bearing no solid shape at all, then it slowly took form, color, and finally, solid matter from nothing but pure energy before their very eyes!

He stood before them as he would probably be, had they not undergone such changes at the very threshold of oblivion during the tachyon storm. He was a fine young dragon, his smooth reptilian skin nearly the same orange hue of the sands of his home, yet having an almost chameleonic quality about it that seemed to just begin to grab at the colors and textures he approached, without ever making any solid transformation or commitment. It seemed as if he would have but only to think it, and it would be so. His enormous eyes seemed utterly bottomless, containing the collective wisdom of one of the universe's elder races; projecting it only to those who *truly* listen. His strong wings spread out at least as far as Erük's, though he stood before them on his hind legs much as a human would, his humanoid mannerisms seeming neither offensive, nor weak. He was absolutely magnificent.

Kaitlyn took a couple steps back... *way back*... not sure what to think of this creature of myth, now standing before her in the flesh. *"Do not fear me, young one. We are closer than you know..."*

"Who... said that?" She looked quickly back and forth between Thor and Ar'Jvikkah, starting to hyperventilate.

"Calm down, Kait! He won't hurt you... *It's OK!*" He held out his hands, sword already replaced in its sheath. "This is Ar'Jvikkah... and he's a very good friend of mine. He wouldn't hurt you if his life depended on it!"

"H-He t-talked to me through... through-"

"Telepathy. It's just telepathy." He looked directly into her eyes, sensing she had calmed down significantly. *"You'll learn to do it as well, young Sky..."* He smiled at her as he sent her this message and he could tell from her returned smile that she understood. He gazed at her for a moment, absolutely astonished by her beauty, yet a little taken aback at how young she seemed to his eyes when it wasn't but a few short years that separated them, even now.

Caught up in the moment, he started noticing something changing about her. The air around her seemed to be distorting similarly to the way the area around Ar'Jvikkah did when he materialized. At first, it seemed quite random, and seemed to have no real form at all, but this quickly changed. She was still smiling, almost frozen in time as if completely unaware of what was transpiring. It was then that Thor recognized the energy signatures. She was being seduced unknowingly, and in her sleep, by the ethereal creatures that Thor had bonded with back in the caves! He rushed over to her, quickly, looking to Ar'Jvikkah for help.

"She needs to wake up! They will take her, mind and spirit, to a place she can't return from! Help me!" Thor yelled at Ar'Jvikkah, shaking Kaitlyn like a ragdoll, only to see them swarm around her all the more. Having bonded with them before, he could feel their pull even from another plane of existence, and he let go of his physical self, grasping at her very core in an effort to keep her rooted to something.

"Forgive me," Ar'Jvikkah said to her, functioning on her level, as Thor faded into the ether to defend her. He shifted his physical form from a dragon to something infinitely more terrifying, then roared ferociously right in her face, causing her to jump back, screaming in terror. Fearing for her life, she first regressed back into herself and temporarily away from the ethereal beings, then as he let loose a giant fireball from his mouth directly at her, she snapped completely out of the nightmare, and found herself back in the darkness of the cave.

She struggled to catch her breath. She couldn't believe how real the whole experience had seemed. Never before had she come out of a dream to such a vivid memory of what had transpired. She struggled to find her last light-stick, still seeing the face of the terrifying, fire breathing demon, and the kind eyes of this stranger she was sure that she somehow knew. She found the stick and snapped it, shaking it profusely. All she wanted was the safety and warmth of her home and family. *What she saw was something altogether different!*

Swirling all around her was a vortex of ghost-like beings, apparently locked in some sort of melee with one of their own kind. The largest one was viciously attacking three others, dragging them off one at a time by the extremities and slamming into the rock walls with them in its grasp, a sort of glow emanating from them each time, as one by one, they became extinguished and the large one was all that remained. She stared in amazement as she witnessed it materializing directly in front of her after returning alone from somewhere *within* the wall.

"Oh my God!" She stared in disbelief at Thor, who now stood before her in the flesh, looking exactly as he did in the dream she was having not five minutes earlier. "Are you real?" She shook her head, making some kind of moaning sound as she started rubbing her eyes in disbelief. "I gotta be losing it... So that was all real? Now, wait a minute... I've been dreaming that place since I was a kid!"

"So have I." Thor started to look confused, himself. "Are you serious?"

"Dead serious. What do you mean, *so have you?* And what about your buddy, Mr. Dragon? Are you going to tell me he was real, too? He tried to torch me!" She suddenly groaned and doubled over, clutching her abdomen. Thor had the terrifying feeling that something was going horribly wrong. Everything seemed to be slipping away, and he was quickly losing his foothold on his very sense of reality. He felt like he was losing *himself.* It occurred to him that he may be causing a temporal paradox of some kind, triggered by giving young Sky too much information.

Surely he wasn't supposed to let the ethereal creatures take her, but what would she have done had he not been here to save her? He remembered her telling him that when they found her in the caves after the three day search, she was in a mild coma that caused temporary amnesia to follow, making her memory of the entire plight a little vague, to say the least. The rest, especially the part about her parents, she blocked over time as part of an involuntary defense mechanism, and only recently had started unearthing the memories, piece by piece.

He decided to do something rash, rather than risk any further complication. He focused his thoughts entirely on Sky... her mannerisms, her physical look, her voice, and most importantly, her energy. He closed his eyes and adjusted his pitch; body, mind, and spirit, accordingly. When he heard her scream, he knew he was there, and slowly opened his eyes, staring directly at what looked like a mirror right before his eyes. "Wh- wh- w- w- what the hell are you?" she asked shakily, almost in a whisper, as if not wanting to upset him.

"Oh, I'm just a girl," he sung sarcastically, remembering the song from his youth as he danced gaily around in front of her, *"Poor little ol' me..."* Knowing he was close to his desired effect, he reached out and grabbed her hand, holding it softly as he kept on dancing around and around, secretly draining her energy mentally the way he used to for Kait back in the underground to help her get to sleep. It was a simple "pull" of energy from one person to the other until the recipient loses consciousness. She slowly collapsed into his arms, and he laid her gently down in the softest place he could find, close to the main opening where he was sure they would immediately come across her when they started the search. He knew that when she woke, her memory of this incident would be vague and unbelievable, and she would question its validity herself, regardless of how real it seemed, most likely assuming it was just a "dream within a dream," or something.

He took a moment to stare at her innocent form; so young and uncorrupted by the transgressions of their leaders. Knowing the pain she faced so very soon at the cruel hand of fate, he took a moment and prayed for her protection, thanking God for this rare opportunity to see the one he loved in such pristine form, and for the opportunity to be a part of her evolution into the remarkably strong woman she is today. He breathed in deeply through his nose, then exhaled audibly, centering himself and then bending his very soul to the place where he came from... bypassing the Astral dream state, and the ethereal flux he traveled through to get here, and arose very successfully in bed next to Sky, as if he had never left.

He wasn't sure whether he had ever physically left at all, or how long she had been awake, but Sky lay next to him, his hand still on her belly, with her eyes wide open, staring at him with wonder and admiration in her eyes. "How long have I been out? I've been having the most intense dreams I've ever had in my life! Holy shit! Whew!" She exhaled loudly, stressing her words with a comical expression and animated gestures.

"Well, let's just say you gave us a pretty good scare.... Ar'Jvikkah and I went to investigate, in a manner of speaking." He smiled coyly, patting her belly softly. She looked absolutely stunned, at first, then smiled back, just enough to let him know she had some memory of what transpired, even though it happened to her, technically, over 20 years ago. "I think I'm starting to understand why some of my memories from childhood are a bit blank.... I think you were there all along, I just don't think I realized it until now! I also think our coming here may have been unavoidable! Our destinies are definitely intertwined... regardless of what choices we make!"

Thor suddenly looked at her very seriously. "I think you may be right about that... I just wish we could see the full breadth of the wake we create with our involvement here. There's just no telling the true effect of even the smallest ripple... and even the slightest screw up could be our undoing!"

Her gaze shifted, and she suddenly looked thousands of miles away, obviously thinking about something very deeply. She arose, slowly walking about the room at the foot of the bed. When she finally spoke, she did so softly, and with much resolve, as if she had finally reached the painstaking conclusion to an epic dilemma. In short, she sounded exhausted in every possible way. "The screw up *could* be simply *doing nothing. Apathy* can cause lives to be lost forever... and a lifetime of guilt to atone for...."

"It seems to me that fate has put us exactly where we were meant to be, with the tools and skills to get the job done... *I'm with you*, Sky, whatever you decide to do." He knew she was referring to the situation with her parents, that she intended to try to save them, and though this could dramatically change both of their lives thereafter; by his love for her he was willing to risk it all for even one chance to help her. He stood up and gave her a long, passionate kiss.

As they embraced, eyes closed, Sky started to have flashes of images and people... places she had never been and memories that weren't hers. Thor sensed it as well... a glimpse at one possible outcome: a rift in the temporal design of the universe... the first possible wave of a reality changing paradox, brought on simply by the *decision to act* being made!

She took a deep breath; eyes still closed, and forced a vague picture of her parents into her head. They were smiling. It was warm outside and they were all at some sort of park having a picnic. No Fleet. No responsibility. A perfect day. She could feel her younger self very intensely lately, figuring this was probably due mostly to their proximity, but it just as well be her all over again. She was so carefree. So full of wonder. So sensitive, loving and playfully naïve.... So totally unaware that her life was about to be ripped apart at the seams forever. Forever changed in the blink of an eye... awaking to a life of loneliness, guilt, and regret. Though she had built herself strong in the wake of this tragedy, she would trade it all to bring them back.

"Thor, we have to do something," she said shakily with her eyes full of tears. "I can't bear the thought of letting them die again, right before my eyes. I can't sit back and let that little girl lose everything and grow up with nobody but these corporate whores to call family… not on my watch! I'm just afraid of what it might mean for *us*...."

"Don't you worry about that," he said quietly, right into her ear, "If there's one thing this life has proven to me, it's that all the Gods, they cannot sever us! We were meant to be together, and so we shall. Don't you worry about it… don't you dare! Let's do what needs to be done… let's go save your parents…" He grabbed her hand and took off toward the utility locker to pick up some supplies on the way to the shuttle bay. Unnoticed by both of them, sitting high in the trees of the biodome, silently looking over the tops of the partition walls down at their quarters, was Erük, deep in thought and troubled beyond words by the loss of his planet and people. He sat as still as a picture, finally having come to his own decision… one that was larger than them all.

CHAPTER 18: THE LONG ARMS OF FATE

Out over the Eastern Plains, the seventh sun, Asterope, the sister who never sleeps, was casting her faint glow over the relative serenity of the eye of the great polar storm that had now nearly doubled in size since its breach of the settlement's perimeter. The great storm had all but crippled the Fleet's activities, but it did not stop Connor and Regina Davies from attempting a ground search for their missing daughter.

They broke through the edge of the inner wall of the eye, an almost solid mass of extremely high wind carrying water, vegetation, sand, and debris of nearly every conceivable kind at speeds faster than any other part of the great storm. Flipping over twice on their side before skidding upright out onto a flat, swampy section of grassy plains, they were once again saved by timing and pure, unadulterated parental determination.

They held each other tight for a moment through their thick EP suits, harnessed to the semi-exposed pilot house for added safety. Connor quickly shook it off, jamming the throttle down to escape the vortex closing in fast behind them, and realizing that they had just cheated death for the second time tonight. He knew they probably wouldn't get a third chance. The first happened not twenty minutes ago, just as they took off in their *borrowed* flatbed mining skiff while still in the encampment at the base of the pyramid mountain....

The winds were howling so hard that the soil was lifting right up off of the bedrock in layers, finally threatening to take a row of flatbeds with it. Connor had been working on getting one of them running without authorization from Fleet's job bank computer; a process that involved a screwdriver, a pair of wire cutters, some electricians tape, the cover of night, and a particularly large pair of balls. Regina was wandering up toward the mouth of the caves, drawn to them like a magnet for some reason, but completely exposed to the weather as visibility worsened and large pieces of debris continued to narrowly miss her on the way by. He finally got it to power up just as all Hell broke loose.

He turned to celebrate, smiling proudly, but couldn't spot her in the maelstrom of weather and confusion. "Gina!" he yelled at the top of his lungs, barely even hearing his own voice over the escalating violence. "Gina!" He searched frantically, suddenly worried that at a mere 120 lbs. soaking wet, she might possibly have been lifted right off her feet in one of the huge upward gusts, then carried off with the rest of the loose supplies, never to be seen again. He could not bear to lose them both.

He turned back to the control panel on the skiff's dashboard computer screen to look for floodlight and loudspeaker controls. He instinctively punched in a warm-up sequence, bringing radar and guidance control online, along with most other flight control systems, and happened to notice a single signature, faint, at best, due to the interference, but coming from the northeast, in the direction of the Great Plains. It was nearly dawn, but still very dark, save for the blue glow always present in that direction. His heart ached with fear for his daughter. If she was caught outside, she would have had to stay within the eye as it moved, outrunning the inner walls as they encroached on her. He became desperate to find them both, and started feeling his last bit of control over this maddening situation slipping away.

Suddenly, a great bolt of lightning lit up the whole encampment as it crashed sideways overhead, both of his fists engulfed in the blackened clouds, but violently penetrating the darkness and shaking the small craft helpless beneath his feet. In that moment, Connor happened to be facing the right way, and just caught her suited silhouette in his field of vision, standing beneath some kind of tall rock formation about 50 yards away with her arms out to the sides, trying to steady herself as she headed uphill against the turbulent wind. "Gina! For God's sake!" he screamed again, to no avail. The speakers in their helmets did little more than crackle beneath the endless interference, and she was simply too far away, with the wind howling too loud, to be heard naturally.

He could make out some large objects in the darkness, spiraling closer and closer, caught in some kind of whirlwind directly over her head, narrowly missing her from above, yet she seemed oblivious to all of it; not even looking back as she remained drawn to the mountain for reasons he couldn't conceive of. As far away as she had wandered, he knew he would never make it to her in time to help her on foot, so he fired up the skiff and backed out of its slip haphazardly, not even looking behind himself as he maneuvered through the rows of parked machinery at full throttle. He came up on her fast, not even slowing down as he approached her from behind on her right side. He held onto the controls of the skiff and leaned way out over the port side of the small craft, scooping her up with his strong left arm on the way by; a large piece of debris narrowly missing her left side as he pulled her to safety and sped off toward the signal.

The clang from a large piece of sheet metal nailed to a broken shoring post as it slammed deep into the hard ground right where she had been standing echoed over and over in his mind for several minutes as he negotiated the deep canyon route on their way toward the plains over which the eye of the storm had settled. She held his hand tightly, neither one of them able to take their eye off of the faint little dot on their scanner as she prepared the harness and lanyard system for both of them, plus a third, smaller suit and harness for Kaitlyn, hoping for the best, but knowing full well that the worst was still in front of them… and coming up fast!

"So, what's your plan?" Thor asked, testing the EP suit's helmet com. His voice came over the speakers within the shuttle, as well as Sky's own earpiece and helmet system, which was still sitting in the vacant seat next to her as she flew the craft quick and low, hoping to stay out of sight from the Fleet's eye in the sky.

"Well, I do know this," she said calmly, never taking her eyes off the rushing ground before her, "They were reported missing, themselves, then Ground Ops crews found the wreckage a few days later."

"Where?"

"I don't know for sure… somewhere out here, I think. Their last transmission recorded by the base said that they were following some signal coming from within the eye of the storm." She started to look pale, then nauseated. "They… thought it was me," she mumbled. Her screen was unintelligible, at best, but they both saw the small energy signature pop up on the scanner at the same time; no larger than most of the debris caught in the inner circle surrounding the eye. It stopped for just a moment, then started moving... *directly toward them!* She switched the view to infrared. There were two obviously separate entities onboard a small craft. This was no RAM probe sent to investigate the signal that they themselves had to be emitting.... *It had to be them!*

"What was that last part?" Thor said, pulling off the helmet altogether.

"I said, they thought it was me... they thought the signal in the eye of the storm was me!" Turning toward Thor, she paused before returning her gaze out the front into the oncoming twilight haze and morning mist enveloping the speeding craft. "Jesus Christ...." She looked like she had just seen a ghost, fixed in her icy stare through the thick windshield as the ground continued to rush by underneath them. "It *was* me..." Thor turned quietly toward her with his mouth hanging partially open.

"What do we do?"

"We send them back!" she yelled, snapping out of it, and preparing the shuttle for autopilot. "I'll not have them die because of me!"

"Look, I cloaked the shuttle's energy signal from the Fleet's equipment, up there," Thor pointed, pacing the short deck and scratching his head, "but the analog gear onboard the smaller ships and RAM equipment must still be able to read us.... Damn it!"

"Hey! I need you to focus! *It's not your fault!* Help me save them... *please!* I can't do this alone, Thor, I need your help!" She was now pacing, herself, her eyes starting to tear up. "How do we get them back to the settlement without being seen?"

Thor looked out to the horizon at the massive wall of violent energy before them, slowly becoming visible against the deep blue glow of the morning sunrise penetrating the debris cloud and the lingering moonlight shining down through the one clear patch of sky straight above. It was absolutely ominous. The clouds surrounding the inner radius of the eye had formed into the clear shape of a vertical wall, nearly a half mile high in places and darkening with solid debris toward the bottom. "Through *that?* It's an absolute miracle they made it through in the first place! To go back through in that little flatbed skiff they're flying would be suicide! Utter suicide! We could give them the shuttle, but that would only improve their chances slightly-"

"And then we'd have the whole Fleet onto us... no thanks, this is bigger than just us," she contemplated, rubbing her belly and thinking about Erük and her promise to him regarding her role as the carrier of his race's legacy. She cringed, unable and unwilling to separate her duty from family loyalty. She had always been hugely empathic, and the bond between her and her mother transcended all modes of normal communication. They could nearly read each other's minds, but moreover, they could feel each other's feelings. Her newly acquired skills were adding a new dimension to this, entirely, and as she closed her eyes, reaching out with her mind, she could definitely feel them approaching.

Her mother was crying, concealing her severe physical injuries from her husband in order to keep him on track and focused. He was like a machine, mind and spirit bent only on the mission at hand, and concern for her immediate safety was the only thing that could possibly deter him once he was set into motion. Sky smiled a teary smile, honored to be the focus of so much love... so much sacrifice... yet she wished she could tell them it was all okay, that she was fine. She homed in on their energy, deciding at last to give them a moment of relief: a sign that everything was going to be alright and they no longer needed to torture themselves.

She had a sudden vision. A moment's distraction... *so much blood!* Her father had spotted the wound! He lifted the flap on the back side of her EP suit to reveal a large piece of shrapnel piercing her kidney and protruding through the front, just under her rib cage on the right side. Sky gasped, understanding more the feeling of shock her father was experiencing than actually *seeing* the circumstances. Her mother was fading fast. Connor glanced quickly this way and that, one hand on the controls of the speeding craft, and the other holding her collapsed body from falling to the floor. The vector proximity alarm went off and his attention sprang back to the front, seeing only vegetation and water as it beat him from all sides.

Sky gasped and grabbed hold of Thor's arm as he was just finishing the seal on his EP helmet, pulling him down and pulling hard on the steering control as she fell to the floor, then everything went dark. It was as if time had slowed to a fraction of its natural speed, and he was the only one who could see it. This was the second time he had experienced this sensation, the first being on the bridge of the Phoenix, during the tachyon storm. His balance was being seriously disrupted as he fought to get back to his feet, and he knew he had only moments, even at this augmented rate, to prepare for what was coming.

He picked Sky up off the floor, strapping her into her seat with the five point harness. As he reached for her helmet, which was already flying in slow motion toward the front, he noticed the nose of the shuttle had already started digging into the soil beneath them. The windshield was fogging over from the inside and beginning to crack as debris flew across it sideways, then upward, and finally downward as Thor clung desperately to Sky's chair for support, his feet now almost straight up in the air.

Out of the nearly useless windshield, he momentarily caught a glimpse of something shiny, something manmade go flying by; just inches away from getting pulverized by the shuttle. He looked quickly to the safety of the copilot's chair, but it was too late. As fast as the whole process began, time seemed to accelerate at a frightening rate; sound, light, movement, and even the sensation of urgency and fear all returning to normal on a sliding scale that seemed to speed right past all known levels as it returned, thrusting Thor headfirst into the conflict... into the crashing sounds of broken glass, wind, and metal tearing and screaming, compressed into one horrific moment in time... a lifetime of movement, intention, strife and triumph... turned into one singular moment of silent despair... then as quickly as it ended, it became movement again... one pulse; one shifting of the tide into a new pitch... *into the light.*

CHAPTER 19: A VISIT FROM AN OLD FRIEND

"What's up, bro?" Thor recognized the voice instantly, but was having a little trouble getting his bearings. Everything was *so* bright. He looked all around, feeling the warm sun on his face, and a cool mountain breeze that smelled so good... so utterly fresh. He could count on one hand how many times in his life, even growing up on the coast in the underground he had experienced such a clean breath of air. He smiled hugely, turning to look at his brother, Tyr, who now sat beside him in a patch of short grass on the hillside as if nothing had ever happened. He realized at once that this was not a dream, but rather, a crossroads; a place that could not be ravaged by time. A place where time did not exist. This was as real as any experience he had memory of in his head. How it came to pass, though, was still a mystery he could not wrap his mind around, but for now he did not try... *this was good.*

"That's the real question, isn't it?" he grinned, sharing a warm, weightless smile, as they had so many times in the past. Thor stood up, stretching, but still not sure what was going on. He did notice they were both wearing their swords.

Tyr noticed Thor's eyes avert and quickly returned the gleam in his eye, grinning devilishly. Thor reached for his katana and attacked, slashing at neck level across from left to right as he drew it from its sheath in perfect form. He struck nothing but air, as Tyr had already rolled backward, pulling his pair of straight Ninja To swords, one from above his right shoulder, and the other from below with his left hand, held reversed.

Tyr feinted with his left hand in a whirlwind lash, followed by a strong overhead attack, stepping toward Thor as he came over the top toward his head. Thor stepped toward him with his right foot, hooking the tip of his blade down and to the right with the pommel straight above his head in a defensive stance. As Tyr's blade fell straight down upon him, he let the tip of his katana drop even lower, keeping the pommel up high and strong. Tyr's sword glanced loudly down the entire length of Thor's block, then as it slipped off the end, Thor spun all the way around to the left, twisting his sword without moving it from its position, until the edge was facing Tyr, then followed through with a slash all the way through his midsection.

Tyr's left hand block was already in place, tip straight down as sparks went flying through a long cut that would have undoubtedly severed his torso from his waist and slashed him right in two. Thor smiled, rolling his blade around with his right wrist as he stepped back and bowed with his sword resting behind his right arm, the tip showing just above his shoulder. Tyr did the same, showing his brother the same respect, neither warrior displaying the least bit of rust in his technique.

"I just had to know it was really you," Thor smiled, sheathing his katana and stepping forward to give his brother a strong hug, grabbing his right forearm on the way in.

"Who else would I be?" Tyr smiled back.

"Let's just say, things have not been what they seem lately... In fact..." Thor became perplexed, as the more he tried to identify where and when he actually was, the fuzzier things became. Tyr put a comforting hand on his shoulder.

"Don't worry about it, brother... This doesn't make a whole lot of sense to me, either, but it's a good thing! I'll take it!"

"You were-"

"Yeah, I know..." Now Tyr started to look confused. "Dagaz... that punk! Uruz..." He closed his eyes, nose twitching with anger and a pent up darkness of a most unsettling kind. "Kait...!" His eyes jarred back open, as he suddenly flashed back to the recordings on the laptop he and Uruz were reviewing just before the knock on the door that sealed their fate.

"She fine!" Thor smiled, leaning in toward him, "Brother, she's fine! I can't really explain it, but she's here... now..."

"Where exactly is that, my brother... I'm a little fuzzy at the moment. One minute I'm on the floor with a mouthful of blood, in excruciating agony, and now, here I am with you!"

"Yeah, I'm a little fuzzy, too," he mumbled, still dazed and confused, not really sure how to explain the time that had elapsed in his world, and not really sure if he even should. "Sky! Her name is Sky!"

"Who? What are you talking about?" he grinned, slapping Thor's shoulder again. Thor suddenly had a déjà vu, and one of remarkable clarity. He even knew exactly what was about to be said, so he spit it out, changing the subject.

"Do you remember when Ragnar told us about the 'ghosts' that the government sent after my father and the rest of the AFG? You know, the assassin's guild with the marks on the back of their necks?"

Tyr looked at him very solemnly, staring deep into his eyes before answering. "Yes. They were known in the underground as the *Vindicators*. Part of that brand on the back of their necks was rumored to be a number, in barcode… their personal ID, so to speak, and the rest was the phrase, *'ipsissima verba,'* Latin for *'letter of the law.'* Why are you bringing this up, bro?" Tyr looked at Thor strangely, as if he had torn into an old wound.

"I've got one after me."

Tyr took a deep breath, exhaling loudly as he bowed his head, pulling his hand through his long brown hair. He looked up at Thor, extremely concerned. "That's just fucking great… You know there's no stopping those guys, don't you?"

"Yeah, I kind of noticed that about this guy. His name's McGinn. Kieran McGinn. He's been following me since… well, let's just say he's got one hell of a reach! I thought I killed him once already, and he just keeps coming!"

"Kill him?" Tyr laughed, "Shit, bro, you can't just kill these bastards! You need to kill them, then follow them to Hell itself, and kill 'em again!"

Thor laughed, realizing Tyr was just trying to be funny while illustrating a point. "That's probably more true than you know, my brother." He laid on his back, staring at the sky. There were quite a few more clouds than he remembered just a short while ago, while they were sparring. He had so much he wanted to talk to Tyr about, but for the life of him, he couldn't put the thoughts in his head to words. It was so good to see him again, yet he couldn't remember where he had just come from, how he got here, or why he hadn't been able to speak to him in so long. Time, it seemed, had no meaning in this place… Here, they simply *were*.

CHAPTER 20: THE RESCUE

The clouds began to cover the entire sky and it seemed like he was starting to lose his air. He started to gasp, pulling harder and harder, but not getting any oxygen into his lungs. "T-Tyr..." He strained to lift his head, and as he did, he saw water rush off a surface in front of his face. To his complete surprise, he realized it was the face shield of his EP helmet! He had the sensation of floating, and as he leaned to the left to reach up and release the seal on his helmet, he sunk completely underwater, no longer balancing on the buoyancy of his air filled EP suit.

He popped the helmet off and shoved his arm through the face mask so he could swim. His mind still racing over the events of the last 10 minutes or so, he quickly paddled to the shore of a very slowly meandering river. It was deep, but not wide, and seemed to stretch and snake all over the plains where he now sat, reflecting on what had just transpired. He was suddenly and solemnly brought back to full cohesion in this reality as the brunt of his bodily damage hit him like a runaway locomotive. He gasped, doubling over from the pain. He forced himself to stand; this shock on his system being the catalyst that reminded him in full detail of what had just happened to the shuttle, and how everything thereafter needed to be put into slightly different context.

Worried about Sky, he scanned the horizon, unsure how long he had drifted down stream. He could see the edge of the storm, looming close now, and he picked up the pace, forcing himself to run as he stumbled along the riverbank, upstream, as fast as his damaged body would allow. He started gasping for air after just a few bends, remembering what he heard about the atmosphere on this planet.

It was then that he realized that he wasn't gasping for air when he was floating in the river from being out of O2 in his suit... he was gasping because the filter damper was underwater! He quickly put his helmet back on. This was good news, as it also meant that not nearly as much time had elapsed since he was knocked unconscious! He took a couple deep breaths of clean O2, and took off on a run at a new pace, wiping his visor with his glove as he ran.

Sky moaned, slowly opening her eyes and seeing the damage all around her. She looked wearily through the smoke filled cockpit at the empty chair next to her, then through the gaping hole in the thick windshield at the water slowly flowing by and the mud and grass protruding onto the control panel in front of her as it sizzled and popped, throwing sparks this way and that. She tried to scream for him, but could immediately tell that several ribs were broken and she had a collapsed lung on her left side.

She put one hand over her abdomen and closed her eyes, fearing the worst. To her surprise, and joy, and thanks to Thor's quick thinking and lightning fast reflexes, Ar'Jvikkah was still alive! She popped the center release on her harness and fell toward the sparking control panel, holding her side in great pain as she tried to look out the front of the shuttle for

Thor. She couldn't spot him anywhere, and after a brief and painful reconnaissance, she returned to the relative calm of the interior shuttle to try and assess her situation. It was obvious that she would have to dive into the river to get out if she couldn't get the shuttle hatch to open, and given her condition, that wasn't sounding too appealing, so she quickly decided to focus on just that.

The control pad was barely functional at all, and after a few attempts to punch in a key sequence, the pad actually burst into flames, adding to the acrid and stifling smoke in the cockpit. Not sure how much longer she could stand it, she tried to activate the voice command feature, having quite a bit of trouble with that, due to the intense pain in her chest and her diminished air capacity. She finally got the computer to recognize her voice, but to her disappointment, the hatch was damaged from the wreck or pinned shut by the landscape or debris, and wouldn't open. Sky stared nervously at the flowing water, splashing inward in rhythmic laps, as over and over again it tried to find its way inside through the broken windshield in front of the control panel and the two cockpit seats only to recede back the way it came, like a child continuously pushing their boundaries, but each time gaining just a tiny bit of ground on the distracted parent.

Nose buried downward into a sandy bank in what appeared to be a winding and relatively shallow river, the tiny shuttle burst into flames out in the open plains of this small planet while the ominous storm closed in around them, cutting them off in every direction but backward. Staring at the jagged opening again, she could see the ominous glow of the flames on the river bottom below the surface of the water, and she knew she had very little time. She nudged herself forward, building up the courage to dive in, despite her diminished lung capacity causing increasingly shallow breathing and deepening pain. No sooner had she pictured in her mind what it would probably feel like and resolved to actually do it, than she found herself immersed in water and literally standing exactly as she was on the shuttle floor, helmet and gear in hand, but *outside* the shuttle, bobbing around randomly in the water as the air trapped in her suit brought her quickly up toward the surface.

She suddenly remembered the incident back onboard the Phoenix in the Biodome when she literally teleported across the room... *twice.* She realized now that this was no freak and random occurrence or anomaly, but rather a gift that needed to be studied and cultivated. She could feel that it was most likely a power borne of Ar'Jvikkah's race, and that it was probably transferring through to her from him, but she seemed, at least in part, to be in control of it... *to one degree or another...* at least for now. There was also the distinct possibility that he was acting out in both of their defense without being able to *see*, except for *through her eyes*, as it were. Whatever it was, she was eternally grateful!

Thor was finally nearly out of breath again as he ran directly into an increasing headwind at nearly a full sprint across the tall marshy grass of the plains toward a pillar of black smoke spiraling upward into the sky from behind a large knoll of bushes, tall grass, and short, wind-bent trees. He lost focus for just a moment and actually tripped, falling face first onto the ground just as the huge explosion rocked the relatively serene air, sending a small shockwave outward in a spherical dome of instantly displaced moisture, fog, shrapnel and fly-rock as the main transformer's cooling coils erupted, mixing ionized nitrogen with the compressed, liquefied crystal fuel they used for their frictionless repelling technology. The high nitrogen content in the atmosphere, combined with its oxygen, and the millions of iron and magnesium particles in the air stripped from the soil during the storm, created the perfect recipe for a shuttle-sized thermite bomb from Hell.

He continued to lay on the ground for a moment, realizing that a large chunk of debris had missed decapitating him by only a couple of inches, and this was due only to his momentary clumsiness. He looked upward toward the sky, thanking God for what could only have been divine intervention, then his heart sank, as he knew there was no way anyone anywhere near the blast could have survived! He watched for a few seconds, continuing to lay on his stomach on the ground and counted, instinctively putting his head down and waiting with his hands behind his head, fingers interlocked. Pieces started raining down all around him; small pebbles at first, then larger and larger stones and pieces of shuttle steel, aluminum, plastic, mud, glass and flaming debris of every kind.

He quickly put his helmet back on after shaking a small pile of leaves and debris out of it. He hadn't picked up a sound through his helmet since he emerged from the water, and had actually deactivated it completely after falling to the ground in order to conserve air, but now he faintly heard what had to be a cough from the other end. "Sky!?!" He quickly looked all around, jumping to his feet and sprinting for the wreckage like it was an Olympic event. "Sky!" He screamed, turning the tuning knob on the side of the helmet while he ran, trying to bring her back. He heard nothing but silence and static on the other end.

He could feel her presence as if she was standing right beside him, so his first fear was that she was dead and it was her spirit he was feeling, but then it started to fade slowly in intensity. He struggled to see through the dirty, mud smeared visor on the helmet as he turned 360 degrees in a slow sweep of the horizon, producing nothing. As he stood with his back to the river, still looking toward the smoke and wreckage, he failed to notice Sky's lifeless body float silently by behind him, drifting downstream on her back.

"Sky! Goddammit, answer me! I know you're out there!" He dropped to one knee, pulling his helmet back off, and started to scream with rage and frustration. "God, help me! Do NOT take her again!!!"

The last thing she saw as she faded out of consciousness from lack of oxygen with her suit's intake damper still completely submerged in the river water was Thor standing next to the river, not more than a few feet away on the bank with his back to her. She tried desperately to hail him, and it seemed to her as if she succeeded. She relaxed finally; things seemingly back to normal... *so warm and bright... back to normal.... Going to be OK.*

She was jarred from her euphoric shock and endorphin induced state of serene near-sleep and peacefulness by a series of violent convulsions as her body tried in vain to pull air that wasn't there into her good lung, while the other one twitched involuntarily and the pain in her body escalated to levels she had never before experienced. She closed her eyes as tight as she could, focusing all of her energy on one thing... one single thought. *"Thor! Please help me!"*

He jumped, not only hearing her voice telepathically, but literally feeling exactly what she was feeling. He grabbed his side, falling over in agony, then forcing himself to stand, knowing she did not have long. *"Where are you? Let me feel you!!! Please, God help me!"*

"I'm gonna... I can't- I'm... w-w... water."

Thor had the sudden sense and rush of falling a short distance, then the pain returned, reaching a desperate, nearly unbearable level... then nothing. The connection was severed. He looked around again and again, starting to panic as he knew in his heart he was simply out of time. He took a deep breath, centering himself so that he could think. He had never been the type of person who panicked in a crisis, but she had a way of disbalancing him at his very core.

He stood in a patch of scorched earth that he knew had to be the crash site. The loose soil had been cooked to a pale grey color, and was actually still warm from the blast. Looking around, he could spot only bits and pieces of the shuttle's framework and chassis among the blackened vegetation, but no sign of Sky. *Water....*

He turned his attention back toward the river, quickly retracing his run in his mind and he remembered a small waterfall, maybe 15 to 20 feet or so in height, not 50 feet downstream... *this had to be what she just felt!* He yanked his helmet all the way off so he could see clearly and ran as fast as he possibly could for the site. As he drew close, he heard the low rumble of the waterfall, but there was also something else... something he had heard before, starting to build in intensity deep in the background. He ignored it for now, hurdling several large stones just before reaching the crest of the falls.

Looking downstream, he backtracked with his eyes, desperate for any sign of her in the water or on the shoreline. It was there that he spotted her, nestled in tight among the floating debris of the river! The unmistakable stone grey of the EP suit stuck out in the crystal clear, bluish water like a sore thumb, vividly contrasted by a large halo of blood stained water that surrounded her, slowly oozing away downstream. She had gone over the falls and was now caught in the currents, face down, in the pool of water beneath; a 30ft diameter basin of slowly swirling water and floating debris that looked as if it went down forever before continuing to snake its way across the Great Plains. Thor accelerated, running full speed, straight at the crest of the waterfall.

He dove out and over the falls, as far as he could reach toward her, dispensing with all possible form and grace, then made up the rest underwater, focusing his will and coming up almost directly underneath her. Remembering the pain in her side that he seemed to have empathically shared, he lifted her carefully out of the water and laid her on the grassy shore. She was bleeding profusely through a tear in her suit near her lower rib cage on her left side.

She was completely unconscious and he was starting to become truly scared for her as he detached her helmet, remembering the trouble he had with his own gear underwater. It seemed they were designed to be sustainable filters for nearly any kind of toxic environment or atmosphere, but without the advent of air tanks, the limited supply of O2 in the suit was grossly inadequate for prolonged independent breathing. They still required the intake of fresh air to function properly, and hence, could not be used underwater without holding one's breath just as if the suit wasn't on at all.

He leaned in close and realized she wasn't even breathing! Terrified, he blew a breath into her mouth, noticing immediately that something wasn't right. He had never experienced a collapsed lung before, but he could certainly feel that forced-air breathing was certain to disrupt and damage something inside her. He knew he had to stop. He was just about to start pulmonary compressions for CPR as he remembered it, but then noticed the bruising and deformity of her lower ribs. He felt sick to his stomach, literally, finally having found her, only to sit here powerless, watching her quickly slipping away from him. He delicately began compressions anyway, carefully keeping away from her lower rib cage, and trying to center directly over her heart, buying himself time to think.

Starting to get extremely light headed from the events that just took place, Thor quickly put on Sky's helmet, unsure where he dropped his own. He paused only briefly from his work on Sky to take a few deep breaths as well, knowing he would be of absolutely no use to her unconscious, and if he even blacked out, she would surely die.... It may have been his own diminished state, or just wishful thinking, but he could have sworn that her chest slowly moved, just as if she pulled a long, deep breath on her own. He watched closely, waiting for another, but it didn't seem to be coming, so he quickly continued with her CPR, desperately trying to keep blood pumping upward into her brain.

He had somehow managed to cut her suit all the way open on the wound-side with a sharp stick he found floating in circles nearby, while continuing compressions, and was holding a large strip of the suit's insulation fabric, some sort of synthetic cotton-like material, directly over the bleeding wound with as much pressure as he felt she could take if she was awake. He closed his eyes, continuing his rhythmic pulse; able to hear his own breathing a little through the helmet's speakers as he huffed and puffed, as unrelenting as a machine, but quickly approaching the point of breakdown. It was then that he heard a faint crackle in the helmet....

He paused. Just to be sure it wasn't his imagination he even stopped the compressions and just listened. All he could hear was the faint hum and rhythmic pitch oscillation that had been present all morning; most likely some kind of magnetic field anomaly from being in the eye of such a storm, combined with being so very near to the southern pole of the planet. When they first departed, Sky joked about it sounding like an "alien fart," a new kind of radio code used by the hostile "Blue Boneheads of Alcyone," fueled by inhaling gas from the nebula... Thor cracked up again, starting out laughing hysterically through his nose, then gradually decaying into sobbing, his eyes tearing up in frustration, confusion and sadness as he resumed his compressions, noting, for what it was worth, that she was still quite warm.

"Is anyone out there...? Pilot of the shuttlecraft-... -ome in-... ayday. Mayday. Mayday..." The message, though distorted and fragmented, was very loud and made Thor jump nearly out of his skin! *The man on the other end had to be Sky's father... and to be receiving this at all in this storm's interference meant he was close!*

"Yeah! Copy that! This is shuttle craft! We're stranded... one pilot seriously injured! Shuttle is destroyed... need assistance!"

"Our skiff is still functional... Where are you?"

Thor had to think for a second... If he hit the homing beacon on her helmet, they would undoubtedly show up on the Fleet's screens as soon as the search party for Connor and Gina got here... even though their short-range analog communications were completely shrouded by the storm, the blast from the shuttle would have gotten their attention, and they would most likely be sending someone directly. He looked at Sky, feeling her slipping away, despite the serious help she was apparently getting from Ar'Jvikkah. "Skiff pilot! Is your scanning computer operational?"

"Yes, Sir!"

"I'm hitting my rescue beacon... Please hurry! I'm losing her!"

Connor saw the light pop up on his otherwise scrambled screen, and knew there was at least a chance that the "her" this man was referring to may be his young daughter... *Maybe they were a S&R Mission who beat him here to rescue her, and were on their way out when they almost collided...* He didn't know, and at the moment, didn't care. He was terrified for his daughter, and now for his wife, as well, who was slipping away right before his eyes. Now the shuttle, probably their only chance for getting her back alive, was destroyed. The little bit of faith he had been grasping in a choke hold since they stole the flatbed was slipping away from him by the handfuls. All he could do was B-line for the mark on the scanner and pray...

Thor listened close to Sky's heart, feeling for a pulse as well. To his astonishment, he could hear no activity from her heart, yet she was extremely warm, *and seemed to be breathing just fine!* He could only speculate, at this point, that it was Ar'Jvikkah keeping her alive... using his own connection with her and his telekinesis to keep her blood flowing continuously, everywhere it needed to go! The only question was, *how long would it last...?*

Reading through the ships archives, Thor had encountered record of a species of parasite encountered on Titan when the Fleet was still in Earth's solar system that would do the same basic thing to its "host" by fusing itself inline with the victim's circulatory system, then upon reaching full gestation, would simply vacate the host, and the human being would die from cardiovascular failure, having developed a dependency on the artificial stimulus of an otherwise involuntary muscle and breathing function. No matter what the ramifications, this seemed to have saved her life, but they definitely didn't have much time.

Thor laughed a nervous, relieved laugh, fueled by a release of endorphins unlike anything he had ever felt. As he heard the skiff approaching, he took off the helmet and put it on her, no longer needing the radio. He knew they would be speeding across the plains toward the lake again, and it would become very hard for anyone on a skiff to draw breath in this environment. In her weakened state, she would never make it, and there was no time to go back and look for his helmet.

Thor waved Connor in, and just as he started to descend over the crest of the hill with the waterfall, Thor noticed the sound again: a low rumble, almost subsonic, seeming to come from above, yet from everywhere all at once. This time it was closer, and as he realized what it was, he became extremely nervous. The last time he heard this sound, it was immediately followed by the unleashing of absolute "Hell on Earth." It was the unmanned drone sent over Erük's home caverns just before they were firebombed into oblivion. The shuttle explosion had apparently brought this section of the map under immediate scrutiny. He could only pray that Mr. Davies was running silent to keep off the scanners himself, or they were as good as found, and would be leading the Fleet straight to the Phoenix!

Connor set the skiff down right next to Thor and immediately jumped down to help him hoist Sky onboard, laying her right next to Regina, who was also still unconscious. Connor started choking back tears as he explained what they were doing out here, and what happened to his wife. Thor cut him short, putting his hand on his shoulder, and assuring him that things were going to work out fine. Although he didn't recognize Sky as being his daughter yet, Connor, being pretty good at reading people, saw something hopeful in the gleam in Thor's eye, and seemed to regain his focus and faith immediately.

"These two need medical attention immediately... Lets go! Just stay off the radar, if you get my meaning..." Connor looked at him quizzically, then nodded, glancing at his wife quickly as she lay under the shelter of the semi-enclosed pilot house. He punched it in the direction Thor showed him to go, with no further questions asked. Thor was absolutely unsure how to handle the situation regarding Sky's identity, and for the moment, just stayed as vague as possible about a great many things. All that mattered at this point was saving their lives and getting everybody underground as quickly as possible.

Thor was kneeling down over the women, keeping a close eye on their situations when they came up on the outer fingers of the labyrinth of canyons leading to the lake. Connor slowed way down, looking frustrated as he glanced all around from above, carefully staying close to its outer perimeter, not seeing any ship, encampment, or even a sign of life. He started to get visibly upset.

"Hey, *Mr. Krey*, was it? What the hell is going on? There's nothing here! We got lost out here earlier, before we got ourselves caught in the outer shell of the eye while trying to transmit." He gestured up toward the sky, starting to get emotional as he was reminded why they were here in the first place. "Your analog signal was the only thing we could read out here... it has the same type of signature as a set of communicators we share with our daughter." His eyes started to tear up quickly and his breathing got very shallow. Thor put a hand on his shoulder and leaned forward, looking him in the eye.

"You'll see her again," he said, a little too matter-of-factly. "Have faith, Connor, let me see your helmet..." Davies handed it to Thor, too upset to realize that he hadn't told Thor his first name. Thor put it on, listening close for any possible chatter that shouldn't be taking place. He stood still for just a moment, then signaled for Connor to move out. He circled around the perimeter, counterclockwise, staying carefully above the deep maze of canyons until he came upon a large bridge of earth and stone, nearly 20 feet high and jutting straight into the center of the spider web and into the side of the lake, about 50 yards straight inward toward the center. "Coast out toward the end of this bridge... then power down."

"Power down? What are we doing here? I mean, do you not see *THAT*?" he shouted, pointing at the closest part of the storm's edge, already hitting the farthest shore of the lake and causing a series of small water spouts to form along its deepest edge, just past the canopy of vegetation conglomerating over the center.

"Trust me," Thor said, stepping out onto the nose of the small craft and waving Connor forward. When he reached the end of the outcropping, Thor looked down at the water's surface. He could still detect the slight hum on the water when he looked closely, assuring him that they were still down there, probably trying to get a solid read on the craft they were in now, but getting scrambled results from the interference. He turned to Connor and smiled, waving for him to set it down, then pulled off the helmet and tripped the homing beacon.

Connor lowered the landing pads and set the craft skillfully down, then sarcastically killed the engines and main power, looking to Thor for the next step. Thor just grinned, looked over the nose of the skiff into the depths of the clear water below. He held the helmet up high, checking to see that the small blinking light underneath its rim was on, then gave it a big sloppy kiss on the face shield and tossed it right into the lake. He watched as it sunk immediately below the surface, then sat quietly next to Sky, checking her pulse and slowly caressing her hair.

Connor stood for a moment, staring off the nose of the skiff into the water with a dumbfounded look on his face, then turned to Thor, enraged.

"Are you mad? What the hell did you do that for? Now we're as good as stuck! I can't hold my breath like you can, young man, and we're a long way out here with nothing but trouble on the horizon! God dammit! What the hell were you th-" He was cut off short by the deafening sound of the URCAT personnel shuttle rising slowly out of the water directly behind him. He jumped to the side, almost falling off of the embankment as he turned around to watch it hover over them, showering them with cold lake water, then set down right next to the skiff and open up. Thor just smiled at him and slapped him quietly on the shoulder as he stood up, then carefully started loading the women aboard the heavily armored, unmanned transport.

"Christ, why didn't you just *tell* me you stashed a CAT!?"

Connor started to lighten up just a bit, but Thor continued to keep a close eye on him, not sure if he could be trusted not to freak out when he realized what was really happening. As far as what to do with them for the long term solution, Thor was starting to get an idea how this all fit together in the grand design.

Just as they were almost loaded into the transport, Connor and Thor both jumped from the sound of the drone sweeping just above the thickening cloud layer that was all that hid them from the Fleet's view. It had slowed down, probably picking up the faint, yet unique signal from the skiff as it undoubtedly was being sent to look for just that. Mr. Davies appeared overjoyed, not understanding the danger or the real situation. "Hey!" he yelled, jumping up and down while flailing his arms as if they could see him. It was obviously more out of excitement, than any real attempt to be seen, but then he rushed over to the skiff and popped the utility box on the back.

Fishing around, he quickly produced what Thor was afraid he was after, and it was all he could do just to get over to the skiff fast enough, as Connor already had the subsonic flare gun out and pointed at the sky with a great smile on his face, ready to save the day. Just as his finger found the trigger and began to squeeze, Thor swept up behind him, mirroring his body position almost exactly. He reached straight up Connor's arm to the pistol, grabbing it and blocking the hammer from falling with his thumb, while twisting it immediately toward the water, in case of accidental discharge. He pulled back on Connor's left shoulder with his left hand, putting tremendous downward pressure on him and kicking the back of his left leg, causing him to drop to his knees in a very quick and controlled motion, while simultaneously removing the pistol from his right hand and turning him slightly face down by twisting his right wrist and applying downward pressure at the same time. Connor winced, caught completely off guard and completely clueless as to the reason for this attack.

"I'm sorry," Thor whispered into his left ear from behind.

"For what?" he grunted, still immobilized with pain.

"For this." Thor struck him hard, directly on the back of the head, so as to render him unconscious, but absolutely no harder than was necessary to accomplish this. He lifted the large man up and laid him in the transport next to his wife, then secured the three of them in with restraints.

Thor disarmed the power chip on the flare gun and put it into one of his suit's cargo pockets for safe keeping, then jumped up onto the skiff. He powered it up just enough to bring forward coast capability online, as if it was going to be hooked into a convoy as part of a cargo train. He knew this wouldn't require main engine and computer warm up and should keep them from popping up on the drone's scanning computer now that it had closed in on so tight of a search pattern.

He hit the button and jumped off the skiff toward the CAT. The skiff slowly rose up to about a foot and a half above the rocky ground beneath it, then started gradually gliding forward. It reached the end of the outcropping, then gently dropped right off the end and sunk quietly into the lake where it continued at an almost 90 degree angle, straight down into the abyss. Thor looked around quickly, then jumped into the CAT and sealed the door, allowing its remote driver back onboard the Phoenix to take it from there as he laid down next to Sky and strapped himself in, sighing with relief. As the slender, capsule style transport slowly submerged itself into the water, "flying" deep into the depths of the lake toward the submerged Carrier, he closed his eyes and grasped her hand, taking a moment to thank God that she was still alive... still by his side.

Thor stood beside Sky as she lay on the examination table, hooked up to a fluid drip to help rehydrate her and spur tissue regeneration after the extreme blood loss she suffered. Astrydd was going over some X-ray films of her rib cage and typing some information into the computer next to Regina, who was in the bed next to her's. Thor could see clearly that the bottom two ribs were broken, but what really concerned him was the skeletal form of Ar'Jvikkah, vividly shown on the monitor in front of him.

The X-ray only caught the top half of the young alien's body, but it was clear to the casual observer that this was indeed the skeleton of a fully developed human fetus! He just started to open his mouth to ask Astrydd her thoughts on the subject when Connor, laying in restraints in another observation bed, beat him to the punch.

"Looks like she was very lucky that the baby boy wasn't injured," he commented to Thor while trying to stay calm, "those ribs broke right into his zone, yet he seems to have been miraculously shielded somehow. He *is* yours, yes?" he asked politely. "I mean, you seem to be obviously deeply concerned for her..." Astrydd glanced at Thor, then quickly looked away, trying not to give him away.

"Yes, they're mine," he smiled warmly, feeling a sense of pride in the statement he did not expect. "Thank God they're all fighters!" He gestured also at Regina, rolling his eyes and exhaling in relief. "This was a scare I won't soon forget!"

"Yeah, I know what you mean...." He started to look impatient and pulled against the straps on his wrists as he lifted

213

his head to look Thor in the eyes. "Anyway... did I miss something? One minute we were about to get rescued, then you attacked me, and now we're here... why? I mean, it looks like they came back for us, right? We're onboard one of the Carriers?" Thor looked at him for a moment, silently deciding what to say to him.

"Remove his restraints," he said to Astrydd, who set down the handheld diagnostic scanner after passing over Regina again and complied. Connor quickly sat upright, rubbing his wrists and then winced, feeling the back of his head.

"Ouch! Damn it, man," he complained, getting stuck for a moment on the large knot left behind from getting pistol whipped with the flare gun. "Alright, now can you please tell me just what the fuck *this* was all about?"

"Fair enough," Thor replied, walking slowly toward Connor as he spoke. "Let me ask you a question first. Imagine there was a chance to fix something... something terrible that someone else brought upon you. You would be saving lives... hell, even saving an entire race from extinction, perhaps... and possibly even reuniting loved ones who had lost each other... *family who had been lost, forever!* But to do it meant that you would be hunted, hated, branded a traitor, and separated from your people for the rest of your life, would you do it? Would you do what you knew was right? Would you have the courage, despite all the consequences?"

Connor sat for a moment, reflecting hard on what Thor just said, trying hard not to assume too much. "I think that throughout history, there have been many times that a mere conflict of interest between parties resulted in separatism and war, with little reason to justify it but money and greed. To go to any extreme for the things you mention would not only be the actions of a free mind, but also an example of the kind of courage and nobility worth following. I am no simpleton, my friend... *talk to me straight!* What's going on here?"

Thor took a deep breath. This decision should belong to Sky, and Sky alone... yet he could clearly see the larger picture transpiring here. If they wouldn't have intervened, her parents might have gone another way to search for her, having never seen the signal that brought them here, *because they intervened!* Like it or not, they *caused* this to happen, and therefore also caused everything that followed as a result, because they knew it was *going to happen*, and nothing, and *no one* could have prevented it.... From their point of view, *it already took place!*

The only decision left was whether or not to let them leave here without the knowledge of what really happens to them and risk a paradox while most likely sending them to their doom. Thor was pretty damn sure he knew where Sky would stand on that issue. If he did, he knew in his heart they would never make it home to their little girl anyway. Keeping them here wouldn't be *changing* anything... to the contrary, it would simply be filling in, on an old canvass, the final parts of a painting that had already started so many long years ago, but was missing some vital sections.

"Let me tell you about your daughter," Thor said with a humble smile.

CHAPTER 21: ERÜK

Thor had been walking around the ship for the better part of an hour, stuck mostly on the mental topic of Ar'Jvikkah's recent development into humanoid form. He greatly wished to have Erük's take on the subject, but his alien brother seemed to be nowhere to be found. He had tried a few times to summon him telepathically: once in the Biodome, once when he was close to the supply warehouse cargo bay, and once more only moments ago in the elevator, but he seemed to be completely unavailable. In fact, Thor was having trouble picking up on his energy at all, and was starting to become concerned.

He hit his belt com. "Hey, Bjorn... Would you locate Erük, please?" Thor closed his eyes, trying once again to home in on his energy.

"Captain, it appears he's not on board!"

"What the hell do you mean, not on board?"

"The computer scanned the entire ship... I even punched in the biorhythm analysis sequence we came up with the other night to account for shape-shifting... His personal signature is simply no longer onboard this ship!"

"Has there been any RAM or shuttle deployment?"

"No... but something that might be of interest... it appears there was a slight flutter in the shield parameters less than 10 minutes ago... similar to the reshaping of the parabolic deck shield just after an energy related attack. I didn't think anything of it, given the multitude of unknown life down here... just figured it was an electric eel of some kind, or something."

"Let me know immediately if it happens again, okay?"

"No problem. Anything else?"

"Yeah... How's Mr. Davies dealing with his new assignment? Any problems adjusting?"

"Not that I've witnessed. He's like a kid in a candy store! I think he's tickled pink to be able to do everything *his* way for a change... I think he was constantly living under the shadow of that asshole, Captain Parnell, who you dispatched! He's mentioned him several times now as if the man was his boss back on their CSE vessel. I haven't told him anything, but I'm getting the impression he'll deal with it just fine, anyway... I think he loathed the guy, and he's glad to be free from his stranglehold."

"Good job! Thanks, brother. Just do me a favor, will you?"

"Keep an eye on him?"

"Yes... Two when you can afford it! I'm not so sure his *de-programming* will stick, especially considering what he's leaving behind... He needs to see Sky awake. They need to talk. *Everything* might depend on it... this was *very* risky."

"I agree."

Erük swooped down as he swam, lower and lower through the canopy of plankton, fish, and small water creatures until he was back in the relatively calm waters of the deep lake, home to the stranger, more complex life forms of this planet. His race's accelerated genetic evolution had already kicked in again since fleeing the apocalypse on his home planet, and he had even developed the ability to breathe underwater. A small section of flesh behind the thin scales of his lower jawbone, just below his ears, had opened up like a sore, then scabbed over. A couple days later, when the scabs healed, they fell off, revealing a small set of gills, which he now used to breathe instead of holding his breath for long cycles as he tried to explore beyond the ledge the ship was hiding on.

Despite his kind's unbelievable lung capacity, and the ability to hold that breath for a ridiculously long time, and despite ignoring pressure differentials from depth, he had still been confined to short radius trips for the last couple days, returning to the safety and oxygen of the shield perimeter or surface for air, but now he could roam as far as he wanted. Something was driving him to find out more about this place. He was at ease here. He didn't know why, as it couldn't possibly be any more different than the dry, sandy plains and hills of his home world, but he felt connected to it somehow; comfortable. It simply *felt* like home.

As he swam deeper and deeper into the abyss, he started to notice that not only were the creatures here getting bigger and bigger, but they were also getting more intelligent. He was pleased, at least at first, that they were no longer running from him in terror; fleeing the very sight of him before he could even try to make any kind of contact, or really observe them close up. He could certainly understand this from their perspective, as down here, even more than other places in nature, *everyone* was in constant danger of being eaten alive by something larger, and at least within reasonable proximity of the canopy near the surface, Erük was among the largest being swimming these waters. Down here, he realized as he continued his decent, he wasn't among the largest by a longshot, and as he looked straight down at a large shadow that seemed to be growing beneath him, he became awash with a newfound sense of humility.

He looked around for a good direction to flee, and noticed every other creature that was just swimming nearby had already scattered completely, making him the only available snack in sight. "Shit!" he exclaimed out loud through the bubbles in English, which was quickly becoming more natural to him than his own native form of communication, for its simple vulgarity and addictively humorous nuances. The shadow seemed to envelop him entirely before taking any kind of actual form, and then he realized the nature of its true form... the source of the darkness. It wasn't really a shadow at all, blocking the light with a veil of darkness, but rather a cloud in the water itself... some kind of ink like that of Earth's octopi, jettisoned probably as camouflage for some kind of attack that was still imminent. He swam as fast as he could, knowing that at any moment, he might be in serious trouble.

He stretched his wings outwards, mimicking the motions of a creature he saw swimming extremely fast yesterday. He bolted for the surface, using his entire body to produce one big pulse at a time. This really seemed to enhance his speed, and within a few seconds, he was close to the edge of the darkness, finally able to see around himself again. He was just about to open his inner eyelids to clear his vision just a bit when he started seeing dead fish and other creatures all around him. Passing very close to one rather large creature, a manta ray type of bottom-feeder, he noticed that the cloud was actually a myriad of tiny parasites devouring the large creature, blood and all, as it slowly floated toward the surface, already reduced to skeleton in several places.

Its eyes were completely gone, as if that was the first thing "dissolved" in this morbid display of nature's fury. Now completely out of the cloud, he opened his inner eyelids, focusing in close on his own skin to make sure he wasn't being gnawed upon right now! He could see them trying here and there, but his skin seemed to be impervious to their attacks for some reason. He sighed, relieved, but felt a cold chill go up his spine as he realized that his eyes would have been devoured right out of his head, had he but blinked to try and focus while inside the cloud.

Looking back toward the floating corpses, he noticed that they were almost completely gone now, fully eaten and digested by these voracious microorganisms. He focused hard back toward the cloud, also noticing that the color of it, as well as the density, had changed dramatically. Zooming in as close as he could on just one of the little fiends, he could actually see it transforming right before his eyes! It went from something resembling a microscopic piranha, to what looked almost like a very small seahorse, now swimming quite independently, rather than swarming with the cloud, like part of a collective hive. He could actually see them growing before his eyes, appearing to continue to feed on the aftermath of the onslaught of devastation and rebirth they imposed upon the ecosystem not two minutes prior, until not one particle remained, wasting literally nothing in the process. Having grown to nearly an inch long each by this point, he realized he was witnessing a display of a rare level of efficiency seldom achieved in the universe!

Numbering in the tens of thousands, they scattered in every direction as a barrage of larger fish, knowing the drill, swept in to feed on this surplus of fledgling, unprotected orphans. Erük suddenly realized he was caught in the middle of a cyclic feeding frenzy that was unlikely to stop until it had run its course all the way to the top of the food chain, and though he deeply appreciated the academic stimulus he was being tickled silly with, he decided it might be prudent to move along and thank his lucky stars that he was just a tourist.

He spread his wings again and bolted for safer waters, this time down, past the Phoenix, straight toward the tunnel where he saw the flock of small creatures like the one they encountered through the shuttle's glass on their way into this underwater world. As he neared the Carrier, tucked safely away in the shadows beneath the canopy's many rock formations and tunnels, he heard several voices in his head... the loudest being the concern of a dear friend. He sent back only his love and reassurance that he was alright and would be back to join them as soon as he found whatever it was he was searching for.

Thor smiled, as right in the middle of his response Erük went speeding by, nearly straight down, looking as if he was truly enjoying himself. Even though he could sense for days that something was eating at Erük and that there was almost definitely something deeper driving him even now, it was still good to see his friend enjoying even the most fleeting moment of personal "fun." Thor turned and walked slowly and enviously back toward the cargo hold door, staring upward at the millions of gallons of displaced water above the deck that their shields were effortlessly and automatically keeping back, and he smirked, as he couldn't help but think of the many times he had witnessed complete electrical malfunction on any of the hundreds of cars and machines he had operated in his life.

Sky emerged from a drug induced dreamscape of groggy, displaced, and abstract images, fueled by the ambient voices and electronic sounds in the Medical Bay, the trauma and stress of the shuttle crash itself, and a strong regimen of morphine and heavy sedatives. For the first time in quite a while, she was actually quite sure she had just been dreaming, rather than experiencing another cosmically significant, first hand vision or shift to another plane of existence.

She blinked several times, having some trouble adjusting her eyes to the bright lights. Not really sure what had happened, or how long she had been here, she struggled to lift her head. She did fine until she started to pull from her abdomen to sit up, then screamed in agony as the pain from her broken rib cage became obvious. She gasped for air, becoming aware of some medical machinery hooked up to her that seemed to be helping her breathe. Starting to recall what happened, her mind flashed through a few scenes from the crash, and she forced herself to calm down.

Slowly, she relaxed her body, then started looking around the room. She could hear Astrydd banging around in the supply room, and was about to call for her when she noticed someone else. Laying on the bed to her other side, just starting to stir from all of her commotion, was her mother, rough as hell around the edges, and looking like she had been riding shotgun in the same crash, but it was her; as young and beautiful as Sky remembered her, having not aged a single day since the last time she saw her, nearly 20 long years ago. She gasped, tears instantly welling up in her eyes. She struggled to keep them clear, still not completely trusting her own vision after the psychedelia she just awoke from.

As Regina slowly started regaining consciousness herself, Sky's heart raced. She didn't know what she should do. She was too groggy to think straight, but was keenly aware that bringing her parents back here wasn't part of the original plan. She nervously glanced around the room for her father, but didn't see him. *What about paradox? What if we changed the past? What about the Fleet?* As her mother's eyes opened and slowly made contact with hers, she broke down completely, and suddenly none of it mattered. She was home.

Reaching an area surrounded almost entirely by small caves, he knew he was there. The hard part would be knowing which one to use. He tried to open his mind to their mundane chatter, but all was silent. It was as if they were hiding. He hovered for a moment out in the open, looking for what might be the intuitive choice, then he saw it.

One cave mouth, out of the dozens before him, was dark beyond dark. Two feet into the void and one could elude even the keenest predator. He tuned his senses into the *sound* of the place; the tiniest difference in the sound of his wings passing through the water, a grunt or chirp, or the resonant echo of his own beating heart allowed him to almost "see" the walls before coming into contact with them. He let out a long guttural hum, bobbing around in pitch and volume like the whale songs of Earth. Suddenly, but temporarily, he could "see" the entire cavern quite vividly.

He dodged a large pillar, a stalactite running full course into its corresponding stalagmite, giving evidence that perhaps this cavern wasn't always underwater. This truly intrigued him, but not so much as the rumbling of voices he was beginning to pick up on in his mind. He chose between two forks in his path, gravitating toward the chatter he was picking up on, and as it still grew in intensity, he learned to trust his instinctive navigation and focus only on what he was "hearing."

He became aware of a level of sophistication in their language he did not expect. In all the forms of communication he had come across in his very long life, including the language of the humans, he had never before bore witness to a race capable of this level of articulation… other than his own. It was because of this dynamic that his kind developed the predominant use of telepathy to begin with. Verbally, in his tongue, the same word could literally have over a hundred different meanings, or *intentions*, depending on the simplest, most minute difference in pronunciation or emphasis, tone, or placement... making verbal communication with any other race nearly impossible. It was simply too hard for any other race to ever learn all the nuances of their language. With telepathy, however, all these things simply became *feelings* conveyed through the mind of the recipient, and after only a short time, even a relatively primitive race could display a high degree of mastery using this technique, making deeper communication possible, and thereby avoiding so many chances for potential misunderstanding... the crux of the fundamental flaw with all communication.

Erük had stopped using his voice for sonar, and instead slowed way down, relying on the quiet subtlety of his own presence again for navigation, while being careful to appear as benign as possible to this reclusive race, who he could now sense were in full focus on him, and preparing to treat this as an invasion. He did his best to communicate with them telepathically, and apparently did it too well, as it seemed there was some confusion as to who was actually doing the speaking. He couldn't seem to get them to shake the notion that he was just some sort of water borne beast, wandering in here looking for food. *If only I could see their eyes... If only there was light!*

No sooner had he thought this to himself, not even trying to project it onto the surrounding creatures, when one by one they started to glow. It was a warm blue light that seemed to come from deep within their body, as if it was some sort of self-generated electrical field. It was particularly bright right around their abdomen, but it also caused their eyes to light up, which sort of defeated the purpose for telepathy, as he needed to be able to see and feel the subtlety of the changes in pupil dilation and facial expression in order to delve into the deeper concepts conveyed through *unspoken* communication.

Passing close by one of them, he started to notice that something was replacing their fear. It wasn't aggression, just yet, but something more akin to bold curiosity. The small creature swam right up behind Erük and touched the tip of his tail, counting coup and shocking him in a quick and painful way, exactly as the one on the front glass of the shuttle had done to Thor. Erük spun around quickly, but the little devil was nowhere to be seen. His glow was apparently composed of a buildup of internal electrical energy, and as soon as released, would need to be built up again.

He looked outward, back in the direction he was originally headed, and saw a very unnerving sight. Emerging from every nook and cranny, from holes in the ceiling and floors, and coming toward him from right out of the darkness itself were literally tens of thousands of these creatures! Still, Erük did not sense an impending attack, and could almost feel their emboldened curiosity growing as their leader drew near. *I come in peace! I will not harm you... and I will not fight you.* One by one, they started to fade to black, leaving Erük in the dark with three very obvious revelations.

They were undoubtedly capable of energy manipulation, if not transmutation itself, and they lived and operated as a hive with a collective conscious very similar to Erük's hyper-evolved race of dragons. Floating weightless in the darkest of dark, surrounded by thousands of kindred spirits, he stood apart; left to his own devices due only to his different appearance... just as with the humans. Despite the wondrous nature of this incredible discovery, he had never in his long life felt so utterly alone.

Gazing deep into her mother's eyes as she awoke, Sky understood completely what Thor had done, and understood the fact that this was the only way. Some part of her, albeit a slightly selfish part, had greatly desired this outcome. *Had I caused it in any way? We had no choice, did we? This already happened... We caused this to happen by being here now... 20 years ago... This is where they went when they disappeared! They didn't die, they left with me... that's why it never felt right... that's why I never felt closure...* "That's why I blacked it all out!" she smiled, nearly shouting as she became awash with genuine happiness... excited, not only at having her mother back, but also at finally beginning to understand the connectivity of these events, both past and present, that had left such a gaping void in her being throughout every single day of her troubled young life.

Astrydd looked down at her while preparing a shot for Regina's I.V. tube and smiled as if she had any idea what Sky was talking about. Regina, however, started to look a little scared. She was obviously in a lot of pain, and since Astrydd had her on heavy medication, she was having a very hard time keeping her eyes open, let alone focusing on this person lying next to her bed... looking so very familiar, yet so totally different.

Suddenly the door slid open and her father burst into the room, nearly hysterical. He ran up to her, then paused, having a hard time with what he was seeing. "I heard you were awake! Jesus Christ, baby girl, this is so strange!" He gazed deep into her eyes, seeing his daughter instantly, but seeing so much more. "My God, have we really missed so much?"

"You've missed nothing, Dad... but I have. I've missed you both so much! You've been gone *so* long! I honestly thought I'd never see you again... I thought you both died!" He wrapped his arms around her, suddenly noticing the large protrusion in her stomach again, and jumped, trying very hard to take it all in stride.

"Yes, I think I definitely missed *something*," he said, sarcastically looking down at her belly, then back up into her ice blue eyes; the one thing about her that hadn't changed a bit. "You'll have to bear with me... with us," he gestured toward Gina's bed, "it doesn't just *seem* like yesterday... for us it *was* yesterday!" He started to get choked up, having trouble getting the next part out. "And Captain Krey tells us that you're actually stuck inside that cave, the pyramid mountain, *right now!* That our little girl is going to grow up for the next 20 years without her parents... Suffer all the grief of losing us... and there's nothing we can do about it! That if we try, we'll either cause a paradox that will erase *your* reality, or we'll be denied in every other attempt, and probably die ourselves, still leaving you on your own! I don't know what to do! Kaitlyn, my love, I can't just leave you there..." His eyes started welling up with tears as he hugged her tightly.

"You already did... but it was *my* fault, Dad! Don't blame yourself! You don't need to *do* anything! You're back! *I'm* back! Just stay with me! I couldn't bear to lose you again! You don't know the pain that has caused me!"

"The last 24 hours have given us a pretty good idea what that feels like, Kaitlyn, to be sure!" She smiled, closing her eyes, and pulled him in for another hug.

"What is it?"

"No one has called me Kaitlyn in a very long time... since you guys disappeared."

"A seer onboard the Helios told us that was your name when I was pregnant with you... said you were an old soul reborn by her own free will. Kaitlyn means-"

"The pure. I remember... in Gaelic." She looked over her father's shoulder to see her mother, now fully awake and coherent, looking deep into her eyes for something.

"Your ancestors were from the northern shore of Ireland and the Scottish Highlands... descended from the Norse who drove out the Saxon occupation."

"I changed my name to Sky after you d-... after you left."

Her mother closed her eyes, smiling warmly, "You always had a fascination with the sky, in every picture, movie... book. I'm not surprised! Cheops was the first sky you ever witnessed with your own eyes!"

"It hasn't been the last... We have some serious catching up to do!"

"Jesus, Mary and Joseph, it's really you, baby girl..." Sky ripped the I.V. out of her arm and struggled to get up out of bed, first taking a long breath out of the oxygen mask next to her, then setting it back down on the end table. She sat up, as did her mother, both dying to embrace the other, but both internally wounded, and having serious trouble standing.

"Hey!" Astrydd yelled from across the room at them, rushing to their side.

"Hey Doc, help me out, they're both too stubborn... they're going to do this no matter what we say, so let's make it easier for them!" He started pushing Sky's bed toward Gina's and Astrydd quickly backed him up, removing the bedding and fluid lines between them and helping to straighten the gap between the beds. The three of them held each other without saying a thing for what seemed like another 20 years, each of them positive, for their own selfishly justified reasons, that defying fate was the correct thing to do. For whatever reason, they had been given a second chance at a life together, and no amount of protocol or temporal-quantum hypothesis was going to deprive them of this. Family was simply more important.

Perched high in the trees, still depressed and dripping wet from his "eye opening" swim, Erük looked calmly down through a crack in the air ducts above the Medical Bay at the reflection in the mirror of Sky and her parents' heartfelt reunion. He thought of the agreement between them all regarding temporal intervention and timeline interference... how any possible paradox was simply not worth the potential gain. Though he felt like he understood the logic behind their decision, he couldn't help but feel that the source of it was ultimately nothing more than an opportunistic knee-jerk of hypocritical privilege afforded those who are truly in control, and so often, denied those who are not.

After stewing on the situation, then slowly coming to peace with it and becoming truly happy for Sky as he knew he should be, he caught the reflection of her internal scan on the monitor next to her bed. He forced his vision to focus closer, opening his inner eyelids for clarity. It was Ar'Jvikkah, of course, but he had quickly adapted to her metabolism and pure-form DNA, evolving in a very short time to an almost completely human form. He was astounded! Though this seemed to be an anomaly of extreme genetic importance, it also marked the end of his species, as Ar'Jvikkah was the last of their kind capable of reproduction, and now he was no longer like them.

Suddenly he was back in the cave, surrounded by life, yet utterly alone. He stared at Sky and her family, thinking hard about the last star scan he conducted with Bjorn, and how he scanned back in the direction they came from to see the binary twin, Algol, still intact a full 20 years before the impending supernova that would seal the fate of his entire species, and he understood now why Ar'Jvikkah didn't evolve into a queen to preserve the species. He sighed... the weight of an entire race of beings resting squarely on his very shoulders. *They were all still alive...* for now.

CHAPTER 22: THE VINDICATORS

"Why am I still here?" McGinn asked, almost at a yell in order to be heard from the top of the mountain peak he now sat still on. He was sitting in seiza position, deep in meditation with his eyes closed for nearly an hour before they answered him. Looking down through the clouds on the small settlement in the making, he knew the persistence of time could only be his ally.

You are not finished, the voice boomed into his mind, perceived, but definitely not imaginary.

"I was cut in half, my Lord, there are limits to what I can achieve from the planes to which I am confined!"

Confined? It would appear to us that you are anything but confined! We have had no choice but to imprison others who have achieved what you have done! Do NOT take this lightly! Stay on track... you will find a way. We have foreseen it. There is a reason we sent you above all others, but do not underestimate him again!

"Forgive me, my Lord, it's just that this would be so much easier with my body still intact..."

Then get it back.

"I will, my Lord, I will. I have a plan."

Do not harm the young traveler, he is of great importance... and above all else, beware of paradox! Be sure you do not tear the fabric of this plane any further... Krey could use this to his advantage.... He could use it to free his father. The Usurper must NOT be allowed to escape! See to this matter <u>immediately</u>. His strength is already growing! He must not be allowed to learn transmutation... he must not be allowed to reach Earth!

Kieran exhaled loudly and opened his eyes. They were still glowing slightly from his severed connection, making his physical vision a little blurry. He strained to see the goings on of the busy human settlers at the base of the mountain below the cloud canopy, but couldn't make out much detail. They seemed to be taking advantage of the break in the weather as the storm shifted to the east to kick production into high gear, shuttling supplies into the caverns at an almost ant-like rate and moving the displaced earth from the newer shafts further and further downward toward the construction site as they laid the foundation for a new colony of some serious magnitude.

He took a moment to gaze out over the valley. Being at the pinnacle of the tallest mountain on the planet, he could almost see *over* the storm's center, clear across the plains to the lakes and marshes of the great wetlands; soon to be frozen over entirely by the giant tempest that engulfed the southern hemisphere. It was a last look at what would then all be terraformed beneath the ice to produce a type of thick vegetation in its wake; an ultra-resilient, rugged, moss-like ground covering altered genetically to use the exact levels of radiation from the surrounding stars to its fullest efficiency in order to produce more oxygen than even the plankton of Earth combined with its former blanket of plant life... a milestone marking the shift in its global tide, bringing with it a new era of potential life to Cheops while simultaneously marking the dawn of its eventual demise. *The coming of mankind.*

He pulled his energy toward his center, allowing his molecules to swirl loosely but purposefully in the wind. A warm ethereal glow surrounded him as he relinquished his hold on the material plane and became as the other spirits of the great mountain. He was amazed at how easy it was here. He had nothing more to do but to will it, and it was done. Something here allowed him to linger in the material plane in whatever form he wished, crossing back and forth as easily as drawing breath. He didn't understand it, but it felt good. He closed his eyes and smiled broadly. It felt *very* good.

He knew now why the thousands of other souls had gravitated toward this place, but he could never find solace here. He, above all else, required purpose. To him, life was a ladder. You are either climbing up, or you're climbing down. You never stay in one place longer than is necessary to rest. Life was a ladder, and this place… this crossroads in space and time was a doorway; and in his upbringing, it was considered rude to linger in the doorway with the door open. *Walk through and close it behind you!*

He continued to swirl in the wind, picking up speed as the wind did, gradually turning into a visible whirlwind of some size. He pulled his energy tight to his core, focusing his will in an arrogant, but solid manner, into the form of a large raptor, something akin to an eagle, yet larger and many times more aggressive in stature. He let out a squawk that was heard by nearly everyone working below, then turned his attention downward, swooping toward the ground at terminal velocity. He pulled back at the last moment, gliding carelessly over the wind-torn treetops of the foothills, looking only with his periphery and feeling his surroundings as he coasted safely across the terrain.

He started following a small convoy of flatbeds with one shuttle for a leader heading up a small, winding valley toward the backside of the mountain. Gliding safely in the blind spot of the soldiers and miners riding on the flatbeds, he could hear their thoughts and some of the chatter and gossip between them. There was talk of the little girl, Kaitlyn, turning up at dawn from within the front mouth of the main caverns, full of stories about spirits, ethereal creatures, shape-shifters, and visitors from the future. They all laughed, but then started trading stories themselves of the ethereal doppelgangers they had all been hearing about since day one.

They finally conceded that they were probably all barking mad from extended space flight, but the hard fact was that nearly every deep recon trip through the mines had ended in someone coming out of the caves hysterical about seeing movement in the walls, people they knew who were dead, or just a thick mist, twisting and writhing in a most peculiar and human-like fashion. Then there was the issue of the true origin of the pyramid itself... It had been revealed in a couple places after the gale force winds had eroded much of the topsoil from the mountain's crest that beneath the mundane camouflage of thousands of years of natural deposits from windstorms and heavy, mineral rich rainfall was the shell of an actual manufactured pyramid! Though its origin was unknown to Fleet scientists thus far, it very closely resembled the great pyramid of Giza back on Earth for which the planet itself was named, and was carbon dated as having been manufactured very nearly at the same time in history, giving rise to a flood of speculation and curiosity.

Management couldn't afford to shut down operations for a full investigation, so these stories were almost invariably discredited by reason of "ether outgassing" in the soil causing hallucinations and dizziness while small teams of scientists were sent into different parts of the structure after they were opened for mining to investigate further. This infuriated the Science Division, as the potential for discovery was being utterly stifled by the contamination of every archaeologically significant finding in the entire pyramid by mining operations. As far as Admiral Reid was concerned, the acquisition of fuel and advancement of his Fleet was all that really mattered, and though discovery and possible contact with another species of intelligent life was intriguing, the only *real* purpose the scientists' research was serving was to provide stability to the myths and gossip about the beings living within, and keep the worker bees in line.

The scientists' findings were always intercepted and filtered through Reid's desk, where he put whatever spin on them that was necessary in order to maintain a veneer upon the whole operation that everything was under control, and that the creatures were harmless and possibly nothing more than the "ghosts" of the same race of being who built the pyramid in the first place. The more educated among them knew better, but for most, this made enough sense for them to continue working without fear since no one had yet been attacked by one; but the level of curiosity could not be so easily contained.

Workers were signing on in record numbers hoping to get a glimpse of these "ghosts." Much to the Admiral's shortsighted satisfaction, this did help speed up the mining effort, but it also succeeded in feeding into paranoia all the combined theories and speculation, pushing the effect of the entire situation, fueled by an ever growing mob mentality, right to the hairy edge of a complete social meltdown and Fleet-wide panic. They had already been continuing on about their work for some time like this… teetering on the brink, and needing only the slightest nudge to ignite the powder keg. Kieran smiled on the inside, resisting the urge to mess with these men on an epic level, considering his treatment while onboard the Phoenix under old management. Lucky for them, he had more important things to accomplish.

As they reached the backside of the mountain, a stormy, flooded impasse of fallen rock, trees and mudslides until just a day ago, they started parking and unloading gear into the mouth of a large cave under a section of the mountain that was so shielded by the surrounding topography that you could almost pass within ten feet of it without noticing it was there. The high wind and flooding of the storm had unearthed the roots of a couple large trees and exposed it from straight above to the view of H.O.R.U.S., and after a quick Ground Ops reconnaissance mission and a day of road excavation, it was ready for exploration and mining to commence.

By the time their equipment was loaded into the caves, and power lines put into place from the generator on one of the flatbeds, it was near mid-day, the one time of day when all three of the closest suns were visible at the same time. It only lasted for about twenty minutes, depending on the season, but during that time the UV's became unbearable and the temperature rose nearly forty degrees Fahrenheit. Kieran decided it might be prudent, given his present connection with ether, to get as deep into the caves as possible before this happened, but first he made a quick detour to the lead vessel of the convoy: a shuttle craft sitting just under a sheltered outcropping near the base of the mountain.

He flew down from his perch in the trees and when he was sure no one was left outside, he whisked into the doorway of the shuttlecraft, regaining the form of a very opaque, glowing version of his former self. Seeing his reflection in the shiny metal surface of one of the security panels for the wiring harnesses, he became enraged and looked away as quickly as possible, seeing flashes in his mind's eye of the fight on deck during the tachyon wave that cost him his human body. He closed his eyes and took a huge breath... soothing, though completely unnecessary in this form. He relaxed a moment, then got back to business.

He sat in the pilot's seat; unable to disengage the fail-safe's for accidental ignition, as there was no actual physical weight in the chair. He became frustrated all over again. "KREY!!!" He yelled at the top of his lungs. Sitting there, mentally exhausted, he suddenly noticed something of particular interest tucked between the panels on one of the consoles. It was a photograph of a pilot, probably the man he just saw landing this very shuttle, standing next to Captain Parnell on the deck of a Carrier. Parnell was pinning a medal on his lapel, and in the background he recognized the bulkhead around the bay door to the cargo hold on what was definitely the Phoenix.

He grinned devilishly, studying every detail of the photograph: the lines on the man's   face, his expression, his eyes, how he stood, how he smiled. Looking very close, he could make out the name "MacAave" on his uniform. He flipped the picture over. There was an inscription on the back from Captain Parnell, reading:

Nicolas, Welcome aboard, old friend! Good to have you at my six!

"Yes, welcome aboard… *old friend!*" he chuckled to himself, smiling from ear to ear.

––––––––––––

The cavern was very unique and very stable, requiring little or no shoring, except for the new branches the men were mucking out as they followed what appeared to be a 9 foot wide vein of pure rhodochrosite, a deeply red crystalline mineral that has the same properties as iron pyrite, but is vastly more pure and pound for pound was worth more than gold back on Earth! It didn't show up on the preliminary scans of the mountain due to all the interference and the thickness of the pyrite in the soil, but upon opening the mountain's backside, it seemed to be in extreme abundance, and might have even accounted for the shape of the original structure, itself, as rhodochrosite actually grows in the shape of a pyramid.

Given its reputation with the mystics and battery-like properties with electricity, it could easily have been the source of all the paranormal activity they were experiencing here. To the Fleet, however, it represented something vastly more important. It was another step in the evolution of their technology, as it seemed to far surpass the ferrous crystal they now harvested from planet after planet as a fuel source, as well as show promise for use as a magnetic "repellant" capable of keeping even the largest Carrier hovering over a large planet with little or no thruster burn. The only substance that had ever worked even half this well was intercepted and harvested from a series of small meteors that were believed to have broken off of a larger planet during some sort of cataclysmic storm or solar disturbance. It was the quest for this very "crystal" that sent them in this direction in the first place, backtracking the path that the meteors originally came from.

The crew had worked the last few days right through the storm to expand one of the natural rooms in the cavern into a large staging chamber, tunneling downward and installing platforms as they went; utilizing large timbers they hauled in from the surface, and returning to their quarters on the CSE mother ship just long enough to get 3 to 4 hours of rack time per night before they were right back on it the next morning. This small group of professionals were Parnell's Journeymen: a highly trained and highly capable elite task force of men and women worker/ soldiers that CSE sent in before anyone to establish the preliminary plans for the development of any potentially dangerous site. Though they were usually sent in to specific hotspots immediately after Ground Ops did their first reconnaissance sweep of a new area, then moved into the office to draft designs and oversee operations, they had been sent back into the field this time after the discovery of this new "back door" to the pyramid.

McGinn slithered through the darkest shadows of the cave, zeroing in on the noise of the crew as they inched the project forward. Three of them were putting a large, full sized timber into place in the staging room, hoisting the massive tree, branches still jutting out here and there, all the way to the top of four levels to be used as a support beam for the upper floor. It was here that they were setting up to store, separate, and transport all of the good ore, and send the debris back outside via railcar to be dumped out of the mouth of the mine onto a great muck slide. Two of them had a hold on the lines, supporting its weight, while the third struggled to line the end up with a notch cut into the wall itself. He took note of each of their faces as he slid by them, feeling the cold, damp wall slowly change to air again as he passed into the corridor leading toward the other ones.

As he came around a large bend in the tunnel that was necessary to get around a very solid deposit of granite, he felt a difference in the composition of his surroundings. Everything had a kind of looseness to it, as if the entire zone was incredibly unstable. Hearing their voices only twenty feet or so down the corridor, he instinctively faded back out of sight, realizing after just a moment that he had faded so deep into the rock face that he was starting to emerge out from behind the giant boulder into another corridor running almost parallel behind them! *Perfect,* he grinned to himself, slowly approaching the trio of engineers diligently working at clearing the fallen debris from a cave-in that separated these two corridors.

He allowed himself to transcend the physical boundaries of this place entirely, seeing for the first time that he wasn't the only casual observer here. Standing within a stone's throw of the unsuspecting humans who only aided their efforts at concealment with their devotion to the blinders they donned with their superior intellect were several of the ethereals, now visible to him for the first time for exactly what they were... *a race of lycanthropes!* Originally very similar to the werewolves of Earth legend, it was probably a good thing that the humans could not see them until they shifted their appearance into something else. Humankind had an annoying tendency to attempt to annihilate anything that frightened them, so this species would have undoubtedly been scheduled for genocide without a second glance!

It seemed they were no longer in their prime material form, and yet they were unable to take on their true form. Somehow their shape-shifting energy had trapped them in this place between places; unable to die and unable to move on, as they seemed to be pinned to this place and its powerful battery for spiritual energy. It was like a magnet to them. They were lost souls from an already ethereal race, set adrift on a rogue body from another world that had been caught in the intense gravitational pull and destroyed by the blue giant.

It was obvious to McGinn that they could see him, but for some reason they seemed uninterested; their attention glued to the humans as if they were in awe... as if they *envied* them. He turned his attention back toward the crew, jumping back a bit when he realized the female was now facing him, waving her light-stick around and looking right *through* him. Though he was entirely invisible to them, he had root in their world to some degree, and her keen female intuition had picked up on it! For a moment, her eyes actually seemed to be looking directly at his, and he started to wonder if she saw him, at least in some capacity. To her it just felt like that nagging sensation of being watched; so common, so misunderstood... so easily dismissed.

Her eyes were beautiful. In this artificial light, he couldn't really tell if they were green or brown, but they were deep; vast portals into the mind of a person wise beyond her years. Her hair, though only slightly beyond shoulder length, flowed like a river of warm sunshine and her lips seemed to be on the verge of a soft whisper at all times. He found her intoxicating. He realized his feelings were probably being amplified by the fact that she was entirely beyond his grasp, but he had never been so utterly distracted by a woman's beauty before.

"Hey Angela," one of the two men spoke up without pausing his task to turn around.

"Hey, *Nick*..." she said back with a playful, yet snotty aire about her.

"You know what really burns my arse?" he asked loudly.

"A match?" the other man answered for her.

"Flames, this high!" He turned around toward her, pinching her ass and laughing loudly with a sarcastic, pompous, guttural laugh that sounded something like the combination between a snorting pig and a drunken gorilla at a frat party. His face shown in the light for a moment and Kieran knew, even from the old, badly shot photo onboard the shuttle, that it was MacAave. There was absolutely no mistaking that pointy-nosed, buck toothed mug that reeked of British, White Anglo-Saxon Protestant heritage, handed down with a fading Scottish accent from his father's side, and an undeserved sense of entitlement he had probably been wearing like a cheap suit ever since he was old enough to spell.

"I've got a match," the other man continued, unconcerned with the fact that he had completely missed his cue, "my ass and your face!" He smiled proudly as MacAave shut up instantly and glared at him while Angela burst out laughing uncontrollably.

"Very funny! If your pickaxe was as sharp as your wit, we'd be past this cave-in already! Seriously, people, I'm going back around to the other side to pry on the boulder, and I want you two to stop giggling like schoolgirls and try to muck this loose from this side with poles, shall we? Or do we need to make a match out of my *boot* and your arse?" He grabbed up one of the 10 foot steel poles used for mucking out collapsed areas and reopening closed mines after a cave-in, then started down the dark tunnel, brushing rudely past Geoff, his partner, and leaning in toward Angela on the way by. "Give us a kiss for the road, Lass?"

"Yeah, I've got somethin' you can kiss," she said rudely, flamboyantly turning her backside toward him.

"Careful what you ask for..." MacAave sneered as he turned away and started to walk down the dark corridor toward McGinn while fishing in his pocket for a light stick. Kieran was seriously starting to dislike this asshole. McGinn was many things... an assassin whose job forced him to lie, cheat, steal, and kill; but lewd conduct toward women was one thing he could not abide. In fact, he despised rudeness, in general, more than just about anything. There were many things he was guilty of, but he lived by a code, and would kill or die before breaking it.

Kieran stood in the middle of the corridor as MacAave approached with a shit-eating grin on his face. He cleared his mind, expanding his awareness to include everything around him. The lycanthropes had backed off, all but disappearing into the vastness of the mountain around them, and he was free and centered, absorbing everything about Nicolas MacAave as he passed right through his true core of energy. McGinn smiled, instantly becoming aware of even the most sorted and obscure of personal details of this man's life: his fears, his insecurities, his mannerisms, and yes, his memories. He felt great satisfaction in realizing that he had been repeatedly shot down in flames by Angela for well over a year, and though he was liked by most for his sense of humor, he had become a bit of a laughing stock over his unrequited infatuation with her.

"Seriously, Nick, we *do* need to hurry! There's a lot more mapping left to do before we reconnect with the others," she yelled out at him as his dim light faded around a corner into the darkness, as did the sound of his steps. Geoff was already hard at work again, practically lying on top of the loose pile of mud and rock, stabbing with the barbed end of the steel pole up at the small hole atop the pile, next to the ceiling. There seemed to be a large boulder protruding downward from above, wedged geometrically between two other large pieces of granite that kept it from falling any further.

He kept stabbing at it and stabbing at it, until he had most of the hole expanded to about a foot in diameter, and about three feet inward. "Pass me up a light, ma'am," he grunted down at Angela, who was trying to back him up by removing as much debris as she could from below, and clearing everything new that he was kicking down her way as he proceeded.

"No problem, Sir," she said with the same light hearted respect, mistaking his old school manners for playfulness. She quickly handed him a light stick and he cracked it, shaking it until the blue light combined with her's brightening their whole side of the cave-in. He crawled up as tightly as he could toward the hole by the ceiling, light stick in his mouth, and struggled to see into the hole. He reached back toward her, snapping his fingers on his right hand, while clinging desperately to the point of the protruding boulder with his left. She quickly handed him the pole. He aligned it with the hole, pulling way back in preparation for a powerful thrust.

He bit down on the light stick and belted out some kind of loud battle cry through his teeth as he started his thrust. All at once, it exploded; dirt, rocks and debris spraying him in the face as the point of MacAave's pole came bursting through from the other side, knocking him over backwards from his own over-reaction. He tumbled to the bottom of the small rockslide, embarrassed, but laughing hysterically, as Angela scrambled to help him to his feet. "I think we're there!" she exclaimed, laughing herself, and helping to brush the dust off of her partner.

"Right," Geoff grunted, as dignified as was possible, then picked up the light stick and continued from ground level to loosen the rocks at top of the pile. The glow from MacAave's light stick shone strongly through the gap at the top, and tasting blood, they turned up the volume, clearing more and more out of the way as he worked at it from the other side. The obstruction was a good three feet wide at the top, and they now had about two feet of working room cleared away, the majority being done from Angela and Geoff's side, since due to their ability to clear the debris out of their own way, MacAave was pushing it through to them, rather than pulling inward toward himself.

This made strategic sense, but had Geoff in a pretty compromising position, his whole body now lying atop the muck pile at an upward angle, trying hard to reach up with his pole and pull down the pieces MacAave shoved through to him, while the giant boulder loomed overhead, now touching him right between the shoulder blades as he worked. Angela was behind him and to his left, trying to assist in clearing the larger pieces, while staying out of the way of Geoff's right elbow and the steel pole as he thrust repeatedly at the roof of the small opening in an attempt to dislodge a section of rock that seemed to extend off to the right. Nicolas picked up on his strategy and started to back him up, smiling at Geoff as he could finally see his face through the opening.

Geoff felt a slight vibration, something akin to the bass rumble in the abdomen during a good concert, then nothing.

He wasn't sure what it was, and was just about to ask MacAave what he thought, when it started again. He was staring directly into Nicolas's eyes when he felt the tickle of movement between his shoulder blades. All he could remember was seeing it change to pure terror as he shot straight backwards, knocking himself unconscious on the protruding rock point as he mowed right over Angela, sending them both tumbling down the pile, backwards into the open corridor. The last thing Angela saw before the lights were buried in rock and mud, and a giant dust-cloud filled the cavern, was the enormous, wedge-shaped boulder falling through the ceiling and slamming into the ground right in front of them, missing them by only inches as it displaced the entire muck pile.

She sat up in the darkness, dazed, extremely disoriented, and unsure if she was injured or not. She quickly felt around for Geoff, her instincts taking over, and lifted his arm when she found him. She felt that he had a strong pulse, then called out for Nicolas, realizing there was no sound coming from his direction. Her voice echoed in both directions. After checking his body quickly for blood or broken bones, she propped Geoff into a slightly more natural position and started crawling toward the cave-in, hoping for the best, but fearing the worse. She could feel something wet and sticky on the rocks and feared it was blood, but then she found the broken plastic shell from a light stick immediately afterward just a few inches away and sighed with relief.

The opening seemed to be constricting and she started to turn around, when her hand rested on what she realized had to be the bottom of a boot! She started pulling on it as hard as she could muster, but realized it wasn't going to budge, and she started to understand why. She became overwhelmed and started to get very dizzy, temporarily losing her sense of up and down, along with the obvious lateral confusion. From a few feet away she heard a familiar, very exhilarating groan.

"Geoff!" she yelled, crawling back toward him as quickly as possible. "Jesus Christ, Geoff, Are you okay?" She reached him from the legs first, and quickly grabbed at his feet to see if he was still wearing both of his boots. Fearing the worse for MacAave, she found them intact.

"My God," he groaned shakily, feeling around for her, "did that really happen?" Angela started laughing hysterically out of nervous delirium as he fumbled in his cargo pockets for something. "There it is," he said proudly, the shakiness still in his voice as he cracked the last light stick and shook it with what little strength he could muster.

As soon as the blue light started to fill the corridor again, they both saw him. Down on one knee and shaking his head just a few feet away from them was MacAave. He stood up, looked at both of them and smiled, then started picking through his pockets and straightening his clothes as if nothing had happened at all. "Thank God!" Angela exclaimed, helping Geoff to his feet, "I feared the worst! What a mess!"

"I'm alright," Geoff explained, shaking free of Angela's hold, then gratuitously brushing the back of her hair and jacket in return. "Thank you, ma'am... Now, let's get the hell out of here, shall we?"

"After you, Sir..." She gestured with her arm toward the direction of the shuttle, back down the dark corridor. She turned to MacAave and smiled as he gestured the exact same way, extending the courtesy to her and offering to take up the rear. Feeling like they were about to forget something, she took a quick look around before following Geoff down the tunnel, still very dazed from the incident, but utterly relieved that they were all in one piece after a close call like that.

They emerged from the series of tunnels and scaffolding to a picturesque setting of the last sun for the day, only minutes away from dusk on Cheops; a fascinating twilight comparable to the false dusk of the western fjords of

Norway or Alaska in the summer, when the sun never quite sets, but rather, just dips its tail into the hazy waters of the great oceans of Earth, only to rise back up for another cycle. Here, this season lasted but mere weeks, but then is replaced with several different degrees of bluish "summer" and one weeklong eclipse of near total darkness, save for the constant glow of the great blue nebula, as the sisters change places in an ever evolving dance around the blue giant, their father, Atlas.

The other skiffs had already retired to the compound for the night, but the shuttle remained untouched, and quite frankly, had never looked so inviting to them. Geoff, being the copilot in charge of pre-flight inspection, was naturally the first on board, practically running up the ramp to the warmth of the glowing cockpit. Angela stood aside and gestured for Nicolas to go next, as was protocol, MacAave being the captain and main pilot of the craft. He smiled at her and started up the ramp.

She was humming a tune she had stuck in her head for most of the day, when she looked down and saw something disturbing, having almost forgotten about it entirely. His boots were both on! She flashed in her mind to the struggle with the boot in the debris back in the cave, and realized that he couldn't have possibly gotten it back on in the time it took for them to see each other... *could he have?* She started to question herself as he slowly ascended the ramp.

Suddenly it became very clear to her. An action repeated a thousand times comes to bear... She had literally walked up *this* ramp behind *this* man so many times, she could not count, and there was not *one single time* that she did not compulsively listen to the purposeful thump and clack of his heavy leather combat boots stomping their way boisterously up this metal ramp on the way in. Every time... *except this one!* As he neared the top of the ramp, she realized he hadn't made a sound! Wide eyed with amazement, she quickly focused her vision on the boots themselves, and noticed that as he stepped, his feet weren't even quite touching the ground... *he was floating!*

She screamed for Geoff as loud as she could muster, and her amazement turned to horror as MacAave, now aware that she knew, stopped at the top of the ramp and turned around slowly to face her, his eyes beginning to glow as he rose up another foot off the floor. She started to back off, sensing that something terrible was about to happen, and caught her heel on a tree root that was protruding up through the soil, tripping and falling flat on her backside, still facing the imposter in terror. He slowly turned his hands palms out with his arms stretched out to the sides and began to raise his pitch as his eyes glowed brighter and brighter.

Suddenly his body thrust straight forward and his head whipped backward at the neck as Geoff slammed into his backside, focusing all of his momentum right between MacAave's shoulder blades. He flew straight outward from the shuttle without falling toward the ground, then seemed to lose his physical body altogether as he whisked around them in the form of a dense mist, regrouping a few yards away into an opaque version of Nicolas MacAave again, and then flew quickly back into the mouth of the cavern without a sound.

"What the fuck was that! And where's Nick?" Geoff yelled hysterically as he looked over at Angela.

"I have no idea what that was, but Nick's dead... and we need to go, NOW!" she sobbed, terrified, staring back toward the mine as she bolted up the ramp.

"Right behind you!"

CHAPTER 23: THE WEIGHT OF A WORLD

Erük concentrated deeply, trying to channel the wisdom of his elders in this time of intense tribulation. He had seen with his own eyes the destruction of his entire race and their homeworld, just as he had also seen how the determination of one single minded warrior could change the destiny of an entire race. *Our destinies were as large as we chose to live, and our reality truly is just a reflection of that choice... for better, or for worse!* Thor had taught him that. As he climbed closer and closer toward the surface of the lake in the shuttlecraft, he tried very hard to keep that one universal fact clearly in the center of all of his thoughts.

There would be a revolution on his planet, regardless. Of this he had no doubt, but the outcome was going to have to change. He would see to that if it killed him. Having come from a long life of servitude and communal, collective thinking, the level of independent grandeur and heroism he was about to exhibit was truly to carry the weight of an entire species on his back; the souls of a hundred thousand strong, held in the balance of his actions on this day, giving him

248

strength like none other in history, and the wind under his wings to accomplish the unthinkable... to overturn the universal verdict of fate, itself.

A myriad of lives hung in the balance: lives who, thousands of years earlier, were the very soul carriers of the human race. His kind brought them out of the darkness once already, and for their trouble, eons later, after they chose to live in harmony with nature once again, forsaking the technology that would have saved them, along with its demon seed light years from their sunken continent back on Earth, the father had hunted down the prodigal son and returned to damn them all.

Erük had spent weeks grappling with this inner conflict in his soul... right and wrong, the concept of paradox and fate, his own personal journey with Ar'Jvikkah and the new hope for their race that existed with their new family onboard the Phoenix. Thinking about the lives that still existed as of right now, lives that were already doomed by this savage race to be extinguished in just a few short years, lives like his own wife and child... he knew he had no choice but to try to save them. Thor and Sky had rigged this particular shuttle and one other, as a backup, for long range flight, just in case anything ever happened that would require them to leave the Phoenix and continue on their journey, since there was no Fleet to "scoop them up" should they have an accident or unforeseeable complication. He felt bad taking it, but more than that, he felt bad leaving without saying goodbye.

Upon seeing the large security detail's lights rushing toward the mountain like it was on fire, McGinn fled out one of the front openings, no longer having any real use for the approach he was attempting. The miners were simply getting too skittish of the ethereal creatures, and as soon as this evening's encounter got reported, there would probably be no getting onboard the CSE vessel from this side. He needed to find another small crew in some kind of isolated situation so that he wouldn't find himself up against the entire Fleet. Stealth was everything if he wanted to retrieve his physical body, still in cryostasis onboard the earlier version of the Phoenix.

In the blink of an eye, he ascended the mountain again for a better perspective. Upon reaching the top, he felt a small tingle of pride in seeing the sheer number of people trying to track him down below. It reminded him of the old days. At one time he had even called the penthouse of one of his victims, a Senator from Washington State who had been scheduled for termination by his own party after he sold them out during an investigation. The police were all over the house, and McGinn, using the Senator's own cell phone, called from an adjacent building top just to gloat. He actually truly enjoyed killing dirty politicians. To him, it always seemed like he was doing the world a favor, but the truth of the matter was, it really didn't matter who you were... if he was sent after you, it was either you or him. Simple. No questions, no pleading, no decision to be made; this was just an object in motion that will stay in motion until acted upon by an equal and opposite force... a black and white situation with only two possible outcomes.

He looked all around, staring out over the eastern plains in the direction the great storm had shifted, trying to figure out where to go from here. Amidst the flashes of light erupting from the dark pockets of activity swirling here and there behind the large center of the storm, he noticed a small beacon of light, pulsing up at him in a cyclic cadence from a tiny spot in the canyon that appeared to be moving. He could tell from the slow speed and the floodlight glow on the surrounding rock formations that it was a search party of some kind. They were too far away to have anything to do with the mess he had just caused, but they were definitely looking for something or someone in particular.

He tried to latch onto MacAave's memories to see if he knew anything about this, but seemed to come up blank. Remembering the way everything hit him all at once back in the cave, he decided to give something else a try. He focused all of his thought on the energy of Nicolas MacAave. Transforming entirely, right on the highest point of the mountain, he felt a rush of memories and emotion swell over him, just as before. In essence, he *became* Nicolas MacAave, in every way that mattered at the moment. He looked down again and it became much clearer. This was a small search party... *three people sent out to look for someone... for the missing parents of a little girl...* Sky!

He rushed down the mountain, floating several feet above the surface as he dodged between rocks and trees on his way toward the small craft. He had the vague memory of her speaking of this on the bridge of the Phoenix, but he had dismissed it at the time, and now it seemed the closest thing he could find to link him to his quarry. He would have to postpone his quest to be whole again if they were indeed hiding this close to the Fleet, and their former selves and focus on his primary mission. They were hiding on the edge of a razor, and this was the paradox that his superiors had warned him of. To stop it from happening and to retrieve Thorsson Krey or eliminate him was now his primary concern.

Erük emerged from the water near the center of the lake at an angle, speeding nearly wakeless across the surface of the electrified water as he used this cover to scan for visitors. To his surprise, there was a signature emanating from a mile or so to the southwest, in the direction of Thor and

Sky's crash. Too small to be any ship larger than a small skiff, he almost ignored it, but after some thought, he decided it wasn't worth risking their position if it turned out to be another search party. He altered his course, keeping as low and smooth as he could. He knew his repulsion thrusters wouldn't be seen from above, especially in this low light, but if he hit the mains, the heat signature from the burn would undoubtedly be spotted by the infrared scanners on the H.O.R.U.S..

"Hey Red! This doesn't look good," the young woman said through the com system on her EP suit, turning toward one of her two partners who were busy combing the landscape for any sign of their friends out here looking for their missing daughter.

The older man was kneeling in a tight little ravine, close to the stream, pawing around in the thin vegetation. "Well, someone came through here. The storm nearly wiped all trace of them clean, but you can definitely see signs of some sort of crash at this site. Look at how charred some of the ground plants are… way too many, and too large a radius to be lightning!"

"Then where's the wreckage?" Laura posed, gesturing out to both sides in a frustrated stance, then putting one hand on her hip, waiting for a reply.

"I don't know… tornado maybe? Or else, maybe there was-"

"Guys!" their other partner interrupted from just down the hill, near the pool of water at the bottom of a small waterfall. He was holding something large in his hands, examining it closely. "Check this out!"

As soon as their helmet lights were both pointed toward their friend, they could clearly see that he was holding an EP suit helmet in his hands! "This must have been the source of the signal!" Red and Laura both started spotting madly all over the rugged terrain with their lights as they approached their friend, still examining the helmet with a concerned look in his eyes. "Now that's odd…"

"What!?" Red demanded, a little short with their young pilot as he was growing increasingly concerned for the safety of his two best friends and their daughter. The man turned it sideways to reveal the insignia of the Phoenix, then lifted the face shield, revealing the print inside, confirming it. This helmet came from a suit issued onboard the Phoenix, which wasn't the home ship of the married pair of science officers, Connor and Regina Davies. They were both stationed onboard the CSE base ship and home office under John Parnell, as was their daughter, Kaitlyn.

They looked at each other quite perplexed, as the suits, and more specifically, the helmets, were coded upon issue to their one and only user for life, partially due to the personal nature of the water recycling function of the suit's hardware, but also so that in the event of a garbled transmission or operator in distress, the party receiving the transmission would be able to instantly identify who they were speaking with directly on their console. This was a bit hard to explain, because as far as they knew, the Phoenix was still in orbit, and had yet to even join the three other Carriers on the surface being outfitted as Harvesters and deployed out on the plains for mineral stripping.

"Doesn't make any sense," Red muttered, "Connor wouldn't risk that kind of trouble by using an unauthorized suit, not when he's got one of his own…"

"Could there have been another rescue attempt? A halo drop straight into the eye from orbit, maybe?" Laura posed.

"I've been on active duty since before they left," the young pilot asserted, "there was no such mission cleared for our airspace... I would've heard it!"

Red closed his eyes for a moment, then sighed heavily. "Let's call it in and ask."

"Whoa... Red, seriously... You know damn well they took that skiff illegally to get out here way before we could have! Fleet doesn't even know they're here! We'll be getting them in a world of shit!" Laura warned, grabbing Red's arm to stop him from stepping over to the skiff.

"I know, I know! I fear we're beyond that, now, don't you think? We need to be thinking about saving their lives by using every resource available! He did what any father would do! The Tribunal will consider that... if they're still alive!" He broke free of her grasp and walked purposefully toward the skiff, still parked next to the river bend, almost exactly where Sky had plowed into the dirt and water when she crash landed earlier. The young Ensign continued to scan all about with his small, hand-held spotlight, his keen instincts telling him that there was still much more to this than meets the eye.

––––––––––––

Sweeping quickly up on the source of the signal, Erük was running blind, using his superior night vision and homing in with intuition alone. He had killed all running lights in an effort to stay out of the view of the orbiting Fleet as the turbulence from the trailing end of the massive storm was starting to have a temporary clearing effect on the skies above. For the first time since their arrival, he could actually see a decent swath of sky, the millions of stars in an unusual pattern above him reminding him just how far from home they had actually strayed.

The ever-present blue glow of the nebula and Alcyone still radiated from everywhere like the light of a harvest moon, but beyond that were shapes he had never before witnessed. This system was alive with literally thousands of bodies, some dark, some colorful, some dead, and some so brilliant you couldn't stare directly at them without seeing spots afterward, even at night. One planet, in particular, caught his eye and he could not take his eyes off of it. From where he sat, almost glued to the inside of the windshield as he piloted the shuttle through the darkness, it looked like an almost exact twin of Sigyn, save for an intense glow about its many rings. It was apparently revolving fast enough that he could almost see the movement with his naked eyes, as was most everything in this system; the mark of a relatively young solar system, to be sure.

He was so perplexed by what he was witnessing here, along with its raw, savage energy, that he almost forgot what he was doing. He jumped, actually becoming startled by a crackle on the radio. They had been running in silence, due to the presence of the Fleet, but also void of chatter due to the storm's interference for so long that he had forgotten it was even turned on. The voice was unfamiliar to him, but extremely clear, undoubtedly due to the very close proximity of its transmitter.

"Search crew Alpha to CSE base... Come in.."

"CSE Base here... Commander Parnell. Go ahead, Alpha." Parnell? Erük couldn't believe his ears! His heart filled with rage as he pictured the man who fought them in the cargo bay of the Phoenix, resulting in the death of Ar'Yiisah, the sacred princess and successor to their Queen. This man's treachery knew no bounds, and in collusion with the evil one, Admiral Reid, himself, it was the direct cause of the annihilation of his entire race! Though he always knew that history would repeat, and these men were alive and well in this time, it still astonished him to actually hear his voice. He slowed his craft to an almost full stop to buy himself time to think, not wanting to be reported.

"Sir, There's no sign of any of them, but we found a helmet..."

"That's not a good sign... With this weather, no one can survive without a sealed EP suit! The carbon fiber in the air is toxic! Start running tight radius sweeps... then widen till you find them! They can't have gotten far! Whose helmet is it?"

"Sir, that's just it... It has the insignia from the Phoenix stamped on it!"

"Impossible! No one from the Phoenix has even set foot on Cheops yet!"

"That's what I said, but I know the stamp, sir, it's the Phoenix, I'm sure of it!"

"What's the name? Have you checked it out by cross referencing its signal ID?"

"Negative, Sir, the console on the skiff is too primitive..."

"Right... right... Well, put it on and call me! Right away!"

Erük cringed, realizing he couldn't be more than a half mile from the crash site. He knew as soon as their conversation was ended his craft's signature would be spotted on their scanners, as well as the Fleet, if they were searching for Sky's parents. He suddenly realized this whole thing was a very bad idea, or possibly a very good idea with horribly bad timing! He had just jeopardized the entire crew... his friends... *his family!* He quickly focused on Thor's energy, not knowing any other human that these people wouldn't recognize. Taking on his shape, he sat down in the pilot's chair, then started slowly forward, toward the site.

"John, it's Red. I've got it on... Who is it?" There was an uncomfortably long pause before Parnell finally responded.

"Is this some kind of fucking joke, Red?"

"Wh-what...? No! What's up?" There was another long pause, then Parnell spoke up, very plainly; very concisely.

"Are you absolutely positive that the insignia on the side of the helmet, as well as the stamped lettering inside the visor, are both from the Phoenix, Red, 100% positive?"

"Absolutely! On my honor, John... believe me, I know it's strange! They haven't left orbit!"

"That's not the half of it..."

"What's going on, John? Who's is it?"

"The computer says it's mine!... and the rank is listed as Captain!" It got very quiet for almost a minute, then Parnell keyed back in. *"Did you hear me?"* Another long gap without any answer from this end. Erük looked out toward the horizon in the direction of the crash site, sensing something was amiss. *"Red, do you copy?"*

Erük sped up, catching sight of a dim glow just over the next small rise. As he approached he saw a lone figure standing, awkwardly enough, without any kind of EP suit or helmet. As he got closer, he looked around for the helmet they were discussing on the radio, which he knew had to be the one Thor said he lost after the shuttle crash, but didn't see it anywhere. It was among the many things Thor "borrowed" from Parnell's berth after taking over the Phoenix, and given the confusion and attention it was apparently causing, Erük knew he needed to retrieve it immediately!

He pulled up next to the skiff, trying hard not to kick up a great deal of particle matter at the poor fellow standing out in the open in nothing but street clothes and combat boots. Erük lowered the shuttle's ramp and walked out slowly, keeping his guard up and paying as close attention as possible to everything going on around him. Upon seeing him there, the man looked like he just saw a ghost, and immediately began to talk incessantly to try to cover for his underlying nervousness. A little afraid that his guise had flaws, Erük looked at himself in the mirrored part of the electronics cabinet, but only saw Thor's likeness in the reflection.

The man introduced himself as Nicolas MacAave, a Journeyman mining engineer who apparently got stranded out here during the storm, and now, lost and starving with a broken down skiff, was greatly in need of a meal and a trip back to his home ship, the Phoenix. Erük knew immediately that he was lying, and tried to ascertain for himself what this man was really after.

He found the man incredibly difficult to read, and could only feel malice as an underlying theme throughout the proceeding conversation and interaction. He knew, based primarily on the man's knee-jerk reaction to the very sight of him, that he definitely shouldn't take him back to their Phoenix, and something told him intuitively that he shouldn't let him near the old Phoenix either, which was still, so far as any of them knew, the home of Thor's frozen body, still safely in cryostasis.

He took off, figuring at this point that if the Fleet had been paying attention at all, they would have seen this ship arrive, then unaware of Erük's arrival under the cover of darkness, it would appear that the same ship was now departing. He stayed low for a moment, circling around the site with full flood lights on looking for any sign of the lost helmet, while engaging in small talk with the man who was now strapping himself in to one of the rear seats just in front of the small cargo hold. It made him uncomfortable that the man was seated directly behind him, but he did his best to simply stay vigilant and maintain eyes in the back of his head, as the man had a very unnerving way about him.

After circling the site twice, Erük was just about to take off when he spotted something very disturbing on the ground next to the broken down skiff. Too far away for human eyes, he allowed himself to shapeshift just slightly in the face to gain the use of his dragon eyes again. Zooming in close he noticed what had to be three pairs of combat boots sticking out of the loose cargo at such an angle as to pretty much guarantee they were on someone's legs. Erük took a deep breath, knowing that if they were still alive, he would have felt their presence while they were still back on the ground. He was now sure that he had not only botched his stealthy take off, but now had a killer on board... one who needed a ship and was seated directly behind him!

He set course to seem as deliberate as possible and continued to fly away from the Phoenix across a large, impassable ocean of tumultuous storm waves, unprecedented ground swell, and deep, unpredictable maelstroms, toward the uncharted side of the planet, hoping for a little bit of luck to intervene and offset his sudden stroke of misfortune and seriously interrupted game plan. He refused to let this unexpected variable ruin his mission to save his people... it was simply too important. He just hoped that the Fleet wasn't tracking his every movement; but as MacAave appeared to have finally dozed off to sleep in his seat, yet the persistent feeling of being watched didn't cease, he feared the worst. He decided to make a break for it just as soon as he could dispose of his malignant passenger in some manner that he could live with.

———————

Thor slowly opened his eyes, looking exhausted from trying desperately to reach his brother telepathically. He shook his head in defeat. Sky and Bjorn sighed, exchanging glances as Astrydd changed her bandages one more time.

"Let me try," Sky proposed, grunting a little in pain as she stood up from her seat with one hand over her dressing on the wounded rib cage. She sounded frail, but Astrydd insisted that her lung was improving by the hour and her condition was as stable as could be expected. Her mother was taking a bit longer to heal, not having the benefit of a powerful extraterrestrial psychic sharing her body. Sky had spent the last day in the Medical Bay getting caught up, or rather getting Regina and Connor caught up, and was finally at peace with what had happened. Her parents, however, were having quite a bit of trouble finding balance in this outcome, as there was always the unresolved matter of the little girl back at the base, thinking they were dead.

She came over to where Thor had been sitting while he tried to channel Erük through the massive crystal Erük used during the tachyon storm to amplify his effect on the shields. It was awash with his energy still. She sat down, placing the large amber chunk of translucent stone across her lap and closed her eyes. She felt a massive kick from Ar'Jvikkah that almost caused her to vomit. She doubled over in pain, taking several deep breaths, and then stared at Thor with a determined look in her eyes, building up the courage to try again. He placed his hand on her shoulder.

"You don't have to do this, Sky! We can find another way... He can take care of himself! Do *not* put yourself in danger over this! Please!"

"Don't worry... This little guy will protect me. He already has... He's just feeling Erük instantly from the stone! That's why this will work." She took a deep breath, then closed her eyes again, this time accepting the flash of energy as they were almost instantly connected. "He's in the long range shuttle!" She paused for a moment, breathing heavier as she listened carefully to him. "He's not coming back... He's going back to the Algol system to try to save his race... Says that he's very sorry, he just has to try...."

"Sky! Tell him the data I processed showed the system going supernova *anyway*! Even if the mining never destabilized the planets, they would still suffer the same fate!

It is only a matter of time! He'd be risking paradox to extend their lives by only a short time! Tell him *please*, come back and let's talk about this! He's making a *grave* mistake!" Sky fell into a deep trance, dug in so deep that Thor wasn't sure how much of his message had even been heard.

"I heard you, my brother." Thor jumped and turned completely around from pacing the floor to stare at Sky, who had apparently uttered this through her own mouth, but it was definitely Erük's voice. He was speaking through Sky because of Ar'Jvikkah's powerful connection to him. Thor suddenly became aware of another presence… one he had become quite familiar with. He quickly glanced all around the bridge, unsure where it was coming from. Approaching Sky, he became keenly aware of its source.

"Erük, are you alone?" Thor spun around to Bjorn, who was typing madly on one of the console computers. "Bjorn, track that shuttle! The storm's interference shouldn't be an issue anymore…."

"I'm already on it."

"Strange you should ask, Brother… given the secrecy of our visit… The answer is no. I picked up a man who was stranded near the site where you crashed. It's a long story, but I think he killed a search party before I arrived. He's unconscious now."

"Who is he?"

"An engineer named Nicolas MacAave." Upon hearing that name, Bjorn dropped his drink on the floor, the glass shattering as he spun around toward Thor with a terrified look on his face, shaking his head back and forth. Thor looked puzzled, unsure where he heard the name, but he knew it sounded familiar.

"Captain, Nicolas MacAave went missing 20 years ago and was never seen again! And he was no killer! Remember the story Sky told us? He was spotted trying to jack a shuttle, then it turned out that it was one of the ethereals, impersonating him! He almost succeeded!"

"Erük, did you hear that? I don't think that's even MacAave!"

"Thor, we've got trouble! There's a small group of ships breaking away from the Fleet... They're heading toward Erük!"

"Erük! Are you still there? You've got company! Erük!?"

Erük lost his connection with them just as he started to spot movement in the direction of the Fleet, then enhanced his scanners to reveal a squadron of fighters and one Carrier breaking away from the rest of the Fleet on an intercept course with him. He heard Bjorn rambling on about MacAave just before the connection was severed, so he glanced back at him through the reflection on the edge of the console. He started noticing that his skin wasn't exactly right. It seemed something akin to the effect on his species' Jvikkahn camouflage that extreme distraction, or even sleep might have; temporarily causing a disturbance in the illusion and revealing just a glimpse of the true nature of the being beneath. In MacAave's case, however, Erük was shocked to see not the flesh of another being, but rather, nothingness. It was as if the entire man did not even exist... at least not in this plane!

He became alarmed, but was immediately distracted again by the rate at which the ships were closing in on his position. He decided to do something rash to try to lose them. He waited until he was directly over a particularly large set of seas, reaching upward nearly 100 feet before they broke randomly as storm waves often do, then he cut straight down into the water, plunging the shuttle directly into the turbulent ocean, and hopefully, off their grid altogether. He piloted the tiny ship deeper and deeper, until he started to see bedrock and sand, hopeful that he wouldn't have any problems with the shuttle's shields, as at this depth, failure would mean instant implosion from the extreme pressure.

He positioned the craft under an outcropping, similar to the manner in which the Phoenix had stayed invisible, then turned to check on his passenger. Erük jumped back at the sight of MacAave standing directly behind him now, having somehow not sensed his approach. He was grinning a devilishly familiar grin and slowly revealing himself as the assassin, Kieran McGinn. Now fully realizing the gravity of his mistake, he decided to face his destiny with purity, truth and honor, smiling with great satisfaction as he received the same look of astonishment and shock from McGinn as he abandoned his own disguise to reveal that he was not actually Thor; slowly transforming back to his true form and towering over the little man with the glaring eyes of an entire warrior race with nothing left to lose.

CHAPTER 24: BENEATH THE MAELSTROM

"You should be directly over him right now. He stopped all lateral movement at this exact location just before disappearing from our sight entirely," Commander Lewis barked from in front of a wall of sophisticated computers tied in to the Hubble telescope and Command computers on every Carrier and Flagship in the Fleet. "I'm sending you his last coordinates as well as the interior life scans on the ship itself. I've never seen anything like it! I'm not sure *what* they were!"

"What are you saying? The shuttle was being piloted by something that wasn't human?" Captain Chen replied sarcastically from onboard the Phoenix.

"That's exactly what I'm saying! Exercise extreme caution and capture that ship intact and its pilot alive! The Admiral thinks these are our dissident aggressors, and he wants to interrogate them personally!"

"Roger that. Chen out." Captain Chen sighed as he clicked off the com, then flipped the holographic viewer around to show an isometric real-time rendering of the squadron of fighters circling over the hostile ocean waves.

Scheduled to retire from active duty this year, Ming Chen had been Captain of the Phoenix for as long as anyone on board could remember. He was extremely intelligent and respected for his many accomplishments, but lately he had become the subject of much scrutiny from his fellow Captains, as well as the subject of gossip among his subordinates, Fleet-wide. He had started to develop a bad, and unfortunately highly visible, case of "Hot Shiver," a reactionary condition seen throughout the Fleet primarily in the oldest generation of citizens, usually civilian, that was believed to be caused by prolonged exposure to the low level artificial gravity present in long term space flight assignments without the benefit of cryostasis cycling.

Since this phenomenon was typically seen in lower level personnel not worthy of expensive cryostasis investment, but who performed a necessary Fleet duty, such as human waste management, recycling, material couriers, or general errand execution, it was unusual and somewhat embarrassing for a Carrier Captain to develop it. He simply did not agree with cryostasis, nor the idea of machines running his ship while he slept, and avoided it like the plague whenever possible. Chen was also nearing 80 years old, and though he still commanded the respect of his crew, some of his judgment calls of late had started, for the first time in his illustrious career, to come into question. One such call was the decision to bench Commander Parnell.

He transferred John Parnell, his would be successor, just after their arrival in this system, and though Parnell was happy with his new charge; running the entire CSE operation, as well as captaining the CSE vessel itself, it wasn't his true calling. Admittedly it was a rash call, but one that Chen stood by and refused to reverse; tuning out the many voices of criticism as he continued to train his new would-be Commander, a staunch disciplinarian named Bellows.

Only Parnell and Chen knew the truth... Parnell had *requested* the assignment so that he could get closer to his biological daughter: a young girl born to a couple without the husband ever knowing about his wife's indiscretion. Even though their short affair had long since run its course and they had both vowed never to speak of this again, he couldn't bear to spend years on deep space assignments as young Kaitlyn grew up without him even around to watch over his daughter from the sidelines.

Parnell was one of those irritating individuals who seemed to be a natural at everything, and was immediately good at everything he tried; but he was, first and foremost, a top-notch fighter pilot. He had flown hundreds of missions with MacAave as young men before being thrust into his role as an officer and leader of men, and even though that was a long time ago, when Captain Chen or Admiral Reid needed anyone trained, or an important mission led with strength and experience, they always sent John.

Captain Chen watched now, with a smile on his weathered face, as the leader pulled his squadron in a tight formation closer and closer to the surface, readying them for the order to submerge. He felt the warm blanket of reassurance in knowing that his trusted friend had agreed to take point in this pressing matter, but as he turned to look at the empty Captain's chair on the bridge of his beloved Phoenix, he worried for the future and once again regretted his decision to allow John to stray.

———

Thor was stressed out in a way Sky had never witnessed, frantically tweaking the computer settings in an effort to keep tabs on Erük and monitor the situation with the Fleet ships now hovering over his head. He was pacing the floor in tight, angry cycles in between attempts on the computer, and banging on every solid object that came into reach while muttering obscenities in languages he didn't even speak.

They all witnessed Erük's swan dive into madness; spiraling straight into the large maelstrom like force-feeding a 3 ton stool into the largest toilet in the universe, in what will undoubtedly be referred to in training manuals for future generations as "The Twist and Flush Evasive Maneuver." Now, for love or money, they could not locate a trace of him on any scan available to them. He hoped for Erük's sake that it was the same for the circling vultures, but somehow he doubted it. Even though Erük submerged before the Carrier had even completed its atmospheric entry, they were clinging very tightly to one particular spot. Thor switched his view over to the holographic table and started pacing around the stand with his arms crossed as he always did when he was strategizing.

They all jumped at the sound indicating receipt of an incoming Fleet Command Message, a sound they hadn't heard since their falling out with the rest of the Fleet. Thor stared wide eyed at Bjorn, the closest officer to the communications console. He bolted over to the console, reading, then double checking the information before turning around toward Thor and Sky with a very confused look on his face. "It's Erük's exact coordinates," he somberly informed them. "I just don't-" He stopped in mid-sentence with a baffled expression. "I get it! Shit! That other Carrier *is* the other Phoenix!" he exclaimed proudly, once again showing his heightened intelligence, despite his young age.

"What makes you so sure?" Sky asked, still a little groggy from her taxing experience with channeling from such a great distance.

"That message was sent directly to the old Phoenix... Each vessel in the Fleet has its own personal code, controlling everything from message decoding, to shield parameters, to waste dumps," Thor added, remembering how it worked first hand, from having been assigned with the task of tying in shield control parameters to the other Carriers remotely from the Phoenix during the battle over Erük's home planet.

Bjorn pointed at him, "Exactly! And we _still_ _are_ the Phoenix! We have the exact same transmission code as the Phoenix that Erük must be dealing with right now!"

"They sent the Phoenix after him... Shit! This just keeps getting better and better!" Sky laughed, looking over at Thor, who remained locked in his own personal orbit around the holograph stand, circling around and around with his arms crossed as he struggled for a way to help his dear friend. Suddenly, he paused, looking very worried.

"The Phoenix! The _old_ version of the Phoenix, with McGinn and myself in cryostasis onboard!"

"Yeah...?" Bjorn fished, "So...?"

"McGinn is on Erük's shuttle!" Thor explained, "He doesn't give a rat's ass about Erük... He's after his own physical body!"

"Yeah, that and _your_ body," Sky said softly, obviously very concerned, "in pieces!"

Bjorn looked somberly at them both. "And if he succeeds?"

Erük struck first, raking his mighty front talons across the breadth of McGinn's front-side as he roared aloud, following the left handed strike with a shadow blow from his right arm, both of them open handed with claws outstretched, swinging down and to the left. Though some part of McGinn seemed to be untouchable; holding on to this physical plane only by the slightest grasp, the sheer _intention_ of Erük's attack transcended this barrier and struck him hard, on every plane in which he still held sway. He reeled, crying out in pain as he spun around two full times on his way to the floor of the small craft.

Picking himself up off of the ground in more ways than one, he glared at Erük, tearing off his torn shirt and wiping some very real looking blood off his chest before discarding it directly at Erük's face. As the bloody rag flew haphazardly through the air, the mighty dragon smiled, already sensing McGinn's next attack. Kieran flew straight at him, both fists clenched out in front of him as he spun his body in a lightning fast corkscrew straight at the massive warrior's solar plexus. He squinted as he approached the moment of impact; focusing his will on transcending the barrier between the ethereal and the material plane so that he would be able to inflict damage on his foe.

Feeling nothing, he became shocked for a moment as his fists slammed into the bulkhead directly behind the large beast, without even the feeling of passing through his body. As far as he could tell, he hadn't lapsed, even for a second, in the continuity of energy in his attack, and by all rights, should be mopping the floor with his enemy's unconscious body. He shook his head as he stood up a second time; sparks popping and flying from the damaged console behind where Erük was standing not one moment before as he slowly turned around.

"Oh, you'll have to do much better than that," Erük taunted from just a few feet away, his arms out to the sides, palms up, in an aggravating invitation.

"So it would seem..." McGinn held his arms out in a very similar manner as Erük, tilting his head back and closing his eyes. No sooner had Erük began to feel his connection to his enemy's energy dissipate, as McGinn began to vanish from sight altogether. Then, as Erük looked around the cockpit for his foe, there seemed to be a *living* aspect to the circuits of the ship starting to emerge that flowed from console to console, sometimes visibly, sometimes not. Erük followed it closely as it made its way around toward him, then paused; sparking and shorting out everything around where he was standing. Erük thrust his huge hand into the violent array of electric activity, and for a moment, he could feel his enemy again.

Somehow McGinn had managed to turn himself into pure electrical energy, fusing his life-force with the computer banks and circuitry of the ship. The proximity alarms were going off as if they were under attack, and as he stepped forward to get a better look at the screen on the front console, he sensed an attack coming from behind. Erük ducked quickly, narrowly dodging an access ladder as it swung down from above, triggered electronically by McGinn. Carefully keeping his distance from anything that had computer control, including the cockpit seats, he leaned over the front control console and saw that the proximity threat was real. According to the scanners, there were several ships approaching quickly from above.

The shuttlecraft lurched forward, propelled by McGinn in an effort to make them completely visible to the Fleet. Erük scrambled around, looking for anything that might help him regain control of the ship before the squadron of fighters arrived, and instead noticed the warm, red warning light fill the inside of the ship. The warning announcement made him jump, and he started, for the first time, to worry.

"Cargo door open... cargo door open..." A flood of water started to rush into the small chamber, sucking the air out and readjusting the pressure for the worse almost immediately. He ran back to the door, prepared to evacuate, then noticed it was only ajar, somehow jammed just a few inches open. He struggled, to no avail, to pry it further, then gave up and prepared to teleport himself out of the craft and into the surrounding waters to take his chances.

He flashed toward the wall, but no sooner had he disappeared from this spot, as he reappeared right on top of the wall of the electrified bulkhead, stopped in his tracks from traveling past this border by McGinn. He bounced violently off of it, landing in the quickly deepening pool of frigid water on the floor of the ship. The shock had taken a lot out of him, and he struggled to his feet, glancing out the front window as he noticed McGinn turning on the flood lights to signal the fighters as the small craft slipped off its ledge and slowly sank, face up, toward the true bottom of this freezing cold, dark abyss.

He gasped for breath, unable to use his gills properly in this extreme pressure as the shuttle impacted the sand at the bottom of the ocean, sending him reeling backwards over the pilot seats into the darkness of the cargo hold. He scrambled back up, swimming over all of the floating equipment and debris and took one last breath. He approached the front glass and called out desperately to his friends, signaling them with everything he had as the water finished filling up the cockpit entirely, shorting out the interior lights and leaving Erük in his cold, dark tomb, pounding on the glass with clenched fists.

Thor stood on deck, looking frantically around as he struggled to figure out a way to help Erük that wasn't suicide for the entire family onboard. He closed his fist, slamming it on the knee wall, cursing his brother for not having the trust to counsel with him before setting off on such a dangerous quest. He stared out into the depths of the lake above him, noticing that many of the small, monkey-like creatures that they saw through the shuttle's glass on the way down were congregated here and there, not too far from the ship, seeming to be keeping tabs on the goings on of the humans. He couldn't blame them. They were invaders, and though they had no choice but to run their shields, sending its disruptive energy through this pristine environment, he was sure they interpreted this as an attack on their way of life.

He was standing there, just about to go back inside to the bridge, when it hit. The most powerful psychic premonition he had ever felt in his life.... *It was Erük, and he was in grave trouble!* Thor scrambled to the stairwell that led back to the bridge via the outer mezzanine, unsure what the feeling meant, but definitely not mistaking its urgency.

As he reached the top level where the airlock door was, above the lights of the lower cargo bay doors, he fumbled the small light-stick he was twirling around in his hand, and he spun around to catch it, narrowly missing as he watched it fall, then bounce off of the top of the light hood and shoot right out through the shield; floating slowly upward toward the surface. He cringed a little, realizing he had just sent up a beacon, however small, directly over their position.

He watched for a moment as it illuminated all manner of fish and small creature, drawing some of them in like a lure. Seeing an area of intense movement, above him and toward the edge of the caves, he hit his com and ordered Bjorn to flood the area with light. As soon as he did, Thor could clearly see that the monkey creatures had all converged on the same hole: a large opening across from them that looked like it probably went on for some distance. There was something special about these creatures that Thor had noticed during his first encounter; and as the last one in turned and looked directly at him, he was sure that to whatever end, they were reacting to Erük's call.

The feeling persisted, nearly causing Thor to double over with nausea as he rushed to help, then, as suddenly as it began, it became silent. His heart sank as he hit the panel to open the airlock door and burst onto the bridge, making everyone jump nearly out of their seats. "Bjorn! Pilot us into that tunnel at the maximum speed attainable with the side-scan sonar imaging as you receive it... Just don't get us stuck in a bottleneck! This material is very soft... it could easily result in a cave-in and bury us alive down here!"

"Aye, Sir! Full ahead!" The small crew jumped into action, scrambling for the designated posts to which they had been assigned. "Captain, where could it possibly lead us? We're in a lake!"

"Are we?"

"Captain Chen, we have the craft in our scopes. It appears to have lost lateral control and has fallen to the ocean floor. They must be in trouble... they keep signaling with their floodlights. S.O.S. in Morse code... over and over."

"Thank you, Commander Lewis, we'll take it from here... Good job!" Chen turned in his seat and hit a button on the arm of his chair. "Commander Parnell, H.O.R.U.S. says they're signaling distress down there... do you have a visual?"

"Affirmative, Captain Chen. He's flashing us with his lights... sensors show his shields are down and the compartment's flooded! There's no sign of any survivors nearby..."

"They may have flooded on impact, or they may have bailed... Let's pull him up!"

"Captain, we'll have to deploy divers to attach tow lines... That can be very dangerous at this depth, especially given the size of that maelstrom! Sir, with all due respect, it's just a shuttle!"

"Do it! That's an order! I'm sending down a dive team now... You and your men stay close... something doesn't feel right about this. I want to know who this pilot was! Chen out."

Parnell sighed heavily, obviously unsatisfied with the Captain's methods at the moment, but very used to his judgment calls panning out. Usually when he said, *"something doesn't feel right,"* something turned out to be very wrong. This time, however, his vibe had Parnell submerged in a single man fighter at a very compromising depth in an uncharted ocean on an uncharted planet during a polar shit-storm the likes of which they had only dreamed of, with a giant, unpredictable whirlpool sweeping this way and that overhead! He took a deep breath, closed his eyes for a moment, then centered himself only on the mission at hand.

He slowly opened his eyes, expecting the same view he had only a moment ago... of the bottom of the deep ocean valley with fish and other life scattering this way and that above a sunken shuttle, sitting face up with its lights flashing steadily into the darkness... three short, three long, three short; but instead he was startled right out of his constrictive pilot seat, scrambling backwards for every inch he could put between himself and this intrusive creature with large, penetrating eyes that was now directly in front of him, its mouth pressed against the glass of his cockpit windshield, holding it in place. His heart pounded as he struggled to catch his breath, cracking up laughing as he realized that it was only about the size of a small chimpanzee and probably offered no real threat to him at all.

He started to calm down a bit and catch his breath, when the strange creature suddenly came right through the glass as if it wasn't even there and shocked him right on the nose with its tail! "Shlihtbuh!" he exclaimed through numb lips, slobbering on himself and struggling with the creature as it climbed all over his face and head, causing him to completely miss the large swarm of them swimming right by the front of his ship toward the shuttle. Dazed almost to the point of unconsciousness, he frantically looked around the ship, desperately clinging to his weakened hold on the situation, as well as his own sanity. From where he was, he couldn't see a thing outside, but judging from the radio chatter in his headset, he could tell his entire squadron was experiencing the same unexpected interference from these nasty little tricksters.

He reached down to his right boot and produced a large diving knife, swinging it madly at the nimble little creature in an effort to regain control of his craft. It was too late. In a frenzy, it scrambled away, stepping all over the ship's controls and managing to accidentally eject them both from the cockpit into the deep of the ocean; jettisoned in a momentary bubble of protective air, but from way too far down to make it to the surface unassisted.

He clung desperately to the inside of the cockpit lid, dropping the knife out of necessity and holding on for dear life as he rose toward the surface. The dome gradually flipped over sideways and filled up with water quite a long way from the surface, and releasing his grip on it, Parnell worried that this was the end, having only gathered about half of the air he could hold in his lungs in the first place. He looked to the surface, praying to see the divers that Captain Chen had said were being dispatched.

———————

Erük gazed up at the action above him, seeing only flashes of chaos in strobe as the ships that were converging on him seemed to be engulfed in some kind of swarm of indigenous activity. He was starting to have extreme difficulty with the pressure of the water. His breaths were getting shorter and shorter, and his vision was fading into a tunnel of darkness. He could feel the intensity on his head, like a constricting belt he couldn't remove, causing pain like he had never felt. He roared with all the energy he had, fighting desperately to hold on one moment longer… then another…. He felt something inside his lower back collapse and he groaned from the pain, convulsing and clawing at the glass as the last bit of light slowly faded in his diminished field of vision.

As fast as he lost consciousness, he reawakened to the sensation of being shocked repeatedly in the face, and he opened his eyes to see one of the small creatures he had followed into the cave actually completely *inside* the shuttle, holding him up by his arms with two of his legs, while "flying" with its wings to remain aloft in the water. It pulled him toward the glass, then spun around, literally *pushing* him right through the thick windshield. Erük could feel a tingle in his spine as this diminutive creature was actually able to manipulate his atoms energetically in the very same way that he did with energy fields, yet he was somehow able to do it with *solid matter*!

This was a type of transmutation Erük had only heard mention of by the elders of his race... a practice they had abandoned before they had even left Earth after the sinking of their great city. The repercussions were said to be too drastic. Too many had died trying to perfect this skill, and yet these benign little beings could apparently not only do this at will, but even effect a crossing for another being in their contact! Erük was fascinated, staring at the creature as it pushed him clear, then began emerging from the other side, himself.

As if it was only a blur in his peripheral vision, in his weakened state, Erük saw the shiny diving knife come out of nowhere, from straight above them as if an arrow from heaven itself, and pierce the small creature straight through his back, just as he was about half way through the glass. Blood flowed slowly outward into the water in a crimson cloud and Erük reeled, looking madly around for the attacker, this murdering coward who had taken the life of his brave and innocent savior, but he sensed no one nearby. He gave a steady pull, focusing his own will and trying hard to free the creature who had just saved his life, but it was stuck in the glass as if they were one in the same. Still feeling the intense pressure, he knew he must flee, paying his final respects, then bolting with a heavy heart for the surface with what little bit of energy this noble creature had afforded him with his selfless sacrifice.

Thor cringed as the passageway narrowed and widened, split, then split again. Frustrated with the delay involved with giving orders, then having them repeated, he had taken manual control of the massive Carrier and was "flying" through the waters with the blind fury of a demon possessed. Having practiced this maneuver before, just for a cheap thrill, he was already tuned into the response time and impulse capability of this ship in zero atmosphere, and even a little bit within the parameters of the low gravity condition of Erük's planet, but this was definitely a little different.

The ship reacted pretty well to the serious encasement in water, but now, in the confines of these oddly shaped, and constricting caverns, there was a whole world of new dynamics to adjust to. Given the sheer size of the vessel, water displacement was paramount. There was simply nowhere for the water to go in a hurry once the ship was in its place. As it moved, being instantly displaced, the next problem was the turbulence caused by both the erratic shape of the walls and pillars throughout the cave, as well as the hemispherical air gap created by their energy shield, which was actually causing "jumps" in their movement and seriously jeopardizing his ability to steer at all. This, combined with the silt blackout being caused by the disruption of the cavern walls and ceiling, was making it increasingly difficult to navigate safely.

Experiencing one "drop-off" too many, and almost ramming the ship directly into a huge, wedge-shaped pillar that would undoubtedly have cut them nearly in two, Thor gave the order to drop the shields. "Are you out of your fucking mind?!?" Bjorn yelled, suddenly very defiant, for fear of his own life. "We'll be flooded the first time you so much as drag your ass on a sandbar, or bump into *anything*!"

"Do it now! That's an order!" Bjorn closed his eyes and sighed, then complied, quickly hitting a series of buttons that caused an audible alarm to engage, then a strong rise in speed and smoothness. "I know the risk... The flooding will be very minimal unless I crash. Erük is running out of time, I can feel it! *Trust me,*" he added, smiling and winking at Sky, who was sitting by his side, strapped into her seat with a nervous look on her face.

She stared at Thor and returned his smile, taken a little aback by his confidence, trying to ascertain if it was a guise, or if he really knew what he was doing. The whole thing just seemed so damned familiar to her, but she couldn't really tell why. They turned nearly 90 degrees on their side coming around a corner in order to shoot through the middle of two massive outcroppings, and Thor executed the maneuver flawlessly, never taking his eyes off of her. As they sped toward what looked to be a nearly impassable labyrinth of some kind of interwoven coral and vegetation, the vines nearly half the diameter of the ship itself, Thor smiled again, gazing right through her, as deep as only one who *truly* knows someone can, and clearly mouthed the words, *"I love you."*

She was instantly overcome with a flood of emotion and memories as she flashed back and forth repeatedly from this life to the one they were denied, all those years ago. She was suddenly back in the stolen car, speeding down the highway with her friends, but her entire world had slowed to this moment alone; the same moment they now shared again all these many light years away.

Looking straight upward as he swam, Erük could almost see the surface. There were shimmering rays of blue and green light penetrating the turbulent mess above. He swam higher and higher, starting to pass the aftermath of some kind of chaos that apparently took the lives of several of the human fighter pilots. The little indigenous sucker-monkeys were scattering here and there, celebrating some sort of victory, and apparently were very proud of themselves for something that had to do with Erük. He truly wished he understood what had transpired better, so that he would know whether or not he should feel indebted to them, but something was blocking his ability to read them, which, until recently, was as keen and sharp for him as reading his own kind.

He passed by several human bodies, suited in uniforms similar to Sky's and Bjorn's, but with a few subtle differences, and aside from the fact that none of them were still breathing, there didn't appear to be anything wrong with any of them.... they had all simply drowned. He quickly dodged to the side and narrowly avoided being pummeled nose first by the front end of a two ton single-man fighter just like the ones that fought in the skies over his lair back on his home planet. He turned his head and watched it descend toward its final resting place; a cold and watery tomb on the ocean floor. Just like the others, the cockpit hatch had been blown and the pilot was nowhere in sight.

He strained his neck to see it go all the way by, then turned back toward the surface again, nearly getting kicked in the face by a sinking soldier who, judging from the bubbles just above his head, had apparently just exhaled his last breath too far from the surface, and was flailing about, preparing to die a somewhat gruesome and unglamorous death... a decorated pilot and Fleet officer, veteran of numerous missions for God and his brethren, and trainer, leader, mentor or inspiration to almost all who knew him; jettisoned into the deep blue, accidentally, by a spastic little monkey-like water clown who got inside his cockpit and wreaked havoc before being caught. With no help in sight, he would face his end without glory, without reverence, and without heroism. Not rescuing defenseless children from the clutches of evil, nor smiting his nemesis in one last blaze of strength and justice; but rather, he would descend wide eyed and fearful into the silent darkness, kicking and thrashing as he convulsed his way toward his last moment of life... cold, in pain, and alone.

Figuring from the trajectory, and noticing that the man's knife sheath was empty, Erük assumed this was the man who killed his savior, so he violently lifted him up to his face to have a look into his eyes before he died. His heart skipped a beat or two as he suddenly realized this man was the former Captain Parnell! The same Captain Parnell who used to pilot the Phoenix over his world as it strip mined the precious life from its heart... The very same Captain Parnell who led the attack against his people before Thor relieved him of the tremendous burden of carrying the weight of his head on his shoulders!

He could see the man had taken his last breath, and though nothing would give Erük more satisfaction right now than looking at him face to face and watching the light fade from his eyes forever, he knew this man was also responsible for thawing Thor from cryo in the first place, and setting off the chain reaction that ultimately led to Thor and Sky's redemption and his own demise. He put his large palm completely over the small man's entire face to keep him from involuntarily inhaling a breath of water, then charged for the surface like some kind of possessed manta ray, steering clear of the maelstrom, and returning the man to the surface as fast as his exhausted body and wings would allow.

Thor started to pick up the signature of the shuttle and realized they were getting close. There were warning lights and sirens going off across the grid from the internal flooding going on ship wide. Due to the fact that they were running a skeleton crew with literally no damage control men on board, the only thing Thor could do was seal off section after section and hope they got there very soon. It was then that he saw it....

His heart sang as he realized the channel was getting nothing but larger, expanding in a funnel shape until it ultimately opened up into the large chamber in the ocean valley that the signal was coming from. He quickly glanced at the damage schematic one last time, then sighing with relief, he gave the order to raise the shields. The water around the ship was displaced almost instantly in the shape of an elliptical sphere, creating an air gap that the internal water could then flood out into. *"Shields are back up... open the airlocks! I repeat... open airlocks immediately to alleviate flooding!"* Thor ordered ship wide through the loudspeaker. The mighty Phoenix breathed a sigh of relief as the water gushed outwards toward its proper place outside the shield wall and balance was restored.

The small crew scanned everywhere, picking through the debris ridden scene in an effort to find their friend. He had already piloted close to the submerged shuttle craft, now with two fighters apparently suffering its very same fate, and was preparing to come about to gain a frontal view, when an awful feeling swept over the crew like a wave. They all held their heads, stomachs, or clung to neighboring objects in an effort to stabilize themselves long enough to understand what they were feeling. It was like thousands of voices all chanting out of key and all in unison... a song of utter despair and sadness. Something, or someone was manipulating the minds of them all; but it was so loud... so powerful. The Phoenix drifted to port just slightly, finishing the arc Bjorn had started, when they saw the front of the shuttle.

Thor strained his eyes, trying desperately to overcome the tunnel vision this psychic attack had inflicted on him, when he saw the small creature, just like the one who attached himself to their shuttle's windshield in the lake, staring blankly at them from just in front of the ship, muttering, word for word, everything that was now entering their heads, as if he was the source of the psychic transmission. The ambient light, shining down from above in a soft blue that intermittently lit up the entire floor was starting to fade prematurely, becoming darker and darker as the feeling of doom and despair overpowered their natural sense of good fortune bit by bit, until it was nearly unbearable and all-consuming.

Looking desperately around the ship, they noticed the source of the impending darkness. The small creature was mentally connected to all of his brethren, now as thick as a swarm of locusts, and was controlling the entire hive through their collective consciousness. They were descending on the Carrier in droves; blacking out the surrounding view with sheer numbers as they encroached as close as they could to the shield, which at this point, was the only thing keeping them out of the ship. Miraculously, though they had no trouble tuning themselves right through solid objects, being of this underwater world, energy fields of this nature were completely alien to them. As resourceful as they seemed, the crew all feared that it was only a matter of time until this obstacle was overcome.

Briefly remembering back to the intelligence and benign energy of little guy who had shocked him through the glass on their shuttle ride down into the lake, Thor knew in his heart that there was no way they were perpetrating this on their own, even to protect Erük somehow, and he started staring hard at the one who seemed to be the leader.

"Zoom in on the shuttle!" he ordered, starting to understand this a little better. Bjorn brought the view of the front of the glass into close focus, and they were all stunned to see that the creature was not only badly injured, but was somehow stuck halfway through the glass, with his bottom half dangling around inside the water filled shuttlecraft. "Flood it with light!"

Upon the intense light hitting the front of the ship, Thor immediately noticed two things. One, the creature's eyes were entranced... its huge pupils were not reacting to their flood lights in the least, as if he was nothing more than a vessel for some higher level being that was using him to amplify a signal through the collective to all of his brethren. Secondly, he caught, just for a moment, a glimmer in the glass; a reflection from the *inside* of the cockpit of a human-like form, arm outstretched, holding tightly onto the creature's tail with his hand. "Freeze! Right there!" The view changed slightly, and he lost it, but upon backing up the view, he retrieved this very incriminating piece of the puzzle.

"Bjorn, can you enhance this image at all?" Bjorn brought it up on his screen and hit a few buttons to reveal a closer look at the perpetrator's face concealed in the shadows. "McGinn!" Thor took a reactionary step backward, shaking his head again to try to get rid of the effects of the trance as the transmission became louder and louder. Looking at the hapless puppet in the glass one more time, Thor jumped slightly as he turned his attention back toward the real view of the front of the shuttle, skin crawling on the back of his neck as the creature looked directly at him with those blackened eyes, smiling.

Suddenly, Thor caught Erük's desperate cry for help again, this time much closer. He looked straight up and saw what appeared to be a fight of some kind taking place at the surface. Bjorn had already zoomed in on Thor's screen view, trying to assist while holding one hand over his head in agony. Sky had all but shut down, and was now lying on the floor holding her stomach, barely conscious at all. Looking closely at the view on the screen, Thor could clearly make out Erük, barely moving at all and being dragged down by the legs by over a dozen of the diminutive winged creatures. Just above him there appeared to be the legs of a human pilot kicking about in the water just below the surface as they pulled Erük downward, apparently completely uninterested in the human.

Thor could see by the somewhat satisfied look on his brother's face that he had just saved the man, and was now prepared to meet his end with honor. For whatever reason, he could also tell that Erük had no breath left in him, be it the conditions being placed upon him, or the composition of this particular body of water, it didn't matter. There wasn't even enough time for them to reach him and get him on board, providing they could even break free of the grasp of the myriad of collective "worker bees" that were physically blocking them in and projecting this overbearing shroud of negativity and despair perpetrated somehow by McGinn from within the shuttlecraft.

Looking back in the direction of the shuttle, Thor could see the slight fluctuation of the lights and the internal glow of the instruments come into play, somehow connected to the pulses of malevolent energy being used against them. He smiled, seeing clearly what he needed to do. "Bjorn..." he gasped, having a very hard time focusing his thoughts, much less projecting them into verbal communication. Bjorn was almost unconscious, hanging over the back of his navigation chair. Thor stood up, clearing his throat and shaking his head, then he yelled loud and sharp, "Bjorn!"

The younger man jumped, shaking his head and regaining his composure for a moment. "Yes, Sir!"

"Fire one of the front cannons directly at the creature in the glass... the non-exploding anti-tank rounds... Then follow with a short radius EMP blast... one of the torpedoes rigged for shorting out minefield sensory equipment... Do you know the kind?"

"Yeah! My father and Sky's parents designed them! It was back when we were just-"

"Bjorn!"

"Sorry, Sir, I'll tell you later!"

"Fire them back to back!"

He punched a few commands in the console and the screen lit up with activity. A loud *"thump"* was heard and a large projectile tracked through the water toward the small shuttle. A second before impact, the little creature sprang to life, struggling to break free of the glass by pushing with his arms and legs from the inside. His eyes grew wide as the projectile approached in slow motion, and he became frightfully aware that he could not break free. His eyes widened as he saw the round coming straight at his face, then in one instant, whatever was controlling him simply vanished, leaving behind a slight disruption in their field of vision, a dangling corpse stuck in the window, and a flooded, but otherwise undamaged shuttlecraft.

The large round slammed into the creature, taking out the glass behind him and causing the entire shield to crack and explode inward from the force. Thor cringed, hoping to minimize the damage to their shuttle as much as was possible, but be sure to expel the assassin who caused this mess. He didn't truly believe that destroying the shuttle with McGinn inside would kill McGinn, any more than cutting him in half on the bridge did, so he decided not to risk the destruction of one of their last shuttlecrafts, nor the effect that the shockwave caused by the detonation of the energy core underwater would have on this entire hive of innocent beings who had been pulled into this by McGinn to further his malicious cause.

The EMP torpedo flew gracefully through the open front-side of the drowned craft and exploded, sending an electromagnetic pulse in a controlled small radius, shorting out any and all electronics in its path, and stopping just short of the neighboring Phoenix. The lights shut down, and the signal stopped on their scanners, leaving nothing but a lifeless shape in the darkness, soon ignored even by the fish. Thor immediately turned his attention upward toward Erük.

He couldn't see him from where he was, but the mass of creatures had already dissipated entirely, most of them fleeing back into the surrounding caves where they lived. A few of the larger, older, more intelligent ones stayed behind as if to try to understand what had just happened, and were picking through the downed fighters, equipment, and bodies, both human and of their kind. Worried for Erük, Thor sped for the surface in the last direction where he had seen him being towed downward.

Dodging back and forth, trying to avoid disrespectfully mowing over the fallen soldiers from both sides, Thor spotted him! He was floating on his back on the surface, getting tossed about madly in the huge storm waves. As they came up from underneath him, needing only to envelop him in their energy shield in order to get him to safety, they spotted the other ship. There was a rescue effort taking place from above, as well. Looking closely, they could just make out the forms of several men pulling another man out of the water. The man being rescued was leaning away from them hysterically pointing overboard toward Erük as they fought to pull him away from the side. Thor knew there wasn't much time.

Rushing out the airlock onto the deck of the ship, he climbed the catwalk and tower, taking exactly the same route that he did the day he jumped... The day that Erük saved *his* life. He knew that if Erük was "rescued" by the other Phoenix, they would pick at him and pick at him until his life was utterly ruined. It may even have serious ramifications well beyond that, due to the events that they all shared. Thor scrambled up the mast in an effort to reach him before he was simply "repelled" by the energy shield, unconscious and unable to tune into it and slip inside to safety without the aid of his friend. Reaching the top of the mast, he calmly stood on the same platform that he dove off of while the Phoenix hovered over the beauty of Erük's home world the day he was reborn into this life.

He reached upward toward Erük, able to visually see his back and tail floating to and fro in the water as lifelessly as the kelp-like weeds that surrounded him, helping to keep his body from turning over in the water and drowning. He was just too far. He called to him and called to him, knowing that if he just regained consciousness, he could pass through the shield himself, and there would be no further problem. He was just too far gone… It would take a serious jarring to wake him from his state in time. Thor needed to physically wake him, and the only way to do that was to reach him in the water….

Thor had analyzed the shape of the shield before, with regard to clearances in tight areas, and he knew this was as close as he was going to get. He tapped his com and told Bjorn to stay put, then took a deep breath, closed his eyes, and jumped outward with his arms outstretched to the sides, just as before… and just as before he smiled, knowing full well from somewhere he could not identify that a higher power was at work here. *He knew he would be O.K..*

As he flew downward, alongside the edge of the ship in the small pocket of air, with water looming beside him like a giant living wall just outside the barrier, leaving him very little room to either side, he knew he would need to tune into its energy before hitting the edge of the shield at this speed, or he would be torn apart as if he was hitting a concrete wall. He closed his eyes and accelerated his pitch, and as he did so, he felt a push from the edge of the wall that changed his trajectory entirely! The Phoenix, now being targeted by the Carrier above them as an enemy, had been forced to take evasive action as a depth charge had just been dropped into the water from above. Thor was now falling at terminal velocity, not toward the convergence with the shield's edge, but directly at the large deck cannon which was now straight beneath him!

He opened his eyes wide and spread his arms like an eagle, not having time to accept or resist his fate... to fear or embrace it... but merely to experience it in its true suchness. He closed his eyes at the last second... *"Sky,"* he said, unsure if it was aloud or projected. He had the sudden sensation, brief and painful, of being knocked sideways... Then it was dark.

"Yes, my love?" she answered. Her voice was so loud... so clear.

"Sky, where are you?"

"I'm right here... on the deck! I'm O.K.!" she laughed a little, sounding relieved. "Jesus Christ, Thor! You gave us a scare!" Suddenly he heard her verbally, and his senses came alive as breath returned to his lungs. He could see light all around him, and he could see her face, looming overhead like a beautiful angel; her ice blue eyes looking deep into his soul like only she was capable of doing... just like she did the day he was being brought out of cryostasis. Suddenly he was back there again and the entire world was nothing but possibility.

He smiled, laying exhausted on the floor, then winced, feeling a very sharp, very familiar pain in his ribs and side. He twisted himself sideways to see the deep talon cuts in his flesh, almost exactly where his scars were from the first time Erük had saved his life by catching him just before he hit the ground. He smiled, suddenly understanding what had happened. The sudden movement of the Phoenix had jarred

Erük to action and for the second time, he had saved Thor's life... as they had saved his. Thor felt as if he had been reborn through his sacrifice, and every day from this day forward was now a gift.

"Where the hell is he?" Thor spoke up, clambering to his feet and looking all around.

"He's headed down to the cargo bay to help get the shuttle onboard... and check it for traces of McGinn." Sky answered softly, giving him a long hug.

"I'm not sure where he slithered off to... but he's got nowhere to cling to on that ship, I'll tell you that much."

"Just the same..." Sky answered.

"Yeah," Thor said with raised eyebrows, "just the same...."

———————

Captain Chen stood in the airlock, personally interrogating Commander Parnell as the Emergency Medical Crew was pushed out of the way. "Seal the door! No one comes in until I say! Never mind quarantine protocol... We were attacked! Now give me a minute!" He yelled at the young EMT who seemed unwilling to leave the soldier's side.

"Yes, Sir!"

"Commander-"

"Captain! Listen to what I'm telling you! There is another Carrier! The shuttle we were following was being piloted by someone... by *something* that was NOT human! It was some sort of dragon..." He was shaking, partially from hypothermia, having just been pulled, barely breathing, from frigid waters after swimming to the point of exhaustion, but also partially due to the residual effect of having a very close encounter with something that one only hears of in stories.

"A *dragon*," the Captain repeated, smiling skeptically. "A sophisticated spacecraft being piloted, in a most skillful manner, I might add, by... *a dragon!* Are you sure you don't want to rethink this experience before making your report?"

"Oh, *definitely!* You bet your ass I'd like to rethink this experience, but between you and me, I promise you, this is what happened! The damn thing even saved my life, Captain! Believe me, I got a *very* good look him! It was a fucking dragon!"

"So where did it learn to fly a shuttlecraft?"

"Sir, it... *spoke* to me! There was a moment when our minds seemed linked together, when-"

"Commander, this *thing* killed a whole squadron of our best pilots... nearly killed you! You're damn lucky to be alive! It stole one of our ships! If this thing got into your mind, you can bet that whatever it put there was misinformation, and it probably took information from you that could put us all in danger! Don't make the mistake of thinking that it *wasn't* the enemy!" The young Commander, now on his feet and trying to dry off, shoved his way by the shorter Captain, hitting the airlock panel and opening the door. "Get cleaned up and meet me on the bridge!"

"Aye, aye, Sir," the Commander shouted from about 10 feet away, saluting him without turning back around as he continued to walk off. Suddenly, and without warning, the entire ship shook and the people onboard, along with anything that wasn't bolted to the floor, flew quickly upward and slammed into the ceiling before returning to the floor with great force; the obvious result of losing power and careening downward about 50 feet to the ocean's surface before slamming back down onto the deck like sacks of potatoes. People were screaming and everyone had suffered at least nominal injury as they struggled to regain power to the ship before it sank into the ocean.

Captain Chen was running for the bridge, just a few feet behind Commander Parnell, when the comforting hum of the primaries firing up could be felt all around them. Almost instantly there was another sound, like a giant popping noise, then a long rattle as the rest of the power was restored and the giant ship thrust upward out above the breaking whitewater of the stormy seas. The Captain hit his com as he continued toward the bridge. "What the hell just happened, people?"

"Sir, someone just shut us down with our own input code!"

"What the hell do you mean, someone... the only people who have that code are us and Fleet Command!"

"...And apparently the Carrier that just blasted right by us without a fight!"

CHAPTER 25: A NEW CHARGE

Hope, it would seem, is the defining characteristic of civilization, and as Erük lay next to Thor in the Medical Bay, it did not take a telepathic mind to deduce that his had been restored. Not just for himself and his own personal sense of purpose, but more importantly, for his entire race, who he now understood were never meant to rest forever in their quiet, peaceful corner of the universe; but rather, they must evolve as they always had, and become the great teachers and soul carriers they once were, back on Earth. Once again, they were *needed*.

Thor laid there, staring at him as his relieved and somewhat renewed look slowly transformed to pure joy and an unhindered smile. "Oh, shit, Erük! What did you do...?" Thor knew him too well to not notice even the slightest change in his demeanor. There was nothing slight about this, however, so Erük opened a channel to him mentally, and laid it all on the line.

He realized now that everything had happened for a reason, and couldn't have happened any other way. He felt truly honored to be in such a position as this... to be responsible for playing such an integral role in the Great Prophecy of his people. Apparently he had passed on the knowledge and set things in motion that would change the fortunes of his people forever, as the ancient writings on the wall within the core of his planet finally became clear to him. The human being in the center of the drawings, who would come to them and bring them out of darkness, their Great Savior, or Ar'Savaant, as they referred to him in stories, was not Thor. It was not Sky, and it was not even Ar'Jvikkah....

It is said that the biggest killer of the world's greatest warriors throughout the ages isn't war itself, or a more skilled opponent, or even the ravages of old age. The biggest killer of the world's greatest warriors is *peace*... to be rendered obsolete. It is within this crux that all warriors dwell... to seek peace in order to achieve one's own uselessness.

He will kill only when maiming isn't enough... He will maim only when hurting isn't enough... and he will hurt only when words aren't enough. But suffer no delusions, when it becomes time to kill in order to defend oneself, or the defenseless, he will kill without a moment's hesitation. He will offer you his life in exchange for victory. Slap his wrist, but he will break your arm... Break his arm, but he will take your legs... Take his legs, but he will claim your life. It is the conflict, the duality, and the paradoxical nature of the true warrior to live his life with only this one possible outcome.

To be on this path and carry it through to fruition can result in only this one possible outcome. This is why a true warrior considers himself to be dead already. It is because he enters every battle a dead man, having already made his peace with this outcome, that there is no distraction, hesitation, nor fear.

Warriors are often misunderstood and accused of being obsessed with death... of placing no value on life at all. This could not be further from the truth. Although he appears to be obsessed with death, a true warrior values life more than most others, because though his intimacy with death, he is endowed with a very real understanding of the true nature of life and a deep love for the world's natural order. Because a true warrior is at peace with his own death, considering himself to be dead already, every moment, every breath is a gift of immeasurable beauty and grandeur. An entire lifetime experienced in each breath... to *truly* live in the moment.

The path he is on is a circle. There is no point of origin, no start... as is there no end. *There is only the path.* This is also his paradoxical nature. It is only because of death that life becomes so very precious. It is also because of his paradoxical nature that a true warrior is always alone, even when he is surrounded by those who love him... by those whom he loves. He carries this burden because this is simply who he is. It is the very core of his existence. He could no more change this fact about his true nature as he could change the color of the sky or the very nature of the whole of mankind. He did not choose to be on this path... his only choice was simply whether or not to start walking.

John sat in silence in his old quarters, staring with a slight smile on his lips at the droll décor the Captain had replaced his own effects with upon his transfer to CSE, realizing for the first time that Chen must have always held out hope, if not an actual plan, for his return to his former post. The plush berth had maintained the illusion of occupancy, but it was obvious to him now that it had never accommodated anyone but him. He felt flattered and deceived at the same time... deceived by his own desire to live a life that was

294

beneath him. He had to admit, it felt good to be back in the saddle.

So here he sat, doing his best to recall and process the events of the day in a manner that could be swallowed without regurgitation. After being ejected into the water, things became admittedly fuzzy. He had all but lost consciousness; but then there was a surreal element at play, as if the whole experience was preordained and he was simply its casual observer. The more he mulled this encounter over in his mind, the more it began to unveil itself from within his subconscious memory. This being that saved his life was unlike anything he had ever dreamed of, much less encountered. It was absolutely terrifying; but then upon looking him in the eye, it became his benefactor... moreover, it had actually *done* something to him.

He was very near death when he first became aware of the creature's presence. He had been swimming for the surface for all the life he could muster, holding desperately onto the hope that someone, or something, would save him, so when the creature appeared, he wasn't all that surprised. He was, however, quite sure in that moment that he was about to be eaten, rather than saved! He wasn't happy about it, but given the convulsive and painful death he was staring in the face, having just exhaled his final breath utterly spent, it did seem the lesser of two evils, and at the very least, a relatively quick release.

He remembered closing his eyes as the mighty creature swept magnificently upon him, covering his entire face and head with one giant taloned hand. As he braced for the pain he was sure would follow, he was instead transported, literally, it seemed, to a world of orange sand... twin suns and twin moons. There were tens of thousands of his kind here, not water demons, but majestic flying dragons, living peacefully... filling the skies, the hills, the water, and even the caves of the earth; and prospering without the intervention of humankind.

Now he could feel the pulse of the planet, itself. He could literally see the world through the eyes of the planetary spirit; feel its joy, its connection to all of its inhabitants... *its pain*. He was a newborn child, seeing the eyes of his mother for the first time and gazing in wonder at the vast beauty of this pristine entity. Watching her eyes close over the hills, winking at him one last time before they tucked themselves away in the valleys beyond, he turned to look behind him, out over the endless sea of orange sand toward the rising fury of the demon head, Algol.

He cowered as it revealed itself in the morning air, lighting up the faces of his children and making known his presence in unmistakable fury. The ground started to shake and flames shot down from the heavens, delivering retribution upon the already pulverized fields before him. The dragons stood their ground, bravely watching the fiery twin serpents as if they knew something he did not. It was then, right on the cusp of attrition that they were saved. She stole his fire and quelled his wrath for another passing... the great mother, Sigyn, the planet's twin sister.

As if she was following him all along, she rose out from behind the same veil... a towering, haloed goddess filling the sky with her deepening violet beauty. She lifted not only the heat from the soil, but the very loads from their backs, connected as deep as the very core of the planet in a dance through the cosmos, restoring balance and maintaining the ebb and flow of a timeless union... as ancient as life itself. He smiled as a giddy child would smile... finding all the beauty and contentment of the entire universe manifested in this one delicate moment of equilibrium.

He became acutely aware of all other things around him, from the deep breath of the creature closest to him, to the wind and the sky; playfully whisping around in the sand and tying it up into whirlwinds all across the plains. He could even feel the wind kick out from beneath the wings on one of the dragons nearly a quarter mile away! He stretched outward, feeling all of them, one at a time... then even the smaller creatures of the world, one by one, until he was at last one with the entire planet, from the largest and most advanced elder of their species, to the most insignificant speck of dust lost in the winds that whipped the hillsides. Its pulse became his own. There was harmony here, so ancient as to have transcended time entirely, existing in such a precarious balance, just as these beings existed... *teetering on the very edge of a razor!*

Now he felt something terrible approaching. Looking out over the horizon, he saw the ships coming. One, then two... only visitors taking safe haven from the perils of the cosmos, similar to their race, not so very long ago. But something was different about these visitors. The old ones could feel it in their intention. They were malignant... a random outbreak from a world that they had neglected to the point of unstoppable decay. They only looked inward... obsessed with only themselves, they couldn't see outward at all... to the ripples caused by their selfish and voracious lifestyle. They were a virus from ancient Earth who devoured their mother without regard, and were now here to do the same to theirs.

There was apparently a puppet master behind the scenes, controlling their actions without any real resistance... unchecked and unchallenged because of their weakened state of desperation and instability. Things were not at all as they seemed, and certainly not how they should be. Someone in power was perpetrating a massive cover up of information in order to achieve the unchecked molestation and mineral rape of the planet, despite its rare state of environmental balance and its hugely misunderstood and uninvestigated indigenous population.

At first, the identity of this perpetrator eluded him, as if it was always shrouded in uncertainty and emotion, as so often the future is veiled. He could see him scheming in a private meeting to bypass their own Indigenous Species Protocol in order to speed up timetables for departure through unabashed and careless mining tactics. He could almost make out his face as he made his conscious decision to firebomb the entire race right off the surface after the resistance grew and he received proof of their intelligence, rather than wade cautiously through the months of public sympathy and diplomacy that was inevitable once they were no longer being demonized. Looking in at him through the windshield on the front of a shuttle as if through the eyes of this creature, he knew the man, at last; identified unmistakably as he cowered back to his flagship on the eve of destruction after deciding to deceive their own best warrior and savior and use his unique skills to aid in genocide, rather than for self-defense and communication for scientific advancement. It was none other than their own leader, Admiral Reid!

He mounted a great war against them, giving himself the authority of martial law once more to silence the dissidents before they could so much as whisper with the voice of reason into the ears of those with the power to stop the madness. The peaceful dragon race, or M'ahk Tehríll, fought back to preserve not only their homes and way of life, but the very existence of this fragile world, as the humans threatened to bring the entire system to a point of critical mass that would destroy everything in an unimaginably vast radius. As the dragons took to the skies and tried to stop them, they fell like flies to the superior technology of the human machines... only managing to take down a few of the monstrous metal beasts for every hundred of their kind who were slain.

Then came the great flash in the sky, and all was silent. During the three days that followed, the few who remained were scattered to the wind as the beasts devoured their precious mother, gorging themselves on her flesh and wounding her so deeply that she would no longer be able to defend herself from the routine attacks of the poison twin serpents. They took all they needed, scorching those who resisted from the face of the planet, and left those who survived to their darkened fate, as the Usurper was revealed; arriving to claim everything and pull the world into eternal darkness.

He grew and grew, pulling everything into his center while lashing out at them with a fury unbound and unchecked. Sigyn tried to shelter them once again, but was devoured as well, as the planet was pulled closer and closer to the demon's head; the twins finally becoming one, and showing the true face of their master in an infinitely deep and sudden reflection that stretched ominously through the cosmos, consuming everything in its path. Armageddon had come to this world, and it was *his* people who had blown the final trumpet....

When he awoke, he was being pulled from the water with this vision still very vivid in his mind. He could still feel the warmth of the fires on his face and hands. He could still smell the scorched earth and burning corpses as if he was standing right there. He had no doubt that this grand vision was not only very real, but had been entrusted to him for an equally grand purpose. There was no protocol for the transport and relocation of an entire species, but he was sure that the message in his head, repeating over and over, was telling him to bring them *here*... to Cheops! He wasn't sure why, but this benevolent creature had chosen him to prevent what appeared to be nothing short of an interstellar apocalypse.

Kieran grasped the loose skin of his neck between his fingers and pinched it together with all his strength, flinched from the pain, then smiled, closing his eyes and basking in the moment. This was the first time since he had been rendered formless by Krey on the bridge of the Phoenix that he could recall feeling truly "alive." He clenched his fists, took a deep breath, then exhaled, standing up and looking around his new quarters while stretching every muscle group in his body, one by one.

The room looked almost the same. Oddly enough, he had ended up in the very same quarters that Thor afforded him just after his liberation from centuries of cryo-sleep. The first time, it was an easy pick, given that almost all the staterooms onboard The Phoenix had been recently vacated. This time, however, it was simply to be his. Now, it seemed, *he* was to be in control.

He could not have hoped for such a convenient turn of events as he lingered just below the surface of the turbulent water, shifting his form to resemble the outstretched arm of a wounded soldier. All that was needed for a "bait and switch" was for the one who tried to save him to be pulled under, absorbed, then mimicked and disposed of. He grinned again, realizing the long odds of this hapless person being who he turned out to be. He burst into a fit of boisterous, self-indulgent laughter, parading around the room in a momentary display of pent up immaturity, as uncharacteristic of him as for the officer whose likeness he had assumed.

He strutted around the perimeter of the room, gazing at the various pieces of artwork and memorabilia. On the desk was a treasure, to be sure. Possibly a family heirloom, a small stand made from varnished Indonesian mahogany that held a finely sharpened Darn Dao, or Chinese broadsword, in its sheath, with its mate running the opposite direction in the same sheath. These were no replicas, but antiques well over 2,000 years old, and utterly priceless.

Several incense burners and religious figurines carefully placed around the desk, along with the surrounding wall full of pictures from all aspects of eastern philosophy made it obvious that this man held his heritage in the highest regard. This soldier was a warrior from both worlds, just as was he, and for only the second time in his life, he felt a sharp tinge of shame for having ended the man's life so indiscriminately.

The first time it was the girl in the alley.... There was a fire in her eyes that would not have been so easily exhausted, had it not been for the cowardly tactics of a lesser man. He closed his eyes, remembering her staring back at him from the other side as she crossed over... something he had *never* before seen. The poor girl had an extremely brilliant fire in her eyes, and absolutely no idea what was happening to her. *Had they but met in another life... Could things have been different...? Are we doomed to make the same decisions over again, if given the same opportunities...?*

As he reopened his eyes, he stepped over to the mirror, just above the nightstand by the bed. His face was now very distinguished; an older man... weathered, but not broken. He was very short, but still had the build of a soldier, obviously the result of a lifetime of good dietary practices and a brutal workout regimen. He prepared himself for visitors, having still maintained his keen knack for premonition, regardless of what form he assumed or what plane he visited. Just then, his door buzzer sounded.

"Captain Chen, your presence is requested on the bridge, Sir..."

CHAPTER 26: CONVERGENCE

Though their original trajectory was an exact reversal, back toward Algol, as soon as they were shrouded from the sight of the H.O.R.U.S. by the vast blue nebula, they changed their course, running blind and as unpredictable as possible in an effort to throw off the disoriented Fleet who would undoubtedly be coming after them. Even though Thor was ecstatic to have his brother back on board with them, he could sense that something far worse was still brewing. Never before had he experienced a foe as relentless, nor as powerful as McGinn, and he knew, with every fiber of his existence, that this man would simply find another way to get to him. This was far from over.

Thor stood in the mirror, changing forms from one person to another, one creature to another, as fast as he could muster the energy and focus to continue. He stopped when he appeared to be an elderly man, possibly of African-American decent, but for the dirt and grime on his hands and face, it was nearly impossible to be sure. He was wearing tattered clothes, ripped and filthy from living for God-only-knows how long on the streets of the underground back on Earth. He turned towards Sky, who was relaxing on the bed with her hand over her belly, stroking it softly in circles.

"Well?" Thor asked, gesturing inquisitively with his hands out to the sides, awaiting her approval. "Do you like the jacket?"

She burst into laughter as he stumbled around in character, even mocking his voice in great detail. "Nice! That suits you!" She sat up and scooted to the edge of the bed. "How the hell did you come up with this guy? Holy shit!"

"He was an old friend of mine," Thor sighed, changing back to himself, "well, more of an acquaintance, really... but we shared some laughs! Even in impossibly hard times, he was one of those rare people who never let things get to him. He was like a drunken ray of sunshine to everyone who knew him."

She smiled at Thor, somewhat stricken by his uncharacteristically sensitive display of emotion as he got a little choked up while touching on his past, and had to wipe a tear from his eye. She could sense that his mind had drifted slightly off to the side to include thoughts of his family, as well. This brought a warm smile to his lips, and he suddenly shifted into the semblance of Tyr. He stood in front of the mirror, absolutely blown away, even himself, at how totally realistic this was. It was as if his brother was truly still here, standing in the flesh before his very eyes.

The more he thought about it, he was increasingly taken aback at the ease of the transformation... *all he had to do to achieve it was remember Tyr's energy.* The rest was quickly becoming instinct. He knew in his core, however, that no matter how good he got, he would need to expand his skills to stand even a hope of beating McGinn. Simple parlor tricks were simply not going to suffice.

"What did... *she*... look like?" Sky asked somewhat reluctantly. "*Me*, I mean... I guess."

"You don't yet know?"

"I think so, but I'm not entirely sure if what I'm seeing is the product of my own mind... or maybe something else." She thought long and hard, scratching her head in confusion. Although he was definitely attracted on a very powerful level to her strength, confidence, and warrior's skill, Thor found himself drawn in an intoxicating manner to this vulnerable, inquisitive and demure side of her that he scarcely encountered. It reminded him of Kait when she first came to the North Clan needing their help so desperately and so completely, following the horrible tragedy that befell her entire family. It was a lifetime ago, yet for Thor, it was still as fresh a memory as any in his head. Suddenly, she smiled broadly. "I've had some dreams lately where I'm her again... *I can see her now....*"

"*Show* me," Thor said, taking a seat next to her on the edge of the bed.

"Yeah, right! And just how the hell do you expect me to be able to pull that off, eh? I think we all developed different... *gifts*... after the tachyon jump. I think that one is yours, my love, not mine!"

"Don't be so damn sure," he whispered into her ear. "I think we've all been irrefutably... *altered*.... Just clear all other intention from your mind... allow it to fade away on its own... *release* it... don't attempt to clear your mind forcibly... this will just replace the old thoughts with the thought of clearing your mind!"

Sky laughed for a second, then took a deep breath and closed her eyes. "Now," Thor added, "simply focus on *her*. All aspects of her.... Her energy. Her humor. Her personality. Her anger. Her fear. Her complete outward appearance.... Her hair. Her face. Her eyes. Her clothes. Her very *style*.... Now, *allow* your pitch to *become* hers," he paused for a moment, watching in anticipation as she seemed on the cusp of transformation, his perception of her physical form being slowly called into question as she became harder and harder to define. "Allow her *energy* to *replace* yours.... Think only of *her*... *Become* her!"

She stood up, taking a step toward the mirror, then turned around, smiling. To the last detail, it was Kait! She could tell by Thor's look of absolute astonishment as he rubbed his eyes and shook his head that she had pegged it, which completely reaffirmed what they already knew, because she had never before so much as laid eyes on Kait's likeness, except in her dreams and visions.

"Wow," she said, turning back toward the mirror, "nice trick! It really *isn't* that hard, is it?"

"No, not since we-"

"Captain... Sky... You guys better get up here!"

"On our way, Bjorn," Sky answered first, Thor still sitting on the edge of the bed with his mouth open, staring at Sky's backside like a horny schoolboy as she transformed back to herself. Thor reached out and took her hand, standing up to give her a kiss.

"Poetry in motion.... I just got to watch you go from fine, to finer, back to finest!"

"This is too weird!"

"I know what you mean! We all need to find the time to discuss these changes," Thor said, quickly donning his battle gear and bolting for the door right behind her.

"I agree!"

There was an awkward moment of silence as they hit the button for the bridge deck on the elevator wall, then stood attentively, waiting.

"Well, I can definitely see what you liked about *her*!" Sky smiled coyly.

Thor looked at her, grinning. "Well, I would certainly *hope* so! Shit, just look in the mirror! The beauty of your soul is exactly the same in both forms, and in both times you've been just as hot on the outside!" She smiled broadly and hit the wall a couple times lightly with her forehead, her cheeks turning slightly red.

"Thank you," she said softly, awkwardly responding to his flattery by looking up at him through her shiny black hair with her big, ice-blue puppy dog eyes, flirting like a teenager with a crush. As the elevator slowed to a stop and the door whisked open, they were simultaneously hit with a horrible feeling, deep down in the gut. They looked at each other, confirming the terrifying notion, then bolted for the bridge door.

Erük and Bjorn were both pouring over charts of the entire quadrant, expanding it in every conceivable direction, then focusing in on each system with great detail, apparently in a big hurry to find a direction to flee. Thor could sense the tension in Erük, but Bjorn was wearing it on his sleeve. The genius level navigator/ helmsman was literally trembling, and though it was a temperature controlled 70 degrees Fahrenheit on the bridge, he was sweating profusely.

"Okay… spit it out, guys!" Sky exclaimed, starting to get tense, herself.

"It's the F-F-F-Fleet," Bjorn stuttered, still trembling as he spun the holographic image around toward Thor and Sky to be read from their perspective. They could see from the sheer numbers that it was the entire Fleet, and that they weren't that far away….

"Jesus Christ!" Thor yelled. "They sent the entire Fleet after us? How could they have mobilized so fast?" He scratched his head with a puzzled look in his eyes. "Well, I guess that's in our favor… I mean, they can't possibly keep up with us with that kind of baggage!" Thor looked around the room at the dumbfounded expressions on everyone else's faces, "Can they?" Then it suddenly clicked. *"Oh my God!"* he yelled, zooming in on the ships to realize that the Icarus wasn't among them, nor was the Helios leading the way.... This was what was left of the Fleet from *their* time! Sky just stood with her hand over her mouth and a horrified look in her eyes.

"They must have caught the same tachyon wave!" Bjorn offered.

"And somehow stopped at precisely the same spot in history as us? Within two weeks of each other? *Really?*" Sky asked, skeptically.

"Sure... why not?" Bjorn replied. "They would have most likely stopped at Cheops, as well, especially if somehow they were scanning us *en route* as we approached this system! The destination target *time* was merely a function of how far we all traveled *at that speed*, before coming to a stop, which was nearly the same for them... within two weeks!"

"Alright, I get it! Now what? If they didn't go forward to the next system like they had planned, then they want vengeance... and our fuel!"

"They'll get my boot heel up their arse, and that's all they'll get!" Thor snarled, slapping the holographic viewer into a spin that caused the image of the Fleet ships to turn into what strongly resembled a toilet flushing just before it turned off automatically. "Beat to quarters!"

"What...?" Bjorn laughed.

"Sorry, wrong century... even for me! Battle stations!"

Kaitlyn sat on the edge of her top dresser drawer, with the drawer itself pulled out and flipped upside-down in order to turn it into a flat surface. She gazed out the window at the converging weather, slowly, but surely, closing in around the lone patch of clear blue sky left directly over the eye of the original storm.

The weather had evolved as originally predicted by the meteorologists onboard the H.O.R.U.S.. The main storm cell had begun moving, but rather than following a straight line and pulling away from the centripetal pull of the polar region, it had circled about, now turning back on its original vector just in time to fuse with a completely separate storm cell that sprouted up in its wake, out over the ocean, and was moving fast.

The smaller, hurricane level storm cell was due to make landfall sometime in the middle of the night, and would then join the original cell on its return pass sometime in the afternoon. It would be centered directly over their current position, reaching critical mass almost immediately and turning the entire southern pole into one massive vortex of natural destruction. Although the shelters and equipment built by the CSE crews for initial colonization were designed to take it, or virtually _any_ natural abuse, given the chain of events that took place regarding the appearance of this rogue Carrier, the decision was made to depart, Fleet-wide, immediately.

Kaitlyn's personal effects could be stuffed into one or two laundry bags in a matter of minutes, but she hadn't even begun to pack. It seemed simply too much like giving up on Mom and Dad, who, as far as her young mind could deduce, were still alive and waiting for her somewhere on this rock... possibly just detained, or maybe injured and unable to respond to any of the many sorties that flew over the areas in question in the days that followed their disappearance. Without bodies, it was simply too hard for her to give up completely, and she just didn't _feel_ them to be gone. Closure, it seemed, wasn't all it was cracked up to be, anyway. At the risk of being painted a masochist, she found that the naïve and fleeting aftertaste of hope, however slight or contrived, still tasted a touch sweeter in its vague familiarity than the solemn bitterness of defeat.

She stared at herself in the mirror, turning sideways to examine her profile. She held her abdomen in tight and thrust her modest breasts outward, recalling the dreams of herself as an adult she had been having more and more in recent days. She had always been content with her progress, and was never really in a huge hurry to grow up, but as things had progressed lately, she found herself strangely jealous of this woman she was to become, and struggled with feelings of inadequacy every time she looked closely at herself. She felt like she was already an adult, yet was treated by nearly everyone as a mere child.

Frustrated, she covered up the mirror with a jacket that was sitting on a small table by the door, then poured herself a glass of juice from the small personal fridge that Captain Parnell had installed in her quarters when he took over command. Though it was totally unnecessary, and even frowned upon due to the communal availability of food in the central cafeteria, it was a very nice convenience, especially during times such as these, when being around a lot of people was very difficult. He always did seem to favor her; and she played on this to the fullest, nearly taking advantage of his generosity and interest in her, despite the fact that she did genuinely appreciate it and respect him deeply. In some ways, he always seemed to her to be more of a father figure than her own dad.

She had her eyes closed, savoring the naturally sweet taste of the bizarre juice from one of this planet's only edible fruits: the *"mangalay"*... a strange, water rich, softball sized melon of sorts, that grew all over the sunny side of the beaches from vines that protruded out into the water, literally growing just underwater until they were ripe, at which point they became buoyant and rose to the surface. Though the water itself was too salty to drink without pulling it through a desalinization filter, these hand sized treats were loaded with all the fresh water one needed, and were as sweet as French vanilla, quickly becoming a favorite of the settlers.

She had her head tilted all the way back, letting the very last of her mangalay juice drip out of the glass and into her mouth when the door slid open, making her jump right out of her skin. She fumbled the glass and it fell, hitting the hard floor with a clang and bouncing around on the hard surface before coming to a stop.

"Don't you guys ever fucking knock!!?" she screamed at the officer and his two man security detail who now stood behind him in her doorway.

"My apologies, Ma'am, but time is a luxury we do not have! We've been ordered to escort you to the Phoenix immediately for reassignment," the man said matter-of-factly, stepping just inside the foyer. His two subordinates followed him in, stopping when he stopped.

"Cute. Look, Mr.-"

"Lieutenant Daniels, Ma'am."

"Lieutenant Daniels. I'm not ready to leave here! My parents are still missing, I just got assigned to this ship, I don't want to leave yet!" she pleaded, having no visible effect on the man's resolve.

"Grab only what you can carry," he said plainly, "we don't have much room on the shuttle." She stood for nearly a solid minute staring the man down, to no avail, then realized she would not be able to sway his mandate in any direction at all… he was very simply under orders.

"Shit! Alright, where's Commander Parnell?"

"He's onboard the Phoenix already. The order comes from him! Now let's go! We need to beat this storm out of here! They're waiting!"

Thor's pacing was starting to get to Sky, who, aside from the fact that she was uncomfortably pregnant, was fairly relaxed and sitting casually in her copilots chair staring at the hologram in front of her. "Will you *please* settle down? I love you, baby, but you're driving me nuts!"

He took a deep breath and sat down, albeit on the edge of his seat, but it was a step in the right direction. "Sorry."

"Now, let's think this through," she said calmly, glancing over at Bjorn and Erük as well, "shall we?"

What started out as a casual glance evolved into an elongated stare that seemed to transcend the boundaries of the room. She stayed like this just long enough for everyone to take notice, then her eyes slowly rolled back into her head and she slumped over sideways in her chair, awake, but hardly conscious at all. Thor rushed to her side, and as he grabbed her by the arms and cradled her back into position, she twitched once with her whole body, mumbling as she stirred.

"Don't you guys ever fucking knock...?" she mumbled in a slightly higher voice.

"Hey! Sweetie! Come back to us, babe, you're scaring me!" Thor whispered a couple inches from her ear, lightly slapping her on both sides of her face and shaking her torso back and forth softly.

"Cute. Look, Mr.-"

Thor smiled, suddenly realizing that she wasn't hearing anything he was saying. "Mr. Bond... James Bond." Bjorn, obviously an old American movie buff, burst out laughing through his nose, spilling water from his glass down the front of his lapel.

"Lieutenant Daniels. I'm not ready to leave here! My parents are still missing, I just got assigned to this ship, I don't want to leave yet!" she mumbled faintly, as if she was talking in her sleep. Erük came up to her and put his hand across her forehead, closing his eyes. He began to move as she moved,

see what she was seeing. She spoke one final time, and Erük's lips moved in sync, right along with hers. *"Shit! Alright, where's Commander Parnell?"*

"I sent him to Hell, my darling," Thor proudly interjected.

Erük stood up a bit, then spoke out quite loudly in a voice that wasn't his. *"He's onboard the Phoenix already. The order comes from him! Now let's go! We need to beat this storm out of here! They're waiting!"* He broke away from Sky, breathing heavily. Thor looked at Bjorn with wide eyes and a gaping jaw. The room remained silent for several minutes as it was now Erük who was pacing grooves into the floor while mulling over what he had just seen within her mind.

"So, Parnell's on the other Phoenix right now, eh? Well, I guess I already sort of knew that... hell, so am I, in a manner of speaking... frozen solid!"

"That's not what bothers me, my brother." Erük stopped pacing and stared right at Thor. *"I could feel something else...."* His joking expression quickly changed to shock and anger as he deduced what Erük was about to tell him, speaking for him as he closed his eyes and nodded.

"McGinn is on that ship."

CHAPTER 27: PARALLEL BY DESIGN

Young Kaitlyn gazed out the windshield of the shuttle as they approached the shores of the ocean, just out over the last of the mountain peaks, where the Phoenix lay waiting, hovering out past the breakers no more than 20 feet above the water, inviting her to pursue her true destiny... her new life as an officer of the flight crew onboard one of the Fleet's finest interstellar spacecrafts. She was excited to begin, and yet she was completely inundated in her surroundings at the moment, staring in wonder at the main body of the lightning storm coming from all around them, attracted to their tiny ship like a magnet. Bolts of lightning were illuminating sections of sky randomly as she stared in wonder and relative safety through the front viewing shield at the mountains in the distance, the swirling clouds of gasses dancing violently around them, and the huge water spouts from the tempestuous ocean below, rising up to meet the heavens in a vortex of natural energy unleashed before them by the very gods of this hostile world themselves.

Much too young to appreciate the danger they were all actually in, she absorbed the experience to her very core;

living a lifetime in each breath and for the first time in her life, *truly* living in the moment. "Sky…" she said with a proud grin, trying it on as she felt, at this very moment, her new life just beginning.

"What was that? I'm sorry, I couldn't hear you, Ma'am… the storm's so loud!" the pilot yelled in response.

"Nothing, sorry… I was talking to myself!"

"Understood," he said with a smile, "I do it all the time! The only problem is, I never listen to myself! Oh, well, no one else does, either."

"I'm sorry… what was that?" she mumbled, distracted by the intensity of a nearby blast of lightning.

"See what I mean?"

She smiled politely, trying so hard to look back up the way they came as they descended straight through the furious storm to land precariously on the docking pad just inside the giant shuttle bay of the Phoenix. There were medics and crewmen standing by with fire extinguishers just in case the trip didn't go as planned. She was honored, as well as a bit surprised at the red carpet treatment, as it was usually only the top brass that received this sort of welcome.

No sooner had she walked down the shuttle ramp and onto the floor of the Phoenix, as she could hear the low hum of the primary engines cycling up for takeoff. She handed her bags to the officer next to her and sped up to a trot, looking around for Parnell, but not seeing him anywhere. "Where is Commander Parnell?" she asked the man with her bags, who merely shrugged and continued walking toward the far side of the landing bay. Just as they were approaching the doors to the cargo elevator, another officer, a stern fellow bearing a slight resemblance to a tree trunk, approached them and reached out to shake Kaitlyn's hand.

"Glad to finally meet you, Ma'am. My name is Ensign Bellows. I'll take you to your new quarters. You get the old VIP stateroom...."

"Is that a good thing?" she asked, naïvely.

"That's a *very* good thing," he laughed, "I think you'll be quite pleased.... This room has served Senators, Admirals, famous celebrity entertainers... hell, practically even royalty!"

———————

Concerned for her well being, Thor had Sky moved to the Medical Bay and confined to round the clock supervision. Though none of them really understood exactly how and why it worked, they all understood that she was somehow too close to her former self, and was living vicariously through her eyes because of Ar'Jvikkah's influence. He seemed to be unknowingly causing the two time lines to fuse, and Thor feared that if they did not get her further away from young Kaitlyn, that the two might become one... transcending space-time entirely in some kind of temporal convergence.

She was "awake," so to speak, and was sitting up on the edge of her bed in deep thought when Thor came back in from his duties on the bridge to check on her again. Smiling warmly as he approached, she shrugged and patted the bed with her hand, making room for him next to her.

"How's everything in the real world?" she joked, laughing just a little as he sat down. He just smiled at her with a troubled look in his eye and softly stroked the back of her hair repeatedly, obviously deep in thought and more than a little worried for her. She started to become a little bit entranced by the feeling of him playing with her hair, then all at once she was overcome with a wild sensation, flinching and wiggling about rapidly for a moment from the sensation he accidentally caused along the back of her neck. She finally shook it off, laughing hysterically and punching him in the shoulder. "You gave me the Heebey-Jeebies, dammit!"

He started laughing, then stopped messing with her hair. "What sense does all of this make to you? Are you actually seeing through her eyes when this occurs?"

"It's just as if it was me experiencing these moments for the first time. I've given this a lot of thought, and it seems to me so far that these moments coincide with all of the gaps in my memory as a child.... I had always been told that I suppressed certain memories in my youth... due largely to the trauma inflicted by my parents' disappearance... but I'm starting to wonder if this wasn't the real reason all along!" She looked at him with wild eyes, full of wonder, but most definitely as sane as they come. "What if nothing can be changed by our being here, because this simply *is* what already happened, even before...? So far, everything that has transpired has been exactly what happened, even then, it simply becomes explainable when looked at from our new point of view! For some reason we aren't allowed to know about the source of the influence from our own futures when it takes place, so-"

"So in our minds, these moments were simply *blackouts* until we become an active party to the gaps finally being filled in at a later time," he interrupted, "No shit! Sky, I think you're onto something! That makes *absolute* sense! If we were allowed to know the source of the influence, it would surely influence our life decisions from that point on... possibly causing some serious problems! By that logic, there can be no real paradox, at least not from our actions or decisions... no real change of destiny.... *Can there?*"

"I don't know. There is still the matter of free will... who's to say that a mind bent on changing a particular outcome couldn't pull it off, providing they were willing to pay for it, somehow.... Perhaps they would find out that it simply *happened already*, or else maybe paradox *is* possible! Keep in mind, we orchestrated a good part of the rescue of my parents the way we did *because* we were being careful to avoid a paradox... our every decision here has been based on that level of personal responsibility! Suppose for a moment that it wasn't...."

Commander Parnell sat at his desk, alone in his quarters, and poured himself a second snifter of cognac, relighting the candle on his stand to prepare for heating it ritualistically to perfection as he plunged into deeper and deeper thought. He couldn't seem to shake the visions Erük had delivered to him, no matter how much he drank. It seemed that he was destined for something great, something far greater than himself *or* this ship... hell, possibly even greater than the Fleet, itself. He rested the snifter on the stand, the cognac inside swaying back and forth over the hot candle flame as he leaned back in his chair and attempted to collect his wayward thoughts.

He carefully corked the regal looking bottle of King Louis the 13th with its majestic crown cap and slid the bottle back into its showcase niche on the bookshelf behind him, then pulled out a comparatively ordinary bottle of Courvoisier XO from beneath his desk in a preemptive strike at the doldrums setting in around him, in favor of but a fleeting taste of *"dolce vita"* from which to abstract some level of inspiration; a plan that most often produced little beyond the faintest feeling of youth revisited, extracted and relived in a fleeting and foggy reflection, at best, and nothing more than a vague shadow of one's former glory.

The true measure of good cognac was in the exhale. One could savor a good glass for several minutes prior to the initial sip, enjoying everything dynamic it had to offer before ever tasting it at all. King Louis was no exception... simply exceptional. He held the glass under his nose, swirling the centuries old brew from the French countryside counterclockwise in a ritualistic gesture, until just when it felt like nothing more could possibly be achieved or extracted, then he closed his eyes slowly and approached his lips with the glass... a rare indulgence even in its own day, as this particular brew sold for over a thousand dollars a bottle even in those times. It was absolutely priceless now.

The Commander walked purposefully down the corridor from the bridge, feeling the need to wrap up one last piece of unfinished business before things went any further. He was frustrated and angry, but for the life of him, he did not know why. It simply didn't matter. There was one name repeating over and over through his mind. One name that was to blame. Only one name to eliminate before things would be set right... before they could go back to the way they were... *Thorsson Krey*. He did not understand why, but he knew he *must* eliminate him. Only then would the voices stop. Only then would things return to normal.

He walked directly past the Medical Bay doorway, then hooked quickly through the next opening into the security clearance room just before the entryway to the storeroom for the cryostasis tubes and gear, where all of the Cryos were stored intermittently while in solo flight, or on planet during mining ops, to prepare them for quick and easy regeneration and utilization. At any given time, there could potentially be as many as 30 of them, awaiting thaw out and implementation next door.

He placed his open palm over the security pad and the double doors whisked open quickly and quietly. Upon removing his hand from the pad, he caught a glimpse of the reflection of a man standing just behind him, practically looming over his shoulder with an unusually serious look on his face, whispering in his ear. It was Captain Chen, looking very anxious about something, but not saying an audible word. He was suddenly awash with the intense feeling of déjà vu.

He spun around, defensively, but to his unnerving surprise, there was no one present at all. He felt as if he couldn't catch his breath and his heart was pounding madly. He stepped back from the door and it slid closed as he shook his head, thrashing about madly in an attempt to shake off the overpowering feeling he was experiencing. It seemed as if he was losing control over his own body. He felt a great pull back toward the door and literally had to force his eyes open again, as if his eyelids weighed 1,000 lbs. each.

"Commander Parnell, we need you on the bridge... It's an emergency... Please respond!"
He jumped as he heard the loud voice blasting through the silence of his room, then there was the sound of breaking glass and the lingering sense that something foul was at work here. As things came into focus he realized that once again he was still sitting at his desk... cognac, broken glass and melted wax strewn across its meticulously polished surface, as once again he was jolted from this still powerfully disturbing, yet compelling dream. He was now determined to discover the meaning of this phenomenon that was starting to cost him an equally disturbing amount of fine liquor. He took a straight shot right off the bottle of XO, corked it and put it back under his desk, quickly changed his shirt and headed out his door for the bridge, tapping the belt com on his disheveled uniform. "On my way... Parnell out!"

Kaitlyn sat alone in her plush stateroom as the huge ship heeled in preparation for a jump out of the planet's atmosphere and into true spaceflight. Though most of the living quarters were virtually impervious to the effects of this type of movement, she could feel it instinctively. She always could.

Her teachers were frequently astonished and annoyed at her outbursts in class when she would point such abnormalities out to the class and turn out to be right after some debate. She could even feel the slightest differences in the craft's speed, which always stumped her parents and teachers, mainly due to the fact that in deep space, with no atmosphere to relatively base a speed comparison on, this was theoretically impossible. What she didn't tell them was that she could actually *feel* the vibration of the engine itself, and could therefore tell when it was accelerating or winding down. This had become the source of much gossip, and even more cheap entertainment over the years.

She wiped the glass on the front panel of the small picture frame, then wiped a tear from her eye as she respectfully sat it down on the eye level ledge of the small set of cubby-style built in shelves next to her bed. It was a day she barely remembered, but one that over the last few days, was becoming increasingly dear to her.

Her mother looked so happy, so utterly free and relaxed. Her dad had the same look in his eye that he usually did when he was around her, like he was about to jump in front of a moving freight train, or take a bullet to protect her. This was a serious stress factor and an obsession for him, but in his own way, this was his source of true happiness as well; his ultimate sense of purpose. She stood right between them, as she always did, holding both of their hands and not leaning too far in either direction for a ridiculous and unfounded fear of showing even the slightest favor and displeasing one or the other of them.

To her, family was everything, and now that they had been replaced with a gaping hole in her chest that she couldn't fill in a thousand lifetimes, she found herself crying, not for their loss, but for the regret that she never had the opportunity to let them see her achieve the level of greatness they always wished for her; to see her life finally complete... to see her finally *safe*. After losing her little sister at such a young age, she knew that this was the only thing that truly mattered to them... the only thing they *truly* expected from themselves. She walked over to her closet with a very different, very spirited look in her eyes and started to put on her combat gear in favor of the formal attire she had originally set out instinctively for this occasion.

Commander Parnell stormed onto the bridge with a purpose, not entirely surprised to see that the Captain was nowhere in sight. A security team led by Ensign Bellows was huddled around the holographic monitor muttering to themselves while helm was madly combing through a series of star charts and navigational scenarios.

"Captain on deck!" Bellows called out, gaining the attention of everyone on the bridge, particularly Commander Parnell. They all turned to him and saluted, as would be proper had he been the Captain....

Parnell saluted back, not completely sure what had transpired, but starting to understand the outcome, at least. "Where's Captain Chen?" he demanded, to which Bellows waved him over to the monitor in front of the security team. Parnell turned white as a ghost when he saw the image of Captain Chen locked in the cryo storage room of the Medical Bay by himself, browsing around the room, but making no attempt to leave. His mind quickly raced back to his dream, but he said nothing to the men about it. "What's he doing?"

"We're not sure. More importantly is the question of *who* he is at all! Look closely at his feet, Sir...."

Parnell leaned forward and looked closely at the monitor, unable to see the man's feet, as he suggested, due to the arrangement of the tables and equipment. He continued staring, but softly asked Bellows a few more questions. "How long has he been in there?"

"We *just* trapped him in there... He was milling around outside that doorway, then we saw people approaching, and didn't want him coming into contact with them, so we manually triggered the door release from here. After that, he went right in and we shut it behind him."

"You didn't *trap* him... he *tricked* you! He knew you were watching him, didn't he?"

"How did you know that? Y-yes, he looked right at the camera after we noticed... after we-"

"After you noticed what? Come on, man, speak plainly!" The nervous Ensign shakily pointed his thick finger at the screen. Parnell turned around just in time to see his feet before he stepped back behind another table where he was obviously checking to see who each of the patients were, and noticed what all the fuss was about. He was moving about the room, clearly mimicking the movements of a physical human being, but his feet were simply *not touching the floor*! He was gliding just above the plane of the floor, but not making physical contact with anything.

"Sir, the man you see before you is simply *not* the Captain! We tried to contact him, even before we saw him in the corridor, but he wouldn't respond! We did a shipwide scan, and Captain Chen is nowhere on the ship! Vanished!" Parnell stared at the man closely while Bellows spoke. "Whoever, or *whatever* he is, Sir, he is *not* the Captain! *You are*. Captain Chen is now officially listed as missing in action."

"Understood. Lock the doors to that room! Whatever he is, he appears to be getting what he came for… let's see to it that he doesn't leave with it!" Parnell tapped two of the security members on the shoulder and motioned for them to follow him, then turned and started for the door.

"Already done… Sir, there's one more problem!"

Parnell turned back toward him. "Yes?"

"This…" He spun the holographic monitor around to give him the best perspective of the incoming Fleet just entering the nebula from the far side, then panned out and toward them to include the present day Fleet, locked in on what appeared to be a collision course with them.

"Why aren't they in defensive formation," Parnell asked, "and why haven't we been notified?"

"I'm not sure, Sir, but as close as they are to the blue giant, along with the presence of the gasses in that nebula, it's very likely that their scanners and their ability to transmit and receive messages has been seriously impaired, if not crippled! Either that, or it's being jammed at the source!"

"Keep trying to hail the Admiral's ship… or the H.O.R.U.S…. Any theories as to who they are, or where they came from?"

"None, Sir."

"He's involved with this, somehow! I'm taking him out before he succeeds at whatever he's up to! Keep me on screen… Adjust the Log to reflect that I am assuming command of the Phoenix, and the rank of Captain. You two, come with me! Let's take him alive! We need to know what he did with Captain Chen!"

"Yes, Sir!" they responded, almost in unison, then followed Captain Parnell over to the munitions cabinet near the door. Parnell placed his palm on the pad and the small door slid quickly upward to reveal about a dozen rifles and a rack full of pistols and ammunition. Thinking quickly about his foe, the decision wasn't hard to make.

Though Parnell typically favored the use of conventional bullet-firing sidearms, he grabbed a plasma rifle and both kinds of pistol, not knowing for sure what type might even be effective on this seemingly energy-based doppelganger. He kept the plasma-based pistol in hand, and instructed the security detail to do the same, due mostly to the possibility of a bullet flying straight through the intruder without so much as slowing down, and becoming a rogue projectile capable of great destruction onboard a starship with a sealed hull and environment control. The two security officers with him were carrying a plasma pistol and rifle apiece, as the three of them marched off of the bridge with a purpose.

Ensign Bellows gasped as he glanced back at the security screen to catch Chen's imposter looking straight at the camera, moreover straight at *him,* and grinning devilishly, as if he was fully aware they were coming, and didn't care at all… in fact, he looked as if he *welcomed* it! It suddenly felt as if they were walking into an ambush.

Bellows frantically hit his belt com to warn Parnell, but jumped in surprise as they all heard the feedback from the small device coming from within the room! They looked around quickly and noticed it was still setting on the countertop next to the munitions locker where Parnell removed it while strapping on a shoulder harness.

Erük leaned in close over her, trying to make out her words, as she sang some sort of melody in her sleep. Thor had noticed this before. It was some sort of jingle or simple song that she didn't recognize herself when Thor tried to recite it to her, yet she seemed to dream of it quite often these last few days, and almost invariably with a cute and innocent smile on her face. Erük couldn't quite make it out, but as he got close to her, he definitely realized its origin. Her young self was humming it as she got dressed, and possibly due to some help from Ar'Jvikkah, or maybe simply because Sky was sound asleep prior to their communion, he was able to see through her eyes quite clearly.

She paused what she was doing and looked madly about the room, sure for a moment that she was being watched. Erük realized he was the cause of this feeling, and he toned his presence down just a notch, not wanting to lose this connection if she started to fight it.... She calmed down rather quickly after realizing no one was in the room with her, and continued getting ready. Erük couldn't help but be just a slight bit amused, seeing this diminutive young woman so aggressively strapping her boots on in preparation for whatever was afoot.

As soon as she finished with her attire, she pulled out a case from her personal effects and produced a leather roll-up satchel from within it, setting it respectfully onto her bed. She gave it a push while trapping one end, and the whole thing unrolled, revealing its contents. Stretched across the breadth of her bed was every manner of knife, short sword, hand weapon and handgun imaginable... all embossed with the personal glyph of the young girl's family, a house rune that was a variation of the Futhark Viking rune teiwaz, or "Tyr" the warrior's rune... so named after the Norse God, himself.

She concealed several of the smaller knives and edged weapons on her person in various places within the confines of her attire, then took a pair of long knives out in a ceremonious way and walked toward the center of the room. She stood there for quite a long time, centering herself and breathing deep, long breaths as she meditated in preparation for kata. In a most non-pretentious gesture, especially due to the fact that she was alone in the room, she turned and bowed to a picture of her

Sensei, *or teacher*... her mentor and friend, the new captain of the Phoenix, and unbeknownst to her, her true father, John Parnell. As she bowed, she methodically uttered the phrase, "*Oni Gai Shimasu,*" meaning essentially, "Let us work well together," in Japanese, then erupted into action.

Jumping into the air nearly straight upward, she threw a scissor kick with her right leg, trapping her phantom attacker's head between the side of her right boot, and the palm of her open left hand, creating an echoing "clapping" noise in the otherwise silent room. She performed a surgically precise hand change on the way down, taking one of the blades into her left hand and slashing the full diagonal breadth of her attacker with her right, downward, from right to left at a 45 degree angle from shoulder to waist.

As soon as she landed from this nearly seven foot high kick, she crouched low, her right fist on the floor as she pivoted around to the left, counterclockwise with a complete reversal, ending in a heel kick to the abdomen from down low, followed instantly by another reversal into a foot sweep. The finishing blow was added, then a high overhead block from this crouched position in anticipation of an impending attack from above.

A right handed thrust with the blade becoming an extension of her arm was now delivered, straight as an arrow, directly into the lower abdomen from this painfully deep, *almost* kneeling cross stance, then back to the overhead block, transitioning smoothly and surprisingly into a grab of the opponent's attacking arm with the left blocking hand, followed by springing upward out of the deep stance into a double crescent kick, left heel trailed immediately in the same jump by the right foot, landing with the right side toward the now very stunned attacker, deep into *shiko*, or a "horse stance," with the right arm twisted underhand and backward, forcibly striking with the fingertips and grasping the enemy by the groin while the left hand remains in *woo sao*, or defensive guard near the right side of the face. In mid jump, another enemy, quickly rushing in from the left, was dispatched by throwing the right handed knife, which now vibrated at a solid 90 degree plant, stuck two inches into the corner stud of the partition wall, 10 feet away to her left.

A desperate reactionary strike from the hapless opponent is then hooked with the left hand blade and parried downward and to the left in a semicircle as the right arm lets go of the groin to pivot all the way back up from its downward position to backhand the now overcommitted and off-balance attacker directly in the chin, causing his head to whip backwards as she spins in reverse, slicing straight across the freshly exposed throat of the man, then quickly turns her attention elsewhere. She looks quickly to the left, bringing the right foot all the way across the floor in a massive sweep, remaining low with her left blade guarding her from above as the new attack comes in from the left side…

"Damn it!" she yelled out loud, slightly losing her balance just at that moment… the same exact place in the kata that always gives her a problem. Frustrated, she spun around, throwing the remaining knife into the wall just below its mate, then wrapped it up for now, feeling the pressing need to get to the bridge for her first day of officer training. She took a deep breath to calm her frustration, pulling her arms upward and to her sides as she inhaled then "pushed" downward toward her hips as she exhaled. She turned to face the picture of Parnell, dressed in his own gi and surrounded by students at some sort of martial arts seminar.

"Domo arigato goza imashita, Sensei," she said, traditionally thanking him for the knowledge he has bestowed upon her in the most polite and respectful way possible. In the absence of personal attendance, it was not considered unusual for a dojo to respect its senior members by placing their likeness in their stead, even in the lineup of ranks about the room, or in ceremonies. It mostly had to do with the feeling of gratitude and respect within the beholder being present at all times, rather than anything to do with any expectations coming from the absentee, but was upheld and practiced with strict discipline and devout tradition, nonetheless.

Kaitlyn put away the blades and hid her satchel in its case beneath her bed, then inspected herself in the mirror to make sure her other weapons were still concealed after her quick workout. She wiped the remaining sweat from her brow, then energetically proceeded out the doorway and down the corridor toward the bridge to begin training for her new post... or so she thought.

"Captain!... Thor! What's wrong?" Bjorn yelled as he shook Thor by the shoulders, unsure what was going on. One moment everything seemed normal, then Thor stopped talking in mid-sentence and just stared off into space with a troubled look in his eyes. Nothing he said or did seemed to be penetrating his trance. "Come on, big guy! You're scaring me, now, wake the fuck up, Krey!" He steadied him with one hand, then reached over and slammed his fist down on the console button for the shipwide loudspeaker, afraid to leave Thor unattended for even a second. "Astrydd! We need you on the bridge, immediately! Bring a gurney.... Bring Erük!"
"Roger that... On my way!"

McGinn was fairly new at using solid matter telekinesis while simultaneously maintaining projected transfiguration, all from another plane, but given his present situation, he found himself with little choice as he focused hard on pulling the second cryo tube from its slot in the wall.

He had been forced to flee into the security of the cryo staging lab without the benefit of a puppet to carry out his mundane physical feats through mind control, or in this case, given his current façade, the direct orders from their beloved Captain Chen. To anyone in human form, this procedure was merely a keystroke or two on the computer, followed by the pushing of a button and the turning of a release valve switch.

With each Carrier only rigged to keep 20 cryos in backup storage at a time, it didn't take him long to locate the two he was looking for. The one he really needed, his own, was going to take some time to bring to a staging point he could use, but his prize was nearly done already.... It seemed as if a prisoner by the name of "James Stanton" was already being pre-staged to be one of the next generation workers. He kicked himself for losing so much time using Parnell to search the computer databank in a trance for "Thorsson Krey," when he had all but forgotten that he sat in the CryoKinetics main office and witnessed Thor signing up under that alias!

He stood fast, bogged down by the system as the equipment went through its necessary list of protocol for cellular regeneration in order to replace the dead cells that had to be frozen solid with cloned replicas, bit by painstaking and exacting bit. Kieran chuckled as he realized that due to the built in safety precautions inherent in the system, it was literally impossible to kill a patient without first having thawed and revitalized them nearly to the point of speech, and by the time there was anything flowing to deprive them of, they would be almost conscious! This was fine with him, as he did actually have a bit of a problem with murdering another warrior in his sleep. Something about it seemed cowardly to him, despite the fact that in order to even do that, he was looking at an almost inescapable scenario. He turned toward the glass doorway and grinned at the mass of security and armed officers welling up just outside the door, totally relieved that he had no intention of escaping.

Kaitlyn was humming a giddy little tune as the elevator slowed its ascent and came to a stop. The door whisked open and she jumped back a step, immediately seeing that something huge was going on in front of the Medical Bay. Parnell himself was standing with his face nearly glued to the glass door of the cryo staging lab while his technicians worked on hacking the door lock from the panel circuitry. She stepped right up, just behind Captain Parnell, in order to get a better look.

"Whoa... hold up, sweetheart! We don't know what this thing's capable of! Just keep your distance while we get this door open," Parnell said in a bit of a condescending manner, managing to inflame her curiosity and her rebellious nature at the same time. She leaned forward, just past Parnell's outstretched arm, and peered inside. She jumped back, realizing immediately that something was amiss with the good Captain.

"W-what is he?" she asked without taking her eyes off of him.

"Good eyes," Parnell smiled, "To be perfectly honest, we're not sure. He's sure as hell not Ming Chen, though, I can tell you that! We locked him in here and then he was able to short circuit the lock electronics to keep *us* out!" She looked up at Parnell as if she suddenly had something to say, then held back, turning her attention back to the intruder, who had now managed to get one of the cryo tubes to eject out of its wall slot and onto a prep table without doing anything but holding his hand over the computer terminal.

She could see the man through the glass on his tube and suddenly became very concerned. "Who is that man?" she asked impatiently. Parnell was busy talking to the technician who was working on the door lock panel, growing impatient, himself. She tapped him on the shoulder. Still nothing. "John!" she yelled, kneeing him in the thigh rather rudely and informally, given the presence of his subordinates. He spun around, obviously miffed, glaring at her.

"What!?!"

"Sir, who is that man he's got almost out of cryostasis? He's going to die if this continues! This imposter is obviously not interested in following the medical procedures necessary after this long of a freeze...."

"Yeah, I don't know, but I'm trying to get this door open so we can ask him... do you mind?" He kept his left hand on her shoulder for a moment as he turned his attention back to the technician, who didn't appear to be making any headway. Frustrated, she blatantly shook him off, then stepped back up to the glass, squinting to get a better look at the man on the table. Something about him seemed very familiar to her, but she couldn't yet place it....

He had reached a point of regeneration that from her medical training, she knew required the use of an I.V. drip of nutrients and electrolytes for quick rehydration. Without it, this man would quickly die, as his organs would be going into shock and he would succumb to an accelerated form of pulmonary edema, quickly flooding his lungs with his own body fluids and causing him to drown right in front of them on the table.

She stared at the strange creature that was mimicking Captain Chen. It had an energy she had felt before... *in her dreams!* She remembered her experience in the caves while looking for these creatures and it finally hit her. *The dream!* She started getting flashes from the dream that seemed so real she could have sworn they really happened. First of Thor, standing inside the small cabin with his katana drawn, the very same sword she could now see tucked inside the clear carbon fiber tube in his personal effects compartment! Then there was some sort of talking dragon that she chalked up as just symbolism, at best, after she awoke the next morning in the caves... some sort of delusion... but seeing this man now in the flesh, it was starting to draw a great many things into question.

Only a few minutes from consciousness, he let out a painful and groggy moan from the table and his head slowly started to roll over toward them, giving her a better look at his face. Her heart seemed to skip a beat, and there was no doubt in her mind. It was most definitely him. She banged on the indestructible glass in frustration and McGinn just grinned, not even looking over to acknowledge her as he continued to prepare his coup de grace.

She simply could not stand here, gawking helplessly through a glass pane, and watch this imposter take the life of an innocent man right before her very eyes... especially a man who she believed knew some things about her that not even those closest to her could know. She scoffed at the whole situation, storming off toward the main wing of the Medical Bay.

———————

Astrydd burst into the main recovery room of the Medical Bay where Erük was still hovering over Sky. She stopped herself in mid approach, obviously unsure whether or not to interrupt the connection that was taking place. Erük pulled away and faced her.

"It's okay... I heard the announcement. I think Thor is in real trouble, and only Sky is close enough to help him! But it could kill them both!" She looked confused. Though she had communicated telepathically with Erük before, it was the subtle nuances that were throwing her off now. The pictures

between words... the *real* message. She understood that he was referring to the Sky and Thor onboard the other Phoenix, and that some sort of conflict was underway that could unravel things as they knew them, but what she couldn't make out was the part he wasn't saying... the part that was dominating his thoughts at the moment. The part concerning Ar'Jvikkah.

If something happened to her past self, she dies here, creating a paradoxical rift in time-space caused by a lifetime of experiences and influence that would have then never happened... and Ar'Jvikkah was caught in the flux; an entire destiny still somewhere between the past and the present could die with her. *"We need to get them both together... in here... that's the only way I can do anything to help them!"*

"All right! Let's go, then! He's on the bridge, let's hurry!" Astrydd turned to walk toward the door and Erük grabbed her arm with his talon, holding her fast. He put the other one over Sky's abdomen, breathing in deeply and closing his eyes.

"She's made the decision.... There's no time!"

There was a quick flash of light and a strange odor, then Astrydd doubled over, feeling suddenly as if she had just gotten punched very hard in the stomach, knocking the wind out of her. Erük let go of her arm, slightly off balance himself as he struggled to miss and she stumbled over to the side, nearly knocking Bjorn over with her.

"Whoa! Shit!" he yelled, trying to catch her himself as Erük scooped up Thor and Sky at the same time, cleared the navigation desk off with his tail, then laid them side by side on their backs, both of them still unconscious as their fates were being decided by a chain of events well beyond their control. Erük quickly tuned back in through Ar'Jvikkah to keep tabs on the situation while Astrydd did her best to fill Bjorn in on what was transpiring onboard the other Phoenix.

Kaitlyn grabbed hold of the grate on the floor in the center of the room that ran the full length of the Medical Bay and lifted up on it for all she was worth. The steel cover for the magnetic repulsion strips that kept the gurneys up off the floor for easy transport also served as an access panel for a small utility run that stretched room to room between the various bays. It wasn't meant for travel, and was barely large enough for a small child to traverse, but Kaitlyn could clearly remember playing here with her cousin when he was sick and scaring the pants off their parents by using it to "pop up" in the equipment closet, then come back out after everyone was hysterical from searching for them.

She set the grate aside, then got down on her stomach in the tiny channel, turned sideways with her right arm over her head and out in front of her, then started wiggling forward without an inch to spare on either side. There was a point when she was almost directly beneath the wall when she almost lost it... almost cried out from sheer claustrophobia. She used her military training, particularly the deeper philosophies of self-defense taught to her by Parnell, to calm herself, take a few deep breaths, then proceed with the mission at hand. All that was driving her was the well-being of this total stranger... this man whom she had only seen in a dream, yet knew she had some kind of inseparable bond with. She already knew she would do anything necessary to save him. Anything.

She pressed on, trying to remain as quiet as possible, as she was now almost directly beneath them both. The imposter had a kind of translucency about him that she could now see from her vantage point, looking directly up at him from the bottoms of his feet as he hovered just above the floor. If she had to guess, she would assume he was some sort of ethereal creature... very similar to those in the caves, yet with some kind of fundamental difference. Unlike the curious beings on Cheops, this thing seemed *extremely* purpose driven.

The tinkering noise on the door panel seemed to stop for a moment, then continue even more frantically, and she glanced over to see what was going on; having just the slightest line of sight toward Parnell and the others through the grate above her. To her surprise, John was staring right at her, totally shocked, scared, and pissed off at her for her brash actions. Suddenly it got very quiet above her, as well, and she had a very keen feeling that Parnell's gawking had given her away. She very slowly turned her head back toward her quarry to see him staring straight down at her with a sinister look on his face!

Her heart missed a beat as he bent down and yanked the main grill right off the floor above her with one open hand and effortlessly sent the 100lb. piece of hardware flying into the adjacent wall, nearly 20 feet away with his mind! She was more intrigued that scared, realizing that apparently he did possess the ability to "push" solid objects from his ethereal plane of existence, despite the lack of a physical body... at least for short, focused bursts. As he grasped her torso, more like a magnet than an actual "grab," and yanked her up out of her hiding place, pulling her up to eye level with him, she calmly wondered if this method could be reversed....

He stared into her eyes, smiling as he seemed to recognize her. He alternated from her to Thor, and back again, then began to speak to her without moving his lips.

"This is a most interesting development... unfortunate, but interesting. You cannot st-" Just at the point in his sentence when he was the most distracted, completely absorbed in his own thoughts and dialogue, without the slightest inkling that she possessed the will, much less the skill, to do anything but shake in her boots, she pulled one of her knives from its upside down position in her backstrap and raked it right to left,

directly across his throat as he spoke while grabbing the back of his left hand with her left and twisting the wrist off of her lapel as she pivoted to her left at the hips.

The surprise attack caught him completely off guard and he fell apart for a moment, losing his concentration on staying in his current form, showing them all for just a moment what he truly looked like. He quickly regained his composure, instantly erasing the injury to his throat that would otherwise have been fatal, and pulling her back to his left with force. She resisted for a second as a preamp, then unloaded on him with the hardest left cross she could muster, but hit nothing but air as she seemed to pass right through him this time, sending her sprawling across one of the examination tables nearby. He then grabbed her by the ankle, throwing her forcefully back in the other direction as the men outside the doorway watched on in horror, absolutely powerless to help her.

Just as she was reaching the end of the arc of his throw, she could feel his grip on her skip out just slightly, then finally entirely, letting loose of her just prematurely. She landed almost on top of the mobile resuscitation machine, covering it nearly entirely with her body, then laid motionless. Parnell and the others watched on as he slowly walked over toward her to finish her off.

She gasped for air, then without turning to see where he was, she started to speak, uttering each syllable loudly and purposefully with her limp body blocking his line of sight, in order to cover up the sound of the portable defibrillator as she punched in the buttons necessary to activate it and prepare it for maximum charge. "Why the hell are you doing this to him? What could he possibly have done to you? He's been frozen *forever*…. Shit, man," she grunted, slowly clambering around to face him with her arms concealing the paddles as she held herself up using the machine stand behind her, appearing to be more injured than she was.

"So have I, Sky, so have I. Believe me, it's nothing personal... in fact, I hold Mr. Krey in the highest regard. It truly bothers m-"

The sound of the electronics shorting out as they flickered sporadically, sending arcs of energy flailing in every direction as the paddles made contact with the ether based life form was bone-chilling, combining with a deep wailing sound from the other plane as the electrical frenzy instantaneously erupted into a small gas explosion that sent Kaitlyn sprawling into the utility closet on her back, the door slamming closed right behind her. Though she was in pretty intense pain, she rose to her feet relatively unscathed and couldn't help but laugh as she took note that she got him to fall for the same trick twice.

Cautiously, she peered out of the door, noticing that there was no further sign of him anywhere. She sighed with relief and rushed over to help the man in the cryo tube who had been bridging a very painful consciousness for the last several minutes. His eyes were still closed as he thrashed to and fro inside his tube, convulsing from extreme dehydration and a pain caused by speeding up the thawing process not entirely unlike an ice cream headache from hell.

She knew that there was no way that she would be able to get the door open in time for the medical staff who were standing by just outside the door to help save his life, so for the moment, she focused only on him. She quickly popped the cover on the tube and detached the stasis lines going into his I.V., replacing the main one with a saline bag and giving him a very healthy dose of morphine in the other. His vital signs, appearing on the small monitor on the side of the tube, itself, seemed to be stabilizing to her, so she started to focus on getting him to regain consciousness.

He slowly opened his eyes after some shaking and pleasant speech, seeing her eyes not ten inches from his own.

She loomed over him for a moment, smiling. "Kait...." he mumbled, completely to her surprise. He dozed back off, his arm falling off the table from exhaustion after he had managed to lift it up towards her.

She heard a loud pounding on the glass, having all but forgotten about her audience, trapped outside. The medical technicians were motioning madly for her to stop what she was doing, as was Captain Parnell. Not sure what the issue was, she backed off, realizing they were about to try to blast their way in with small, concentrated shape charges, placed directly on the edges of the glass doorway. She knew any charge strong enough to compromise the shatter proof, impact resistant transparent carbon fiber they used for glass onboard these ships would undoubtedly wreak havoc on the inside of the room.

She held up a finger in order to buy a little bit of time, then gave Thor a sedative so he wouldn't wake up in mid-process. She rigged the I.V. inside the tube, temporarily reattaching it to his stasis lines, and sealed him inside his tube again, replacing it into its slot in the wall and effectively stalling his cryostasis. She then signaled for them to proceed, and walked back into the utility closet, covering her ears and squatting down low while protecting her body as well as possible from any shrapnel that might occur by tipping over a metal table on its side and getting down low behind it with her right side toward the impending blast.

A few minutes later, without incident, the blast went off. It was rather anticlimactic, as the level of precision used in dialing in the appropriate charge kept the whole affair as minimal as possible, causing the giant plate of glass to merely fall inward and land on the floor with a dull thud, the plastic explosive cutting tape having carved through the one inch thick material like butter as it instantaneously bought them entry and her, egress.

The medical techs immediately began to re-prep Thor for continued cryostasis while he was still unconscious, somewhat to Kaitlyn's disdain. She scoffed, holding her arms out to the sides in disgust as she exhaled. "So that's it?" She looked around, getting a response from no one. "What the fuck!?!" She approached Captain Parnell, who was already on a direct course to speak with her. Neither one looked happy in the least.

They both started to speak at once, neither one backing down for a few seconds, then, finally, she gave in out of respect, as well as exhaustion. "You first," she bowed, flamboyantly gesturing toward him with a rolling motion and open fingers.

John took a deep breath, then closed his eyes as he exhaled, shaking his head with a grin. He opened them, stepping toward her and grabbing her up into a very serious bear hug that seemed to go on forever. She made a couple of bleak noises, more grunt and squeak than any actual attempt at communication, but understood for what they were, nonetheless. He finally let her go, still holding her by the shoulders out in front of him like a piece of human artwork to be revered.... "Don't ever do that to me again."

"Is that it?" she laughed, knowing full well there was much more he wanted to say.

He shook his head, chuckling to himself as she laughed. "Not even close!" He cleared his throat, trying to regain his composure as she did, as well. "That was truly exemplary... I couldn't be prouder of you! As a student... as an officer of this ship... as a soldier..." He was starting to get a little choked up, and paused for just a moment and saluted her before continuing. "And as a daughter."

"Thank you, Sir!" She stood proud, returning his salute as she choked back a little bit of emotion herself, despite the fact that she had no idea that he meant the last part anything but figuratively. "

"Please… right now, call me John," he said softly, now well beyond the earshot of anyone who might consider the behavior unprofessional or unethical, "and speak frankly."

"John… *Dad*," she smiled coyly, "why did you give the order to put that man back into cryostasis?" She could immediately tell she had struck a nerve as he nervously looked about, hemming and hawing for a viable answer to her question. Unable to provide her with one quick enough, he instead side-stepped the entire issue, turning it around on her.

"What do you know about him?" John tested, only understanding, himself, that this man was a key part of what was to come, and should be protected at all costs. While the mission Erük had laid out for him was painfully vague, he knew it to be, at the very least, a leap of faith, and one that would reveal itself, as well as the right and wrong choices along the way, as they arose. Something about the mindset bestowed upon him by this powerful and noble creature was utterly reassuring, to say the least. He only wished he had the ability to impart on those around him, particularly his family that were directly involved, the confidence that he had the luxury of carrying like a torch. He simply knew, beyond even the slightest doubt, that when the time came, he would know it, and he would react appropriately. Though he wished for details, himself, he knew that for now, this would simply have to suffice. As above: so below. Things were going according to plan, and couldn't happen any other way.

"I met him in a dream… at least I think it was a dream. It was when I was unconscious in the caves, but it seemed so real! In the dream, *he* saved *me*… I think so, anyway… it's a little vague. I wonder what the creature wanted with him…. I don't get it."

"Yeah, I know what you mean...." Parnell was looking through the computer log as they spoke, then paused. "I don't think that was all he was after... Hmmm... this is strange."

"What's strange?"

"Well, it looks as if there was a final log in entry in the personnel files *just* before the blast. From <u>here</u>... *From this very room!"* He scratched his scalp, looking very confused. "Sweetie, I don't really remember, but did you try to key in just before you jumped into the closet? When you were setting him up... *right* before the blast?"

"Hell no! I'm sure of it! Not at all," she said with 100% confidence. "The only thing I used the computer for at all was to check his vitals, I'm absolutely sure!"

"Yeah, I didn't think so...."

"What did they do?"

"That's just it... they didn't *do* anything... there was just a hike in the vital signs of one of the cryos, as if he was halfway revitalized... as if he was trying to thaw *himself* out with the aid of the computer system!"

"Did he start processing another one while he had this other guy out?"

"No. That's just it... It was just that guy, Stanton, or something. Nobody else was even queried."

"So who's vitals changed?"

"A guy further back in the rotation, but the odd thing is that it looks like they both came from the exact same place and time... It's *very* possible they knew each other. His name is McGinn. Kieran McGinn."

CHAPTER 28: HUNTER'S MOON

Sitting in adjacent seats on the bridge of the Phoenix, Thor came to just before Sky, looking about the room in a very disturbed manner. He had an odd look in his eye, as if he had just awakened from an extremely vivid, albeit manic dream... one he was having difficulty wrapping his mind around, or forgetting, for that matter. He immediately snapped out of his trance the moment the loud proximity alert sounded and quickly started looking all around the bridge. When he got to Sky he paused, stroking her hair as she began to stir as well.

Bjorn and Astrydd stared at each other in disbelief, not sure why the two of them were found in this catatonic state in the first place... but for both of them to emerge almost simultaneously? Astrydd smiled smugly out of only one side of her mouth and grunted slightly, then walked over to aid Sky, who seemed more than a little disoriented and groggy. "Somebody grab her some water! Please!" she yelled out, taking a knee in front of her and staring into her eyes with a small, lighted scope.

"I got it!" Bjorn called out, already close to a small faucet in the corner of the room near the first aid center. He stared at the screen Erük was using while he filled the small glass, over pouring it as he became transfixed on what he was seeing. "Shit!" He poured out the smallest amount to avoid further spillage on the way back, then rushed it over to them and sprinted for his own post at the navigation station he usually manned to get a better look.

Thor became enraged, slamming down his fist on the console as he turned and glared at the entire bridge crew. "Will someone please explain to me how we ended up with the Fleet's flagship close enough to our ass to read the manufacturing date on our thrusters without anyone noticing? They've engaged a tractor beam and will undoubtedly attempt to board us! Apparently they have been trying to contact us for nearly twenty minutes! Twenty minutes! God-dammit!"

Bjorn spoke out first, looking down at the floor with a shameful look in his eye. "Sir, we were *all* distracted... mostly to save you two! It's my fault, mainly... I should've never left my post! We were all just so worried about the two of you! I just wanted to help any way I could." Obviously having a hard time staying angry given the circumstances, Thor smiled a half-assed smile at the young man and nodded, trying hard to think of a way out of this unexpected predicament.

"Well, thanks for helping me, Bjorn," he said sincerely as he slapped the young officer on the back, making him step forward to regain his balance, "I'm sorry for snapping at you all, you're the absolute best at what you do, and I know you all know your jobs. This was just an unexpected surprise we could have done without right now. Now, what the hell to do about this asshole... Any suggestions? We're too close to the blue giant to attempt a hard evasive breaking of the tractor beam, aren't we? We'd be pulled apart ourselves...."

"They've been trying to hail us almost nonstop on the com... Should we respond? They want to know why our override code doesn't work!" Erük yelled out to Thor.

"Yeah, I'll bet they do," he laughed, "They want to know why they can't just shut us down with the typing of one code!" Thor was pacing the floor now, the way he always did when there was something stressful happening, arms crossed, head cocked slightly upward, pacing back and forth... mind like a steel trap.

"Erük, respond verbatim: Attention, Admiral Reid, Our code has been changed to protect this ship and its crew from the imposter we encountered while taking off. It was another Carrier exactly duplicating us in every way... They even knew our defense protocol and attempted to use our code to disable our ship. We are conducting repairs to our long range engine reactor, and request that all tractor beams and magnetic interference cease at once. Captain Ming Chen." Thor winked at Bjorn, who was grinning and nodding in approval, then turned back toward Erük. "Send it."

Thor continued pacing the floor of the bridge like an expectant father, waiting for some sort of reply from the Helios. During one particular lap around the holographic console, Sky intercepted his leg, pulling him toward her chair in order to calm him down. He stared at her nervously. No words were necessary for her to completely understand his concern. To be caught now, after everything they had been through together, would be absolutely inconceivable.

It got so quiet that you could hear a pin drop just before the message came in, causing what would normally have been just another beep or chirp on the computer console, but instead made them all jump nearly out of their skin! Thor spun around and looked eagerly at Bjorn, awaiting his translation. Bjorn turned back toward them with a shocked look, as if a group of larger children had just taken his entire bag of Halloween candy.

"They apologize for the use of the tractor beam... and will deactivate it as soon as the team of mechanics and engineers onboard those two shuttles arrive safely onboard the Phoenix ... They claim the high gravity flux makes this the only safe way for their crews to dock," he said with a smirk, spinning the holographic viewer around to show what appeared to be two well-endowed shuttlecrafts emerging from the main bay of the large Carrier. Both of them were the Fleet's newest hybrid exploration shuttles, equipped with a full array of weaponry, including a prototype unidirectional EMP cannon capable of disabling almost any known technology in one shot.

Thor exhaled loudly, pulling his hand over the top of his brow and through his hair, wiping away the sweat that was already starting to accumulate. He stared at Sky for a moment, perplexed by her stamina; her grace under pressure. She seemed so calm, so confident... so utterly convinced that things would work out fine. Until now, he had found himself using her faith in him as a shield as they paraded through the cosmos like Bonnie and Clyde, without a care in the world. Now, it seemed, he would need to use it as a weapon. *Two newborn children oblivious to the transgressions of man... Invincible. Immortal.*

"Tell them... tell them: *Thank you for the assistance. We are lowering our shields for docking.*" He motioned for Bjorn to send the transmission. The young officer hesitated, preparing to warn him about the likelihood that this was a setup... that they already knew that *their* Phoenix was still way behind, possibly still on Cheops... and that the *engineers and mechanics* were most likely a well-armed team of security personnel with orders to take back the ship at all costs. Thor simply held up his hand to stop him, then pointed forward to send the transmission, saying the rest with his eyes.

"Yes, Sir."

"Now cut our shields and stay sharp! Bjorn...you have the conn. Sky, Erük, come with me. Astrydd, stay put! Bjorn will need help with evasive, plus we may be coming right back with some scrapes!" Thor winked at her, to which she rolled her eyes in anticipation, similar to a mother's worry.

"You got it, Captain."

"Thor, are you guys doing what I think you're doing?" Bjorn called out as they walked through the main doorway to the bridge. Thor turned to him for only a second and just smiled.

Walking quickly toward their private quarters, Thor looked at Erük with a bit of honest concern in his eye. "Do you think you can *see* inside the shuttle closest to us well enough to effect a crossing for all three of us... given that we have Ar'Jvikkah's help?"

"I think so... much depends on whether there is enough physical room or not. Give me a moment." Erük stood entranced in the darkened corridor just outside of the Captain's quarters, the flashing red lights from the proximity alarm adding a surreal tint to the presence of this majestic creature, standing like a sculpture from medieval Earth of one of his massive, fire-breathing brethren.

Thor and Sky quickly darted into their berth and suited up, grabbing, in particular, a barrage of close range weapons including Thor's katana, and Sky's personal favorite since her early combat training, a pair of tonfa, crafted for her by their best metallurgist to her exact specifications, including arm length, gripping circumference, and wieldable weight vs. impulse damage. They were extremely light... nearly as light as aluminum, but even stronger than tempered carbon steel, made from the prized store of Titanium 6V4Mg alloy that the Phoenix had the discreet privilege of transporting.

She never failed to get an envious glance from Thor upon brandishing these traditionally elegant, yet space-aged weapons. He made no secret of his appreciation for the metal, and it was even her secret intention to have a sword made for him as a gift from some of the stock, an idea that wouldn't have settled very well with the machinists who would have been grinding their best tooling to the nubs trying to work this magnificently strong substance into the desired shape. Luckily for her, the machinist in question onboard the Phoenix would be herself.

They finished strapping on the last part of their gear just as Erük came around the corner. *"We can do this, but we'll need to split up."*

"Split up?" Thor exclaimed through a mouthful of some kind of simulated jerky. "How the hell can we do that? I can't teleport yet... especially to a place where I can't see where I'm going!"

"No, but she can..."

"Oh, no... my brother, that's just too dangerous! Is there no other way?"

"Time is short! We must go now... She will go to the farthest ship. There are only four men onboard. Only two of them appear to be soldiers. I have to carry you! She's already a burden for Ar'Jvikkah... Two would never work! Are we ready? They are here!"

Sky nodded as Erük placed his hand across her abdomen, transferring information directly to Ar'Jvikkah, then let go and offered his arm to Thor. Thor hit his belt com. "Bjorn, jam their transmissions to the Helios... now! We're boarding both shuttles!" He reached out and grabbed Erük's arm, taking a deep breath.

As he looked over at Sky, time itself seemed to slow down. There was an unusual tickle in his solar plexus and his nose felt like it was running, yet there wasn't any liquid coming out. He could see her shaking side to side very quickly, yet ever so slightly. If it wasn't for the decelerated rate of his vision, he doubted if he would even have noticed it at all. Then he saw what he had predicted all along.

Originating in her womb, Ar'Jvikkah was raising her pitch along with his own. He did so very quickly... blowing right by the various shades of the solid matter, sound, and then light spectrums, directly into some kind of other being, entirely. He could actually *see* the flux of the ethereal plane as she phased out of the prime material plane completely, leaving only what he called a *shadow* of herself in this moment. Then, as if her shadow was alive, it began to stretch in the direction of the shuttlecraft, stretching the very fabric of the material world toward it in exact repercussion with the pitch change she made toward it. As soon as the exchange of energy was finished, she simply *snapped* out of the room as if she was never there.

Thor was standing with his jaw wide open when he realized just how fast this process actually takes place with the "training wheels" off! The fleeting moment that Erük had been gracious enough to provide him with, mainly so he wouldn't get disoriented and vomit upon arrival, was gone, and they snapped instantaneously into the empty cargo hold of the closer shuttle. As they reappeared, Thor momentarily became dizzy, wobbling sideways for a step, then regaining his composure, luckily without making a sound.

Looking forward, they could clearly see two of the security team members standing just in front of the clear plastic transition screen, so they cautiously approached. Looking past them, Thor counted eight more, including the pilot and copilot. They had the element of surprise, but these men were no ordinary security detail! They were all highly trained officers of Reid's personal guard... his own personal Gestapo, and they were as good as they come. *This would definitely not be an easy fight in such close quarters....*

Thor's mind was racing through every possible scenario that might result in victory without the pilot or co-pilot getting a chance to warn the Helios, but in every case, the odds were stacked horribly against them. He turned to Erük to silently ask him for some input and jumped, a bit startled to behold his friend now standing before him in the full guise of one of them... down to the last detail of their uniforms! He grinned, realizing the obviousness of the tactical advantage this would bestow upon them, then turned back around to prepare his mind for the same transition.

To his shock and momentary dejection, the two guards in the back were both turned toward him, staring straight at him with completely confused looks on their faces. Thor stared back at the one on the left, memorizing his outward appearance down to the last detail. Erük yawned, stepped forward with his arms outstretched, then slapped both of their heads together with lightning speed and amazing strength, rendering both of them unconscious without so much as a whimper. By the time the next pair took a casual glance backward, they were both standing in position exactly where their counterparts were standing having already donned their exact semblance.

Sky snapped into sight just as the small ship was coming about in its final approach, causing her to momentarily lose her balance and fall sideways, adding to the unfortunate fact that one of the pilots was looking back and speaking to the soldiers as the ship heeled sideways in mid-maneuver. She rolled in the direction that the motion was throwing her, effectively bridging the gap between herself and the soldier on the left. As the craft leveled out, she used his momentary shift in body weight against him and swept his legs as she spun herself around to stand up.

She continued with the spinning motion, picking up tremendous inertia as she came around full circle on her way to her feet and leapt into the air, delivering a powerful roundhouse kick directly to the side of the face of the second man that sent him sprawling on top of his partner. She pulled the pair of tonfa from her belt and simultaneously delivered a knockout blow to both men on the back of their heads, putting a direct stop to the groaning and squirming they were starting to do, but being very careful not to kill them. She concluded her attack with a flamboyant, kata-like maneuver that finished with her frozen in a fighting stance at the end, directly after some lightning fast coordinated spins of the tonfa that left the pilots in awe and unwilling to move against her as they looked from her to the two men on the floor and back again a couple times with their mouths hanging open stupidly.

With the enemy having in no way anticipated the boarding of their own ship, the rest was relatively easy. Thor and Erük simply waited for the right moment and then opened fire with the guards' own weapons. Set merely to stun, the shuttle was filled with flashes of blue light from the ends of the confiscated rifles as they mowed the remaining six guards down like grass. They fell sideways and forward, falling on top of each other in a clumsy pile before the pilots could even react to the mayhem.

As they hit the last two, one of the pilots decided to be a hero and snatched up one of the sidearms from the holster of a guard who fell nearly on top of him, and nervously fired off a random round of actual artillery from his archaic looking revolver, nearly hitting Erük in the head as he yelled at the top of his lungs, shooting with his eyes completely closed. Thor quickly took him out, hoping like hell that the plasma discharge didn't wreak havoc with the ship's flight computer.

To all of their good fortune, the man was leaning almost over the back of his seat toward his assailants and away from the console, with no part of his body in direct contact with the metal controls as the blue light engulfed his entire body, sending him shaking uncontrollably to the floor to join his other comrades as the heavy .357 caliber handgun slid across the floor toward Thor's feet. A personal favorite of his, Thor quickly scooped up the ancient looking Colt Python from the floor to add to his growing collection and slid it into his pants, never looking away from the remaining pilot, who immediately put both of his hands straight up in the air and surrendered, so frightened that he was literally shaking uncontrollably.

There was an unusual amount of ambient noise coming from all around them as the console seemed to be going crazy with warnings and flashing sensor lights. The man dropped to the floor on all fours and groveled at their feet as they approached the pilot seats, mumbling endlessly. "Please don't kill me... please! Please! I don't want to die! Please, sir, I'm begging you! I'll do anything! I'm just a pilot... I won't get in your way... Please! PLEASE!" He grabbed onto Thor's pant leg as Thor approached the console, struggling to hear an automated voice coming from the ship's computer.

"SHUT UP!!!" Thor yelled. The man was instantly compliant, quivering on the floor and trying not to make eye contact, as if he was dealing with a couple of wild animals. Thor looked at Erük in horror as he realized what the message was saying.

"Hull breach... aft section, starboard. Hull breach... aft section, starboard. Atmosphere: 40 percent."

"Shit! That bullet must have penetrated the hull! We're purging air!" Looking toward the rear of the shuttle, Thor could clearly see the source of the breach as dust, smoke, and even vaporized moisture from the air was being sucked violently toward a small area on the back cargo door, then blown out into the cold of space. The bullet had torn a small hole, about the size of a nickel, in the thinnest part of the door sheathing and was very quickly decompressing the controlled atmosphere inside the shuttle craft.

Thor quickly punched in a few commands into the console and an image of the Phoenix, the Helios, and both shuttles appeared. It looked as if Sky's shuttle was almost ready for its final approach, coming around behind the Phoenix and synchronizing vector telemetry. Thor looked at Erük nervously as he realized that they had lost most of their speed during the fight, and were now dangerously close to the Helios without a prayer of getting to the Phoenix before reaching zero atmosphere. "Damn it! This prick must have hit the brakes to warn the Helios the moment we started fighting!"

"I'm sorry! I'm sorry... I'm sorry... *please* don't kill me! Please, please, please-"

"I said, SHUT THE FUCK UP!!!" The man cowered at his feet, shaking uncontrollably and covering the back of his head with his hand as if worried he was going to be beaten. *Not a bad idea,* Thor thought, as he pounded his fist repeatedly on the console while trying to think up something fast. "Shit!"

Shuttle RF-2, what's going on? We have sensors indicating a hull breach! We have visual confirmation of breach on aft cargo door! What happened?" The pilot looked up at Thor inquisitively, awaiting his orders.

"Don't answer." Thor grabbed the small, cowardly man by the scruff of his neck and shirt collar and dragged him to the back of the shuttle, just in front of the breach.

"Atmosphere: 20 percent. Internal temperature: 15 degrees, Fahrenheit." The stoic computerized voice almost seemed to project a small hint of sympathy as it resonated in the small compartment; the sound changing in a frightening and surreal manner as the pressure all but disappeared.

"Put your hand over the hole!" Thor demanded, pointing at the breach, already frosted over on the edges from the moisture coming into contact with the cold of space.

"B-b-but m-m-my hand will-"

"NOW!" Thor yelled, pointing the rifle at the man's forehead and jabbing him hard with the barrel. He closed his eyes for a moment and complied, shaking in his boots as he literally wet himself right there and then, the puddle of warm urine pooling out of the bottom of his pant leg, then steaming up in the freezing cold that was quickly entombing them all, as he sobbed and cried out in pain and fear. "You're going to buy us more time! If you let go, I'll kill you... do you understand me?"

"Y-y-y-yes Sir!"

"Atmosphere: 15 percent. Stabilizing... Atmosphere restoring." Thor was mumbling something to himself as he took the controls, staring at the rear end of the Phoenix, momentarily relieved. He hit the thrusters and smiled at Erük, once again proud that things seemed to be working in their favor... then came the slap in the face from reality.

They both lurched forward in their seats; all forward momentum instantly halted, then quickly reversed, as if they had hit full reverse thrusters in mid acceleration. The com sounded out ominously, and Thor knew without asking that it was Admiral Reid, himself.

"Shuttle RF-2... Abort mission, you are under tow. We are pulling you immediately back into the Helios for inspection."

"That gunshot blew it! They must have done a life-form scan right after we were breached! That would mean.... " He ran to the side window, then pounded on the glass in anger as he saw Sky's shuttle being pulled backwards out of the shuttle bay just as it was preparing to dock. He closed his eyes, frustrated, but never beaten. "Shit!"

Suddenly, as if someone flipped a switch, he looked up at Erük with a refreshed, almost mischievous look in his eyes. Erük nodded, reading him instantly. They both walked back toward the pilot, still standing with one hand frozen in place over the hole. He was facing the door, sobbing... so sure that he was about to die... so easily threatened into doing *anything* that would save his pathetic excuse for a life.

"What's your name, helmsman?" Thor asked, placing his left hand on the man's right shoulder, while holding his rifle leveled at the side of the man's head where he could see it.

"Ensign Theodore Percy, Sir."

"Alright, Mr. Percy... First of all, I'm sorry about the hand... you're probably going to lose it. You *are* the one who hit the brakes, though, and seriously complicated things for us. Frankly, you're *damn* lucky we don't kill you right now," he said, leaning in toward the scared man with the tip of his gun as he spoke. "You know how we got here, right?"

"N-n-n-no-"

"No, you don't... Erük!" He gestured to the front of the shuttle and the man looked over his shoulder as Erük snapped from spot to spot, still camouflaged as one of the security guards who lay at their feet. "Now, believe me when I tell you, we can be anywhere, at any time... and if you don't do *exactly* as we tell you, we *will* be paying you a surprise visit... and then we'll visit every one you know and love... *one at a time.* There is no place you can hide, Mr. Percy, no place at all... Do you understand me?"

"Y-y-yes, Sir!"

"Oh, and there is just one more thing about my friend Erük here... in addition to being able to imitate anyone on your ship, there is the small matter of his *true* form..." Erük took the cue and shifted back into his natural form directly in front of the tiny man, roaring loudly two inches from his face, causing the poor man to void himself further... this time, entirely. He jumped back so startled that he didn't realize, at first, that part of his frozen hand was still stuck to the cargo door, keeping the breach sealed for the moment.

Thor escorted him back to his pilot seat, shaking in his boots, as he quickly explained exactly what he wanted the man to do for them, then, as if it was all a bad dream, the man was sitting alone in his own soiled pants next to a pile of unconscious soldiers as the shuttle bay on the underside of the Helios slowly opened to accept his crippled craft.

Sky sat sobbing at the console of the other shuttle, the prototype, RF-1, trying to think of some way to rescue Erük and Thor and break free of the tractor beam herself. She had been monitoring the situation with their hull breach, but was unable to break radio silence to try to contact them or the Phoenix, and was growing increasingly more and more worried. She sensed a shift for the better, but was still shocked into jumping out of her seat when the voice boomed from behind her. "Hey, gorgeous! We gotta stop meeting like this!"

She leapt over the back of her seat and almost knocked them both over, hanging from Thor in a massive bear-hug and bursting into tears of joy and relief. "Oh my God, Thor, I feared the worst! What are we going to do? They have me, too! Reid will have us shot without a trial!"

"Oh, I don't think we need to worry too much about that asshole," Thor smiled, setting her down softly, then approaching the console. "Bear with me for a moment...."

He quickly killed all power on the shuttle and grasped her hand, staring out the side window as the other shuttle disappeared inside the Helios. Thor started counting seconds as he clicked his fingertips on the glass window, then pointed his finger at the massive Carrier, as if he was shooting it with an imaginary pistol. Sky looked at him as if he was losing his mind, crinkling her nose and tweaking one eyebrow as he turned to her and smiled proudly.

The darkness erupted with a brilliant show of blue, white and purple lightning, wrapping itself around everything on the ship as a gigantic shockwave of dark energy shot out in a perfect halo from the shuttle bay, engulfing the entire ship. The lightning continued for a moment as emergency blast shields slammed in place of the aesthetic energy shielding, and airlocks were pulled closed by their own pressure-triggered failsafes until all was dark and silent... rendering the Helios an impenetrable shell, floating through space completely blinded, crippled, and incapable of causing them any further harm.

Thor hit the throttle, speeding toward the freed Phoenix; the tractor beam now incapacitated along with all the other electronic systems onboard the Helios from the highly advanced EMP weapon that Mr. Percy had been instructed, under penalty of death, to unleash inside the shuttle bay as soon as they safely touched down and could aim its unidirectional pulse cannon away from the Phoenix and the other shuttle. After docking safely themselves and taking the small shuttle crew to the brig, they scrambled for the bridge, quite sure that this was far from over.

Within the darkness, noise and chaos of the crippled Helios, mass panic had begun to erupt as small, closed cell battery lights and light sticks were being deployed shipwide, revealing the pride of the Fleet in utter pandemonium, caught with its pants down and defeated by one of their own crewmembers with the mere touch of a button firing their own weapon upon them. Officers and civilians alike were scrambling everywhere, unable to even ascertain if this was, in fact, the end, or simply some sort of temporary power failure. They flailed around aimlessly in midair, deprived of even the benefit of artificial gravity, as the ship itself drifted through the cold vastness of deep space, leaving them without even the reassurance of the Admiral's voice over the intercom to calm them. The crew was quickly turning on itself and becoming a sudden experiment in fear-induced mob mentality run rampant.

"We're a dead stick! Goddammit, ladies, someone get the power restored before we all die out here!" Reid yelled out in the darkened room at his frantic crew. Though he had nothing but the very best and brightest that The Fleet's academic programs could churn out already in place onboard The Helios at his disposal, he knew they were now at the mercy of a higher power, and lost in this fog-like cloud as vast as space itself, with no signal for anyone to track, they would most likely drift on their random heading completely beyond the realm of any plausible rescue before the rest of the Fleet even finished its search for the imposter. What they needed was a miracle, or every one of the nearly 2,000 souls onboard this flagship would be consigned to the oblivion and impending madness of deep space; set adrift as they slowly died, one by one, from exhausting their supplies in the cold dark... a fate that quite possibly awaited them all if things did not get more promising for the entire race, and a new, more life sustaining home found soon.

"Sir, with all due respect, that was a weaponized electromagnetic pulse fired from close proximity... in all likelihood it was fired inside our shuttle bay *from our own shuttle* as it was returning, and it knocked out every single piece of electronics onboard, including the main heliostatic generator coils in our main *and* slave drives!"

"I KNOW what it did to us, Goddammit; I helped design the damnable thing! What I need from each and every one of you is some creative thinking on how we can get back online as quickly as possible before that asshole gets too far away from us! Is this clear?" Admiral Reid yelled to the entire bridge while temporarily nose to nose with the young science officer as they drifted in slightly different directions while rising up off of the floor.

"Yes, Sir!" they all yelled back in unison, saluting him stiffly, then scrambling back to their posts by whatever means they could pull together in zero gravity the second he released them with his salute.

"Connors... Tate... Come with me! We need to find a way into engineering that doesn't require power! We can't replace those coils, but we may be able to bypass them if-"

"Sir! *INCOMING!!!*" One of the young helmsmen, a mere kid of maybe twenty years old at best, was floating just out in front of the clear windshield; an impact proof window made of clear composite graphite nearly three inches thick, and as clear as glass. He grabbed the frame with his right hand and quickly pulled himself out of their way to the right so that everyone could see out, pointing frantically toward the Phoenix at a large guided missile that had been fired and was now completing a return arc of about 270 degrees backward to set it on a locked course straight at them.

"It's too large to be a normal artillery torpedo or incendiary missile... is it a hull splitter? I've never seen one up close," another young deckhand spoke out while admirably maintaining an unemotional combat demeanor and never taking her eyes off the missile.

"I'm guessing a nuke... what else would only take one shot," a security guard added.

"Well, we're about to get a *real close look!*" Reid jeered rudely at the man, "Brace for impact!" The projectile finished its arc, straightened out, and came rushing right at them, leaving no hope for a miss, as they didn't even have so much as automatic evasive maneuvering capability back online yet. "Over 2,000 brave souls... and it comes to this," he mumbled as his eyes teared up with an unbelievably painful combination of defeat, shame, and despair.

Despite the thin veil of egocentric sarcasm Reid was generously heaping on his crew to hide his fear, his voice was shaky as hell. There was no hiding the fact that he was coming apart at the seams in a most unprofessional and uncharacteristically mortifying manner. He took a deep breath and closed his eyes, sobbing out loud as the harbinger of their demise curved inward just slightly and sped straight toward the bridge itself as if it was being guided by a will of its own.

Leveling directly at them now, the missile opened up in the front to reveal its payload, dropping the last section of its delivery shell to expose a shiny, sophisticated piece of technology the likes of which Reid, in all of his wisdom and military experience could not begin to identify. They apparently had the honor of being the first ship in human history to have this new device tested on them, and to his own surprise and temporary self-revulsion, Admiral Reid actually felt a small sting of disappointment in the sudden realization that he wouldn't be around to see the results. The last thing they all heard just before impact was a funny little whimper escape from his throat as he opened his mouth to take a deep breath at the last moment as if he was diving into water and the loose flatulence of an overweight man shamefully and fearfully voiding his bowels as if he was hanging with his neck in a noose.

CLANK!

The familiar sound of metal hitting metal echoed through the minds of every single person in proximity of the bridge onboard the Helios as they anxiously crowded around the small window to see what happened. Most of them half expected to see some sort of undetonated munition, crushed like an accordion from the impact and spinning slowly off on some random trajectory as it drifted into the cold darkness, unspent and unsatisfied; rendered utterly harmless until pecked at in the wrong manner, at the wrong time by an unsuspecting asteroid or other hapless participant in an unfortunate twist of fate. What they actually saw was something altogether different.

Now attached firmly to the front of the hull with a powerful electromagnet and a mechanized system of claw-teeth and wedge grappling appendages was the "missile," evolved in mid-flight into a fully extended distress buoy with a very bright visual strobe, pulsing and transmitting an SOS call in Morse Code, and a long system of antennae protruding from the far end where a self-contained transformer and power boosting transmitter were sending out its signal in all directions and frequencies. This would undoubtedly insure that the Fleet wouldn't pass right by their cold, dead ship in the thick of the nebula, shrouded by magnetic interference and unnoticed, thereby sealing their fate.

"Well, I'll be damned..." Admiral Reid said shakily as he grinned a fake grin and leaned over a bit, straining to see the faint image of the Phoenix slowly disappearing into the dark blue glow of the nebula.

"Jesus, what a disgusting smell," someone below him commented. He grunted as he finally caught his breath, trying to position his body in the shadows of the bright strobe light coming through the thick transparent portal so that nobody would notice the dark, wet stain in the crotch and seat of his neatly pressed uniform.

"A brave man tastes death only once..." Erük said softly, staring at the rear view monitor as the huge flagship fell back and was consumed by the blue haze.

"But a coward dies a thousand deaths.... Alright, Reid, now it's your turn... Go do what you do best," Thor said to the image of the crippled Helios on his main screen, watching with some satisfaction as the bright distress strobe got fainter and fainter as they proceeded deeper into the nebula's thickest, most turbulent zone: an area almost directly in the middle of a natural triangle… between Cheops, the blue giant, Atlas, and its diminutive binary counterpart, Pleione, Atlas's mortal wife.

Erük sighed with relief, being the only one who completely understood how things needed to transpire from here on out. He nodded proudly at Thor, who nodded back with a smile, wrapping his right arm around Sky, who still looked fit to be tied. "It burns my ass to let that bastard go! We had him… dead to rights, we *had* that son of a bitch! He doesn't deserve to live!" Thor just smiled quietly, stroking the back of her hair while looking to Erük to field this one, as for the most part, he totally agreed, and was merely taking it all on faith at this point.

"We will, Sister, do not worry… He still gets what's coming to him… I'll see to that personally! For the moment, though, he is still necessary… do not forget, some things still need to happen as they did before… otherwise…" Erük gestured toward Thor and then toward her enormous womb, gleaming confidence from his eyes. She felt instantly better, wrapping her free arm around him and pulling him in for a group hug which Thor happily completed.

"You know what burns *my* ass?" Thor muttered to Sky.

"What?"

Thor held his free hand palm down, just about waist height. "Flames… this high."

CHAPTER 29: LONE WOLF

Kaitlyn stood proudly beside Captain Parnell directly in front of the giant viewer screen on the bridge, casting only the slightest glance back at the tumultuous sea of water and earth they were leaving behind. For the first time in her life, she was starting to feel a sense of pride knowing that she was now a trusted part of something much larger than herself. She mattered.

The distress call from the Helios was disturbing, to be sure, but the part that was bothering Parnell the most as they sped toward the blue haze was the unusual flood of data he was picking up from within the nebula. It seemed, at least through the increasing interference, that the Fleet was in two places at once! The numbers were nearly impossible to ascertain with any real accuracy, but it looked almost like a mirror on his screen.... There was the Fleet obeying Admiral Reid's last standing order before contact was lost and following a bent parabolic trajectory around the blue giant in order to gain a serious speed boost to accelerate their journey toward the Algol system, and yet, he could clearly see what looked like nearly the same mass of moving objects bearing on an opposing trajectory, as if they had just come from there.

He knew the electromagnetic interference made his scans untrustworthy, at best, but this would put them on a collision course with each other at speeds that rendered evasive maneuvering not only ineffective, but seriously dangerous, due to the extreme gravitational influence of the massive blue giant. Any loss of momentum within the heliosphere of Alcyone would render the craft incapable of escaping its pull before the ship was destroyed. Just as he started to reach for the com to try and contact one of the other Carriers, he felt a keen and gnawing sensation telling him not to interfere.

He knew that from where they were, it was likely that no one would be able to clean up his garbled transmission, providing they heard it at all, so he made the call to head straight in to investigate first hand and assist the Helios and her crew, being the only ship not already underway. He gave the order and put his arm around Kaitlyn's shoulders, feeling the pride of a father, and for the first time, the freedom to openly express it.

———————

Thor stood beside Sky as they sped toward the outer edge of the gas vortex of Alcyone's inner satellite ring, staring out the window at the immense swath of glowing matter spiraling around the blue giant in a state of near-harmony. The innermost edge of this beautiful, would-be planetary ring was being peeled off and devoured, directly into the deep blue core of the bright sphere, fueling its godlike furnace as it is ever replenished by new matter being pulled into instant orbital decay from around the outside edge, giving the entire phenomenon an appearance not unlike a miniature galaxy in formation. It was the most beautiful and wondrous thing either one of them had ever encountered!

Sky grasped Thor's hand and yawned, weary from all the excitement, yet not wanting to miss a thing. She rubbed her eyes, then turned to give Thor a peck on his cheek. He was relatively unresponsive, still staring wide eyed at the once-in-a-lifetime scene stretched out before them as far as the eye could see. "Ass!" she teased, slugging him in the shoulder, "you know better than to snub me... when... I-" She stopped herself in mid-sentence, realizing all at once that he hadn't taken his eyes off the scenery before them since they started standing here... as a matter of fact, she wasn't sure if he had even so much as blinked!

He opened his mouth as if he wanted to say something, but couldn't find the words. She spun her attention back in the direction he was staring and started to notice it too.... The stars all around the outer edges of Alcyone, mainly in the direction they were traveling, were suddenly *not where they were supposed to be.* It was the same phenomena they had noticed as they were traveling into this system from their accelerated state. It looked like something was shrouding the stars in the background from clear view... almost like they were phasing in and out of existence altogether. "Bjorn!" she yelled, gripping Thor's hand tight.

"I'm already on it! I have a bad idea I know what's causing it," Bjorn yelled out while typing madly on the keyboard in front of him, having trouble hiding the giddiness of the scientist on the verge of profound discovery from his voice.

"I figured you might," Thor yelled out, still not taking his eyes off the phenomenon.

"It's like this-"

"English..." Thor and Sky both preempted in unison.

Bjorn smiled sarcastically, rolling his eyes as he proceeded. "As you wish. It's like this.... The last time we witnessed this occurrence, it was because we weren't where _we_ were supposed to be. We were being pushed by subspace tachyon radiation so fast that the light from the surrounding stars literally *appeared* to us to be in two places at once... in short, we were *outrunning* time. If I'm not mistaken, our brothers and sisters did something very similar... they just arrived a little later than we did. Now, we have the old Fleet from about 20 years ago trying to slingshot around the blue giant to accelerate themselves toward Algol at as fast a speed as is possible; but they are inadvertently on a collision course with *our* Fleet, and won't realize it until they are clear of the sun's interference. It is *very* likely that they will run right into each other almost literally, which, as you two have felt very intimately, causes some kind of temporal convergence between the two timelines that very nearly results in time-space paradox."

"Yeah, or at least a tasty déjà vu..." Thor added skeptically.

"You've both felt it whenever any decision is made that would disrupt the natural flow and result in a different *you* than yourself, but I think we are about to have a disruption of unparalleled magnitude! I believe what we are seeing is the aftermath of a very serious rift, or even a *tear* in the fabric of the universe... *before* it happens! The light from the stars in the affected area is *outrunning* the event!

"The *event*? *What* event?" Sky looked nervously back and forth from Thor to Bjorn as they left the window and marched toward their posts on the bridge.

"What do you mean *event*?"

"We need to stop this from happening!" Thor yelled, giving the hand command to accelerate the Carrier to full speed.

"With all due respect, Sir, how are we going to do that? It's *already* happened..." Bjorn gestured at the haze in the viewer again.

"I don't know, but we have to try! There's too much at stake!"

"He's right! We left them all for dead once already, because of the actions of one man... This is our chance to set things right," Sky said forcibly, pointing at the screen.

"Set course to come around the side behind the old Fleet... Maybe we can draw them off, somehow!"

Speeding into the thickening cloud of blue gasses and reflective particles, the entire bridge quickly became enveloped in an eerie, almost underwater glow, flashing randomly with the strobe-like penetration of Alcyone's glare as it found small, intermittent gaps in the thick haze. The scene on the bridge became surreal as the light reflecting off of all of their worried faces camouflaged the sensation of temporal distortion that was starting to influence them. Minutes started to seem like hours, and then without cause or pattern, everything would very suddenly shift the other way in a rush of distorted perception, causing an hour to pass in what seemed to be only minutes. There appeared to be no way to alter this phenomenon; and yet, they were all becoming keenly aware of its increasing influence as they approached the blue sun's horizon and drew ever closer to the impending collision.

Now completely within the nebula, they were flying as blind as the other ships, relying on the one thing they had that the others did not... a clear programming of all the other ships' vectors prior to being engulfed by interference. It was Bjorn's hope that this would be enough to pilot the ship visually through the integration of this data into a simulator program, but he was starting to become a bit skeptical due to the strangeness of the temporal distortion issue they were experiencing. "I hope they're still where they're supposed to be," he mumbled out loud.

"Why wouldn't they be?" Sky asked, more than a little disturbed by his sudden drop in confidence.

"Well, it's as we said... the location of the incoming ships are subject to their own Captain's *intentions*... they *are* decelerating, so who knows, for sure, which way they will try to go... at least until they see us!"

"Yeah, and Erük's keeping an eye on that situation." Thor gestured to Erük, who was sitting in the middle of the floor in deep meditation, trying desperately to keep tabs on any and all changes in the will and intentions of the people onboard the other ships... particularly the Captains onboard the leading few ships from *their* Fleet... *the ones who were hunting them.*

Sky looked skeptically at Bjorn. If there was one strength she possessed above all others that seemed to define her, it was the uncanny ability to see right through people. It went far beyond female intuition... she just straight up could *not* be fooled.

He had been evading her gaze as he ran his numbers and pretended to be much busier than he really was, but it was starting to wear him out. "Oh, hell!" He turned to look directly at her and dropped what he was doing. "I think this temporal distortion thing goes far beyond simply distorting *our perception* of time.... As we all know, time is *very* relative! Simply staying busy can alter one's perception of time significantly! Sometimes an hour can seem like an eternity, while other times it flies by so fast that we scarcely even realize what we did!" His face grew very serious as he changed his candor from the giddy teacher to the bearer of bad news. "I fear this is different, though."

"Why?" Thor asked, "What do you mean? Different, *how?*"

"Yeah, I mean, I'll admit, it's been pretty extreme… but-" Sky was cut off in mid-sentence by Bjorn clearing his throat loudly, counting out five seconds on his fingers, then throwing a large hand scanner from his belt into the air directly in between them all. He threw it as high as he could without hitting the ceiling and as it fell to the floor, his theories were proven true. They all flinched and braced for a loud crash as the expensive piece of machinery started to drop hard, just as one would expect; but then about halfway to the floor, it dramatically *slowed down*! They all stood dumbfounded at this anomaly as it just as suddenly sped back up, actually accelerating far faster than it should have just before hitting the ground with a crash and a slight bounce.

"So," Sky shrugged, nervously, "what does this mean?" She looked at Bjorn with a tense smile, growing increasingly worried.

"I believe it means that as we grow closer to this temporal event, things will continue to distort, quickly reaching a point where they simply *come undone*… Time and space will literally start to unravel."

"Resulting in what, exactly?" Thor asked.

"Who knows…? There are many theories. Some think this type of event will open a worm hole, or Einstein-Rosen Bridge…. Others think these things are some kind of a rift, or tear, in the fabric of the universe itself, resulting in the complete disintegration of anything caught in its wake."

"So then why, exactly, are we still rushing toward it?" Sky asked rather loudly.

Bjorn shrugged, suddenly distracted by Erük, who seemed to be having some sort of fit while in his deepened state of mental bridging. He began to quake violently, with a very distant look in his eyes, then suddenly stopped, as alarms erupted all across the control panel, and fell back into some kind of silent trance; eyes fixated on a spot thousands of miles in the distance. Barely audible through the chaotic ensemble, a call came in from engineering. They hit the com switch and listened closely, as a rather hysterical sounding Mrs. Davies was yelling something loud and garbled into it through the noise; warning sirens obviously permeating her side as well. Sky grabbed the hand mic off of the console and tried to calm her mother, speaking to her very slowly and concisely.

"Mom, this is Sky..." She laughed and shook her head, catching her mistake since her mother had never heard her nickname before their accident, "I mean *Kaitlyn*... Please calm down and repeat your message slowly, and with the microphone further from your mouth! What's going on down there?"

*"*Sweetie! Thank God! I don't know what's going on! People were phasing in and out of existence... and now they're gone... just gone! Ensign DiAnno disappeared right in front of my eyes! It was horrible! Me and your Father are the only ones left! Honey, what the hell is happening? There's still some kind of haze, right where they were standing... like a shadow or something!"* There was a pause as the crew tried to understand what she was telling them, then she yelled into the mic again. *"Kait! Kaitlyn! Are you there!?"*

"Yes, Mom, right here! Sorry... just thinking! Can you two keep engineering running alone on a Carrier this size?"

*"*Yes, Sir! Frankly, Connor and I make a very efficient team by ourselves, anyway. Shit, sweetie, our design team is the reason these ships can run on damn near anything with nitrogen content! We'll keep her floating, you can count on that... but you side stepped my question.... What the hell is happening?"*

Bjorn had been punching numbers and investigating the phasing incident through the ships internal scanners and life-support system and looked very disturbed. "Kait!" he interrupted, holding out his hand as if to stop her. "Tell them to stay completely away from those *shadows*, even if they move... I repeat, do not come into contact with them under *any* circumstance!"

"Mom...?"

"Yeah, I heard... Don't worry, we're one step ahead of you! But, why?"

"*Just don't do it,* Mrs. Davies, the area surrounding them appears to be highly unstable," Bjorn yelled unnecessarily loud in the direction of Sky's hand held microphone.

"Ya think?"

Sky laughed just a little from her mother's familiar sense of humor, something she had been without for so long that even her poignant sarcasm was like a dear old friend. She turned back to Bjorn to try to figure out what these shadow zones actually were, when they both noticed Erük starting to come out of his trance. He was now muttering something about *"the cabin"* and Thor's father, then he digressed entirely into what sounded like Old Norse.

This went on for a minute or so, then, as quickly as it started, it just stopped. He opened his eyes wide, blinking both sets of lids a couple times, then looked at them, apparently completely oblivious just prior to this very moment that he had a captive audience. Rather than embarrassment, he almost looked relieved that they were right there, and he quickly snapped out of it and rushed over to speak to his friends directly; the urgency of his message reaching them before the words.

"*It has already begun! You must stop them!"* He motioned for Thor to follow him, then bolted off of the bridge, the two of them leaving Sky and Bjorn standing there, quiet and confused.

"Was it something I said?" Bjorn joked, looking puzzled and even smelling his armpits and his own breath in a facetious gesture. Sky laughed, slapping him on the back with the open mic still in her hand and heading over to the number two navigational computer with a curious look in her eye.

"What the hell was that all about? Did I miss something?"

"Never a dull moment, Mom... just you and Dad stay on your toes down there! We'll keep you posted!"

"Roger that, Honey... always do..."

Sky started to put the microphone down, paused and cleared her throat, then keyed back in. "Hey, Mom... Dad..." The feeling in her heart was tempered by *true* sensory distortion; the culmination and impact of twenty lost years. No closure... no trauma... no last words. No fight... no harsh feelings.... Just a gaping, aching hole that could never be filled... *until now.* Twenty long years now crammed into one moment. The truest sense of distortion is that if the moment can't expand lengthwise for twenty years, it has to displace time somehow... in this case, it was now twenty years deep. A true second chance to just say three simple words in these uncertain times, lest they go unsaid forever...

"Yeah, Sweetie?"

"I love you."

———————

Thor and Erük stood mystified as the shuttle bay door slid open to reveal the magnificent prototype right before their eyes. it was truly a work of art, both aesthetically, and with regard to its superior engineering and user-integrated design. They were in such a hurry upon bringing it back to the Phoenix that they never really got a chance to stand back and appreciate what their death defying stunt had procured.

Thor helped Erük finish loading the craft with all the fuel it could carry, along with enough provisions to sustain him for a very long flight. He knew that without a copilot, cryostasis would be far too dangerous and would jeopardize this already unpredictable mission, so he would have to stay awake through the unimaginable vastness of his lone journey. This aspect of deep space travel had caused much worse than a case or two of Hot Shiver among pilots, in fact, only a small handful of beings could survive it at all.

Somehow he knew Erük would be fine. Thor had a pretty good idea what he was planning, but couldn't seem to get him to free up any details. It had something to do with his own role in things to come. All he knew for sure was that Erük needed to go back to his home planet *before* the humans arrived. He had been accepting Erük's decision to go alone based solely on trust, and as much as it pained him to part ways with his best friend, he knew that time was of the essence, so he kept the "goodbye's" to a minimum. Thor quickly reached his arm out toward him as he was starting to turn around to ascend the ramp, sensing that Erük was avoiding physical contact for some reason.

"Screw this... Come here!" Thor yelled, jumping up and grabbing Erük in a full body bear hug. As he hugged the seven foot tall dragon for all he was worth, he was taken suddenly aback by a premonition; a flash both visual and audible, revealing in one notion and moment, the outcome of the clash that was about to take place between the two Fleets. It was horrific, yet utterly magnificent to behold; colors, sounds and light transcending human perception as the entire horizon was being engulfed in one massive convergence of life energy. The outcome was the part that was totally unclear, and seemed to be actively and constantly changing.

Normally, a convergence of even two *intentions* would result in a compromised state, to say the least. The outcome finally settling in as an entirely different life altogether, composed of the knowledge and experience of both individual timelines. The addition of even a couple of *bridges*, however, connecting this compromised energy to another one by involving other lives, creates a vast amount of possibility for paradox, this number increasing exponentially with each new addition, leading to potentially disastrous consequences.

This is not a force of destruction, but rather, dispersion. It is the manifestation of the natural law of entropy. Through infinite possibility, even life itself will deteriorate into chaos after starting with perfect order: one simple *intention* from one life form. Through all of the interaction and all of the bridges formed, entropy is inevitable. Hidden away at the very core of the infinite chaos that this exposes is a doorway... A possible rearranging of the lives of all of those who were affected, or in any way were connected to those within the rift. The obvious question on Thor's mind was how to use it.

Erük held his forearm, staring deep into his eyes and took a deep breath. *"We caused the mess that's unfolding, but unlike a normal bad decision that has its consequences, something was allowed to happen here that only I can prevent. I want you to know, my brother, that if something happens and this fails-"*

"It won't!" Thor sternly interrupted, absolutely refusing to hear Erük's grim disclaimer. "Will I see you again?"

Erük took another deep breath, then reached up with his left hand while still holding Thor's right forearm tight and gently placed it across the breadth of his face and temples with his two middle fingers stretched over his frontal lobe. Almost instantly, as if someone had started a video directly inside Thor's mind, he was inundated with one very profound truth... He knew now exactly what these kinds of rifts actually were.

More than a tear in the universe, or a wormhole to another part of space, they were a gateway to the entire web-work of any given lifeline... specifically his own! Time did not matter. Space did not matter. Through the interconnectivity of the entire universe by way of the infinite bridges we all create, one can literally travel *anywhere* at *any time,* provided they know how to access the membrane of this "web."

"I am trusting you with the secret of our elders... the very secret that almost destroyed us. The secret that will make us whole again."

Thor stared at him, remaining speechless as he struggled to digest the deep impact of the transfer of knowledge and energy that Erük had bestowed upon him. Much of it was so advanced that it went well beyond his native tongue and could never be spoken of with any real accuracy, but the possibilities this power invited were excruciatingly obvious and morally testing, to say the least. For him, the one thought on his mind didn't take a telepath to see... it was written all over his face.

"You will have your chance, my brother... Why do you think I chose now to impart this gift to you? You will be able to reach your father. He is not dead. Those that have been trying to stop you have him isolated in a place of eternal darkness. It is unlikely that you can free him without confronting them on their own plane, but if you do not hesitate, you will have your chance to speak with him."

"When? How?"

"When the gateway opens, you will have only moments, but you can stretch this with pure will.... Use your will! You will have much to contend with to keep them safe, but when the opportunity arises, do not hesitate!"

"Will I see you again?"

"You already have," Erük said out loud, waving his arm as the hatch slid shut and the ramp retracted. Thor jogged for the bay door as the engines wound up to full cycle, then hit the panel to engage the airlock. As he stepped inside he was hit with a head rush of new feelings, mostly of familiarity associated with events and decisions that haven't yet happened, sort of like a mass déjà vu. It was just like what Sky had described feeling whenever she did anything that may have altered her past or affected her other self in an unexpected way.

"I bloody knew he was going to say something like that," Thor mumbled.

CHAPTER 30: THE RABBIT HOLE

Parnell stood fast on the bridge with a very confused, young crew at his command, unsure why he wasn't plotting a course for Algol when the rest of the Fleet was already underway. The only person on board who knew of his "conversation" with the dragon and its inherent impact on his decision making process was Kaitlyn, and that was the way he had to keep it, lest he be proclaimed barking mad and promptly relieved of his command. Even she scarcely understood what he was stalling for, but she had decided some time ago to trust him, and that was all that mattered.

Staring out toward their intended heading, he was starting to foster doubts, himself. There was something happening... he could feel it in every part of his body. The "grand purpose" for his wait, as laid out by Erük, was possibly for no other reason than for them to escape some kind of tragedy the rest of the Fleet had somehow fallen into, and that didn't settle well in his gut. He was a military man, a soldier, and a friend to many of those souls now possibly in peril, and sitting on the sidelines waiting from a safe distance while fate had its way with them made him feel like a coward.

"Full ahead! Head for the anomaly, but prepare for a slingshot onto the new vector. Use the Algol coordinates sent by the Helios for the new heading. Bring us as close to that storm as possible without influencing our flight plan."

"Aye, Sir!" the young helmsman responded, looking like a world of confidence had just been restored in his new Captain. Parnell suddenly felt weak. He had a gnawing in his bowels that warned him with every fiber of his being that he needed to stop right now. The dragon had told him that it would come to him as it was needed, and to have faith that he was on the right path, but it was just so damned hard to justify... the presence of mind to overrule one's head based on intuition alone was not something he could easily ingrain into his own psyche just yet.

Grappling with himself and whether or not to order a full stop, he was gazing toward the brilliant blue giant, trying to figure out just what they were all seeing. Just outside the haze of the innermost particle cloud, thickened by the flickering reflective nebula gasses being pulled in and concentrated by the immense gravitational strength of Alcyone, there was some kind of struggle taking place. Amidst what could easily have been written off as a meteor shower gone berserk was a shimmering, two dimensional sheet of lights, prismatic in nature, that seemed to be in front of everything around it... almost as if it was engulfing the other light entirely. He had borne witness to some of nature's most inexplicable phenomena countless times through the course of his illustrious career, but this was definitely something new.

Watching closely as they picked up speed and began closing the gap between themselves and the event, he started to notice that time itself seemed to be fluctuating. The rate that the surrounding stars seemed to whisk by on screen was wildly erratic, seeming more and more distorted and surreal as they got closer and closer. He held up his hand, one finger starting to protrude as if he was just about to give a command to stop, then came his proof....

"Thomas, Thomas, Thomas..." he heard booming in his head just as the small shuttle sped by from behind, swooping in front of their viewer. The voice was unmistakably the same as he heard from the dragon down in the ocean of the hostile world below. Obviously having been pegged as an avid reader, he couldn't help but smile at the Biblical reference given his recent course of action and obvious lack of faith. The shuttle tipped on its side, then changed course drastically.

"Follow that shuttle!" Captain Parnell ordered. Kaitlyn was typing something into the scanning computer, then she turned toward the Captain and proudly announced her revelation.

"I have a way for us to see in this cloud of interference!" She hit a few more keys and then turned the holographic viewer around for Parnell to see. The shuttlecraft popped up on screen, but was a little erratic and delayed, seeming to shift around slightly as they flew on. "I used sound, similar to side-scan sonar!"

"Side-scan sonar? Where did you learn about that?" Parnell asked, looking a little more worried than curious. "We've never used sonar in space..."

"I don't know, to be honest... it just popped into my head! I've been having that happen a lot lately. I thought of sound because of the particle density in the nebula... it vibrates just like water molecules, just not for as long and not as continuous or deep. We have to make-"

"Hard to port!" Parnell yelled, rushing toward his seat as the giant ship emerged on her scanner, instantly confirmed on the main screen. "Full reverse! Emergency evasive maneuvers!" The shuttle had broken wide to the right only moments before, but Parnell hadn't given any thought to the fact that he might be leading them *to* something, and for the moment had all but forgotten about the distorted distress beacon that had been emanating from the Helios!

As he caught his breath, he realized that the Helios was absolutely dead in space, pitching and rolling in an inertial tumble with no sign of life but the beacon flashing bright off the bow near the bridge that they had picked up on their scanners before entering the thick of the nebula. Coming up on the Helios's blind side as they did, they didn't even see that much until they were literally right on top of them. Had it not been for Kaitlyn's innovative scanning technique, they likely would have rammed her from behind at speed and caused catastrophic damage to both ships. "Kaitlyn, scan for life-"

"Sky."

"I'm sorry, what?"

"I changed my name to Sky... And yes, Sir, there appears to be a full crew... alive and kicking, but dead in the water, so to speak. It looks like they were hit with an EMP of some kind! Even life support is offline!"

"We need to start shuttling them onboard. Ensign Bellows, take a mechanical team and a security detail with you and shuttle over. Wear EP gear, full suits! We don't know what's happened! Kaitl-... Sky, I want you with them as medical support."

"Aye Captain," she saluted proudly, excited at having a chance to help at such a young age, so early in her first tour onboard a Carrier.

"EMP... EMP... What the hell could have-" He stopped muttering to himself in mid-sentence as the shuttle sped off from where it had been waiting and turned back around toward the anomaly at full speed. Just then Parnell caught a better look at it and realized that the shuttle was one of two prototypes originally onboard the Helios, both of which were equipped with the Admiral's brand new weaponized EMP charges. He had to admit, it made little sense that his mystery friend would attack the Helios, only to risk exposure by detouring to make sure they were found before drifting off into space. Pleased with his show of good nature and humanitarianism, Parnell made a conscious decision to try and not second guess his new friend's instructions again.

Thor and Sky were holding hands, both excited, and yet very nervous about where this course of action would take them. They knew that at this point there had to be other Fleet ships in proximity, but all they could see was a bright blue light, and the ever changing prismatic shimmer that was stretching across the horizon in front of them. Sky could tell this blindness issue was driving Thor nuts, due largely to his overprotective nature and sense of responsibility for those on board. Suddenly, it hit her. "Sound!"

"What?"

"Check this out," she said, rushing over to the holographic scanner like a giddy little girl on her first tour.

Erük sped directly at the shimmering wall of light, now nearly engulfing the small craft. All around him he was starting to see what appeared to be other ships, caught in various positions and stages of flight, and in many cases, collision with each other. It appeared that the two fleets had run directly into each other, as feared, but somehow they were all caught in some sort of sub-paradoxical state of suspended animation... neither moving past the rift, nor advancing forward in real time. For some reason they were simply frozen; awaiting some kind of decision or some kind of resolution... or simply awaiting the return of those who, in convergence, had become predisposed while the universe sought to rebalance itself.

Looking around, it was obvious as well as disturbing that many of the ships were altogether gone, and doing a very quick tally of the situation, he realized the obvious truth.... The missing ones were the duplicates that, due to their flight pattern, seemed to have collided with their own counterparts! The two seemed to have converged in this time and become one! It was as if physical contact with their displaced counterpart made them fuse somehow, in this place and time. *Perhaps it was this very phenomenon that caused the rift in the first place,* he thought.

As he traveled deeper and deeper into the rift, his fear of being caught in the temporal freeze began to subside. He seemed to be functioning outside of its surface effect, probably, he supposed, due to the fact that he had no counterpart in close proximity. The other him was still back on his home planet, nearly 20 light years from here; and the ship he was in was destroyed along with the other Helios in a fiery cataclysm over his lair, to some great personal satisfaction, as he remembered.

All at once, he felt it happening. The very fabric of space-time was coming unraveled all around him... all *through* him. Sound and light became the very same thing. His vision no longer mattered at all, as he became able to actually *see* his very thoughts. Everything around him became as unreal to him as the most abstract of dreams, and in this moment, *he knew everything!*

He became inundated with the notion that for the first time in his life, he had absolutely no questions! He was whole... he was at peace... he was in complete and utter communion with the All, the Creator, *the entire Universe! This must be Heaven,* he thought, *for without this feeling, how could one ever be truly at peace?* As long as there were *any* questions left unanswered, or *anything* left to learn, he would always be in a quest to obtain whatever he lacked. *This must be Heaven....* It was like taking in a tremendously fulfilling breath of air that completed oneself utterly, leaving absolutely nothing left to desire.

The tendency to remain here, basking in this sensation, was overwhelming. He had to mentally force himself back into *his* reality in order to even remember what he was getting ready to do, lest he stay here in limbo forever. He speculated that this was probably the fate that overcame the rest of them, but given the temporal distortion effecting them all, it was nearly impossible to tell for sure. All he knew was that he needed to break free of this snare at once, lest this become his eternal reality.

He hit the throttle and sped past the others, trying hard not to be dissuaded by the flashes and visions erupting into his mind like clips from a movie, as well as trying to ignore the cries of anguish, pain, and horror he was hearing now in his head; beaconing to him to stop and help... appealing hard to his other side, his honorable side, after losing the battle as his desire for carnal pleasures and personal joy and satisfaction.

As he sped straight into the cluster of lights, he began to make some amount of sense of the distortion around him. What appeared, at first, to have no real shape or discernible color was now starting to take on a very definite visual pattern. As he allowed the brilliance to fade into his periphery just a bit, he clearly made out what appeared to be a spiral pattern in the innermost core of the vortex he was now traveling through. It varied from smooth and bent, winding around seemingly randomly like a wormhole, to rough and pulsing with lightning and strobe flashes emanating randomly in all directions. At times it even seemed to exactly resemble a complete human DNA strand.

He was surprised to find that with his instinctively heightened mental discipline, he had tremendous navigational control. It seemed that in the blink of an eye this doorway was capable of placing him absolutely *anywhere* in *any time*. All he needed to do was will it so. The versatility of this incredible wonder of the known universe had somehow eluded even the Old Ones of his race... the greatest of the Great Travelers... the ones who had been driven from Earth before history itself, because the humans feared their knowledge so much. Even within the collective knowledge of the elders passed down to royalty such as Erük, there wasn't much more than a whisper of such a portal, and yet he could *feel* he wasn't alone. *Someone was monitoring his passage!*

As he swept up on the destination he had chosen: the one event he had always known he must undo, he could feel himself "collect" his former self. He neatly *swept up* and fused with his own past, combining effortlessly with his own body in true convergence on the Eve of Annihilation... the very day his own sense of humanity and compassion cost tens of thousands of M'ahk Tehríll their lives. The day that had haunted him ever since.

————————

Sky grasped Thor's hand tightly as they followed the small shuttle into the rift. At one point the light seemed to refract off of the shuttle's hull and create what appeared to be an Omni directional lightning storm, then it seemed as if it just disappeared entirely. She was staring directly at the back of the ship when it happened, and instantly became pretty shook up and worried for Erük. Unsure what was coming next, she tried very hard to just calm down and center herself. Thor could sense her tension, and still holding onto her hand, made a concerted effort to help calm her mind by bringing himself, and vicariously her as well, to a state of meditative bliss that seemed to help them both significantly.

They stayed like this for a few moments, then, as if it was some sort of dream, everything began changing very rapidly. Visually, everything was coming apart at the seams in slow motion. Thor crouched as the entire bridge seemed to be shaking, and people's voices, particularly those furthest away from him, started to distort just as they did before; going fast, then slow… fast… then slow. This phenomenon was increasing in magnitude, and starting to spill over into even the *feel* of the events as they transpired. This was the first symptom that wasn't merely observed, but rather, *experienced.*

Chaos ensued, and within a few minutes, panic had consumed the entire bridge. Things had accelerated to the point that one couldn't tell if they were about to walk right into someone else, through a wall… or gesture widely and knock someone's head off, so Thor made a flailing attempt at regaining control. "STOP!" he yelled at the top of his lungs. To his total surprise, everything and everyone froze exactly where they were. It was as if time stood still and he alone was its master.

He smiled for a moment, turning to his right to get Sky's take on the situation, but was caught off guard and somewhat frightened by the fact that she was just like everyone else. He could sense that they were all still alive, yet there was no pulse, no movement, not even any warmth to speak of. They were simply reflections of their actual selves, a single page of his life, caught in time. Thor closed his eyes and took a deep breath, trying to come to some kind of terms with what was going on. He felt utterly lost and alone, then he remembered what Erük had told him about the onset of the phenomenon… his one chance. He bent his will in one direction alone…

Not sure if he had actually dozed off for a second, or if the scenery merely changed in the blink of an eye, but Thor was suddenly aware of a cool breeze and the smell of tundra, as well as the sensation of the warm sun beating on his face from a relatively high altitude. He snapped his eyes open and looked around quickly in all directions, half expecting to see McGinn, or Tyr, or a flying bloody leprechaun; but instead, just mountains... the same mountains he had visited many times in his dreams, as well as in the stone-cold-sober, wide awake visions of late where he was able to spar with and hang out speaking to deceased friends. By the standards of his journey thus far, this was so far as tame a vision as could be expected.

"Nice... nothing coming out of the woodwork yet!" He exclaimed out loud in a sarcastic tongue, still absolutely clueless as to why he was here, or where the ship was. All he knew for certain was that this was no dream, and that he was most definitely still awake... that he had followed his brother, Erük, into some kind of cosmic rift or wormhole, and that whenever he found himself at his most lost, this was where he kept ending up.... "That's it!" he said aloud again, "I'm here because I didn't focus on a destination!"

"That doesn't explain what the hell you're doing in my head, though!"

Thor jumped nearly out of his pants, not expecting the loud intrusion, whatsoever! The voice was that of a man, probably middle aged.... He sounded gruff, cynical, and slightly pissed off... much like his uncle Ragnar! At this point, nothing would surprise him.

"Ragnar? Is that you?"

"Ragnar!? Who are you? How do you know of Ragnar?"

Thor paused for a moment, reluctant to answer, unsure whether this entity was friend or foe. Skeptical, but intrigued, he continued. "He's my uncle... assuming we're talking about the same Ragnar, that is."

There was a long pause. Thor could hear the sound of the wind picking up through the trees down the hill in the valley below and shivered for a second as he felt the brisk chill of an autumn breeze cutting through the warmth of the sun as it touched the exposed skin of his face and arms. *"Do you... mock me? He's... my brother!"* the man somberly responded. *"Know thyself..."*

"...But know that we are among you." Thor replied, still deathly afraid this was some kind of cruel joke.

"Th-Thor...? By the Gods, is that you? How can this be?" Thor knew full well in his heart that there was only one person this could be, though he didn't understand the mode by which they were conversing in the least.

"Dad...?" The voice was *so* near, yet looking around for the hundredth time since he first heard it, he could not find its source. It was not just in his head, nor was it coming from any discernible location. It *sounded* as if they were in the same room, just looking at different scenery. "Dad? Where are you? Why can't I see you?"

"What do you see?"

"I'm in the mountains... Somewhere near a cabin I visit a lot in my dreams."

"The cabin... oh yes," he chuckled warmly, *"this is no dream, I assure you!"*

"I've dreamed of it since I was a small child...."

"I've sent you messages of my whereabouts since you were a small child... This place is my home, or at least it was." He groaned for a moment as if in severe pain, then breathed heavily for a second or two before continuing. *"I was betrayed by those who professed to be my brothers! We discovered the secret of immortality... and it consumed them. Now they've imprisoned me. Thor, you're in great danger! They've sent someone after you... they've sent... him."*

"McGinn."

"Yes! How do you know about him? Have you seen him?"

"I've fought him… twice," Thor chuckled, "he's a bit of a handful!"

"For God's sake, Son, don't take this man lightly! He's more dangerous than you know! Beware of The Vindicators, Thor, the order they seek is not what they were founded to achieve. They've become self-serving and corrupt. They want immortality, and they're willing to disrupt the balance to obtain it! That's why I quit, and that's why I'm their prisoner!"

"Why haven't they killed you?"

"There is much I need to tell you… All I can say for now is that they've perfected a weapon… a weapon of unimaginable power! It requires a human interface… one with a very specific skill."

"You."

"Very good… Now understand… for all things there exists an opposite. You are the key to this. You are the only one who can undo what they've done to me! You must find me… and set me free. This they fear above all else, and will stop at nothing to prevent it! They will kill everyone you love just to weaken you a little… Thor, I didn't want to leave you, please believe me. It was the only way I could protect you from what I had already found out. Go now, before they pick up on your energy… Do not stay in one place for too long… He WILL find you!"

"Dad, I- I-"

"I love you, too."

Thor closed his eyes, merely to choke back some pent up feelings he had been storing deep for the last 20 years, but in the instant he visualized the bridge of the Phoenix, and his love by his side, he was there. The setting was exactly where he left it, and the crew was still frozen. Apparently, he was still caught in the rift that made this type of travel possible. He wondered if they were able to do the same thing, and if that was so, then what about all those on the ships frozen outside? *Were they free to travel the vast planes of existence at a mere whim, or were they now nothing but lost souls, trapped in a bipolar dystopia of their own construction....*

He had a pretty good idea exactly where Erük went, so in the interest of progress and unanimity, what he needed now was to exude a little more control and focus. He grabbed Sky's hand and bent his will on the planet of the Sand Dragons, where the M'ahk Tehríll still ruled the skies. The place where he first met Sky. The place where he was born again.

CHAPTER 31: FULL CIRCLE

One second she was standing next to Thor on the bridge of the Phoenix, holding hands as they plummeted into the unknown universal anomaly that lay shimmering before them, and the next, she lay twitching on the ground again, just as she had dreamed before, shaking violently from some kind of electrical weapon used by the man who was now dead on top of her from a single gunshot wound to the head. She had dreamt this all before, sometimes like this, and sometimes from a third person perspective, floating high above herself in the alley... only this time something was definitely different.

The man in black who now stood above her after shooting her attacker in the forehead was definitely Kieran McGinn. He was standing calmly, leveling his single shot pistol directly at her head as she struggled to free herself from the electricity that rendered her helpless. She could do little but stare into his eyes as he reluctantly resolved in a most professional manner to tie up this loose end. It was in this moment that she understood.... *He did not yet know who she was!*

His hesitation cost him dearly, as gunfire erupted from the side alley across from the bar just as he was about to shoot her too. She focused hard on the man, worried that she would be "whisked" out of here without finding out what any of this was about. *Too many unanswered questions... Got to warn the others.* She was pulled, instead, deeper into her body on the ground, where she was continuously stricken with pain, stricken with fear, and convulsing madly, as the device on her wrist shook her to the core.

She focused hard on not passing out this time, as McGinn was sent straight backward, losing his gun instantly as huge wounds opened up in several places on his chest, abdomen and neck. Staring at his twitching body, she gasped as she recognized the wound pattern from seeing his scars during his post-cryostasis examination onboard the Phoenix. *This was real! She truly was in the past... But whose past?* This sudden and profound realization caused her to completely lose her focus on the pitch of the device and she was taken over violently again by the stunner's charge. She started to fade out of consciousness and had to continuously force herself with all the will she could muster to remain where she was.

She tuned into the things that kept her rooted to this time and place: Thor... Dagaz... Tyr... she even smiled as she remembered Uruz, with all of his belligerent, boorish charm. These memories came rushing back into her mind as she reopened the floodgate, even though this life was now a world apart.

Suddenly, several others entered the picture. A few men in tactical gear descended on the bloody scene with military precision, but apparently were uninterested in preserving the incidental integrity of the crime scene. These men were obviously not cops, but instead seemed driven by some other agenda; focusing on covering up the entire incident. The two smaller men started lifting the man in black by his legs and wrists up off of the ground, and the larger man bent down toward her on one knee, analyzing the device without touching her.

He found the control laying in the dirt next to her knee where Stanton fumbled it and shut it down, causing her to relax so much that she actually felt the sensation of pissing herself. She half smiled from the irony, half from the pure relief, realizing this was the absolute least of her concerns at the moment. The huge man tested her joints quickly, making sure nothing was broken, then hoisted her onto his shoulder, fireman style, and quickly started walking off into the adjacent alley. The other two men were having tremendous difficulty with the assassin; fumbling and pulling as if he was rooted to the earth with some sort of immoveable anchor of energy.

Struggling with him repeatedly, they finally made the last minute call to give up and abandon him there when some commotion started from around the corner by the bar. It sounded as if half the bar was coming out to see what happened. They dropped the man randomly onto the ground where he crumbled into a contorted pile, face down, almost in fetal position, and as she stared again at the barcode tattoo on the back of McGinn's neck, she started to wonder where Thor was... and if he was alright. They had somehow become separated, and this was certainly no dream! She could feel her belly, and for the first time, realized that she was no longer pregnant with Ar'Jvikkah. She had no idea what this meant, but as she became more and more convinced that this was actually happening, this single fact disturbed her the most. Her bond with this tiny creature was already as real as that of any mother to her child, and as deep as the universe he came from.

She started to fade off again as the large man carrying her walked quickly into the dark alley, and was slowly losing sight of McGinn's body lying there, close to the intersection, when she suddenly noticed him twitch and start to get up, bleeding profusely. She tried hard to get the attention of her savior, fearing McGinn would rise up and shoot him in the back, but once again, for some reason she couldn't influence anything. She now seemed unable to do anything but observe.

He looked around himself, now up on one knee, struggling to rise. He looked in their direction and her heart missed a beat. She seemed suddenly able to focus to an outstanding degree of clarity, and not just her eyesight, but her thoughts as well! Her animal-like vision zoomed in on his cold stare as if he was right in front of her, close enough to reach out and touch.

Her eyes focused in on his, looking deep into the windows of his soul and seeing something not entirely human, and not entirely sane.... There was something to this man that couldn't be easily qualified, quantified or explained. It was almost like looking into the eyes of someone who knew you better than you knew yourself, knew your thoughts before you did, and then suddenly realizing they didn't like you in the least. She started feeling vulnerable in a whole new way.

He was still struggling, but almost on his feet, never taking his eyes off of her. She was growing increasingly worried, not so much for herself, but for Thor and the Northclan family. A vision of her childhood home flashed through her mind, mixed with thoughts of the attack on her own family in the underground... then of Thor, and how he took her in without question or expectation. She had a flood of thoughts spilling over from her life now, backward into the past. Her parents searching for her on Cheops... the Fleet... Erük and Ar'Jvikkah and her new abilities... Thor and McGinn fighting on the bridge. *Thor! He was the one constant.*

Suddenly she had the sensation of being "read" and she realized her thoughts had betrayed her... *had probably betrayed them all!* McGinn was staring deep into her eyes, from all the way down the dark alley, reading her like a book!

A devilish grin started on the edge of his mouth and he winked at her just as the man who was carrying her rounded a corner and took her out of his line of sight. As he kicked a door open to an abandoned building and started up some stairs with her, she pulled away with all her will, needing to warn them. This time she didn't float out of her body. This time she didn't wake up next to Thor. This time it didn't stop.

Upon reaching the top level, she caught a better look through a pane of broken glass in an old office doorway at the man who was carrying her. He was dressed in some sort of official looking uniform with a utility belt, brandishing a sidearm and several magazines of ammunition, as well as a large knife and a couple miscellaneous tool pouches. He was huge, probably very nearly 300 lbs of solid muscle, and he had a full head of carelessly styled, medium length dark hair. She got the feeling from the look in his eyes that his charity was entirely circumstantial. This man was all business.

He reached out and put his hand on a sensor pad next to a solid steel sliding door, and she cringed, knowing full well what was coming. It beeped, then whisked open, revealing a room with about 50 people in it, all of which she was sure she knew... *All of which were deceased!* She became frightened all over again as once again, she gazed into the eyes of one of them, in particular... her little sister. Her heart missed a beat as she realized that she had been in this situation before, or at least she had dreamt of it... *and it did not end well at all!*

The five year old girl standing before her had died in her arms when she was just a child herself from complications with a severe flu attack, and now, as she lived and breathed, here she stood, before her! Sky could immediately tell something was amiss. It *was* her, down to the very last detail, but her energy was somehow different... a cheap copy, at the very best. She was, quite simply, someone else. The gnawing feeling in her abdomen intensified as she turned to her benefactor: the man who had turned off the stunner and carried her here, only to realize that he was no longer in the room. This was particularly disturbing, because she knew full well what came next.

She tried to speak, but no words came out. Now she was very scared, and she spun back around to her sister. Involuntarily, she realized she was hovering a few feet from the ground; the sensation of energy permeating the air around her. The hair stood on the back of her neck, and her arms slowly rose out to the sides, palms up. Something was happening as she mentally recorded the looks of awe and terror from everyone in the room. She was becoming more and more detached from them. Within a few seconds, she didn't even recognize her own sister, and she had elevated her pitch to a point well beyond that of anything she had ever experienced, or even imagined.

Turning her palms back over toward them, she unloaded. Screams of terror and the crashing sound of lightning and destruction filled the air as she tore the entire room and everyone in it asunder, leaving not so much as a remnant bone to tell their story. In the metal sheathing of the opposite wall, she could hazily make out the reflection through the smoke and debris of someone she no longer recognized, hovering a few feet above the floor with glowing eyes and wings like a dragon gently flapping in the air out to her sides.

Sky hovered above the aftermath of the carnage that had just been unleashed through her; huge dragon-like wings flapping gracefully, instinctively timed, even as the transition back to her conscious self progressed.

Ceasing her wing flapping, she landed softly back down on the floor, quickly regaining her sense of self. She was utterly blown away by what she had just done to them… *but then, they weren't real… were they? She wasn't real. This was a dream. It had to be.*

"Does it?" the voice boomed in her head, strong, yet somehow gentle, and strangely familiar.

"Does it, what?" she asked back without speaking.

"Does it have to be a dream?"

"I was just taken over by someone who destroyed everyone I know who already died... I am not even me... I think that it does!"

"Then, so be it."

"Who are you?"

"A friend."

"Why would a friend put me through this?"

"You can only move forward with your back to the past."

"Am I dead?"

"No, but you have no further use for this plane..."

"Who are you?"

"A planeshifter, as are you."

"Will I see him again?"

"You already have."

She was consumed by an overpowering feeling of déjà vu... that she had been here before... in this exact situation, yet somehow, something was different. Straining very hard, she could almost *hear* a conversation taking place in a faint whisper... from beyond the thin veil of her perceived reality... *perhaps the same one who was just-...* It was starting to come back to her.... The room. The voice. Gaining closure through the annihilation of the *illusions* of her past ghosts....

She became consumed in the guilt of the sudden realization of one despicable fact... that the people she just slew were absolutely *real*! Most likely common street people, captured and set up for her so that whoever was perpetrating this façade could test her ability for use as some kind of psychic weapon... *one of unimaginable power!* The rest was nothing but smoke and mirrors; a ruse designed to make her stand utterly alone. By taking her back to her own past, they planned to effectively erase her bond with the future... her bond with him. To attempt to untie the very bonds that destiny had kept secure across the vast span of death itself.

She glanced around quickly, looking for a way out, then realized that even the door she came in through was no longer there. Not understanding how this could possibly be, she started feeling all the way around the room with her hands, starting with where she remembered it being. An overwhelming sense of desperation and hopelessness combined in her head, and she knew she was trapped. She started to cry. The smell of burning flesh was overpowering, reminding her that this was no dream, and yet still she begged the Gods to wake her.

McGinn was standing behind a loose partition wall halfway up the stairwell when the large man came back down from the cell to speak with him. People had been congregating all around the scene of the shooting for several minutes now as Kieran remained hidden and dressed up his wounds, but they were mainly gossiping locals and were already getting bored with the situation and dispersing on their own.

"Do you think that they bought it?" McGinn asked the man as he held out a small envelope toward him.

"I know they did. They're reporting your death as we speak. Only the Vindicators will know of your involvement. The AFG will be completely in the dark."

McGinn snatched the envelope from the man's hand and opened it immediately. His face got very serious as he stared at the photograph inside. He closed his eyes and took a deep breath, then opened them slowly, staring at the man without saying a word.

"Now you know... This is your last assignment. The one in the middle is-" He was interrupted in mid-sentence by the thump of two silenced subsonic rounds hitting him square in the ribcage and piercing his heart, followed by the jangle of the brass shells bouncing down the stairwell. The wide eyed man reached out toward him, grasping nothing but air as he dropped to one knee and slumped onto the stairs face down.

"The son of General Krey... I know." He pulled out the accompanying letter from the envelope, memorized the address, then lit his lighter and caught all of it on fire, leaving it in a smoldering pile on the ground. "We have a very special plan for him."

First there was the *sensation* of light; a warm glow, starting from a pinhole in the dark, then growing larger. Next, the sensation of cold beyond cold, and slowly becoming aware of his own body, then himself. Pain. He cringed, suddenly aware of some kind of sound, possibly himself crying out. The pain was nearly unbearable. He tried to call out, but couldn't move his mouth. Even the light was now becoming unbearable. He could feel his eyelids moving and tried to focus on just that. He was becoming aware of people moving around him, but he still couldn't hear right. There were muffled noises and voices coming from all around him, but he couldn't make out any words or even tell what language they were speaking.

"How are they coming along?" the male doctor asked one of the two females that were assisting with the patients.

"This one's moving... He keeps trying to speak. Should I give him another shot of adrenaline?" she asked.

"Do it! What about the other four?" he yelled over the sound of running water, while preparing something in a vial over by the sink.

"This one's not responding!" yelled the other woman. Neither one was dressed like a nurse or doctor, but more like some sort of soldier.

"That's what I was afraid of..." the doctor grunted, shoving his way past her with a syringe full of some kind of dark liquid. "I keep telling the asshole! We're going to lose every one of them!" He shot the fluid directly into the man's heart, slamming down hard with the large needle to puncture the chest plate.

Thor's vision started to widen slightly, and he began to make out a set of eyes. Female eyes. Beautiful, like the eyes of an angel, unblinking and cutting through the haze with a softness he could feel even through his desensitized numbness. Then the contours of her face and hair began to take shape. She was starting to smile.

"He's coming around!" she yelled out, turning to the other two, who were busy pumping on the chest of the older man, who still wasn't responding. She looked back down into his eyes. "Hang in there, it'll pass... You're doing great." He could just make out the stinging sensation of her grabbing hold of his hand. He tried to grab back, but couldn't even tell for sure if he had moved it at all. He grunted something audible, but unintelligible from the strain. She leaned down with one ear to listen. He clearly grunted out one word...

"Sky...."

He dozed back off, his arm falling off the table from exhaustion after he had managed to lift it up towards her. The military uniform she was wearing had a small device attached to the lapel that looked like a rectangular metal clip with a button on both ends and some sort of speaker or microphone perforation across the face. It made a chirping sound and she squeezed the ends together to stop it. She squeezed again and spoke into it, "I'll be right there."

She stared at him quizzically, unsure if she actually just heard what she thought she heard. She turned to the doctor and said, "This one's exceptionally strong... be careful with him, I'll be back to check them out in a while, right now I'm needed upstairs." She started walking toward the automatic door, stopping briefly to correct her partner's hand position while she gave another patient an injection. The other woman nodded in compliance.

"Did you hear what he said?" Astrydd whispered to Sky on her way by.

"Who?"

"That cryo."

"Yeah, maybe he heard someone call me by my name...."

"If you say so... Is that why you've been waiting diligently until he was next rotation for thaw out?" Astrydd smiled at Sky and winked, leaning toward her so no one else could see.

"I really don't know what it is... I've seen him in my dreams. I feel like I've known him... ever since I was just a child. I even knew he would speak my name! How weird is that?"

"Yeah, we've all been experiencing a rash of déjà vu and unexplainable memories since we left Cheops. No one seems to know why."

EPILOGUE: ERÜK AND THE M'AHK TEHRÍLL

      Erük came out of his shift as close to his desired destination as could have been hoped for. His focus was a singular force of will, and his power over his environment was always uncanny, so not even he was surprised by this fact. All there was to do now was accomplish what he came here for, then his life would be forfeit. He would have served his ultimate purpose, and each day thereafter would be a bonus.

      There was a warmth in his heart from being home again. Night time on his home planet was always such a treat. He used to sit for countless hours atop the highest plateaus and stare out over the endless sea of orange sand, turned violet by the warm glow of Sigyn overhead; keeping them safe from the menacing duality of their own warmth and light giver: Algol, the binary sun... the two headed demon lurking just on the other side of the planet. The twin wolves, their moons, Vali and Nari, played overhead as usual, trapped in a dance of brotherly frolic, kept in perfect balance like everything else in this delicate system... forever teetering back and forth on the cusp of oblivion. He would sit quietly and bask in his solemn charge as the high protector of this delicate world… a duty he now brought home with a vengeance.

Admiral Reid always chose to pilot himself in any shuttle he was riding in. Being a lifelong military man in a mobile fleet, he had spent his time in the cockpit of just about every type of craft they had, and he was damn good, but the main reason he always took the stick, plain and simple, was that he was an insufferable control freak. He was actually incapable of letting anyone else become responsible for him in any way. Sometimes this was a quality that served him well, but most of the time it just pissed people off, disrespected his associates, and undermined the authority of his officers.

The other Fleet Captains were already back onboard their respective ships after the emergency strategic meeting concerning the last minute implementation of Thor's unifying "living shield" interface into their defense against the huge Sand Dragon incursion that was about to take place when the Fleet finished backing them into a corner over their main nest and home. Reid was prepared to betray them all, as he had no intention of using his typical "firebombing" technique as a fall back, but rather, as an opening tactic for nothing short of the total annihilation of Erük's entire species.

The last time he was here, Reid managed to escape Erük's clutches after Erük believed he had "force fed" enough information into his brain to provoke a change of heart, but based on the outcome, it was obvious that Admiral Reid *had* no heart, was incapable of any kind of decent act of humanity, and was therefore not worthy of a second chance. This time, Erük was here to prevent a genocide… nothing else. *No hesitation. No quarter. No regrets.* He hung back and let the former version of himself handle round one….

As Reid banked hard in his single manned shuttle, coming around for final approach behind the Helios, there was a sudden flash like something passing right in front of the forward lights. He quickly looked at his radar screen, which he had been neglecting for a while as he was enjoying manual control, but nothing showed up. He shrugged it off as a small vapor flash from a passing cloud or something and was just starting to drift off and get back to enjoying himself, when it happened again, this time seeming to come from above and flash downward very fast.

"What the..." Reid said aloud, standing up and looking out the small shuttle craft's front window, trying to see downward at what blew by him. His face was almost press-fit on the glass when it hit straight on; a massive Sand Dragon slamming into the front of the craft and clenching its window frame from the sides with its huge front talons. Reid jumped nearly out of his skin, finally landing almost directly on top of the control stick, causing the craft to pull straight up in a gravity bending vector with the Admiral pinned over the controls and onto the pilot seat on his back, with his neck still bent toward the window, staring the creature right in its huge, dark, penetrating eyes.

Caught in a giant back-flip with the Helios right below him, and the Icarus and Achilles coming up from behind, neither the Admiral, nor the creature even so much as blinked. He was involuntarily caught in a mind-lock with the creature, trading thoughts completely out of his control. The entire course the Fleet had laid out in the meeting flashed through his mind, as well as the firebomb, fighters, sweep mining, and the supernova... all his knowledge on what was really causing the planetary degradation, along with everything else of any strategic importance was now utterly compromised. He had a flash in return of large groups of indigenous creatures living in caves; wonderful caves, with waterfalls, rivers, phosphorescent light, etc... Whole families of these creatures coexisting with other life forms down below... *even underwater*!

With no more than a few meters to spare, he managed to pull out and back around toward the Carriers. His eyes were instantly and instinctively combing his entire field of vision for the creature that seemed to have vanished as quickly as it had appeared. It was not showing up on his radar, and was not to be seen anywhere. His heart was racing as he set course right behind the Helios, ordering them to start the docking sequence immediately.

Hanging back in the darkness, just beneath the landing pads and disruptive magnetic flux of the Phoenix, concealed well beneath the radar in the cover of darkness, Erük watched in admiration as his former self exercised the constraint necessary to spare this insignificant human's life and send the tiny shuttle off on its way after their face to face encounter that revealed Reid's sinister intention... one that had actually come to pass after the occurrence of a slightly unpredictable chains of events. It was too bad that his faith was misplaced, and now it was because of this that he was here again. To prevent this great atrocity from happening was now his new mission... his sole purpose... his destiny.

He swooped down from above, intercepting his former self from behind like an eagle's attack on a rabbit from above. As he recalled, he had just broken off his engagement on the shuttle window after a long enough mind-lock with Reid to make him truly believe that this warped little man would have a sincere moral change of heart. Not a chance. Not only did he *not* repent, but he actually took the incident as a personal attack that, in his mind, he "skillfully" evaded, thusly strengthening his resolve even further.

As soon as he collided with his former self in this place, a very intentional, as well as predictable convergence took place. From Erük's perspective, he was merely stricken with an overpowering sense of déjà vu, accompanied with an eye opening new vantage point, similar to waking up and suddenly remembering what you did yesterday, or for the last week, in place of what seemed to just be a blank.... Adding a length of time to his memories and experience, nothing more. Before it was added, it was simply as if it never existed... just as the future doesn't exist until it happens. He smiled, realizing he could repeat this process so very easily, should the need ever arise again.

He continued his decent straight *through* the other him, collecting himself, literally, as he slammed into the back of the small shuttlecraft, causing it to career right past the open docking bay, spinning sideways out of control. Reid had already switched off his thrusting engines and was running solely on magnetic repulsion for his docking maneuver, so steering was only possible at the slowest of speeds, making it impossible for him to correct the craft's trajectory in time.

The small craft spun around slowly to the right as it descended toward the two adjacent Carriers looming below, picking up speed from the planet's gravity. Erük flew up alongside it, making sure to keep himself close enough to the shuttle so as not to appear as a second blip on the radar screens, but also careful to remain in the blind spots, just out of line of sight from the other Carriers as he crept up on the thick reinforced polymer glass of the front windshield. The terrified Admiral sat alone inside, absolutely clueless as to what was really happening.

Erük locked eyes with him again, unloading directly into his mind all of the pain of the entire war... the anguish of every torn family... the pain of every disfigured, burnt and dismembered soul... the senseless loss of a culture more timeless and dignified than any other race encountered in the universe thus far. All utterly destroyed, because of the greed, vanity and lack of compassion of one individual. Erük held on to the edges of the window again, looking for a sign of true leadership... *the humility to change.*

Tears started welling up in Reid's eyes. His face, reddened already from the shock that Erük was putting him through, was starting to twist with deepening emotional strain. There was guilt in his eyes, but there was something much deeper behind that. He reached down to his gun belt that held the 18 inch long disruptor gun: any officer's main sidearm next to the traditional Colt 1911 bullet firing relic he kept cocked and locked in his shoulder harness. Operating with a high tech blast of electricity and highly augmented sound waves, the disruptor gun was capable of doing horrific damage to any tissue-based organism with minimal collateral influence on the surrounding environment. The military originally developed these for crowd control without any danger of hull breach or damage to the domes that used to exist over Earth's last few metropolitan centers to keep the poisonous air out, but they quickly became the standard issue sidearm for officers onboard Fleet vessels for obvious reasons.

Admiral Reid solemnly lifted the polished weapon from its holster and stared coldly at Erük as he raised it toward his head, the tears in his eyes making him nearly impossible to read. His hand was trembling; and though he seemed full of remorse at first, his disingenuous nature prevailed as his deep hatred for anything he could not master drove his hand straight past his own head and pointed the gun at Erük through the glass. To Erük's great fortune, he had never seen enough of Reid's humanity to completely trust his intentions, and he had already preempted just enough, coupled with a shifting of the shuttle's inertia, to cause Reid's shot to miss.

The blast hummed in a very low pitch as it went straight through the front windshield, hitting the shield of the Icarus just a few meters away from his current position, causing the large Carrier's shield pitch to lower in order to absorb the energy. This caused what the engineers refer to as "pitch hardening," creating an area of the shield that is essentially solid and electrified for a few moments until the harmonics can reset themselves back into balance, making even the passing through of other Fleet ships, which is normally permitted, utterly impossible.

Erük could hear Reid scream in terror as the shuttle slammed into the hardened area just milliseconds later, tearing through his hull like a cannon ball through an aluminum hulled fishing boat, leaving the explosive fireball and the crushing of the shuttle body around him to finish the job.

McGinn sat quietly in his cell, finally awake and pretty disgusted with his apparent state of affairs. It seemed, for as much as he could tell from what limited contact he had been afforded, that he was once again locked up and imprisoned in the brig of a Fleet Carrier, most likely the Phoenix again; and once again, he was going on a solid week without word one from his captors or his handler, who, at this point, should have been communicating with him though his dreams. It seemed to him, so far as he could remember, that he hadn't even had any dreams lately. It seemed as if something was actually blocking them from happening in this place.

As near as he could tell it was the ship's own infernal power source that seemed to be keeping all of his abilities in check, much like Kryptonite to Superman. The source, so far as he was able to discern, was the power core in the center of this, and many other rooms... one of this level of the ship's many glowing blue pillars at the center of the room that acted as a tether for the electromagnetic signal used on the work levels and the brig for everything from cell shielding security and environmental control to communications and personnel and prisoner scanning for security purposes. This type of system was nearly fail-safe, as it's circuitry was independent of the ship's computers, and ran on an independent network as well, such that outside breach was logistically impossible, and in the event of total power or system failure, the brig and work levels, including the cargo hold, would automatically go into lockdown protocol, and remain completely active and functional, otherwise. This was another one of Admiral Reid's profit ensuring ideas that gained all the support it needed to become standard issue onboard every Carrier.

He remembered it well from before... when he was pulled from cryostasis nearly two weeks after Thorsson Krey had already been assimilated into the crew for his mental talents, leaving his rotting carcass withering and utterly dreamless before this infernal blue glowing usurper and soul-sucking battery for the machine that the other inmates flocked around like it was some kind of magical campfire. It was not even a type of energy he could draw strength from, so here he sat by himself in the corner of his open cell, waiting for someone to fill him in... waiting for a chance to influence his own life once again... *waiting for someone to make a mistake.*

The last thing he remembered before ending up here was fighting with a very skilled young warrior who had to have been none other than Sky herself, at a younger age, while he was locked in the Medical Bay. He was trying to find, and forever alter the frozen body of Thorsson Krey before he could be thawed in the future and create the support mechanism for himself that seemed to grace his every move and make him such an impossibly hard mark. The only setback, as McGinn remembered, was that he had no physical body at that point... a problem that he apparently rectified when he fled into his own frozen one at the last minute through the machine interface. From all he could tell from the events that had transpired so far, he should still be onboard the Phoenix, during just about the same time in the future that he was thawed before… awaiting a second chance to finish what he failed to finish on the bridge during the tachyon wave.

He grinned in a most sinister manner as the conversation going on around him suddenly rang a bell! He wasn't just having a ridiculously long string of déjà vu, he was actually back in the same situation onboard the same Carrier, full circle, and if he wasn't mistaken, this was exactly what had transpired immediately before Krey's voice went out across the shipwide loudspeaker, announcing his appointment as the new Captain of the Phoenix. Shortly after that, if the players were none the wiser, he would get his second chance to kill Thor, as the new Captain would pay him a visit inviting him to join them on the bridge, and showing him his new quarters where he was able to dig up the weapons he used before.

Looking around the room anxiously as he waited for the crackle of the loudspeaker, he started to get a little nervous as he saw someone he didn't recognize… then another… then someone else! He listened closely and even noticed that their conversation had shifted slightly to include some gossip about Parnell where he could have sworn the inmate, one of the brown nosing trustees named Rydell, referred to him as "Admiral." He quickly stood up, worrying for the first time that the timeline may have changed, and that things may have just taken a sideways turn! Then, it came. It was like someone let the air back into the room. He was overjoyed, and listened closely to the shipwide transmission as he could suddenly breathe again.

"Ladies and Gentlemen of the Phoenix… anyone still left onboard, free or imprisoned… Captain Parnell is no longer in command of this vessel. I am Captain Thorsson Krey. Lieutenant Commander Davies and I have assumed command of this vessel, and are attempting to make right some of the atrocities of the previous administration. Our journey

will take us far from Fleet, who at this time are in the process of trying to track and project the outcome of a large supernova and the birth of a new black hole. It is very possible that our paths will never again cross, so if you have family or loved ones on other ships, please consider strongly the possible outcome of staying with us...."

*"Anyone who wishes to remain with the Fleet will proceed to the shuttle bay immediately and wait for Commander Davies, who will see to it that you are given the opportunity. If you are detained and unable to get there, someone will be by to retrieve you. Identify yourself by laying a towel by the entry to your quarters, or your cell, immediately. Thank you very much, Godspeed, and good luck to us all in these uncertain times... Captain Thorsson Krey, out."**

Kieran smiled devilishly and threw his towel over his right shoulder as if he was headed to the shower, knowing that there were enough others littering the open walkway right in front of him to at least gain him brief audience with Thor prior to being thrown onboard a shuttlecraft full of scared crewmembers. Somehow his identity must have escaped Thor's attention, or this would certainly have been the death of him! His assumption was absolutely correct, and for once, he didn't even have to be patient for things to play out... the door to the brig slid open within a few minutes of the announcement being played shipwide over the airways.

McGinn noticed several inconsistencies leading up to this moment, but everything seemed closely enough tied to the original timeline for him to successfully plan his *coup de grace*, once and for all. Kieran was usually all business, and did very little jawing for the sake of mere jawing when he was at work, but at this moment, he was as giddy as a high school girl, and was already chewing on a mouthful of questions and statements he felt compelled to bombard his nemesis with as soon as he had him at his mercy.

The door slid open and a small security detail entered, led by Sky, who walked straight through and bent her course directly in his direction in a most unassuming manner, both unannounced and unexpected. She was looking straight into his eyes as she approached and Kieran couldn't detect anything but the slightest feeling of familiarity, as if she barely recognized him at all! This was either one _very_ convincing acting job, or she actually _did not_ remember him! Thor came through the doorway a moment later, going over some charts on a pad being carried by one of the guards. He didn't even look at the prisoners as he entered the room into full view, taking up his place next to Sky. McGinn slowly rose to his feet, grinning slightly, and staring at Sky as if he'd seen a ghost.

"So, Mr. Krey, or was it Stanton?" he asked, assuming now that they were both from this timeline. "So, the NSA sends agents this far into space to dispatch crooked ship Captains, then? I'll go for a ride with ya, how 'bout gettin' us outta this cell, then, eh Boyle?" he said with a thick Irish brogue and a rather convincing smile. Thor walked in a little farther and peered into the cell. Sky looked confused as Thor suddenly burst into laughter.

"McGinn, was it? Well I'll be damned! You're a sight for sore eyes!" Thor reached out to shake his hand, but when he reciprocated, Thor gave him an unexpected shove with his right palm, hard enough to catch him off guard and knock the wind out of him. He flew back a few steps, hitting the cell wall with his back, then fell forward onto his hands and knees. Thor reached up and hit the panel on the wall, causing the intense energy field to regenerate, trapping him in his cell. "Erük and I made a few modifications to the signal transmitted here in the brig... I'm sure you'll find it to your liking... especially when you try to shift out of here! Go ahead and enjoy your stay, asshole, 'til I decide what to do with you!"

He turned his back to him and closed his eyes, grinning. Sure enough, his taunts caused the enraged McGinn to attempt to pitch-shift through the shield and attack Thor. As soon as he started to transcend the barrier, its pitch changed abruptly, causing him to be shocked and sent flying painfully backward into the wall behind him with some force. Thor burst out laughing, reopened his eyes, then grabbed Sky's hand and headed for the door without looking back. "Just beg whoever it is that you pray to that I don't blow your sorry ass out the airlock, McGinn!"

Meanwhile, the guards evacuated the other cryos, leaving McGinn trapped in his cell by himself. Upon reaching the doorway, Thor paused, turning around momentarily to see McGinn glaring at him with saddened eyes, panting like a freshly caged beast who was unable to comprehend its predicament. "By the way, my father says, Hi…" Thor winked at him, adding insult to injury, then walked out of the brig without another word.

"Where do you know him from?" Sky asked, strangely concerned, "It's just that he has even more scars than you do. Do you have any idea what he did for a living?"

"I met him in the office at CryoKinetics… Let's go somewhere quiet and catch up on a few things… There's a lot I need to tell you."

They began walking down the corridor toward the bridge, trying to remain next to each other in spite of all the commotion as they dodged one person after the next… the human crew members still a little wary of the M'ahk Tehríll who chose not to adopt a human form for the ride, but rather kept their physical body in the form of a dragon. It seemed that only about half of the population had the ability to shapeshift… the others seemed to possess a myriad of different unique skills that they had developed over several millennia of peaceful coexistence and the open sharing of ideas through collective intelligence.

They were not happy about having to abandon their home planet, but as Erük explained to the Queen, the supernova was inevitable. The humans had not *caused* it in the other timeline, but rather, they *accelerated* it. The planet, the sun, and everything surrounding it, were ultimately doomed. It didn't take her long to give the order to take the humans up on their offer to help them relocate. Their new home was nearly 80 percent water; and since they possessed the ability and resilience to transcend any dependence on surface dwelling in its harsh environment, Cheops would ultimately provide them with everything they could ever want or need.

Upon reaching the bridge, Thor hit the front viewer, revealing the familiar sight of Sigyn one last time as they sped toward Cheops, accelerating boldly. They would never forget the beauty of this hostile world, nor the lessons they were lucky enough to have a second chance to learn. He turned the view manually, panning straight forward as the engines wound up into their final cycle.

From the edge of the screen, they could make out the edge of the Helios, looming in the viewer, nearly twice the size of a normal Carrier like the Phoenix. Thor let go of Sky's hand and approached the Captain's chair. "Bjorn, patch me through to the Helios."

"Yes, Sir."

"Parnell here...."

"Admiral Parnell! How are your new passengers getting along?"

"Well, let's just say it's going to be an interesting trip, to say the least... I have someone here who wants to talk to you."

Thor smiled warmly. "Put him on!"

"Thank you, my brother. Do not worry... we'll find a way to free him. Together."

"I know we will. I know. Thanks, Erük... for everything."

"The young one has just arrived, Brother... We will talk later. Get in there!"

———————

Thor and Sky dodged people, dragons, and equipment, all the way from the bridge to the Biodome in anticipation of Ar'Jvikkah's arrival. For Thor, it also marked the possible arrival of the Sky he knew better than anybody, and had been through Hell and back with. He had been growing increasingly disturbed over the last several weeks since their shift that brought convergence to the two timelines. Sky seemed to be "off" in far too many unforeseen ways, and though he loved her no matter what, just for being who she was, he wanted her back... the "her" he had shared so many memories with. The way she was... *before* all of this happened.

There were literally dozens of crewmembers Fleet-wide who were experiencing major identity problems... in some cases, even total amnesia; but Sky had been standing *right next to him* when they went into the rift. It didn't make any sense... *and she was carrying Ar'Jvikkah in her own womb! This <u>had</u> to be it!*

Thor and Sky quickly rounded the last corner and hit the panel to open the Biodome door. In the darkest part of the Biodome, where the small rivers converged into a cave, the Queen Mother sat peacefully, consoling her daughter, Ar'Yiisah. Though she had seen her species evolve right before her eyes in her own lifetime, this child was special... she could feel it in every fiber of her being. He was not just an old soul, he was the future of the M'ahk Tehríll: a Wind Walker, the son of the Queen's Royal daughter, a Jvikkahn King, and with

Sky's gift to their race, he would always be every bit a child of two worlds. As he emerged from her womb, quickly cleaned off by the Queen, then handed to his anxious mother, he opened his enormous ice blue eyes and it was obvious that beneath his beautiful dragon wings that he folded instinctively around himself for warmth and protection, baby Ar'Jvikkah was one more thing... *human*!

Thor squeezed Sky's hand as they shared this wonderful moment together, but in the back of his mind, all he could think of was her. Logically, she should be here... going blank and even falling down from the rush of convergence, then basking in this moment with all the heartfelt intensity of a new mother, herself, given her very intimate connection with this child! He already felt his answer in her energy, but dared a glance up at her face. She looked over at him and smiled warmly back at him, more charmed by his display of sensitivity than anything else. She could tell he was starting to get upset, and though she did understand why, she couldn't help but be upset by this. Having no true knowledge of what they "were" together, she had only her very real feelings for him, *as things were now*, and couldn't help but feel as if it was someone else entirely that he was in love with.

"I'm so sorry..." She broke off from his tight grasp on her hand and headed for the door before he had a chance to see the tears welling up in her eyes. Ever since Thor had undergone awakening from cryostasis for a second time, she seemed like the old Sky... from *before* the supernova. It was as if there had never been a convergence for her, and the other Sky ended up somewhere else. He knew these things didn't work on a linear timeline, so he had been patiently awaiting her arrival, but since Ar'Jvikkah's birth? *Where could she be?* Suddenly, he remembered the peculiar look on McGinn's face when she stood next to him in the brig... *he knew something*.

414

Thor was sure of it! God as his witness, he would pry it out of him... one way or another.

———————
————
——
—
.

ᛰᚼᛚᛊ ᛈᛁᛏᚼᛰᛏ ᛏᚼᛗ ᛒᛰᚼᛤᛊ ᛰᚠ ᚠᚠᛗᛁᛚᛊ ᚠᛤᛗ ᛈᛗ ᛏᛤᚾᛏᛊ
ᚠᛏᛰᚼᛗ

ᚲᚼᛰᛈ ᛏᚼᛰᛊᛗᚾᚠ ᛒᚾᛏ ᚲᚼᛰᛈ ᛏᚾᚠᛏ ᛈᛗ ᚠᛤᛗ ᚠᛗᛰᚼᛜ ᛊᛰᚾ

www.novelty-fiction.com/garisson

**SHAPESHIFTER
FICTION**